CHILDREN
KILLING
CHILDREN ...

GANG VIOLENCE INVADING AMERICA'S HEARTLAND — These are the headlines behind William J. Reynolds' latest Nebrasaka mystery, DRIVE-BY.

"Not long ago, many Americans dismissed the slaughter as an inner-city problem. But now the crackle of gunfire echoes from the poor-urban neighborhoods to the suburbs of the heartland. Omaha, with a population of 340,000, is just an average Midwestern city, which is why the story of its armed youth shows how treacherous the problem has become...

"On any Saturday night, Omaha's police radio betrays the city's image as a bastion of conservative heartland values: 'Caller reports two youths with guns in a parking lot...Anonymous caller reports shots in her neighborhood...Drive-by shooting reported...Officer reports at least 10 shots...One young male wounded by gunfire.'"—Jon D. Hull, *TIME*, Aug. 2, 1993

Darius LeClerc, gunned down on an Omaha street, seems to be the victim of one of those random shootings with which the media have made us all too familiar. But having been appointed the young man's unofficial guardian angel, the writer-detective Nebaska is not so sure the murder was unplanned.

He teams with Darius' uncle, Elmo Lammers, to find the killer, and their quest leads them through the streets and alleys of an Omaha as alien and dangerous as a foreign land, teeming with fascinating, richly drawn people. The climax is as exciting as a classic western shootout, but with the gritty reality of today's urban milieu.

DRIVE-BY is a must-read for Nebraska fans and a glorious introduction for readers new to the series.

DRIVE-BY

Also by
William J. Reynolds

The Nebraska Series
THE NEBRASKA QUOTIENT
MOVING TARGETS
MONEY TROUBLE
THINGS INVISIBLE
THE NAKED EYE

Nonfiction
SIOUX FALLS: THE CITY AND THE PEOPLE

DRIVE-BY

A NEBRASKA MYSTERY

William J. Reynolds

EX MACHINA PUBLISHING COMPANY
SIOUX FALLS, SOUTH DAKOTA

M

For reasons that are probably obvious, many of the people who contributed to this project prefer to remain anonymous. They know who they are, and they know they have my thanks.

Special thanks also to John Kerwin and Robert T. Reilly.

DRIVE-BY, A Nebraska Mystery, Copyright © 1995 by William J. Reynolds.

Published by EX MACHINA PUBLISHING COMPANY,
            Box 448,
            Sioux Falls, SD 57101

First Edition, First Printing, July 1995.

Consulting Editor: Gayle Emmel

Library of Congress Cataloging-in Publication Data

Reynolds, William J.
    Drive-by : a Nebraska mystery / William J. Reynolds. -- 1st ed.
        p.   cm.
    ISBN 0-944287-14-X (alk. paper)
    I. Title
PS3568.E93D75 1995
813'.54--dc20

                                        95-1513
                                        CIP

*This one was always for
Meredith Abbie Reynolds,
and all of them are for her mother.*

CHAPTER

1

At two o'clock on the last morning of his life, Darius LeClerc parked the old, battle-scarred Plymouth Duster in the first available spot along the curb, under a dead street light, and hustled the two and a half blocks to the housing project.

The night was mild by the standards of a Midwestern winter; still, Darius's breath preceded him in pale clouds as he moved along the broken and littered sidewalk. At least Omaha hadn't had too much snow that winter, and it hadn't been all that horribly cold—nothing like the winters back in Detroit. The thought of those winters made Darius hunch his shoulders inside his jacket and cram his fists deeper into the side pockets. Damn but those Detroit winters were cold sons-of-bitches.

Darius LeClerc was nineteen years old, a slender, almost skinny young black man, nearly six feet tall. He was dressed in dark colors: black fake-leather bombardier-style jacket, gray acid-washed denims, black Puma high-tops. Under the jacket he wore a black T-shirt and a gray hooded sweatshirt, hood down. As his long limbs propelled him quickly along the sidewalk, Darius pulled his left hand out of its pocket and checked the cheap "sport watch" strapped to his wrist. He had bought it for $14.95 at the K mart on West Center Road. It was mostly plastic, but it worked well enough, he guessed, though at the moment it would have been nice if it had had a luminous dial. Still, there was just enough light for him to see that he was late.

He stepped up the pace, half-jogging toward the street light, the working street light at the corner, near the eastern entrance to the project.

He stopped there, puffing white clouds into the cold night air, scoping out the territory. No signs of life. Was he *that* late? He moved to check his watch again. It'd be easier to see under the street light.

He probably never realized that he would be easier to see, too.

A car engine grumbled awake up the block, back in the direction from which Darius had just come. He turned automatically toward the sound. It was a big car, a Caddie or a Lincoln, maybe, pulling away from the grimy curb across the street, coming down the block, toward the pale illumination at the corner. Its headlights were doused.

Darius LeClerc's first thought was that some damn fool was going to get killed. His second thought, when he saw that the car was veering toward his side of the street, when he saw that the windows were rolled down in defiance of the chilly February night, when he saw that gun barrels were resting on the window frames, was that the damn fool was him.

CHAPTER
2

It's easy to get a private investigator's permit in the State of Nebraska, hard to lose one, and even harder to get one back. How I managed to lose mine is a long story. The fact is, I did lose it—or, more accurately, had it taken from me—back in November, and by mid-February I was hip-deep in the appeal process. As near as I can tell, this process comes down to a series of delays running as close to forever as can be managed. The goal, I think, is to frustrate the appellant so thoroughly that he decides his suit really isn't worth pressing after all and goes home. Guys like me, who get their backs up at such treatment and decide it's the other bastard who'll have to blink first, must be a rarity. That's the only way I can make sense of having had my latest hearing date moved back four times since the first week in January.

When I shared this opinion with my lawyer, Mike Kennerly, he smiled tolerantly and told me not to worry. When a lawyer says not to worry, worry is what you should do first. If we didn't make any headway with the secretary of state, our next stop would be District Court. I had no reason to expect that to be cheap. What I had were serious doubts about whether it would ultimately be worth the effort and expense.

I was telling all this to Elmo Lammers on the short drive from the Omaha Municipal Airport to my apartment on Decatur Street. Elmo laughed. He has a low, lazy laugh that is

9

well suited to his speaking voice. "You worry too much, Nebraska," he said. "You always did."

"I like to think it's one of the reasons I'm still around to meet old friends flying into town."

"Probably something to that," Elmo said.

Late-morning traffic was light this crisp, semi-clear Thursday. I risked turning my attention from the street to Elmo. I couldn't get used to him with the whiskers, a full but close-cropped beard liberally flecked with white. His brown hair was going white, too, and thinning at the temples. But otherwise he was the same slightly built black man I had met a hundred thousand years ago in a hot, wet jungle on the other side of the world, courtesy of a mutual relative: our Uncle Sam. Over months of griping about the crappy weather, crappy rations, crappy equipment, and all-around crappy situation Uncle had handed us, we became friends. We hadn't kept in touch as much as the long-distance companies might like, but it was the sort of friendship that didn't depend on constant or even frequent contact.

When Elmo had called me the previous afternoon to say he was flying in to Omaha today, my only question had been what time should I meet him at the airport.

"Anyhow, what's so great about being a private detective," Elmo was saying. "Pay's lousy, hours stink, and most folks figure that when it comes to ethics you're right up there with the used-car salesmen."

"Yes, but on the plus side, people occasionally get pissed off at you and send bullets, knives, and various blunt instruments your direction."

"Only if you're any good at it." After the army, following stints with a sheriff and a county attorney, Elmo had joined the Chicago office of a medium-sized regional detective agency. He was now what they called a field manager, which, incongruously, meant he spent hardly any time in the field. "What's going on with your writing career, Nebraska?" he asked, out of the blue. "Couple years ago, I went and put up a new bookshelf in my den, for my autographed collection. Still only got one book on it."

My reply was delayed by a small woman in a large Buick who turned from a side-street when she should have waited for me to pass, and then who proceeded to tool along ahead of me at eight miles an hour. She had a bumper sticker pasted on the back end of the car: IF YOU DON'T LIKE THE WAY I DRIVE, STAY OFF THE SIDEWALK! People who put messages like that on their cars are giving you fair warning, which you ought to heed. I made a detour at the next corner to get away from her.

"My publisher had about given up on me, too," I finally said. It had been almost two years since my first novel, forever in my heart The Book, had appeared. It did reasonably well for a first effort. Well enough that my publisher spent a few months pestering me for a follow-up before evidently deciding it was futile. "I surprised him with an early Christmas present a couple of months ago. A new manuscript. It's not the sequel he wanted—he sort of had his heart set on a detective series—but he liked it. He hopes to bring it out this winter. What on earth are you doing?"

What he was doing was moving his long, almost delicate fingers in the air. "Counting. Your first book was about an inch thick, give or take. My bookshelf is four feet long. Figure a little space on each end for looks…shoot, I'll have to put up another shelf in about thirty-five years, you keep cranking them out at this rate."

"I'd forgotten what a one-man laugh riot you are."

"Seriously, Nebraska. I always thought the plan was you'd dump the PI racket, make it as a writer. Maybe this is your big chance, man."

Mike Kennerly had said the same thing. So had other friends who had suffered through the long years of my saying I was going to ditch my day job as soon as I felt I could support myself as a writer. The private-eye dodge, I said, was just a fall-back. Problem with having a fall-back, though, is you're tempted to fall back. And I had—more than once. When the magazine writing assignments didn't come fast enough, when the books didn't get done, and when the wolf was at the door, I would scare up a snoop job. Just to pay the rent, you understand. Strictly temporary.

After a while, something occurred to me. If PI work was so crummy, why didn't I just walk away from it? I had quit other jobs, other careers before. Why the reluctance to give up this one? The only reasonable conclusion was that, my protestations notwithstanding, I liked it.

As soon as I reached that conclusion, the gods reached down from the mesosphere and lifted my license.

Even your closest friends don't necessarily want to hear all the gory details of your pothole-riddled journey to self-discovery, so I spared Elmo and merely said, "There's a difference between giving something away and having it taken from you."

"Yeah," he said after a long moment. "I hear you."

Elmo Lammers was Darius LeClerc's uncle.

By now we were on Decatur, bumping down the long, rutted hill at the bottom of which was my apartment house, a red-brick building built like a motel and set back from the Northwest Radial Highway, which it faces. I steered my old Impala into a space in the miniature lot on the north side of the building. We got out and went up the open-air stairs. Elmo traveled light: a canvas briefcase, a small soft-sided suitcase, and a zippered garment bag that matched the suitcase. I toted the garment bag while he carried the two cases.

"Drop 'em anywhere," I said when we got into the apartment. "You have your pick, this couch or the fold-out bed in the bedroom." In an effort to reclaim my dining table, which had doubled as my work table, I had gotten rid of my bed several months back and replaced it with a convertible sofa. When folded up, the sofa-bed left enough room for a standard office desk in the bedroom. "They're both comfortable, the bed just gives you a little extra room."

"Couch's fine," Elmo said. "I don't want to put you to any trouble."

"We had this conversation yesterday. You're staying here, it's no trouble, end of discussion. What's the agenda?"

"First I need to use your bathroom, then I need to use your phone. I want to let Julie know I got in okay."

"Bathroom's the first door on the left. There's a phone in the bedroom, on the desk, in case you'd like a little privacy while you talk to your wife. Straight down the hall. Don't worry about me, I can eavesdrop on the extension out here."

While Elmo went to his chores, I went to work in the little kitchen. I ran a handful of Eight O'Clock Bean through the grinder and started the water boiling for coffee. As I watched bubbles begin to form in the bottom of the tempered-glass teapot, I thought about Darius LeClerc.

I had known him. More accurately, I had met him—twice, to be exact, and talked to him on the phone maybe once more than that, at the request of his uncle, my old friend Elmo Lammers. Darius had come to the Big O about eight months ago, from Detroit, where he had lived with his mother, Elmo's younger sister, and where, I gathered, there had been "some trouble." Elmo hadn't been specific about the "trouble," and I hadn't asked. If he had thought I needed to know, he'd have told me. Darius was going to be staying with a paternal aunt and uncle, but Elmo asked me to "touch base" with the kid anyway, let him know there was someone else in town he could turn to if the need arose. It wasn't the sort of thing that made me leap up and do cartwheels, but I agreed. A friend's a friend, and like that.

I gave Darius a week or so to get settled, then called him up. Since I had previously telephoned and introduced myself to his aunt and uncle, Susan and Jack Reedy, and since Elmo had alerted them that I might be getting in touch, no one wondered why this old white guy was calling to invite the kid to lunch. No one except Darius, maybe. He was eighteen at the time, tall and too skinny by half, and he wore his attitude like chain-mail. He made it clear that he was meeting me only because his Uncle Jack insisted, and then underscored his indifference by refusing to make eye contact with me as he slouched on his side of the restaurant booth, answering my questions, if at all, with guttural monosyllabic utterings.

After ninety minutes of that sort of balderdash, I kicked him free. Or kicked myself free. Who's to say? I had done my duty to the friend of my youth: I'd made contact with the kid, given him my card, told him not to hesitate to call if he needed anything, et cetera, et cetera. I knew the kid would never call, and that was all right with me. I'd done my bit and that was enough.

Except it *wasn't* enough. I knew Elmo must have been worried about Darius—real worry, genuine worry, as opposed to normal avuncular concern for a nephew's general welfare— or he'd never have asked me to check on the kid. And my twenty-year-old friendship with Elmo was such that I couldn't have simply told him I'd bought his nephew lunch and so had fulfilled my obligation. I mean, I *could* have—Elmo would have asked nothing more of me than that—but I couldn't have.

So a couple of weeks later I called Darius to "see how it was going." Evidently it was going "okay"—that one word being about all the detail he was prepared to part with. From his aunt, Susan Reedy, I learned that Darius was "adjusting," but that it wasn't easy. She volunteered no specifics, and I didn't press. It was none of my business. For that very reason, and because there's a difference between being interested and being nosy, I waited three months before I called again.

That time, I got a different Darius LeClerc. He was friendly, even loquacious. Said he was "in treatment"—drug treatment, I assumed, having somehow formed the impression that drugs were part of the "trouble" back in Detroit—and doing well; said he had found a part-time job that he enjoyed, and was thinking of taking some classes at Metro Community College come autumn; said he'd been meaning to call me and recipro- cate for the meal I had bought him when he came to town. A week or two later, we met for lunch. Darius had put on a few much-needed pounds, had abandoned the slovenly too-hip gangsta look he had previously affected, had learned how to look a guy in the eyes. I was, frankly, amazed at the change in him. Amazed and impressed. Despite my original lack of zeal, I was glad I had met young Darius LeClerc.

And I was sorry, genuinely sorry, when I heard of his death. He had seemed to be a young man on a downward spiral, and then he seemed to have reversed direction. At the risk of sounding sappy, it was downright inspirational. The future, a landscape which once had been bleak and limited, had begun to stretch out before him. But now he would never travel it. A random act of mindless violence had prematurely ended Darius's journey.

If it had been a random act.

If the violence had really been mindless.

If, if, if.

The circumstances of Darius LeClerc's death were not yet clear. There were questions, questions as yet unanswered, questions which Darius's uncle, Elmo Lammers, had come all the way to Omaha to probe.

Would my old friend feel better when he found the answers—if he found the answers—or worse?

That's the problem with this line of work. One of the problems.

The water in the teapot rumbled to a violent boil, and I spooned the coffee into the glass beaker of the coffee pot. I had been searching for the properly balanced formula that would reduce my caffeine intake, but not so far that I'd end up on the ceiling if someone handed me a cup of full-strength coffee. This week's mix was about one-quarter decaffeinated to three-quarters real. I put the coffee beans back in the freezer and pulled out the hamburger patties I had made earlier, a three-to-one hamburger-and-ground-turkey mixture laced with dried onion bits and liberally doused with Worcestershire sauce. There were six of them. I shoved them under the broiler. I split the oversized buns from Benson Bakery and arranged them in the oven; enough heat rises from the broiler to turn the oven compartment into a warmer. I opened a jar of pickles and set it out on the table along with spicy mustard, ketchup, and a bowl of industrial-strength potato chips.

By the time Elmo emerged from the back room, the burgers were ready to be flipped and the kettle was hissing angrily on the stove. I poured the boiling water over the grounds and fit the plunger-filter assembly into the top of the pot. "I'll let that steep a minute," I told Elmo. "How's Julie?"

"Good. Did I tell you they moved her over to the commercial-loan department last month? Took her a while to get up to speed, but she really enjoys it now. Lot smoother than consumer loans."

"Having a wife who's a loan officer should come in handy in a couple of years, when the girls decide they want to go to nice expensive top-ten colleges."

"Having a wife who's rich would be handier." Elmo bit into a pickle and made appreciative noises.

"There's an eighty-six-year-old widow on the first floor of the building who's adopted me," I said. "Mrs. Galas. The landlord lets her keep a garden out back of the building. The garden occupies a geographic area somewhat smaller than Rhode Island. During the summer she's out there about every day—in a long dress, wool sweater, bobby socks, and Nikes. She almost needs migrant workers to help with the harvest. Among other things, she gave me about nine hundred jars of pickles that she put up herself. I can send a few dozen jars home with you, if you like. Meanwhile, coffee's ready, there's beer in the fridge, stronger stuff in the cabinet up there, Coke, 7-Up, orange juice..."

"I told you not to go to any trouble."

"And I told you not to worry about it. Fix yourself a hamburger."

He did, and I did, and we sat down and went to work on them. We were each on our second burger before Elmo came around to the reason for his visit. "I talked to your police again yesterday. From Detroit, after the funeral. They don't have anything new. Don't know any more than they did Sunday night—Monday morning, I guess—when Darius was killed."

"I'm afraid these street-gang drive-by killings aren't anything new in this town, Elmo. Within the past four-five years, the Bloods and the Crips have spread out from Los Angeles like some sort of infestation and found ready markets in smaller, 'second-tier' cities. Portland, Denver, Minneapolis, Kansas City. Omaha. They've brought their coke and their crack, their semiautomatic weapons, their colors and their smack and their turf wars."

Elmo grunted. "I thought all of that was supposed to be ancient history now, what with the big post-riot truce."

"Yeah," I said. "Right." When the smoke had cleared—literally—after the L.A. riots, the major rival street gangs, the Bloods and the Crips, had declared a much-ballyhooed truce. Maybe it was doing some good in California, but out here on the lone prairie its noticeable effect had been exactly nil. Locally, the gangs were still at each other's throats—which might not have been so bad if all they did was bump each other off. Unfortunately, that wasn't the case.

"As with any war," I said, "there are innocent victims. Kids shot because they were out playing when a drive-by went down. Kids knifed for wearing the wrong color shirt on the wrong block. Kids, and adults, killed because they were sitting in their living room watching TV when a stray bullet came through the window."

There was a plain manila file folder on the kitchen counter. Now I reached behind me, retrieved it, and handed it to Elmo. "Here are the newspaper accounts of Darius's death. I also went downtown to the public library and copied stories about local gang doings going back about six months." There were perhaps two dozen sheets of photocopier paper in the folder. Elmo was giving them quick but interested glances.

"Kinda all start sounding the same after a while," he said.

"It gets to be like the reports about Sarajevo or Rwanda or

Londonderry. You want to be interested, but time passes and nothing changes and you find yourself skimming the headlines on your way to seeing what Winnie Winkle's up to." I got up and went after another mug of coffee for me and another Harp for Elmo.

He had finished skimming the file and gone back to the *World-Herald* account of Darius LeClerc's murder. It had started in a small box on the front page, lower left, and jumped inside to page five. "Youth Slain in Drive-by Shoot" was set in the same size type as "Clean-up Costs Worry Sarpy County."

"Nothing here the police didn't already tell me."

"And no more in the follow-up in Tuesday's paper. Youth slain, cops investigate, no witnesses, no leads, gangs suspected. I clipped it anyway, just for completeness' sake. Nothing at all in yesterday's paper. Or this morning's."

Elmo closed the folder and leaned back in his chair, sipping his beer, contemplating the Gulden's Mustard bottle on the table.

"I still have one or two friends at OPD," I said. I used to have more, but cops like defrocked private investigators about as much as Dan Rostenkowski likes the Justice Department. "What they're giving you is straight. They don't know who killed Darius or why. No one in the project or the surrounding neighborhood saw or heard anything useful. They heard the shots, sat tight until they figured it was safe, then ventured a peek out their windows. Some of them could see Darius lying on the corner. A couple of them called nine-one-one. The first patrol car was on the scene six minutes after the first call came in, and Darius was already dead. The MO makes them think gangs. The location makes them think Crips: the project is Blood turf. No one's taken credit for the shoot, which is odd, but speculation is that a carload of Crips went down there to cause trouble. Darius came walking by, they figured him to be Blood, gunned him down, and took off."

Elmo looked at me. His brown eyes were expressionless. "Wrong place, wrong time," he said.

"Looks like it."

"Uh-huh. Pretty damn convenient, isn't it?" He stood up and went into the living room. That sounds like more than it is: the living room is separated from the kitchen–dining area by imagination and little else. He went over near the picture window and looked down at the four lanes of the Radial Highway. The nine-to-fivers were on their lunch breaks, and traffic was heavy. The apartment house was perhaps a hundred feet back from the road, and the distance plus a number of big old maples in the yard were enough to blunt most of the traffic sounds; it was quiet in the room. Two minutes passed. I know because on every circuit I could hear the bent second-hand on my kitchen wall clock scrape a whitish smile near the nine.

Although Elmo had tried to be his usual jovial self when I picked him up at Eppley Field, I could tell he was forcing it. I chalked it up to grief over the loss of his nephew and travel fatigue after the journey from Chicago to Detroit and Detroit to Omaha. But there had been something else in his voice just now: anger.

I said, "I know the cops in this town, Elmo. Some of them are lazy, some of them are stupid, and some of them just don't give a damn. But the other ninety-nine percent of them are pros—responsible, committed, all that Cub-Scout-oath stuff. That certainly applies to the ones I spoke with about your nephew. If they say they're investigating, then they're investigating."

"The boy was killed Monday morning. This is Thursday afternoon."

"It's not their fault they don't have anything to go on."

"*Heavens* no," Elmo said.

I refilled my mug and took it into the living room. I sat in the big uncomfortable chair that usually serves as a coat rack, when I haven't tidied up for company. "Look, Elmo, I'm not OPD's favorite at the moment, but the cops I talked to wouldn't lie to me. If they didn't want to talk, they just wouldn't take my calls; they wouldn't lie." I paused a moment and then went on: "And they tell me they have some blank spots where your nephew's concerned."

He turned away from the window. "Go on."

"No one can figure out what he was doing in that neighborhood at that hour. It's clear the hell on the other side of town from the Reedys' place. It's only so-so by day, bad news by night. It's a center for gang activity. And you know as well as I do that Darius's record isn't exactly unblemished."

"Ah." Elmo smiled. "Black kid, bad history, bad neighborhood, middle of the night. What business's he got there? Must've been a wrong dude, probably deserved what he got."

"The cops tell me Darius was a known user and probable dealer back in Detroit." I hadn't been surprised to learn that: I figured that was part of the "trouble" Elmo had alluded to back when he first asked me to look up his nephew.

"Like I said, probably deserved what he got."

"Dammit, get off that. What the hell do you want, anyway?"

He looked at me for a long time. "I want someone to give a damn," he finally said.

"Okay, you got him. Now what? You gotta work with me a little here, Elmo. What is it you want? What are you doing here?"

His beer bottle had rested forgotten in his hand during this time. Now he rediscovered it and took a long pull. "Yesterday afternoon I helped my sister, Francine, bury her firstborn child. I helped her grieve. I grieved with her, Nebraska. I didn't know Darius very well, I didn't see him very often, but he was family. You know?"

I said that I did.

"Francine's widowed these past four years. Raising three kids. Two, now. James is fourteen. Sara is twelve."

"I didn't know. I'm sorry, man…"

He half-smiled an acknowledgment. "What hurt more than burying that young man was seeing what it did to Francine. How it tore her up. My baby sister…" He put his head back and squeezed his eyes shut. Still, a tear trailed down his right cheek, disappearing into his beard. When he finally opened his eyes again, they were red and wet. "I promised Francine I'd come down here, see what I could find out. See if I could come up with a *reason*, some way to make sense of Darius's death."

Elmo took a powder-blue handkerchief from his pocket and wiped his eyes. He cleared his throat. "What your friends told you is true. Darius was a user back in Detroit. Pot, pills, and, most recently, crack. Maybe selling a little, too, to help finance the habit. Dealin' and stealin', you know, that's how they do it." He smiled unevenly and carefully folded his handkerchief and tucked it away. "That's part of the reason for him being out here. In Omaha, I mean. I figure you guessed that much back when I called to ask you to look him up, eight months ago."

I nodded, and made some coffee disappear.

"I told you there was trouble back in Detroit. I never said what sort of trouble 'cause I'm not real clear—'cause Francine wasn't real clear either. We know he was using, know he was mixed up with the wrong sort of people. Anyhow, and here's where it gets fuzzy, something happened. Something blew up in the boy's face. He didn't tell his mother exactly what had gone down, just that there were some people looking to hurt him. He said he had to get out of town, like right away. He was scared, Francine said—so scared that she got scared too. She thought of sending him out to me, but Darius didn't think Chicago'd be any better for him than Detroit. Darius had an aunt and uncle and some cousins here in Omaha, his father's sister and her people—the Reedys—so Francine put him on a Greyhound that very night."

"What sort of trouble do you think the lad was in?"

He laughed, and sniffed wetly. "Lad? You know, Nebraska, it's okay to call him a boy. He *was* a boy."

"You mean I can call a spade a spade?" I said innocently.

"Whoa, now there's where we draw the line."

I smiled and emptied my mug. "Fair enough. What sort of trouble was the boy in?"

"Can't say. If he was dealing, maybe he crossed somebody. Or somebody just thought they'd been crossed by him. If he was stealing, maybe he ripped off the wrong people."

"Gangs?"

"Darius wasn't a member of any gang. But you know how it is these days—at *some* level they're always involved with drugs. I called the manager of our Detroit office when this all hit the fan. He's okay, I've met him once or twice. Asked him to do me a favor, check with the local badges there, see if he could tumble to anything." He shrugged. "Inconclusive. There had been a shooting the night Darius got scared. Small-time dealer, ripped off good and left in a parking lot with a pair of bullets in his gut. He died next morning without waking up. Big news in Detroit, huh? Someone said they saw two black kids in the next block about the time the police think it went down. Running like the devil himself was after them."

"And you think one of them was your nephew."

"Maybe. I can't make myself believe Darius would participate in a killing, but maybe he was there for a buy. Saw the dealer get whacked, and panicked. Maybe he knew the shooter. Maybe he was with the shooter. Maybe he was afraid the shooter would come after him. And maybe not. Far as I know, the case is still open."

"Darius came here to hide and cool out, but Detroit caught up with him. Is that how you run it?"

"The guy who died, the dealer, was strictly small-potatoes. Doesn't seem real likely anyone'd go to the effort to track his killer down."

"These gangbangers hire out." When I was a kid, *gangbanger* meant something different.

"Doesn't seem real likely anyone'd put out a contract on him either. And a lot of time has passed since Detroit…"

We let it hang there awhile. I went for another dose of coffee and silently asked Elmo if he wanted another Harp. He silently told me no. I went back into the living room and sat down. "All right, I'll be the one to say it first. Darius was on that corner at that time of night to make a buy. It got messed up. Maybe the deal went sour. Maybe the shooters thought he was someone else. Maybe he really was just in the wrong place at the wrong time. It doesn't make your nephew look too good, Elmo, but it works."

"That what your cop friends think?"

"They think it's a possibility. What do you think?"

He put his feet on the coffee table, crossed his ankles, and studied his shoes. They were soft-soled cowhide loafers, polished to a high gloss. His shoes were always shiny. Even when we were slogging through the jungle, Elmo somehow kept a shine on his boots. He could probably raise a shine on a pair of suede shoes, if he set his mind to it. He said, "Did you ever meet the people Darius was staying with here—Jack and Susan Reedy?"

"Not really. I talked with Susan on the phone a couple of times."

Elmo nodded. "Me neither, really. I met her at the funeral yesterday, but only for a minute. I understand they're good people. Agreed to take the boy in, no questions asked. On one condition. He get his head straight. Get into a program, stick with the program, keep his nose clean. Anything short of that, Jack Reedy said he'd bounce Darius out on his butt. No second chance."

"Tough love."

"Reedy's a drunk, recovered, recovering, whatever they call it. And you know what hard-cases converts always are. Also, the Reedys have two kids just a little younger than Darius, and like most of us parents they're scared to death the kids'll get messed up with drugs and booze and shit. Point is, Darius had no choice. Take the cure or take his chances. He was in a program practically the minute he stepped off that Gray Dog. And know what? It took. I understand Darius never was a real heavy user, but they still had some tough weeks with him while he got cleaned out. That crack is bad shit, man, gets you hooked like right now. But the point is, he *did* clean out, and he stayed clean. He stuck with the program. Hell, you saw how he'd changed in the last half-year. He got a job at some

submarine-sandwich joint. He was looking into vo-tech classes, thought he'd see about learning something when the next
term started up. He was on-track, Nebraska. On-track."

"One thing about junkies, Elmo. They're damn good liars."

"And I know it," he said fervently. "And that's the first thing
that entered my head when Francine was telling me all this
stuff the other night. She's telling me her boy had got it all
together at last and I'm telling myself he fucked up. He had a
second chance and he blew it. He conned everybody, his
mother, his aunt and uncle, his counselors—you—probably
even himself. Got himself right back into the shit-can he was
in back in Detroit, and this time there was no pulling him out."

"If that's what you think…"

"Then why am I sitting here drinking your beer?" He
smiled. "Because I've got a sister who's hurting. She defends
her son, she really *wants* to believe he was getting straight when
he died. But she knows him too well. And I know *her* too well
to think she'll ever sleep good with that kind of uncertainty
churning inside her."

"And?"

He looked at me. "And what?"

"This is *me*, man. I know you. You could sell long underwear in the Sahara. If all you had wanted was to ease your
sister's mind, you'd've done it. You'd've made like butter on
hot toast, reassured her about her boy, and convinced her that
his death was just one of the cruel ironies of life. For that
matter, you could still do it. There's that file of newspaper
stories about innocent people getting blown away by the
Bloods and the Crips. There's the phone. Call her and read her
some of it."

Elmo stared at the phone, which was on the counter that
separated the living room from the kitchen. He has always
been an unhurried conversationalist. Sometimes you think
he's ignoring you, but he's merely considering his reply. Now,
however, he took a long time even for him, and his beard was
not so thick that I couldn't see his jaw muscles working as he

sat there silently. Finally he said: "Whatever Darius might have been back in Detroit, whatever he may or may not have become here, he was family. My family. And somebody shot him down like a dog in the street. That throws everything out of whack, Nebraska. You know me—I like things to balance out. Okay, maybe your cops are all stand-up guys. But you know how things go in the real world, man. Case drags on, nothing breaks, meanwhile something else goes down. There's only so much money, so many man-hours… Things get lost in the shuffle. I can't let that happen, Nebraska. Not to my nephew. Not to my baby sister."

I finished my coffee and put the mug on the floor.

"Where do you want to start?" I said.

CHAPTER

3

Elmo got out of the car and slipped on a pair of black plastic sunglasses with neon-green accents. It wasn't sunny, although the haze had lifted a little, or maybe just turned a lighter shade. There always seems to be a little haze anymore. They tell us the air in Omaha is cleaner now than it was ten years ago, but there's always that haze. Not smog exactly. Not quite; not yet. Give us time, though, and maybe we'll work up to it.

I climbed out of the car and walked with Elmo across the street, to the corner, near the wall that marked the entrance to the project, a set of squat block buildings the color of broken dreams. The wall that contained them, crumbling stucco over concrete block, looked like it had been decorated with graffiti, painted, decorated, painted, over and over in an endless ritual. The graffiti artists had had the last turn. The centerpiece was "Blood Thang," spray-painted in big cartoonish red and black letters and set off by lesser works.

Elmo reached into a side pocket of the wine-colored leather coat he was wearing and extracted a pack of the brown-paper cigarettes he favored. He stuck one between his lips and fired up the battered gold lighter he always carried. The lighter was the rich honey color of old 18-karat gold. When he had the cigarette going and had slipped the lighter back into his coat pocket, he gave the project the once-over, a precise right-to-left pan. Then he looked down at the pavement beneath our feet.

26

There was no sign of the violence of fifty-some hours earlier, no remaining trace of the police investigation that had followed it. There were scars on the stucco wall that may have been made by bullets that flew past or through Darius on Monday morning. Or they may have been made at some other time, for some other reason or no reason at all. The only way you could tell that this was where the kid had fallen dead was that the sidewalk was a little less grimy here. Someone had scrubbed it down to get rid of the blood.

Slowly, Elmo raised his head. He looked back at the project. Then he looked across the street, toward where my ancient Impala was parked. Then he looked at me. "I hate to admit it, but everyone's right: What the hell *was* the boy doing here in the middle of the night?"

I couldn't read his eyes behind the shades.

I said, "Either he was dirty or he was clean. If he was dirty, he may have been down here to make a buy. The buy went wrong. Or it didn't, but he was in the wrong place at the wrong time."

"Everyone who's in a position to know says Darius was getting straightened out. You saw it for yourself."

"All right, say he was clean. He's going to or coming from a completely innocent meeting. And he's in the wrong place at the wrong time."

"Then why hasn't the person he was meeting said something?"

"Fear," I said. "This gang shit has got people in this town really nervous, Elmo. People are moving as far west and south as they can manage. The prevailing wisdom is move out to Millard and buy a big dog. People are jittery."

"And even more jittery if they're living in the thick of it all?" He surveyed the surroundings again, the garbage, the graffiti, the careworn buildings, the few tired, wrung-out-looking residents who passed by or loitered here or there. "Yeah, okay, I'll buy that," he said after a while.

I said, "Doesn't make that person or persons not worth

finding. People change their minds."

He nodded, and took a well-worn Leatherette booklet from an inside pocket. The booklet was the kind you slip a small wire-bound notebook into. He flipped through the notebook's dog-eared pages, talking as he did so. "Like I told you, I've been in touch with Omaha Police Division. I talked to a Sergeant—let's see—Banner. Homicide."

"I know her. She's good."

Elmo nodded, as if that verified something he already suspected. "I spoke to her from Chicago on Monday and again from Detroit yesterday. I also called her from your place, let her know I was in town." A good PI always checks in with the local badges when he comes to town on business. "Sergeant Banner told me that the nine-eleven dispatcher received two calls reporting the shoot, almost simultaneously. The nine-eleven autotrace only led them to one of the callers, who said he or she—Sergeant Banner was generous with information but stingy with specifics—heard the shooting and called the cops but stayed away from the windows, so couldn't give any details at all. The crime-scene team canvassed the neighborhood and came up with only two other residents who had anything to say. They said they heard a car speed away; one said he—or she—saw it. A big black car. Didn't know what make or model, naturally. Also saw the body lying here on the corner. At least that's what he-or-she thought it was. He-or-she didn't come out and investigate."

"I don't blame him. Or her. What happened to the other nine-one-one call?"

"Didn't trace right. Some kind of computer glitch, I guess. But the caller did tell the dispatcher that he-or-she saw a, quote, big black car drive away, unquote."

"That could be helpful," I said.

Elmo put away the notebook and went back to studying the other side of the street. I helped him.

The corner we stood on used to be the northwest corner of the intersection of the two streets. When the project went up in the sixties, this half of the intersection became its eastern entrance. Through-traffic was prohibited, creating, in essence, a T intersection. If you're used to orienting maps to the north, think of an H with the right-hand vertical bar missing. The area to the left of the remaining vertical bar—west—was the project. It took up maybe five blocks. The area right of the vertical bar and above the horizontal bar—northeast—was a residential block. Smaller, older homes, some in fair condition, fronted by a parkway strip dotted with ash trees of respectable size; the neighborhood was far older than the project.

The area below the horizontal bar, southeast of us, was commercial. No tree-lined parkway; the sidewalk went right up to the curb. Most of the buildings were one- and two-story affairs with brick or stucco façades. It must have been very nice, when the neighborhood was new, to have a little grocery, and a drugstore with a soda fountain, and who knows what all else right down the street. Today you have to get in the car and drive fifty miles to Target or Food City or what's universally known as The Mall. Still, there appeared to be a few going concerns along the block, and a fair number of the windows displayed hopeful For Rent signs. Some of the windows even had glass in them.

The windows on the second floors of those buildings that had second floors looked like they might have apartments behind them. I looked at Elmo and he looked at me, canting his head toward the houses across and up the street. "Hard to see this corner from over there," he said. "With the trees."

"No trees in that block," I said, nodding toward the commercial buildings. "Or the next one down. Someone on an upper floor, front, would have a nice view of this corner. Especially if this streetlight works."

He turned and looked at the project behind us.

"Not with that wall," I said.

"Unless he's Superman."

"And we both know that couldn't be, 'cause *I* am."

"Uh-huh. Your super-ears pick up what our little friends are saying about us?" He nodded over my left shoulder.

I didn't look. I had spotted them earlier, through the entrance to the project. A cluster of black kids, boys, had congregated around some rust-scarred equipment in a sorry-looking play area just inside the entrance. They had turned out about thirty seconds after we arrived on the scene and had remained there, sizing us up, ever since. Some of them were wearing red bandannas tied around their left forearms. I said, "My guess is that they're not worrying about whether we're truant officers, though they should be. If any of them's older than fourteen, I'll eat my trenchcoat."

"You never owned a trenchcoat in your life."

"Your trenchcoat, then. I don't think they're gangbangers."

"Too young," he agreed. "They like them young, but that young they only want them for running errands and stuff."

"Errands," I said. "The sort of errands that'll get you three to five."

"Only if you're eighteen, which is why they hire the kids." He turned away from them and joined me in looking across the street. "They'll tell the Bloods about us."

"Does that bother us?"

"Hard to figure what we could do about it if it did. You feel like going calling?"

We went across the street.

CHAPTER

4

You reached the upstairs spaces via unmarked doors alongside the storefronts. We tried five of them spaced along the first two blocks. Two of them were locked up tight, their large window openings now filled with plywood. One, though locked, had had the plywood knocked in. Someone had enjoyed a bottle of off-brand liquor at the foot of the stairs just inside the doorway—recently, too, since the door hadn't been patched up yet and the bottle still had a drop of liquid in the bottom.

Two doors were unlocked. They led us, in turn, up steep, unlighted staircases that ended in narrow corridors that ran the width of the building. The second building we entered had a window at the far end. It admitted a little light to play on the cobwebs and litter.

The hallways smelled of dust and cooking.

There were four apartments—rooms, more accurately—in each of these buildings, two front, two back. The corner where Darius had died would be visible only from front windows, so that cut the job in half. We knocked on four doors, two per building.

The first two resulted in, respectively, a man and a woman who were willing to shout at us through their doors but unwilling to talk with us except to say they didn't know anything about anything.

The third produced no response.

The fourth was opened by an enormous black woman minding three small children—not hers, she volunteered—in a space slightly larger than an elevator car. She had heard the shots, she said, and even admitted to having called 911. Had she seen anything? She shook her head and smiled at us, softly, as if we were addled. "You don't be hangin' 'round no windows you hear bullets start to flyin'," she told us sagely.

Back on the pavement, Elmo lighted another cigarette while I looked down to the next block. Half-block, really; while the nearer half was more of the same, the far end had been razed and now stood vacant.

"Couldn't see the corner from that distance, that angle," Elmo said, echoing my thoughts.

"Maybe the one who saw the car isn't a registered guest."

"A squatter?" He scratched behind his ear. "Had to have a phone to call it in."

"Let's burn that bridge when we come to it."

I jaywalked across the street and Elmo came with me. The afternoon had turned out pleasant enough and there was a surprising number of people out and about. Surprising to me, at least. Given the recent gang terrorism, I had imagined more of a siege mentality. Imagining was all I had done: this was not a neighborhood I frequented. But the people of the neighborhood were out going about their business, the kids who had bothered to go to school were now on their way home, mothers with younger children were sitting on the benches around the playground while their kids made the most of the run-down equipment. Except from the youths at the project earlier, Elmo and I attracted only the most casual looks. While the surroundings were definitely lower-income, definitely down-at-heels, it wasn't quite the deserted, bombed-out battle-zone I had pictured.

Still, you weren't apt to catch me standing out on that sidewalk after nightfall.

The afternoon sun had come around enough to begin to glint off the front windows in the two blocks Elmo and I had just covered. I pointed to a second-floor window in the first block we had taken. The building had a coin-op laundry on the ground floor, but the door to the upstairs rooms had been locked. It was the door with the kicked-in plywood panel.

"Window on the left," I said.

"Son of a bitch," Elmo said.

The light was such that we could see a small, unevenly shaped patch on the window pane, where someone had smeared the grime away to make a peephole.

We went back across the street, to the vandalized door.

The stairway and the corridor were repeats of the two we had already been in, with the addition of the heavy hush of vacancy. The window at the end of the corridor was partly open. We walked down to it. There had been a screen, but it was long gone now, leaving only the cheap wooden frame. The sill was free of dust except at the very edges. There was an iron fire-escape landing just below the window, over a narrow dead-end alley. Elmo raised the sash and leaned out. "There's no ladder to the ground. You could jump down, maybe—never up..." He looked around. "Ah," he said.

He moved aside and I looked. There was a narrow iron utility ladder bolted to the side of the building. Roof access. It was an easy reach from the landing.

"They took out the fire ladder to the ground to discourage squatters, vandals, and kids," Elmo said. "No one saw any reason to try and pry that sucker off the side of the building."

"Probably take the wall with it," I said, pulling my head in. "Looks like it's been there since forever."

"These rooms are supposed to be vacant, and the front door's supposed to be locked and boarded up. Someone, kids or drunks or someone, kicked it open, but that's temporary. If you were squatting here, you'd want a more dependable entrance."

"This building butts up to the one next door," I said, "and those upstairs rooms are occupied. Officially occupied, I mean."

33

"That's why there was no hallway window," Elmo said. "But there's probably some other way up to the roof."

"You come in next door, get onto the roof, come across to this building, down the ladder, in through this window, and..."

The front apartment nearest the window had a big Yale padlock hanging from a hasp bolted into the woodwork. Elmo studied the lock. "Landlord's gonna be pissed," he said. He held up a hand. "Wait."

I heard it too, in that same instant. A scuffle and crunch above us, on the roof.

We slid away from the padlocked door and back up the hallway. The doors on either side were set back maybe six inches from the corridor wall; we flattened ourselves into a pair of these hidey-holes, counting on the relative gloom of the hallway to conceal us further.

Elmo eased a small flat Browning automatic from inside his coat. Until the resolution of my permit-revocation appeal, I was allowed to ply my trade but not to carry a concealed weapon. That's why I felt a lot better taking my revolver from the clip-on holster on my hip and having it out in the open.

The dim light in the corridor dimmed even more as a shape blocked the window. I heard the sash slide in its channel, then the scrape of shoes on the sill, accompanied by a faint grunt of effort. I risked the slight movement required to glance that direction and saw the silhouette of a man crouched in the window frame as he angled himself in.

Another shape moved on my left—Elmo, darting up the hallway toward the newcomer. I'd figured we'd wait and see what the window man did, but obviously my friend had other ideas. Maybe I'd have been equally impatient if Darius LeClerc had been my nephew. Anyhow, there was no time to philosophize now. I left my hiding place, half a step behind Elmo. We reached the window man almost simultaneously. Elmo grabbed his right wrist and I grabbed his left wrist and we helped him into the hallway.

He didn't cry out, but he did groan loudly and, pulling away from us, curled into a ball against the padlocked door, his arms up over his head.

"Easy," I said. "No one's gonna hurt you." I put away my gun. Elmo didn't.

The man peeked out between his upraised arms. He was a small, slender white man, thirty or thirty-five years old, with dark hair that hadn't been trimmed in a while and a dark beard that was in similar condition. His clothes were old and ill-fitting, but not threadbare. He looked clean enough. Harmless, too.

"What you want?" the man said. His voice had a whiny, wheedling pitch to it. It was the voice of a bus-terminal panhandler.

"Just to talk," I said.

"You live here?" Elmo said brusquely.

The man looked at me. "You from the county?"

"We're not from anybody. Come on, let's get you up." We helped him to his feet but he still cringed a little, as if he expected us to strike at him at any moment. "What's your name?"

"Jeff," he said after some hesitation.

"Okay, Jeff," I said soothingly, smiling. "This is Elmo. My name's Nebraska."

Jeff looked at me with renewed suspicion. "You from the state?"

"Why the hell don't you get a first name," Elmo growled.

"Got one," I said. "I just don't like it." To Jeff I said, "It's just my name, that's all. We're not from the state or the county or the city, or anyone else. We're on our own. We're trying to find out what happened here Sunday night."

"Sunday?" He acted like he had never heard the word.

"Jesus Christ," Elmo snapped.

"The night that boy got killed outside," I said, smiling twice as hard in an effort to make up for Elmo's gruffness.

Jeff's bearded face brightened. "Oh yeah. Was that Sunday?

35

I saw it. It woke me up. It was real noisy." He thought for a minute. "I called the police, too. Nine-one-one." He recited it the way a kid recites a phone number someone's made him memorize.

I exchanged a glance with Elmo. Despite his slow and childlike mind, Jeff must have seen our skepticism. "I'll show you," he said, and there was a little defiance in his voice. He dug in a front pocket of his jeans and produced a key. It was attached to an otherwise unused belt loop with a thin black shoelace just long enough to reach from his hip to the padlock. "I put this lock on here myself," he said with pride.

"It's real nice, Jeff," I said.

The room was almost identical to the one that had belonged to the black woman in the next building: a square, suffocating space that in its day might have been pleasant, though never pretty and certainly never spacious. It was surprisingly tidy. Not clean, just neat. The front windows were soiled to an almost translucent state, except for the spot that Jeff had buffed semi-clean. Cobwebs hung from the ceiling, holding trapped chips of paint. The corners of the worn and warped hardwood floor were hidden by thick layers of dust. But Jeff's few possessions were neatly stowed. There was a forest-green sleeping-bag folded in half in a corner near the door, a thin pillow on top of it. Next to it stood, side-by-side, two white cartons that had originally contained photocopier paper. On the lid of the first carton sat a plastic lamp that was powered by a lantern battery; on the lid of the second carton, a transistor radio in a vinyl case. He had driven ten-penny nails into the wall above the little set-up, and from the nails hung wire hangers bearing a couple of polyester shirts and a pair of jeans identical to the ones he was wearing.

He had also driven nails into the north and south walls and stretched a plastic clothesline between them. For his laundry, I guessed, though it was a lot more line than he needed for his wardrobe, from what I could see.

There was nothing else in the place.

"Come in," Jeff said in a self-consciously courteous way. "I don't have any chairs," he added unnecessarily. He was busy locking the door from the inside, using the same padlock that had been on the other side of the door. When he was satisfied that we were secure, he went over to the carton that had the battery-operated lamp on it. He set the lamp on his pillow, then removed the lid of the carton, setting it on the floor next to the sleeping bag. He did this carefully, as if these were prized possessions. But he was even more careful when he reached inside the carton and, moving aside what looked like a few items of clothing and some other odds and ends, brought forth a standard beige desk phone. He showed it to us the way a true believer might show a sacred relic.

I didn't dare look at Elmo. I knew if I did I'd burst out laughing, and I didn't want to laugh at poor Jeff. If he really thought he called the cops on a phone that wasn't hooked up to anything, who was I to laugh at him?

Suddenly he shoved the phone at me. Uncertainly, I lifted the receiver. "Hello?" I said into the void.

Jeff frowned at me. "It's not hooked up," he said in disgust. "Just hold onto it a minute."

I took the appliance and he turned back toward the wall, lifting a corner of the sleeping bag and pulling out a length of telephone wire that ended in a modular clip. The other end of the wire disappeared behind the baseboard of the wall.

Jeff got to his feet, plugged the modular clip into the slot on the back of the phone, and put his hand on the receiver. "Now be real quiet," he said in a sharp whisper, although no one but him was making any noise. When we were real quiet he carefully lifted the receiver and put it to his ear. He smiled, and held the handset out toward us. We could hear the dial tone.

"I tied in to the laundry downstairs," Jeff said, still whispering. He silently cradled the receiver. "The line runs through the wall here." He smiled shyly. "I know a little bit about telephones and stuff."

When the 911 autotrace coughed up the number of a

business whose office was closed at the hour the call was placed, the cops naturally blamed it on a computer hiccup. Computers are the great uncomplaining scapegoats of the modern age.

Jeff unhooked the phone and put it away as tenderly as he had unpacked it. "I don't have anybody to call, but I still like to have a phone, you know? In case of trouble? Sometimes I call Dial-a-Prayer, just to like test the phone. But only at night, when the office is closed downstairs. They don't know about my phone. They don't know about me. Nobody does." He put the lamp back on the box and turned to look at us. "'Cept you. How'd you know I was here?"

"We didn't," I said. "We guessed. The door downstairs was broken—"

"Drunks," Jeff said disdainfully.

"—so we came up to take a look around. We knew some people had called nine-one-one Sunday night." He started to look puzzled again, so I prompted, "The night that boy got shot?" and that seemed to help. "A lady down the street said she *heard* the shots and called the police, but we figured someone had to have *seen* something."

"Let's cut to the benediction, okay?" Elmo said. "What did you see that night—the night the boy was killed."

Jeff flinched away from the hard edge in Elmo's voice and looked at me. I nodded encouragement.

"Well," he began slowly, "It was real noisy. It woke me up. I heard this like loud bang-bang-bang. That's what woke me up. I went over to the window..." He got up and moved over toward the bare windows in the west wall. I noticed he didn't get too close to the glass, probably for fear of being seen from the street. I wondered why he didn't seem too concerned about people downstairs hearing him moving around up here, then realized that when washers and dryers downstairs were running, as they were now, they would drown out any sounds from up here.

"There's that street light over there, you know?" Jeff was saying. "So I could see this big car kind of zooming away down

the street"—he swept one arm to illustrate the zooming part—
"and this like body on the ground by the light. So I got on my
phone and I called the police. Nine-one-one. The amb'lances
and everything, they came right away." He came away from the
window and looked at us. "But that boy was already dead," he
said, imparting a confidence.

"We know, Jeff. But that was still a real good thing you did."

Elmo said, "Did you see anything else? Did you see who was
in the car?"

Jeff scratched his scraggly beard. "No. I couldn't see nothin'
'cept like the roof of the car, you know? From up here, I
couldn't see nothin'."

I had drifted over toward the windows and now casually
glanced down toward the street. Jeff was telling the truth. The
angle was such that you couldn't see a thing except the roof of
a passing car. Darius's killers had not had the courtesy to use
a convertible.

Elmo was looking at me. I smiled. He took my meaning. He
turned back to the other man. "What else do you know?"

Jeff shrugged. It seemed to make his head sink even further
into his shoulders. "Nothin'." The whine was creeping back in
there.

"Elmo just wants to know if you've heard anything around
the neighborhood," I said, wandering back toward the other
two. "You know—what people are saying about the shooting.
Who did it. Why. That kind of thing."

He shrugged again. "Nothin'. I kinda mind my own business, like."

"Let's get out of here, Nebraska."

"Yeah, we'd better be running along, Jeff," I said. I extended
my hand and Jeff, after a slight hesitation, shyly shook it. From
my side, it was like shaking a dishrag. "Thanks for your time.
Thanks for showing us your phone," I added, seeing how the
guy was so proud of it.

Jeff smiled, then the smile evaporated. "You won't tell
anybody?" The whine was back in his voice again, and he

lowered his head slightly, hunching his shoulders in a half-cringe. "You won't tell anybody 'bout me?"

We assured him we would not.

"What about my phone?"

"Hey, we told you man. We're not city, county, state, federal, or anything else. We're just a coupla guys, okay?" I gripped the man's shoulder in what I hoped was a reassuring way. "Okay?"

After a while Jeff nodded. "Okay. Thanks."

He unlocked the door for us. As we filed past him, some impulse took me and I handed him one of my cards. At Mike Kennerly's suggestion, I'd had new ones printed to use until my permit suspension was settled. These omitted the dread word *investigations* and my permit number, leaving just my name and telephone number in black raised letters.

Jeff took it, handling it by the edges, the way you would a photograph.

"You ever need to test your phone or anything, you can call me," I said.

Then we left.

CHAPTER

5

The Reedys lived in a standard-issue three-bedroom ranch-style house not far from Pipal Park in south-central Omaha. It was a neighborhood of smallish, tidy houses on smallish, tidy lots, a neighborhood built for and by working people thirty or forty years ago. By the look of things, it was one still populated by blue-collar and low- to mid-level white-collar workers. The Reedy house sat behind a large birch tree that was as dead as a telephone pole, thanks to whatever blight had ripped through the region last year. Afternoon had slid into evening and the evening had turned everything gray, but if I'd had to guess, I would have said that the house was painted antique blue.

Susan Reedy, Darius's aunt on his father's side, answered the front door. She was a trim woman in her late forties, with a wide and ready smile—about what I'd expected, based on my telephone conversations with her. She had been expecting us; Elmo had let her know we would probably be stopping by this evening. She invited us into the trim little house, apologizing for the "mess" although there was none. I told her if she wanted to see a mess, she should see my place, and Elmo agreed a little faster than I thought was polite.

"I feel a little frazzled," she said. "I only got in from Detroit about an hour ago. I should have flown in this morning with you, Elmo. Some part went blooey on my flight and we sat on the runway for an hour and a half while they fixed it."

"Really makes you look forward to the flight, doesn't it," Elmo said.

She laughed. "Anyhow, Jack should be along any minute now, depending on the traffic. I get off easy, days that I work, since I'm just over at Westroads; it only takes me about ten minutes to drive home." I knew from Elmo that Jack Reedy was a communications specialist at Offutt Air Force Base—former home of the Strategic Air Command, when there was a Strategic Air Command, when there was a Communist Threat—while Susan was an assistant manager at Dillard's, the big department store that had filled the void created when our local Brandeis stores sold out to the Younkers chain a few years ago.

Elmo said, "Sorry to be busting in like this. We'll try not to upset your suppertime too bad."

"Don't be ridiculous. What with everybody's schedules, we're lucky if we can get together for supper at all, let alone sit down before seven, eight o'clock. J.T., that's our oldest, he's on the varsity basketball team, so he's got practice 'most every night. With all that practice, you'd think they'd win more. And Anna, our girl, she's in band and orchestra and chorus and I can't keep track of what all else, so I never know when I might see her next." She laughed a trifle nervously. "Listen to me go on. I just made a fresh pot of coffee. Can I get you a cup?"

Silly question, as far as I was concerned.

We were fixed up with coffee and small oblong cookies and making chit-chat again when the back door opened. It opened into a small dining area that was really no more than a nook off the living room, so we could easily see the young black girl who banged into the house with an armload of books and a trombone case that stood taller than she did. She was followed by a very tall black man.

"Look what I found," the man said. You would have expected a booming voice, but instead it was a thin tenor. "Jilly's sister was dropping her off just as I pulled into the driveway." The man peeled off a camel's hair topcoat and

42

draped it over the back of a dining chair. The girl got her stuff deposited on the dining table and shucked off her jacket, a red down-filled number that made her look a little like a Macy's Parade balloon when in fact she was about as big around as my left wrist.

"You must be Elmo," the man said, moving into the living room, loosening his uniform tie. It took him almost two strides, with his long legs. Elmo stood and they shook hands. "Jack Reedy. I'm real sorry I couldn't make it to the funeral."

Elmo introduced me and Jack took my hand. I was relieved to get it back.

The girl had come in right on his heels, wearing a short skirt and a long multicolored sweater and her mother's smile. It was the quick, unabashed smile of someone who genuinely likes people. She stood near Susan, who put an arm around the girl's slender waist.

"And this is Anna," Jack Reedy was saying, "who challenged the first-chair trombone player today at school and won."

"I told you you could if you put your mind to it," Susan said, beaming.

"Hi," Anna said to Elmo and me. She had a high, sweet voice.

Jack loosened his tie and somehow managed to get his six-foot-plus frame folded around the coffee table and onto the sofa next to his wife, whom he kissed. He said to Anna, "Hon, this is your cousin Darius's uncle Elmo Lammers, from Chicago, and his friend Mister Nebraska."

The girl frowned slightly at Elmo and said, "If you're Darius's uncle, then are you my uncle too?"

Elmo smiled. "You know, I've been trying to work that one out too, Anna," he said pleasantly. To someone who had just met him, like the Reedys, Elmo probably seemed friendly and relaxed—which is how he usually was. They might not have noticed, as I did, the tightness at his jaw, the occasional nervous jackhammering of his left leg, the slight tension under his words. Still, he made the effort—more than he had done at Jeff's hovel. "I don't think so," he said to the girl. "See, Darius is related to you because he was your mother's brother's boy—"

"That's your Uncle Curtis, hon, you never knew him."

"—and he's related to me because he was my sister's boy, but I can't see where you and I are related, except that we're both members of Darius's family."

I said, "Don't the genealogy buffs say everyone's related to everyone, umpteen times removed?"

"That's just fine," Elmo said. "Like I don't already have enough relatives wanting me to get them Bulls tickets."

"Are you gonna find out who killed Darius?" Anna asked. Her mother looked a little embarrassed, but said nothing.

Elmo took a deep breath. "We are going to try to find out what happened to Darius. I don't know what exactly will come of that, but we are going to try. Listen, honey, what can you tell us about Darius? Nobody seems to know what he was doing out in that part of town so late at night. Do you have any idea?"

Anna had long, frizzy hair that she pulled tight across her scalp but let hang free from the back of her head so that it bounced when she shook her head no.

"Any friends that you knew of who maybe lived out there? Someone Darius might have been going to meet?"

"At that hour?" Susan Reedy said. "Even if Darius knew people there, what would he be doing meeting them in the middle of the night?"

"That's the sixty-four thousand dollar question," I said.

"The police wanted to know the same thing you want to know," Jack said. "And we had to tell them the same thing we're telling you, that we're just as confused about it as anyone."

"I don't think Darius had too many friends," Anna said. "He knew some people from the treatment place and some people from the sub shop where he worked, I guess, but I don't think there was like anybody he hung out with or anything."

"He can't have spent all his time at the treatment center and at work," I said. "What did he do in his spare time?"

"He worked a lot," Susan said. "Almost full-time, some

44

weeks, if they needed him."

"You have to understand," Jack Reedy said. "I'm an alcoholic. Maybe you already knew that. I've been dry for almost ten years now, but I'm still a drunk, and I know that all the treatment in the world isn't gonna do you a damn bit of good if you don't change. That means breaking all the old bad habits that maybe didn't get you into trouble, exactly, but sort of went along with your getting into trouble. Understand what I mean?"

"Temptation isn't sin, but if you can avoid temptation you may avoid sin," I said.

"That's good," Reedy said. "I'm gonna rip that one off you and use it down at the center sometime. I'm a volunteer, help counsel other drunks two, three nights a week. Anyhow, Susan and I suspected a big part of Darius's problem back in Detroit was that he had too much time on his hands with nothing to do. No direction. No job, no responsibilities, no real interest in much of anything. No self-confidence. Well, we made sure he got his butt into a good treatment program right off the bat. A little later, when his counselors thought he was ready, we made him go to work."

"He didn't want to at first," Susan said.

"But he didn't want to go back to Detroit even more."

"It wasn't long before he saw that he was getting better and he saw that he could do a job, and do it well, and have people appreciate what he was doing. And he started feeling good about himself. You could just see it in him—the way he held himself, the way he talked." Her eyes were wet. She dabbed at them with a tissue.

Jack Reedy patted the back of her free hand and smiled sympathetically. "What we're getting at is, at first we kept Darius busy so he'd stay out of trouble. Then he started to get better, to get clean, and he began to see the pleasure of working. All he was doing was making hero sandwiches, but he was loving it. He'd never done anything worthwhile before. So before long, he was keeping *himself* busy." Reedy shook his head sadly. "He was shaping up to be such a great kid."

There was a long silence. Susan Reedy used the Kleenex some more. Then Elmo said, "This sandwich shop where Darius worked. Is it near the project?"

"Oh, sort of," Reedy said. "Not really. More toward downtown, I guess you'd say." He gave Elmo a street address, not that Elmo knew Omaha.

"Did Darius work Sunday night?"

"No. And anyway—I think I know what you may be getting at—he didn't make deliveries. Not that too many places make deliveries to that part of town. There's just no reason for Darius to've been on that corner Sunday night. Or any other time."

"But there he was," Elmo said.

I said, "Darius went to his counseling sessions and he worked at the sub shop. Set aside seven or eight hours for sleep, you still haven't filled up the whole day every day. What'd he do the rest of the time? Where'd he go? Who'd he see?"

"He hung 'round with J.T. and his friends," Anna supplied helpfully.

Susan nodded. "J.T. included Darius as much as possible. Darius was only sixteen months older than J.T., and they got along real well. Sometimes if he wasn't working, Darius would head over to the school and watch J.T. and the team practice."

"Your son's friends would pretty much all be west Omaha kids," I said.

"I wouldn't guess any of them'd ever been anywhere near that project or any of the others," Reedy said, nodding.

"Any of them been in any kind of trouble?" Elmo said.

"Sure. A couple of 'em. Including J.T. Reedy."

"J.T. got into trouble with drugs almost two years ago," Susan said. "That's why we're so...I don't know, involved with all this drug- and alcohol-recovery stuff. Jack works with other recovering alcoholics, I volunteer on a drug help-line, and we both of us keep our eyes open, after what happened with our son."

"Scared the crap out of us, pardon my language."

"We were like a lot of parents, about half-ignorant, half-afraid. I think we sort of had the idea that if we didn't talk about it, it wouldn't be a problem."

"Plus this is a good neighborhood, good people, good schools, good kids. Not supposed to have this sort of problem out here. But we do. And we did. Now we keep our eyes open, like Susan said. Gotta watch this one every minute," he said, mock-glaring at Anna, who giggled and oh-daddied.

"If Darius was in that kind of trouble, we'd have known," Susan said unequivocally.

"Plus Darius was still going to treatment three times a week, two of them one-on-one with his counselor. Everyone down there agrees, he was on the mend."

"Doctor Nielsen—his counselor—said Darius was shaping up to be one of her best success stories. She was crushed when she heard the news."

"Here's J.T. now," Reedy said, and a moment later the back door opened and a rush of cold night air came into the house, followed shortly by a tall, slender boy in a high-school jacket and baggy corduroys.

"Practice over already, J.T.?"

"Sorta," the boy said, shedding his jacket and coming into the living room. He had the springy, slightly bow-legged stride of an athlete. His face was wide and open, and would have appeared round except for the tall, squarish style of his hair, a "fade" cut that disappeared well above his ears. "Coach got mad, said if we weren't going to play any better than we were we might as well go on home." J.T. grinned, half-embarrassed. "He sorta threw us out."

Susan made introductions. J.T. had a solid handshake he inherited from his father. He sat cross-legged on the carpet while we went back over some of the ground we already had covered with his parents. He echoed their sentiments—Darius had come a long way down the right path, he was a hard worker and a great guy and, above all, he was clean. "I would know," J.T. said. The certainty he had inherited from his mother.

I said, "There's a possibility that back in Detroit Darius was

47

selling as well as using. Could he have kicked one habit but not the other?"

"Could explain what he was doing Sunday night," Elmo told them. "Making a buy that went bad."

Jack Reedy was shaking his head before I even finished my question, and J.T. quickly spoke out against the idea. "There's just no way," he insisted. "I spent a lot of time with the man. He shared my room. I would know."

"Then how come you didn't know he sneaked out Sunday night?" Anna taunted.

"Shut up, midget." They began to tussle.

"That's enough of that," Jack Reedy said sternly.

I said, "Before you came in, J.T., we were talking about Darius's friends. It sounds like mostly he hung out with your crowd." J.T. was nodding agreement. "I know none of them live down around the project, but I'm thinking maybe a friend-of-a-friend thing..."

"Only time Darius hung out with my friends was when I was hangin' out too," J.T. said. "Like if me and a couple of the guys were goin' to the mall or somethin', or maybe some of us were goin' out to Godfather's after practice or somethin', Darius would come along. But he'd like never go out with the guys if I wasn't going."

"But he must have had friends of his own."

"Guys he worked with, I guess," J.T. said with a shrug. "But he never like hung out with them."

"I already told them that," Anna said.

"Well, tough," J.T. said and once again grabbed at her, pulling her giggling and squirming across his lap.

"You have to understand," Susan Reedy was saying, "Darius was only here a few months, and in the early days he wasn't in much of a mood—or shape—to make friends. I'm sure he would have, if he..."

"What about a girlfriend?" Elmo said.

"No..." Susan said thoughtfully.

"What about Shelley?" Anna piped up.

48

"Shelley wasn't Darius's girlfriend," J.T. said scornfully.

"Well, she's a girl, isn't she, and she was Darius's friend, wasn't she?"

"Well…"

"That's enough," Jack Reedy said. He looked at his wife. "They did sort of go out a few times." He turned to us. "Not really boyfriend-girlfriend, I don't think."

"Shelley's Tony Beacon's sister," J.T. said as if that explained something. "Tony's in my class at school. That's how Darius knew Shelley, through me. But they weren't like serious or anything."

"Shows how much you know," his sister said, then stopped short.

"Anna," Jack Reedy said firmly. "What do you know?"

"Honey, if it has anything to do with Darius, you have to tell us."

She slid away from her brother and knelt on the floor, her eyes trained on the carpet. Her voice was almost a whisper. "I promised Darius I wouldn't ever tell anyone."

The Reedys traded glances. "It's important to keep promises, honey," Susan said. "But it's more important now to try and find out what happened to your cousin. If you know anything that can help, you have to tell us."

"And right now," Jack said.

The girl sighed and, haltingly, told her story. A little more than a month ago, Darius had gone out, supposedly to take in a movie with Shelley Beacon. But later on that evening, Anna and her friends, doing whatever fifteen-year-old girls find to do in shopping centers, saw Shelley and a couple of other girls waiting in line for a flick at the theaters in the Westroads mall. No sign of Darius. The next day, Anna teased her cousin about his being stood up, and was startled by his angry reaction. "He told me shut up and mind my own business. But I didn't mean anything by it. I was just teasing."

"We know, hon," Susan said, stroking the girl's hair.

A little later, Darius apologized to Anna for his outburst. He explained that he and Shelley had gotten their wires crossed, and that he was annoyed and embarrassed about it, which is why he blew up when Anna brought it up. He made her promise not to tell anyone, saying he'd feel foolish if people thought Shelley had stood him up, and Shelley would look bad too. Anna liked Shelley, and loved her cousin, so she readily promised, and kept her word until we pried it out of her.

Elmo and I exchanged glances, and he nodded almost imperceptibly. "I think it'd be good to have a talk with Miss Beacon."

"That's not gonna help any," Jack Reedy was saying. "For one thing, the police already talked to her, they talked to a lot of kids who knew Darius. Plus, she's a neighborhood girl, they just live a couple blocks over. Darius wouldn't be down at the project to meet her."

"He wasn't there sight-seeing," Elmo said. "He was there for a reason, probably to see someone. You say he wasn't doing drugs any direction, and maybe you're right. Still, he had to have had a reason to be where he was when he got killed. Maybe he told the Beacon girl something he didn't tell you. Maybe she noticed something you didn't. Worth checking, in any event, 'cause except for her what we got so far is goose eggs."

The Reedys considered this for some time. Then Susan said, "I'll call the Beacons and see if Shelley's home."

CHAPTER

6

Shelley Beacon's family lived in a split-level house about three blocks south of the Reedys. Susan Reedy had warned us that Jan Beacon, Shelley's mother, had not been overwhelmingly receptive to the idea of our dropping by. Chet Beacon, Shelley's father, was even less enthusiastic.

"My girl already talked to the police," he said brusquely. His arms were crossed tightly across his chest, and his feet were spread as if he thought he might suddenly have to take us on. Elmo and I were standing on the front step, in the glare of a floodlight, while Beacon, a broad-shouldered black man with a deeply lined face, stood at the threshold and tried to decide whether to let us cross it. "My boy too, for that matter," he went on. "They ain't gonna tell you anything different than what they told the police. They're real sorry about what happened to Darius, we all are, but we don't know a thing about it."

"I'm sure that's true, Mister Beacon," Elmo said smoothly. "But you have to understand. Did Susan Reedy mention that I'm Darius's uncle?"

"Well..."

"Darius was my widowed sister's only son," he lied, "and now he's been taken from her and nobody seems to know why. Think how you'd feel if it was your boy, Tony, Mister Beacon. You'd want to know. You'd *have* to know."

"The police…" Beacon said uncertainly.

"Of course they're investigating. That's their job, and they're good at it. I used to be a cop, you know, in Illinois. I know that, dedicated as you may be, it just isn't the same when it's somebody else's family. You know what I'm saying to you?"

"Well, I… I don't see how Shelley can help you." He was softening. This is what I had meant when I compared Elmo to butter on hot toast.

"Maybe she can't. Or maybe she knows something that she doesn't know she knows—something that maybe didn't seem important, or that no one's asked her about, or that the police just didn't catch."

"The point is," I said, speaking for the first time, "there's no way of finding out unless we talk with your daughter, Mister Beacon."

He still had to mull it over, but Elmo had softened him up expertly and in the end he let us in. The living room was not large, and was mildly cluttered with the jumble of things you'd expect to find in the average American living room. Beacon shut off the TV set, moved a disassembled newspaper off the sofa, and invited us to sit. I had the distinct feeling he'd rather we didn't accept, but we did.

"Jan," he called toward the back of the house. "Those men are here to see Shelley."

A plump black woman in slacks and a sweater came into the room through an arch that must have led to the kitchen. She was wiping her hands on a checked dish towel and smiling, a little uncertainly. "My wife, Jan," Beacon said, and Elmo handled our side of the introduction.

"Shelley'll be right out," Mrs. Beacon said. "Can I offer you men something? Cup of coffee?"

It was not what you'd call a warm invitation, but even so Chet Beacon flashed her a look that would have reduced you or me to a pile of smoldering ash. Mrs. Beacon was impervious. Nevertheless, it seemed the better part of valor to politely decline her offer, and so we did.

Shelley Beacon turned out to be a newer model of her mother, pretty, with wide, direct eyes, but inclined toward chubbiness. She smiled tentatively as introductions were made. Then we all sat, except for Chet Beacon, who went back into his crossed-arms stance. We got down to business.

As advertised, the girl said she knew nothing about what had happened to Darius. Her father shot us a hot *you-see?* look. Elmo went on, with an occasional two-cents' worth from me, negotiating what were fast becoming the standard questions—Darius's friends, activities, attitudes, habits. Shelley's answers pretty much echoed the Reedys'. Darius was a good kid, she didn't think he was mixed up with anything or anyone he shouldn't have been, she couldn't imagine what Darius would be doing in that part of town.

"Now, Shelley, that isn't exactly so, is it?" Elmo said gently.

She hadn't been real big in the eye-contact department all along; now, however, she seemed to find the denim that covered her left knee to be extraordinarily interesting.

"You callin' my daughter a liar, mister?" the man standing behind her chair said.

I had to hand it to my friend. Beacon's belligerence was beginning to piss me off, and I hadn't come into the situation half-pissed-off, as Elmo had. But Elmo kept his cool, ignored Beacon, and let the silence stretch to where it became uncomfortable. Half of the art of interrogation is knowing when to keep your trap shut.

"Shelley?" Jan Beacon said at last.

The girl looked up and her eyes were wet.

"You *can* imagine what brought Darius to that neighborhood, can't you?" Elmo's eyes were kindly. His voice matched.

We had discussed it on the short ride over from the Reedys' place. There was only one likely possibility.

"Darius was sort of seeing this girl who I think lives up around there someplace," Shelley said wetly.

"Jesus Christ," her father said.

"Honey, why didn't you *tell* anyone?" her mother said in alarm.

"I di-int want anyone to get in t-rouble," the girl hiccupped. She was a quiet crier. She didn't sob or blubber or howl. The water simply flowed down her cheeks and her voice got trembly and thick. She wiped her face on the sleeve of her bright, oversized sweater, sniffling, until her dad handed her a white handkerchief.

"Anyh-ow," she went on after a bit, "I didn't really know anything." She hiccupped and swallowed hard. "Darius and I went out a coupla times. We were ju-ust friends is all. Then he called me one day and said he'd met this girl that he wanted to go out with. Only he knew his aunt and uncle wouldn't approve of her. So he asked me if I would kind of cover for him, you know. Like he'd tell his people that he was going to a movie with me or something, only he'd be going to see this other girl."

"Jesus Christ," Chet Beacon repeated.

"Well, it wasn't like I was doing anything bad," Shelley protested. "Darius was the one doing the lying, not me."

"You were *helping* him."

"Nuh-*uhn*. I never lied to anybody! And I never told Darius I would, either. I said he could do whatever he wanted."

"And what would you have done if someone asked you?" Mrs. Beacon asked.

Shelley's voice was small. "I don't know. But no one ever did. So I never had to lie."

"Girl, a lie isn't just something you do, sometimes it's something you *don't* do. Like tell the police and everybody else you don't know nothin' when you sure as hell *do*!" Beacon had cranked up that look of his again, and the girl wasn't as immune to it as her mother. The water started again.

"Where'd you get such a hare-brained idea anyway?" he demanded.

"I *told* you. It was Darius's idea. But I... Well, I could tell he like really liked this girl."

Elmo and I glanced at each other. It was about as we had guessed. Money, love, and revenge are the human animal's primary motivators. If Darius hadn't been on that corner for some sort of commercial reason—and everyone who knew him insisted that he couldn't have been—then it was time for us to consider an amorous reason. If the relationship between Shelley and Darius hadn't been serious, then what accounted for his outburst when Anna teased him about the missed date? And why should Darius have sworn her to secrecy about it?

Now we had the answer. Or the beginnings of one.

"This other girl," I said, interrupting what I suspected was another oath from Chet Beacon, "what can you tell us about her?"

"Nothing," Shelley said decisively. "That's part of why I never said anything. There wasn't anything I *could* say. I don't even know the girl's name."

"But she lives in or near the project?"

"I think so. Darius said something once about her living in a bad neighborhood or something. I don't know for sure that that's the one. All I know is when I heard what happened, where Darius had been when he was killed, my first thought was he must have been there seeing that girl."

"Why did Darius think the Reedys wouldn't approve of this girl?" Elmo said.

Shelley shook her head. "I don't know. I asked him once, when he first wanted me to"—she glanced sidelong at her father—"help him. He sort of changed the subject. That's when he told me she lived in a bad part of town. I knew he didn't want to tell me anything, so I never asked again."

"Jesus Christ."

We went at it from two or three different angles, but the results stayed consistent. Shelley didn't know where or how Darius had met the girl. She didn't know the girl's age, race, or political party. She didn't know a thing except what she had told us, but she felt that Darius must have really liked this girl, and that was the reason Shelley allowed him to use her as his alibi. "He wouldn't have gone to the trouble if he didn't really like her," she said a little dreamily.

In tandem, then, Elmo and I stood up and thanked the Beacons for their time and, such as it had been, hospitality. Shelley, belatedly, apologized for having kept silent for so long. "I would've said something if I thought it was important."

"Problem is, you never know what's going to be important," Elmo said. "That's why it's always best to tell everything."

"The police who talked with you folks the other day probably left a card," I said, and Chet Beacon nodded. "You may want to dig it out, call them, and tell them about all this. In case it does turn out to be something."

"We'll do that right now."

CHAPTER

7

Jim Marineaux and Robert Olson share the apartment at the opposite end of the building from mine, right down the hall, sidewalk, gangplank, or whatever you want to call the exterior suspended walkway along the front of the place. The layout of their apartment is the mirror-image of mine, which always makes it a little unsettling when I go down there, as I do fairly often. They collect the rent and so on for our absentee landlord, and I guess they must like the challenge I usually present them on the first of the month, because we've gotten to be friends.

The boys—when you're pushing forty, guys who are pushing thirty are "boys"—were in the middle of a pizza and *Citizen Kane* on videotape when Elmo and I stopped over.

"'Rosebud' is his sled," I said when Jim let us in.

Robert hit the stop button on his remote-control box. "Well, that saves us a coupla hours."

I made quick introductions, then told the boys we didn't want to interrupt their movie. "I just wanted to hit you up for the loan of some wheels," I said to Robert.

"Shoot, take the whole car. It'll be good for it to be driven." Three months ago some unsavories had run Robert off the North Freeway, dragged him out of the car, and dented up his skull for him. They had a good reason, at least: they thought he was me. Robert was on the mend now, and his hair was even

57

beginning to look like he *meant* to wear it that way, but the driver's seat was still off-limits to him.

To Elmo I said, "Robert's my stunt double. It saves me a lot of wear and tear. Of course, from now on I make him drive his own car." My poor old Impala was the one he had been piloting when the badguys overtook him. The car had needed a lot of work, but I wished that taking the dents out of Robert had been as easy. Not that I blamed myself for what happened to him. It's been a long time since I could afford the luxury of thinking the universe revolves around me. Yes, Robert and my oldest friend, Pat Costello, had ended up in the hospital because they knew me. But not because *of* me. The distinction may be subtle, but it's an important one to make if you don't want to go stark raving crackers.

"Looks like you're coming back okay," Elmo said.

"About eighty-five, ninety percent, I'd say. The docs say they're shooting for a hundred, but I don't know. I still get the headaches and the double-vision now and then. Never any warning, which is why no driving."

"I told them he was never that good to begin with," Jim said, bringing cold beers for Elmo and me. "Double-vision might actually improve his driving."

"The really annoying thing is these weird memory lapses," Robert said. "Like the night before last. I went to call my folks, just to say hi. Sat down in this chair, picked up this phone…and had no idea what their phone number was. They've had the same number, I don't know, twenty-eight years that I can swear to. It was my number when I was a kid, for cryin' out loud. But there I am, like an idiot, staring at the phone like maybe it'll tell me something. Finally had to look it up in the book. There have been other little spells like that, something I know I know but just can't nail down. I'd almost rather forget something entirely, not even remember that I ever knew it. Be less frustrating."

"Maybe you have," I said. "If you forgot something so completely that you don't even know you ever knew it to forget, how would you know you forgot it?"

Robert looked at Jim. "Who *is* this guy?"

We all laughed, and I said, "If that's going to be your attitude, I'll take my beer and your car keys and leave."

"You guys eaten?" Jim said. "There's plenty of beer, and I can call Pefferoni's and have them send over another pizza."

"What about your movie?"

"Seen it a dozen times."

"And we can watch it any time we like, since it's a copy Jim made in complete disregard of federal law."

Jim shrugged. "They show *Citizen Kane* on cable TV, I tape it to keep in my library forever and ever, the Supreme Court says that's okay. I go down to Blockbuster Video, rent *Citizen Kane*, and make a copy of it, I'm a desperate criminal on the lam from the FBI. Go figure."

"Just the sort of Byzantine calisthenics favored by the Guys in Ties," I said, drifting toward the pizza. "The same deep thinkers who tell me that my leaving the scene of one murder in an attempt—futile, I grant you—to prevent another murder is an irresponsible act that warrants cancellation of my PI permit. If I had said to hell with the second victim and stayed put while the cops went through their drill, they'd've given me the good citizen award. What is that, sausage?"

"I'll call Pefferoni's," Robert said. "*That* number I remember."

The first pizza was history, the second was heading that same direction, and several bottles of Grolsch had fallen like tenpins when Jim said, "I still don't get it. So maybe the reason your nephew was up by the project was to meet this mystery girl of his. It still doesn't explain *why* he was killed."

Elmo looked at me and I said, "Kids today. You have some tomato sauce in your beard."

"I was saving that for later," he said, daubing his chin with a paper napkin. "See, Jim, that's just the thing: we don't *know* why Darius was up there. May have something to do with this girl, may not. May have something to do with the gangs, may not. May have something to do with the scrape he got himself into back in Detroit. Or may not."

"For that matter, there may not even be a mystery girl," I said. "That could be a story Darius made up for Shelley Beacon's benefit, if he was up to something he shouldn't have been and wanted her to alibi him."

"It's just the sort of thing she'd go for," Elmo said. "She's a romantic. That's why she kept Darius's secret even after he was killed."

"All we really know is that he was there when he was there and there was a reason," I said.

"And that somebody gunned him down. At least three somebodies, maybe four, from what the police have pieced together from the physical evidence. Probably another to handle the steering wheel."

"There again we don't know whether it was accidental or purposeful—whether Darius was the intended victim or just unlucky—and if the former, why. Darius managed to keep his girlfriend, if there was one, secret. What other secrets may he have kept?" I drank some beer. "As I keep telling you guys, nine-tenths of this racket is picking up pieces and putting them in your pocket and hoping you can fit them together eventually and make a picture. Now it may be that there is a girl but she doesn't figure into it. She may know something, without even knowing she knows, that will lead us to someone or something else, and so on. The Reedys led us to Shelley Beacon, who led us to the girl, who may lead us…who knows?"

"Frustrating," Robert said.

"No," Elmo said, prying the cap off a bottle and passing it to Robert. "Tiring, maybe. It's only frustrating when this leads you to that, leads you to that, leads you to that—and then you dead-end."

"The reason we need your car is that we want to be able to head out in separate directions," I said. "Cover as many angles as possible in as little time as possible."

"And you're too cheap to rent a car," Robert said.

"Exactly."

He shook his head. "Like I said, frustrating."

"It does seem like a very big haystack and a very small needle," Jim said thoughtfully.

"No argument."

"Then wouldn't it make more sense to just tell the police what you've found out about this girl and let them handle it? I mean, there are a lot more of them than there are of you."

"No argument there either," I said. "But our hearts are purer and that gives us the edge. The Beacons are going to let the cops know that Darius told Shelley he was seeing a girl his family wouldn't approve of. The cops will say thanks very much and take that information and pour it into the big vat containing all the other little bits of this and that they collect, and let it simmer. Eventually it may boil down to something useful. It probably will; it usually does. The cops are good at their work, but they're part of a bureaucracy and bureaucracies are not noted for their mind-boggling swiftness."

"Besides which, we got something they don't have," Elmo said. "Motivation. Nebraska assures me they're all real good people on your police force here, but to them Darius LeClerc is just another name. A number. A black kid with a history who got gunned down in a bad neighborhood. They'll try to find out what went down because it's their job to try. But that ain't motivation, it's routine. The paper shuffle. In the end, it's nothing to them except the year-end crime statistics.

"Me, I got motivation. A widowed sister who just had to bury her oldest child. A dead nephew who has a cloud over him even in the grave. And the knowledge that somebody put him in that grave. Somebody gave the orders, somebody pulled the triggers. Maybe it was a hit, maybe it was bad luck. Maybe Darius was dirty, maybe he was clean. I don't know yet. All I know is somebody killed him. And if those people got a God, they better be asking him to see to it the cops find them before I do."

"That's a little Old Testament, isn't it?" I said, trying to jolly him out of this funk he'd been in all day.

"Damn straight," he snapped. "That's how the game's played. You push me, I push you back—harder. You hurt me, I hurt you worse. You kill mine, I kill you." He set his empty bottle on the edge of the coffee table. It *clunk*ed with the flat finality of a coffin lid closing. "Now if you'll excuse me, I want to call Julie and the girls before it gets too much later. Thanks for the hospitality."

When Elmo had been gone a minute or more, Robert said, "You have one angry friend there, Mister Nebraska."

I was still digesting Elmo's words and, more important, the hard, bloodless way in which he had delivered them. "I knew he felt strongly about this one, of course," I said at last. "Christ, we're talking family. But obviously I underestimated *how* strongly he felt."

"Can you blame him?" Jim said.

"No," I said. "Absolutely not. But if it really is Old Testament justice he's after—eye-for-eye, tooth-for-tooth, life-for-life—well, I can't just stand by and let him go at it, either."

"Kinda sounds to me like that's what he has in mind," Jim said pensively.

I didn't say anything. I didn't have anything to say.

CHAPTER

8

Koosje Van der Beek was waiting for me in front of her place the next morning. Koosje is a Dutch name—she's Dutch by birth—and there's really no English-language equivalent to that double-o. *KOH-shuh* is about the best most people can expect to do. Her last name rhymes with *what the heck.*

Koosje is a psychologist. Up until about nine months ago, she had been my girlfriend. That's a ridiculous term to use when you're talking about adults, but there's no good synonym. Anyhow, I had screwed things up nicely. I managed to forget—I managed to make myself forget—that even when no formal promises have been made, every close relationship is founded on tacit agreements, unspoken understandings. Trust. I violated Koosje's trust, and knocked us off-track. We were working to find a way to reverse that. It wasn't easy. I don't suppose it ever is.

Nevertheless, we were still much more than "just friends," and Koosje had agreed readily when I asked her to come with me when I visited Darius LeClerc's counselor. When you deal with medical, legal, or psychological types, you never know if you'll need a translator.

Climbing into my car, Koosje said, "Where's Elmo?"

"We divided the labor, in hopes of getting results quicker. If there are any results to be gotten. He's gone up to check the project."

"Looking for the 'mystery girl' you told me about when you called?"

"If there is a mystery girl," I said, backing carefully out of Koosje's long, narrow driveway. She had recently bought a house on Blondo, just down the long slope from the four-way stop at Fiftieth Street. A great investment, but good luck backing out of that driveway. I had decided some time ago that the best bet was to wait for the slightest break in traffic and then simply go for it and count on the other cars to stop.

After the cacophony of horns had died down, Koosje said, "Not exactly filled with optimism this morning, are we?"

"So far I haven't come up with anything to feel optimistic about," I admitted. "Darius is dead, which is no good. There's at least a slight chance that his apparent turnaround may not have been as thorough as everybody—including yours truly—had thought, which also is no good. Elmo is out for blood, literally, and I don't know what he'll do if we should happen to find out that Darius got something that was coming to him. Hell, I don't know what he'll do no matter *what* we find out—or don't find out. And I don't know what *I'll* do if he decides to do something rash. Not a lot of room for optimism in there."

"Mm," Koosje said. It's an all-purpose noise she makes, the way some people say "Ah" or "Huh." It's a space-filler, and it can mean anything at all, or, as in this instance, nothing at all. "Then I suppose I might as well point out to you that your gasoline gauge indicates you have perhaps an ounce of gas left in the tank."

"Don't pay any attention to that thing," I said. "It hasn't worked for over a year now."

"Very reassuring. Given your concerns about Elmo, do you think it's a good idea to let him go up to the project alone?"

"Elmo's a grown-up, Koosje: he goes where he goes whether I 'let' him or not."

"You know what I mean."

I pretended to concentrate on the traffic for a moment. I

had doubled back around and was heading west on Pacific. Mid-morning traffic was brisk but tolerable. "Yeah, I know. I suggested that I tag along—'ride shotgun,' as I put it, and I meant it as more than just an expression—partly to watch his back, partly to watch *him*. But we agreed that, given the demographics of that neighborhood, he might make more headway alone than with a white sidekick. And I do think we need to get more of a handle on Darius himself, too, which is why I want to meet with Doctor Nielsen sooner rather than later."

"Mm. You're not convinced Darius was an innocent victim of a random act of violence?"

"I *want* to think that," I said after a bit. "And not just for Elmo's sake, but Darius's too. I liked what I saw the last time I met him, I liked that Darius, and I liked the idea of someone turning his life around and getting it on track. I don't like the idea that he might have been fooling us all."

"Is that what you think happened?"

"That's what I'm hoping we may find out."

Pacifica Counseling Center was a bluish glass cube off Pacific near 105th, more or less tucked back behind One Pacific Place. There's been an annoying local tendency, in recent years, to follow bigger cities' mania for using building names instead of addresses. I'm old-fashioned. I like to look a place up in the phone book and see that it's at One-hundred Third and Pacific, not One Pacific Place. At least Pacifica Counseling Center had a real address. From the bluish cube's top two floors, a team of psychologists and social workers handled any sort of problem you'd ever think you might encounter—pain and stress management; drug and alcohol abuse; sexual disorders; eating disorders; depression and anxiety; divorce, adoption, emotional problems.... The list stretched on. I was reading it from the back of a brochure while Koosje and I waited in the reception area. The brochure and the reception room were both done up in soft, soothing colors; each had a certain reassuring texture to it. Good thing, too. Just reading the brochure was enough to give you more than a few symptoms.

I had called ahead earlier that morning, and Dr. Eileen Nielsen was expecting us.

I had expectations, too, and they were met. Dr. Nielsen was as Nordic-looking as her name suggested. She was tall, pale, and angular. Her hair, which she wore long and pulled back from an almost bony face, had once been blond. Now it was fading gracefully to white. Her face was open and direct, her blue eyes surrounded by a network of crow's feet she was too sensible to try to hide, her wide mouth showing only the barest hint of pale lipstick. She would be about forty-five, I guessed. Fifty at the outside. I started to introduce her to Koosje, but they had met professionally once or twice. We sat in her office, a tiny room that, decorated differently, might have triggered claustrophobia but with the mellow colors was instead intimate and cozy.

"I've spoken with the Reedys two or three times since Monday," Dr. Nielsen said when we had settled in. "They've asked me to help you as much as I can, and naturally I want to. I liked Darius very much. He was a nice young man, and I honestly believe he was well on his way to getting his life in shape. That's what makes his death all the more tragic."

"As you might guess, the big question on everyone's mind is what Darius was doing on that corner Sunday night," I said. "Have you any idea?"

She shook her head and nibbled on the blunt end of a yellow pencil. "I've asked myself that same question a thousand times. What business could he possibly have had there? And I keep coming up with the same answer: none."

"No answer or no business?"

She smiled slightly. "Both. The police talked to me, of course, and I got the impression that they thought it might have been some drug-related business. I've tried to distance myself, tried to look at the facts not as Darius's counselor and friend but rather as a purely disinterested, objective party." She looked at Koosje and smiled. "It can't be done, of course, but I've tried. And try as I may, I cannot believe it. I'm not saying I'm infallible, or that I haven't had cases backslide on me, or that I haven't been fooled by patients. I've made plenty of mistakes, I'm afraid, and I may be mistaken about Darius. But I doubt it. And nearly a week's worth of mulling it over hasn't had any effect on me. I haven't felt any self-doubt, any of the emotional shilly-shallying that sometimes says we knew something was out of kilter but allowed ourselves to overlook it. I haven't had the least inkling of such a feeling. My faith in Darius is solid."

She certainly was convincing. I had to confess that my own confidence in Darius wasn't as solid—I harbored not a few doubts about the totality of his rehabilitation, but was trying to ignore them while we worked to find the "mystery girl" Shelley Beacon had told us about—but I was glad Darius had had a friend like Eileen Nielsen. And not only for his uncle's sake.

Koosje said, "What sort of drugs did Darius use?"

"He started with marijuana as a young teenager. Then amphetamines. He had recently graduated up to crack cocaine. That was in Detroit, you understand."

"Crack was your biggest problem?"

Dr. Nielsen nodded. "Darius hadn't been using crack for very long, but I'm sure you know, Koosje, that crack addicts can develop a strong psychological dependence on the drug, and quickly."

"Crack is sold—and used—mainly in north Omaha," I said. "If Darius had gone off the wagon, he might have gone up there looking to score."

She frowned. "Well, it is true that different drugs are more common in different parts of town. Partly it's economics. Powdered cocaine is expensive—dealers call it 'the rich man's pleasure'—so you're more likely to find it in the wealthier neighborhoods, west Omaha and the suburbs. Crack, on the other hand, is comparatively cheap, and common in poorer neighborhoods such as the north side. But you need to keep two things in mind, Mister Nebraska. First, there are no absolutes. You yourself said crack is *mainly* found in north Omaha. That's certainly not to say there are *no* other drugs available there or *no* crack available anyplace but there. We three could go not five miles from this building in any direction you like and, with very little effort, score enough coke or crack or both—or a variety of other substances—to keep us flying until high noon on Saint Patrick's Day."

"In other words, Darius could score right in his own nice middle-class neighborhood; he wouldn't have to go up to the project. All right. What's the second thing I have to keep in mind?"

"Darius wasn't using drugs." She smiled, which only served to underscore her conviction.

I grinned back, wryly. "You seem very certain."

"I am very certain." The smile stayed in place.

"Let's assume you're right," Koosje said. "Darius wasn't using drugs. Could he have been dealing them?"

"The police had the same question. The answer I gave them was I don't think so."

"Why not?" I said. "You do drugs, they betray you—things you do, things you say, even the way you look. You sell drugs, on the other hand, and the only noticeable effect is a slight limp caused by lugging around a heavier wallet."

Dr. Nielsen laughed. "That may be, but you have to understand that we had spent most of the past six or seven months helping Darius overcome his drug dependence. Darius was quite successful at this, but it had taken time. He hadn't been drug-free very long at all. Frankly, I doubt that he could have been around any appreciable quantity of drugs for any length of time without lapsing."

"And if he had lapsed, you would know."

"I think so, yes."

"Either Darius had made a lot of progress, or he had gotten

very good at pulling the wool over people's eyes."

Koosje said, "It's not impossible for a patient or client to fool his therapist if he really wants to. As Eileen said, she's been fooled before; so have I. But we're trained to be on the lookout for signs, little clues that help us judge whether a patient is being honest with us. It's extremely difficult for someone to go on duping his counselor over a long period of time in close one-to-one sessions. Not impossible. But extremely difficult."

"And as I said, I haven't felt the slightest little bit of nagging doubt about Darius," Dr. Nielsen said.

"All right," I said. "Let's talk about Darius's personal life. If drugs didn't take him to that corner, a personal reason is our next best guess. Do you know of any friends Darius had in that neighborhood?"

She shook her head. "Darius hadn't made many friends yet. Mainly his friends were friends of his cousins and people he worked with."

"Did he ever speak to you about a girlfriend?"

"There was a girl he had dated a few times, I know," she said. "A friend of his cousin J.T., I think…"

"Shelley Beacon. Anyone else?"

"No… No, I don't think so. Why?"

I let it go by. "What about where he worked? Any close friends, male or female?"

"He never mentioned anyone in particular. I don't want you to get the wrong impression, Mister Nebraska. No doubt everyone you've spoken to has really talked up Darius, emphasized how much he had achieved in a short time, and so on. That's all true. But Darius was still a fragile young man, and no one realized that more than he. People in that condition usually are not too gregarious."

"Really?" I said, and my surprise was genuine. "The last time I saw Darius, he was downright outgoing—and I didn't know him well at all."

"But you did know him," Dr. Nielsen countered, "and you knew him from 'before,' so to speak. In a sense, you were part of his support system, albeit a step or two removed. If you had been meeting Darius for the first time that last time you saw him, I doubt whether he'd have been at all outgoing. In fact, he'd probably have struck you as guarded and suspicious."

"Then I take it he hadn't made any close friends here at the center, either" I said. "Excluding yourself, that is."

She smiled. "Thank you for that. I hope I was Darius's friend. As for anyone else around here, I very much doubt it. We have no inpatient facilities, so most of our clients come in for their appointments and leave as soon as they're done. There's not much chance for socializing. Or much desire for it, either, I would expect."

"I understand Darius was in some kind of group session, too."

"Yes, you're right." Her pale eyebrows knitted in thought and her eyes focused on nothing for a long moment, then came back to me. "No, I can't think of anyone there he seemed to be close to, or that he'd be likely to associate with outside the center."

"What are the odds of my talking to the other members of that group?"

She smiled and shook her head and looked at Koosje. Koosje shrugged and said, "Sometimes he asks a question even though he already knows the answer to it. I don't know why."

"Because sometimes the answer isn't what he thought," I said. "But not this morning, I take it."

"Tell you what," Dr. Nielsen said. "The group meets again Tuesday evening. If you like, I'll ask the members whether any of them knew Darius especially well or socialized with him outside the center, or if any of them knows anything else that might be helpful. How's that?"

"Not as good as my talking with them first-hand, but pretty good. What would be better, though, is if I could persuade you to get on the phone to these people yet today and see what they have to say. The more time passes, the less likely we are to get anyplace."

She flipped through the lined pages of a desk calendar on a plastic stand. "If I can rope in a helper, we might be able to manage it," she said. She gave me that direct, unblinking look again. "I can't promise anything except that I'll try."

"Who can?" I said.

CHAPTER

9

"What do you think?"

"Mm," Koosje said. This particular "Mm" meant *I'm thinking*, and when she was done thinking a few seconds later she said, "She was being uncommonly helpful to you," Koosje said. "A lot of people in her position wouldn't have given you the time of day. I'm not sure I would have."

I glanced away from the traffic long enough to make a face at her.

"I think it illustrates what she said, that she has no nagging doubts about Darius," Koosje continued. She thought about it a bit more. "Eileen Nielsen is good at what she does. If she's that certain, I think you have to put a lot of stock in what she says."

Koosje, in turn, is very good at what *she* does, and I do put a lot of stock in what she says.

The morning haze was thinning. Some guy on the radio said we could expect today's high to be in the lower forties. Very un-February-like weather, but then the whole winter had been very un-winter-like. We drove past a bank whose electronic sign said it was thirty-three degrees. Another bank half a block farther on had it as thirty-five degrees. Which bank would you rather have your money in?

I said, "We keep piling up character references for the kid, but that only makes it harder to understand what he was doing out on that corner the other night."

"Still not sold on the mystery girl, then?" Koosje said.

I shrugged noncommittally. "Maybe there is a mystery girl—but so far, at least, nothing says she lives around that neighborhood. Maybe Elmo will turn something up. We're hoping that if there is a girl and she lives in or near the project, then Darius may have spent time around there and someone will recognize him—and lead us to the girl."

"Mm," Koosje said. "I've never been in that neighborhood, but from what I've read in the paper and seen on TV, it doesn't seem like the sort of place where you'd arrange to meet your date out on a corner in the middle of the night."

"Or at any other time of day," I said, "which makes the mystery-girl angle even more dubious. Still, we have to follow it up..." I thought about it for a couple of blocks, then said, "Nine-tenths of the problem is that there are two big question-marks on this case. One, what was Darius doing on that corner that night? Two, why was he killed? You try to make headway on one, all it does is take you to the other and back in a continuous loop. Take Question Number Two first. Darius was killed either accidentally or on purpose. If accidentally, then either he was mistaken for someone else or someone—maybe the Crips—chose that moment to do a drive-by."

"Two in the morning?" Koosje said skeptically. "And a deserted street, from what the news reports said."

"It's a safe bet that any loiterers scattered before the cops arrived, and certainly before the press—the media, as they say these day—showed up. But you're right. These mutants favor the daylight hours on nice, sunny afternoons, when they can count on an appreciative audience." The guy on the radio was prattling on about some asinine call-in contest, so I shut him off. These stations that promise "more music and less talk" should be required to prove it. "It's also funny that no one's come forward to take credit for the shooting," I said. "The conventional wisdom is that the Crips must be responsible, since it went down on Blood turf. But they haven't said anything. I don't recall the Crips—or the Bloods, for that matter—being so modest in the past. Usually they're on the horn to a TV station before the bodies are even loaded into ambulances."

"Remember that one last fall by the Logan Fontenelle project?" Koosje said. "One of the Crips later called a friend of a girl who was killed and apologized."

"But after almost a week now, nothing. An eerie silence, as they say. I mean, you'd think someone would jump in there and take credit for it even if they didn't deserve it."

"Which makes you think…"

"It sure does," I said, and trod hard on the brake pedal while swearing imaginatively at one of my fellow motorists. He was one of these malletheads who has to weave in and out of lanes in order to be first in line at the red light. There was a bumper sticker on the back of his Camry: Don't Like the Way I Drive? Dial 1-800-EAT-SHIT.

"Which makes you think *what*?" Koosje tried again.

"Well, I guess it makes me think that this was not a standard-issue drive-by killing."

"In other words, Darius was killed on purpose. Why?"

"That's still Question Number Two," I said, "and it still remains a mystery. I have the feeling that the answer to Question Number One—what was he doing on that cor-ner?—will point up an answer to Number Two."

"And you don't think the answer to Number One is To meet his girlfriend."

"Doesn't seem real likely."

"Mm. And from what everybody says about Darius, it also doesn't seem very likely that he was there to make a drug buy."

I mulled it over for half a minute. "Let's say he wasn't using. And he wasn't selling. That doesn't rule out his making a buy for someone else."

"The mystery girl?" Koosje said.

"Darius told Shelley Beacon he wanted her to alibi him so he could see a girl his aunt and uncle wouldn't approve of. I've met the Reedys, and I can say they definitely would not approve of Darius's dating a woman who used drugs. Of course, it needn't be the mystery girl. Darius's cousin J.T. had a drug problem. Maybe it didn't go away entirely. But, then, it sounds like J.T. could get all the pharmaceuticals he wanted right on the schoolyard..."

"For that matter, as Eileen Nielsen said, drugs are fairly easily available almost anywhere in town, if someone wants them bad enough. Darius wouldn't have to go clear to the project to buy them. Certainly not at that hour. Be that as it may, though, I have to agree with Eileen. Someone who has been drug-free as brief a time as Darius was is exceptionally susceptible to recidivism—"

"Recidivism, is it?" I said.

"—and doesn't dare allow himself to be around drugs or people who use them. Buying drugs for someone else qualifies too. Darius almost certainly would have begun using again, and Eileen almost certainly would have observed that. Darius's family, too, by the sound of things."

"By all accounts, Darius had made remarkable progress in a comparatively short time," I said. " 'All accounts' including my own. Isn't it possible that that was because he had great willpower, or was highly motivated, or possessed some other trait that would help him resist temptation? Especially if he hadn't been exposed to that temptation for very long yet?"

"Mm," Koosje said. "Possible."

"Uh-huh. In other words, Doctor Van der Beek thinks Question Number One is still up for grabs too. You see what I mean about the continuous loop. Meanwhile, let me try another question on you: How's about lunch? My treat."

The clock on the dashboard had read 2:20 since 1986, so Koosje was forced to look at her wristwatch. "It's barely eleven o'clock," she said.

"Yeah, I don't know, I had a bagel and forty-eight cups of coffee this morning while Elmo and I plotted out the day, but somehow they just haven't stuck with me. I have a powerful craving for a submarine sandwich."

"There's a Little King in the Old Market," Koosje said helpfully. "We could get something to go and take it up to my office."

"Not any old submarine will do," I said. "I gotta have one from the restaurant where Darius worked."

"Mm," Koosje said knowingly. "In that case, would you drop me by my office first? I should spend a little time on my work today, you know."

I had followed Pacific as far east as Elmwood Park, then jogged up to Leavenworth Street, continuing east. Now I veered off onto St. Marys Avenue, tooling along toward the Old Market, where Koosje has an office in a crumbly old brick building that someone picked up for eleven cents on the dollar and, through the sort of real-estate sleight-of-hand that has always been a mystery to me, now managed to rent it out for probably six hundred bucks a square foot.

"All right," I said. "Your loss; you never know when I'm going to offer to buy lunch again."

"Don't I know it," Koosje said.

CHAPTER

10

Elmo Lammers sat behind the wheel of Robert Olson's 1992 Honda Accord. He had parallel-parked facing west, facing the corner where his nephew Darius LeClerc had died. Gunned down like an animal.

He sat a moment, gripping the wheel as if he meant to rip it off the steering column. His jaw was clenched so tightly that his head ached. Not for the first time, Elmo noted, he was a little worried about—and a little frightened by—the anger inside him. He had felt it building since Monday evening, when his sister Francine called with the news about Darius. It wasn't showing any sign of letup; in fact, it seemed to get worse by the minute. It seemed to take every ounce of his strength just to keep the lid on it—to the extent that he *was* keeping the lid on it. None of his coping mechanisms, none of the little switch-off devices that most cops develop for their own survival—to say nothing of their sanity—were working for him. That was the part that frightened him. He was no stranger to anger, but in the past he had always controlled it, used it as a weapon. Now it felt like anger was on the verge of controlling him, and when that happened, it was like pointing your weapon at yourself.

Elmo knew that, knew what most veteran cops know: It isn't so much the stress of the job that'll kill you. It's the anger.

He took it out on the steering wheel until his arms ached,

then he climbed out of the car. He lit a cigarette, and sucked down the smoke like it was the best thing he had ever tasted. At that moment, it was. The Honda's ashtray had been distressingly clean, obviously unused, so as a courtesy to Robert Olson, Elmo hadn't smoked inside the car. Considering his stressed-out condition, considering he got lost on the way over—thanks to the great directions that *someone* had given him—considering he had to visit three gas stations before he found one that not only sold city maps but actually had one in stock, it was a wonder that he hadn't said to hell with courtesy, smoked up the car, and given it a thorough Ozium dousing before turning it back over to Olson.

Now he leaned against the Accord, as if his affecting a relaxed posture might bring on relaxation, and watched his cigarette smoke join the morning's haze. The radio said the haze was supposed to burn off later and the temperature climb into the low forties, but right now it was nippy and, with the haze, clammy. Elmo let his brown cigarette dangle from his lips, buried his hands in his coat pockets, and looked over at the entrance to the project across the street.

What a place to have to call home, he thought grimly. Where the sun peeked through the vapor overhead it glinted on broken glass on the sidewalk and in the project's common area. The playground equipment looked ancient, and abuse and neglect had left it in a dreadful state. The playground itself was pavement, not grass; rough, crumbling asphalt that had been patched so many times that there was nothing to it except patches. Small green areas were left here and there, mainly along the narrow walkways that led from the common area to the buildings. Only they weren't green, they were brown, and not the temporary, dormant brown of winter but the flat brown of bare dirt. The scene was all the more forlorn for being deserted this cold, overcast morning.

Elmo thought back to the house he had grown up in back in Missouri. It was old and it was small, and his family was crammed in there hip-to-haunch, but it was theirs and they took pride in it, keeping it up as best they could during the mean times. But a place like this... Christ, even if you wanted to turn it into a home for your family, how could you? Look what you had to work with. Not just the physical plant, which was bad enough, but your neighbors: the Bloods and the Crips and the junkies, hookers, and other disreputable elements they attracted.

An uphill climb for damn sure.

Elmo could empathize, because he now faced such a climb himself. There were a lot of doors in the project and the surrounding neighborhood. And Elmo had to knock on them. Show anyone who would look the color snapshot of Darius that Susan Reedy had taken last Labor Day weekend. Ask if they had ever seen this young man around the neighborhood; if so, was he with a young woman; if so did they know who she was? A very big haystack and a very small needle, Jim Marineaux had said last night, and he was dead-on. They didn't know whether the mystery girl lived in the project or in the surrounding neighborhood. Hell, they didn't even know for a fact whether she even existed or whether, as they had speculated last night, Darius had invented her in order to con the Beacon girl into providing his alibi for some other business.

Elmo tended to discount that theory. Not that his nephew would have been incapable of pulling a con job like that— Darius was no saint, and Elmo knew that well. It just seemed a little too elaborate for the boy. A lie covering a lie covering a lie. If Darius had been involved in something hinky, he'd undoubtedly have lied about it, but it would have been a more straightforward lie. A smarter lie. Less chance of getting tripped up that way.

Maybe he was as big a drippy romantic as Shelley Beacon, but Elmo believed there *was* a mystery girl. From what Darius had told Shelley, she lived in a bad neighborhood. This was a bad neighborhood, all right, and if she lived around here, it might at least explain one-third of what was on Elmo's mind: why Darius had been here; why he had been gunned down; and who was responsible.

If it got him closer to the answer to that three-part question, he didn't care how many damn doors he had to knock on.

Be nice if there was an easier way, though.

He threw his cigarette to the street and ground it out under his heel, then went across the street and into the project. Best to start there, since it was at its entrance that Darius had been killed. If that didn't pan out, he could work his way into the surrounding area. One foot in front of the other, just like they taught you in the army.

A couple of stringy youths of fourteen or fifteen had now appeared and were monkeying with the playground equipment. They could have been the same kids from the previous afternoon. They had red bandannas on their left arms. Except for the kids, no one was out in the common area. In fact, the whole neighborhood was quite still. The few people, mostly women, who were out and about looked to Elmo to be intent on innocent errands. Gangbangers were for the most part night owls, not eagles—which explained why the decent people in the neighborhood were out early, hurrying to complete their mundane missions before the vermin crawled out from under their rocks.

The boys on the playground weren't playing; they were just hanging around. Elmo wondered if they couldn't hang around school just as well, and maybe accidentally pick up some learning. They eyed him closely as he stood inside the entrance. He eyed them back.

His imaginary coin-toss favored the building to the right, on the north side of the common area. The front door was a slab of dented steel, painted brown and broken by an eight-by-ten wire-reinforced window at eye level. It opened into a small square lobby. There were a dozen mailboxes in the east wall, but they were unused. The doors were missing from most of them, and they were now repositories for garbage. Elmo had noticed several of those free-standing lockbox contraptions just outside the east entrance to the project. You probably couldn't pay a letter carrier enough to bring mail into these buildings.

Elmo went down a garbage-lined corridor that ran along-side a darkened staircase. There were two ground-level apartments at the back of the building, boasting a lovely view of the project's northern wall, which stood no more than three feet out the back. The corridor was festooned with graffiti done in spray paint, marking pen, and, by the look of it, knife or nail. Much of it was unprintable; much of it was unintelligible. At least, unintelligible to me.

Bob Barker was conducting *The Price Is Right* inside apartment number one, but evidently the occupant was too busy to come on down to the door. No answer at apartment two, either. It was dead still inside when Elmo put his ear to the steel door.

He went upstairs. The stairs led to a small landing, then doubled back to a larger one off of which were four more doors; then the stairs repeated the pattern up to the top level and four more apartments. There was a wire-reinforced window on each of the smaller landings. Elmo paused on the first landing and looked down into the common area. The two kids from the playground were gone now.

He went on up.

Two toddlers in grimy clothes played on the landing on the top floor. Elmo wondered how many kids in these buildings had tumbled down the open staircases in the last twenty or thirty years. There was dust, litter, and plain old garbage everywhere. The stairs and landings reeked of garbage, cooking, and hopelessness, reeked badly despite the fact that they were virtually unheated.

The first building was a washout. Elmo's knocking produced answers at three of ten doors. One door closed immediately when the occupant, whom Elmo never glimpsed, saw that his or her caller was not a familiar face. The other two opened as far as their security devices would allow. Through this half-inch gap the snapshot of Darius at a green-painted picnic table passed through and then back, with the resident claiming not to recognize the boy.

The second resident, though—it had been a woman's

voice—actually apologized for not being able to help. Silly little things like that are what you grab hold of when you've got a big and possibly futile job ahead of you.

Elmo went back downstairs and out the front door, and met the welcoming committee.

The question hadn't been *whether*—that was answered when the boys disappeared from the play area—just *when*. Elmo's money had been on sooner rather than later. That was his preference, too. These kids might tell him more than all the other residents of this battle-scarred neighborhood.

There were five of them, including the two who had been on the playground. The other three were bigger kids, but not, Elmo thought, much older than the first two. Fifteen, sixteen, seventeen—in there somewhere. That would make them old enough to be full-fledged Bloods, but Elmo doubted that they were. For one thing, they were up and active comparatively early to be part of a bunch that conducted most of its business at night, all night. For another, they didn't quite have the attitude down, the leaden eye, the heavy lids, the hard impassivity. These kids were a little too excited, even nervous. The smaller two especially, the boys who must have gone to alert the others, looked at Elmo as if he had just materialized in a puff of purple smoke, sporting horns and a pointed tail.

That made them less dangerous. A little.

Elmo smiled, but there was neither warmth nor friendship in it. "Morning, brothers," he said pleasantly enough. "Wonder if any of you young men might help me with something."

"Ain't no brother to you," the biggest kid spat. He was a little taller than Elmo, and beefy. In a year he'd be downright fat. Like the other boys, he was dressed in layers of baggy clothing and unlaced high-tops. He wore a black felt jacket with big leather sleeves, over which he had draped several leather medallions bearing images of Africa in red, green, black, and gold. He had the red cloth around his forearm; they all did. He wore wraparound shades and a multicolored knit cap that hugged his skull, and his wide mouth was a sneer. "Saw you 'round here yesterday with Whitey."

The kid was pushing for a reaction, so Elmo gave him one, though certainly not the one the kid expected. Elmo contrived to look puzzled and said, "How'd you know his name is Whitey?" Then, while the kid was still working on that one, he went on in a level tone: "That white man's a friend of mine, helping me find out what happened to the brother who got killed the other night." Elmo had the snapshot of Darius in his left hand; now he showed it to the big kid.

The kid didn't look at it any more than was required to take it, tear it in half, and let the pieces fall to the ground. "Tell you what happened to him. Got his fuckin' head blowed off, that's what. Now you know, you just shuffle along, Tom." The kid showed his uneven teeth and laughed derisively. The other boys laughed and made rude remarks. They think this is a game, Elmo thought. They think this is fun. Their leader—ad hoc leader of this little group, at least—had scored a couple of points at Elmo's expense, and like cowardly mutts they now joined in, yipping and sniping.

Elmo had copies of the picture, a pocketful of them, printed out at a one-hour photo center the previous evening after they had left the Beacons'. He took another one from his coat pocket and proffered it to the big kid. The gibing died down.

"Take a closer look," Elmo said calmly.

The big kid stole a quick glance over his shoulder, back at his companions, as if to reassure himself. Then he laughed a little. Not the derisive laugh of a moment ago. He tried for it, but all he got was bluster, which didn't quite cover his confusion and embarrassment.

"You ever see him around here?" Elmo continued. "See him hanging out with anyone? Know anyone he might have known?"

"Yo, Tom, why'n'tchoo go ask your whitemeat friend?" This came from another of the bunch, a kid with a bad complexion that he tried to hide behind a thin, patchy growth of peachfuzz. One of the other kids made kissy sounds, and the others joined in—again, like dogs who suddenly sense that the advantage is with them.

The big kid took a step forward. Elmo was standing on the concrete slab that formed the building's doorstep. It was a few inches above the level of the walkway, so when the kid moved in close, he and Elmo were just about eye-to-eye. Elmo could smell the kid's breath; it was surprisingly cool and sweet. The kid stared him down, trying hard to look fierce and dangerous and doing a pretty fair job of it.

"Get outta my face, son." Elmo's voice was as cool and smooth as a pane of glass.

"Ain't no son a you, you got that, Tom?" The kid's voice was husky and heavy, his words a series of body-blows.

The other boys were silent for the moment.

Elmo said, "Then I guess that makes you my nephew."

A collective *wohhhh* came from the group, unmistakably mocking in its tone. Elmo didn't know whether it was directed at him or the kid, but the kid's jaw tightened and his face clouded, either in anger or in embarrassment.

"Motherfu—"

The kid was good. He had practiced. The knife was in his hand almost before Elmo realized it.

But Elmo had practiced, too, and he was very good. The Browning nine-millimeter semiautomatic was in his hand a full ten seconds before the kid realized it. When the realization caught up with him, he froze. Elmo tucked the working end of the automatic against the kid's jacket, just below the ribs, pushing gently upward into the soft flesh.

"Drop the pig-sticker."

He did. Elmo kicked it off the sidewalk and into the dirt.

It would have been easy to pull the trigger, send the kid's innards flying, call it justice. You kill one of mine, I kill one of yours. As far as Elmo was concerned they were all the same—Crips, Bloods, all the others, they were all insects who fed on society's raw wounds. Worse, they exploited their own people, although from their perspective they had no people outside their own gangs, and everybody else was there only to be exploited.

The anger came back, in hot waves that spread from Elmo's chest outward, down his arms, toward his trigger finger.

So fucking easy.

And that very fact stopped him from firing. He let the anger recede, then moved back a pace, taking the barrel of the gun out of the boy's belly. There would be some grisly satisfaction in killing one of them, or all of them, but Elmo knew it would be temporary. He wanted the ones who had been in the car that night. More, he wanted the one who was behind it, the one who gave the orders.

His hand moved quickly, unexpectedly, almost involuntarily. The gun flashed dully in the weak sunlight and the barrel slammed against the big kid's left cheek.

The kid recoiled and a collective gasp of astonishment went up from his friends, who jumped at the sudden move and the cold violence of it.

Elmo grabbed the kid by the collar of his felt jacket, spinning him around to face his friends. The kid was off-balance, reeling from the pistol-whip and Elmo's grabbing him, so it took hardly any effort on Elmo's part to propel the kid forward, stumbling, into his friends.

"Now here's some advice—for all of you." Elmo's voice was steady and calm, completely at odds with his recent actions. "It's free now but it gets real expensive later on, so take it while you can. First, get out of my way. Second, stay out of my way. Any questions? Then *do* it."

They scattered, across the common area, toward the buildings on the other side.

Elmo looked down at the slender pistol, frowning. Then he slipped it back into his right-hand coat pocket. Saving it for later.

There was no doubt in his mind that those boys would report this little encounter to the Bloods. They would embellish it, of course, to make themselves look stronger, braver, and more in control until bad luck swiped the upper hand from them. But they would report it, and then—

And then what? Elmo fished out a cigarette and lit it. His hands shook, his shoulders and neck were tight with tension and bottled rage. The smoke was soothing. He took it in as deeply as possible. *And then what?* It would be interesting to see. Since Crips probably were responsible, you might expect the Bloods to offer no opposition to the investigation—hell, they might even line up to help out. But that was presuming that these people followed the normal rules of logic, when in fact their logic was their own. While they might not mind seeing Crips being nailed, they might nevertheless protest the investigation on their turf, just for principle's sake.

As he pondered these things, Elmo wandered across the common area, toward the building directly south of the one he had just had such glorious results with. There were still doors to be knocked on. As he came even with the wide entrance to the housing project, he glanced out toward the street, toward where he had parked Robert Olson's car. The project sat on ground slightly higher than the block across the street, so Elmo was looking literally down the street that dead-ended at the project entrance, and from this higher elevation now spotted something he hadn't noticed yesterday. The top of a cross rising above and behind the buildings they had canvassed the previous afternoon. A church of some sort, obviously, down in the next block.

With not an instant's hesitation, Elmo turned, left the project grounds, and made for the cross.

He had been doing this kind of work, here and there, for nearly twenty years now, and he had met very few ministers, priests, or rabbis who didn't make a point of knowing as much as they could about the goings-on in their neighborhoods, whether it involved their congregation or not.

If the preacher at that church could save Elmo a little shoe leather—or a knife between the shoulder blades—Elmo was in favor of that.

CHAPTER

11

The church was a small, white stucco building that obviously was a converted house, although the work had been done long enough ago, and well enough, that the only real giveaway was a suspiciously picture-window-sized stained-glass window in the front. That and the fact that the building sat so close to the small houses that made up the rest of the block, houses all similar in shape and size to the one that was now Friendship Christian Church.

There was a small sign in the minuscule front yard, a black felt rectangle in a glass case. Elmo wondered how often they had to replace the glass. White letters were pushed into grooves in the felt: FRIENDSHIP CHRISTIAN CHURCH — REV W R O-NEAL — SUNDAY SERVICE 10 A M — EVERYONE WELCOM.

The Reverend O'Neal had run out of E's.

Elmo went up concrete steps to an open porch, hesitating at the door. You don't ordinarily knock at the door to a church, but to simply walk in would feel like just barging into somebody's home. He had just raised his fist to rap on the door when it swung inward. An enormous black man blocked Elmo's view. He was certainly six and a half feet tall, and Elmo would have bet that it was a constant struggle for him to keep his weight below 300. He had a full head of graying hair cut close to his skull, a slightly darker mustache kept equally trimmed, and a hundred-watt smile. He wore vaguely clerical clothes, black slacks, black mock turtleneck—all black except for a bright red cardigan.

"Come in, come in," he boomed. Elmo would have been disappointed with anything except a voice that rattled the windows. "Don't be shy. Nobody knows whether to knock the first time."

"Reverend O'Neal?" Elmo asked.

"The one and only Walter Raleigh O'Neal," the big man thundered. He had very dark skin except along the left side of his face, where a pigment deficiency left a long jagged patch of pink. "That didn't always used to be true," the minister went on, ushering Elmo into the entryway, "but since my dear dad passed on a few years ago, the world's been down to just one." He laughed at his own joke.

For historical reasons, a good many Americans of African descent have Irish surnames. Whenever Elmo met a black man like the Reverend O'Neal, he thought that that fact was fitting. The man was as full of blarney and bluster as any O'Neal from the old sod could ever hope to be.

"My name is Elmo Lammers." The front door opened into a short corridor. To one side was a tiny room, probably originally conceived as a music room but now a cloak room; to the other side, an archway into the living room, which obviously was where services were held. There was a makeshift pulpit in the form of a portable lectern on a small table near the fireplace on the far wall, a well-used spinet, and perhaps two dozen chairs lined up in rows facing the pulpit. The chairs were beat-up brown straight-back numbers. From the look of them, Elmo guessed they had been picked up for a song when some school district was through with them.

"And what may I do for you, Mister Lammers," O'Neal said genially, shouldering open a heavy double-hinged door on the other side of the archway. Following him, Elmo saw that it led to what must have originally been a small dining room, currently set up as an office or study. O'Neal gestured toward two chairs in front of a wooden desk, low, barrel-shaped chairs done up in ugly orange corduroy. Elmo sat in one, O'Neal took the other.

Reaching inside his coat for his wallet, Elmo said, "It's about the shooting that happened over in the next block the other night. Morning, really." He found and handed over a copy of his Illinois PI permit.

"My," O'Neal said, studying the permit through Ben Franklin reading glasses he had slipped on. He handed it back. "You're a long way from home, aren't you, Mister Lammers."

"The boy who was killed was my sister's oldest."

"I see." The minister's face was no longer wide and jolly, but instead showed earnest concern. All part of the act, Elmo figured. Change the face to suit the circumstances, like changing socks to go with a suit. "My sympathies," O'Neal was saying. "How can I help you? I assume you're trying to find the killers, but I'm afraid I have no idea. From what I've read, seen on the TV, and heard up and down the street here, your nephew was the victim of a drive-by. The famous truce between the Bloods and the Crips seems not to have touched our little community here. If anything, their rivalry seems to have intensified since the Los Angeles riots."

Elmo said, "And what have you been hearing on the street, Reverend?"

O'Neal frowned. "As I told you, that your nephew was killed in a gang incident."

"I assume you would know a great deal about the gang situation in this town, Reverend O'Neal."

The big man stood, and walked behind his untidy desk, and looked out a narrow window behind the desk chair. "These gangs are like a scourge on our community," he said soberly, his voice a hard rumble. "The Lord visited upon Pharaoh plagues of frogs and gnats and flies and rains of heavy hail such as had never been in all the land of Egypt since it became a nation." His voice grew louder and rounder. "But, Lord, I know I speak for your decent people in this city when I say we would gladly be visited by frogs and gnats and flies and rains of heavy hail if only we could be rid of this plague of godless, soulless people and their drugs and weapons and hate."

O'Neal exhaled heavily and turned to face Lammers. "Yes, I know about the gangs, Mister Lammers. I have sat in hospital waiting rooms, and funeral homes, and cemeteries with families whose children were victims of the gangs. I have seen kids, good kids, kids from my own little church here look around at the emptiness and hopelessness of their lives and decide— wrongly—that the gangs offered whatever they felt they lacked. Respect, purpose, love—in a peculiar way, they do find love in their gang families, Mister Lammers. And I have seen the utterly appalling effects of the drugs that are these gangs' stock in trade. Drugs that are far more deadly than any bullet ever molded. Oh yes, friend, I do know the gangs."

"Then certainly you must know more about what happened to my nephew—even if it's just rumors."

O'Neal thought, his brow furrowed and his full lips pursed. "I don't know how familiar you are with the street-gang situation here, Mister Lammers, but this neighborhood is one the Bloods have claimed as their so-called turf. Odds are that the Crips, the Bloods' sworn enemies, were responsible for killing your nephew. It would be like them to lie in wait for someone, innocent or not—I don't say anything against your kin, understand—and then open fire. This being Blood turf, you'll understand that there isn't a lot of hard information circulating about the Crips. Mainly rumors, innuendoes, and insults. Now, maybe your time would better be spent talking to people down in Crips territory…though I wouldn't advise it."

"The Crips haven't claimed responsibility for the shooting, which I understand is unusual. There's nothing to tie them into this drive-by except their rivalry with the Bloods, and that's not much. Given that, our time's better spent trying to figure out why the hel— why Darius was on that corner when he was."

"*Our* time?" O'Neal said quizzically.

"I have a friend helping me. Reverend O'Neal, Darius was staying with an aunt and uncle on the other side of town. He had kicked his habit, or at least he was working on it, and according to his family here—who watched him closely, as you might expect—he wasn't using anything. It doesn't look like he had anything to do with the gangs. So far as we know, he didn't know anyone in this neighborhood."

"Then why was he here the other— Oh, I see." O'Neal smiled grimly, nodding to himself. "Yes. Why *was* he here. But I still don't see how I can help."

"We've found out that Darius may have been seeing a young woman, something he kept secret from his family and, it seems, about everyone else he knew."

"A girl from the neighborhood here?"

"We don't know. We're guessing that she might be, that Darius came down here to rendezvous with her, but we just don't know. My job today is to try and find out whether anyone in this neighborhood knew Darius or had seen him around, maybe with this mystery girl. Someone might know who she is. Or, failing that, someone might be able to give us some other idea of why Darius was where he was when he got killed. Now, I'm prepared to knock on every door within a ten-block radius of here if I have to, but like any good American I'd like to find an easier way. I barely got started before I was accosted by a gang of young punks. I don't mean *the* gang. I don't know if they were members or not."

"Probably not—since you're sitting there discussing it so calmly," O'Neal said with grim humor. "This neighborhood's just full of young men who can't wait to get old enough, big enough, strong enough to join the Bloods. They actually look up to these, these *devils* as if they were heroes!"

"Not hard to understand. They look around, what do they see? Broken families, poverty, neglect, abuse, and absolutely zero prospects for their future. Hold that up against life in the gang, pulling down maybe a grand a week dealing crack—not much of a contest."

"I don't know where that thousand-dollars-a-week business comes from," O'Neal said sourly. "The top dogs, the main players may pull down that much. Some of them do better than that. But your average gang member, he's lucky to deal-and-steal *fifty* dollars a week. You do better than that slinging hamburgers at McDonald's, and you're less likely to end up bleeding in some gutter 'cause of it. This b.s. that says kids sell drugs because honest work can't bring them the same kind of money, that's just so much loose talk. It comes down to they can't *find* work, the jobs aren't there for them. But the gangs are. You take care of the first problem, you take care of the second problem at the same time."

"My little friends this morning didn't act like they wanted me to give them jobs," Elmo said. "One of them tried to give me this, between the ribs." He pulled out the knife he had taken from the kids' leader, flicked it open, and deposited it on O'Neal's desk.

The minister looked at it solemnly. "Then they surely weren't full members," he said, "or they'd've used bullets instead. Automatic weapons are so easy to come by and such efficient killers, these snakes hardly ever waste their time with toys like that anymore." He rested his forearms on the back of his desk chair. "Mister Lammers, I am sorry. But I don't know how to help you. I don't know any more than I have told you."

Elmo pulled one of the snapshots of Darius from his coat pocket. "You know a lot about what goes on in this neighborhood, Reverend. Maybe you saw Darius around sometime. Maybe you can give me some ideas on going about my task without ending up dead on a sidewalk myself." He held out the picture.

O'Neal reached for the photo and his glasses simultaneously. "I didn't recognize the boy when I saw his picture in the paper and on the TV...."

"They used his driver's license picture," Elmo said. "You know how good they are."

O'Neal smiled politely and looked at the photograph through

his half glasses. When he looked up, his smile was broad and genuine.

"Mister Lammers, when the good Lord brought you here, he brought you to the right place."

CHAPTER

12

It was on the fringe of downtown, on Harney a few blocks from both Doctor's Hospital and Lutheran Medical Center. It was a low-roofed blue-green block building with a parking lot that was slightly smaller than the plate-glass window in the front wall of the place. Green and red neon tubes in the window spelled the name of the joint in letters that formed the shape of a submarine. Sub Standard. I liked it.

The interior was as plain and straightforward as the exterior: linoleum floor, plastic-paneled walls, fluorescent lights in a suspended ceiling. As charming as a Styrofoam cup. There was an L-shaped display counter that began with canned soft drinks, fruit, and dessert items, moved on to a variety of breads, meats, cheeses, and other options, and ended at a beat-up NCR cash register. Sub Standard obviously had been designed for take-out and delivery, but somewhere along the line someone decided to accommodate those customers who couldn't get enough of the atmosphere, and crammed a few square tables and hard chairs on the opposite end of the room. A couple of them were occupied.

There was only one person ahead of me in line. I grabbed a can of Coke and an apple from the self-service end of the case, gave my sandwich order to a tall Asian kid with bad skin, and handed my money to a stocky middle-aged guy with wiry red-brown hair over a face as craggy as a coral reef. He wore a plastic badge that said HARRY and MANAGER. "That to eat in?" he said, giving me a plastic tray and eating utensils. "We'll bring you your sandwich." He pronounced it *sannitch*. When I didn't toddle along right away, he gave me a look and said, "Something else?"

I handed him my card and he looked at it. Some guys are good at looking unimpressed. He was one of them. "So."

"So I'd like to talk to you, if you can spare five minutes."

"Mister, it's gonna start getting zooey in here in about fifteen minutes, I got one kid out making deliveries and another who was supposed to be here—"

"Shouldn't take long. It's about Darius LeClerc."

"You a private cop?"

"Something like that," I said.

He gave me a long, close look, then nodded slightly and moved out from behind the cash register. "I'll be with this guy a minute, Donnie," he told the tall kid.

We went to a table near the front window. The table wobbled on its pedestal.

"You lookin' into what happened to Darius?" the little man said right away. "Good. He was a good kid. By the way, I'm Harry Hanley." He wiped a blunt-fingered hand on his apron and held it across the table.

"You know mine from my card," I said. "Everyone just calls me Nebraska. You'd have to be a contortionist to pronounce my first name."

He still had the card in his left hand, and looked at it now, but all it had were two initials and the name that my grandfather adopted shortly after he came to this country. His money took him no farther west than Nebraska, and he didn't like what Immigration back in New York had done to his name—admittedly, a horrendous mouthful of consonants to begin with—so he called himself after his new home. If only he had made it as far as Montana, I'd be hearing *Any-relation-to-Joe* instead of *That's-a-peculiar-name* every time I meet someone.

Harry Hanley let it pass without comment, though, and

said, "Jack Reedy hire you?"

"No. I'm doing a favor for a friend, another uncle of Darius's." I drank some of my Coke and said, "Harry, nobody can figure out what Darius was doing up in that part of town at that time of night."

"Beats hell out of me," he said. He had a raspy voice, the kind that sounds like it gets a lot of use. "Tell you one thing, though. No matter what the cops may say, Darius was not there to buy, sell, or do anything else with any drugs."

This kid had more fans than Elvis.

Hanley gestured to indicate the restaurant. "Most of the kids who work for me are about the same age, teens to early twenties. They're all problem kids. Problems with drugs, the law, the gangs, teachers, parents—cripes, you name it. Nine-tenths of them are recovering addicts. Me too. I was a boozer and a user for more years than most of these kids have even seen yet, and that was back when everyone thought it was your own damn fault."

"A lot of people still think that way," I said.

"Got that right. When I was trying to climb out of the gutter, no one'd help me. No one except this one parish priest. He gave me a job. Nothing much. Broom-pusher. But he showed me some respect and after a while I began to get some self-respect. Then, when he thought I was ready, he got me into a program. I promised myself, if I ever got back on my feet again I was *not* gonna just stand around and watch other people who got the same kinda problem as me."

My sandwich came, courtesy of an appallingly thin girl with the stringy, lifeless hair and almost translucent skin of an anorexic. "You're late, Lynn," Hanley said.

"Traffic was bad, Harry."

"Traffic's always bad, Harry. Leave the house ten minutes earlier." When she was out of earshot he said, sadly, "Tried to kill herself last year. The weight some of these kids carry… Anyhow, that's why I bought this place, to get in there and *do* something. All the hospitals, agencies, rehab centers, churches, they all send kids to me. I put 'em to work. And they *do* work, or they're out on their butts in about forty-five minutes. Likewise, they start screwing around with dope or gangs or whatever, whether or not that's what got 'em in trouble to begin with, they gone." He let a crooked smile split his rough features. " 'Course they don't know what all the people at the treatment centers and what-not know, namely, that I'm the softest touch in the county. They send the kids back to me and I always take 'em back. Long as I know they're *working* at getting straightened out. That's the main thing."

"You ever kick Darius out?" I said around a mouthful of prosciutto.

"Never had a reason to. His work habits were good. He showed up when he was supposed to, did his job, and didn't bitch. As far as the other—I knew all about his situation from his Uncle Jack and from Eileen Nielsen over at Pacifica—I'd bet money he didn't do anything stronger than a cup of black coffee."

"Gee, I'm almost getting the impression that the people who knew Darius best think he was not in front of the project the other night looking to buy or sell drugs," I said. "So why was he there? Did he pal around with anyone who lives around there? Maybe another of your employees?"

Hanley glanced back at the counter. The phone, which had rung fairly often while we sat and talked, now seemed to be ringing almost constantly. The over-the-counter trade had picked up, too, and the two kids were almost a blur trying to keep up. "I gotta get back," Hanley said. "Bring your tray over here by the register."

I followed him, finishing my lunch while leaning against the side of a stainless-steel refrigerator as Hanley went back to work.

"What'd you ask me? Oh, yeah… None of my kids lives around that project. Got one lives over by Logan Fontenelle, but that doesn't help you any. I don't think him and Darius even knew each other that good. Darius was a good kid, friendly and all, but he still kinda kept to himself, you know?"

"Boy, do I."

" 'Fraid I couldn't tell you if he knew anyone from around there, you know, from outside of work. But I know Darius's Uncle Jack, and I doubt he'd stand for it."

"If he knew about it," I said. "Look, do you know if Darius had a girlfriend?"

Business had gotten brisk. The clientele was mostly younger people. Older people prefer a nice place where they can linger awhile over a cup of coffee or two. I knew because I found myself preferring that more and more with each passing year. The girl handled the phone, the boy handled the walk-ins, and Harry assembled phone orders. He didn't have to think about what he was doing, his hands just did their work independently.

"There was this girl used to come in here from time to time. Kid, nineteen, twenty years old. They acted like they knew each other—not the same way you know your regular customers, exactly. Like they were friends. I remember thinking that that was maybe a good sign, if Darius was getting interested in a girl. But I don't know if she's the one you mean."

"Me neither. Got a name?"

He turned to the boy. "Donnie, what's the name of that girl used to come in a lot when Darius was working?"

"Yeah, I know who you mean. I don't think I ever knew her name."

"Well, ask Lynn when she gets off the phone, willya?"

"She live around here, you think?" I said.

"Nah. I think maybe she works around here or something. Seems like most of the times she came in she was kinda dressed up a little. Carrying a briefcase, too, I think. Yeah, one of those nylon cases, you know? Green."

I asked him for a more detailed description, and got it. Black, nineteen or twenty, five-six or -seven, about 110 pounds, brown hair, straightened to a soft waviness. That narrowed it right down.

"You seen her since Darius died?"

He paused a second, thinking. "Nope, don't think so. You know, if she and Darius were close, then maybe the only reason she came in here was 'cause he was here. I don't know that I ever saw her when Darius wasn't on the schedule, now that I get to thinking about it. So then she'd know Darius is dead and maybe she wouldn't be coming in here anymore."

"Cheer me up some more," I said. I pocketed my apple and pitched my debris through the slot of a trash container, parking the tray on top. "Do me a favor. Ask your other kids if they know this girl, or where she may live or work. Maybe she phoned in for deliveries sometimes, who knows? If you come up with anything—or if she wanders in here—give me a call at the number on my card."

"You got it. Sorry I can't be more help. Darius was a great kid."

That seemed to be the consensus. I thanked him and shoved off, weaving through the small mob of lunchers piled up between the display counter and the door. I held the door for a short, solidly built young woman of Hispanic or possibly American Indian ancestry. She had on a nylon jacket with the Sub Standard logo on back and carried a plastic cooler with a bumper sticker slapped on the side: FOLLOW ME TO SUB STANDARD.

"C'mere, Crystal, we got a pile of orders to go out," Hanley said from behind the counter.

I went out to my Impala, wondering what we would do if we did manage to turn up the mystery girl only to discover that Darius had merely been on that fatal corner en route to or from a tryst with her. That would take care of Question Number One but leave Question Number Two completely intact. Worse, we'd probably dead-end at that point. What would Elmo do then? I knew from experience how tough it was to let an investigation just peter out, even when I didn't have a personal stake in it. Elmo wasn't much better at shrugging them off than I was. And he *did* have a personal stake in this one, a very personal stake. That worried me.

Elmo's hard eye-for-eye pronouncement of last night still rang in my mind's ear. That worried me too. Spend any time in this racket and you're bound to find those thoughts and feelings occasionally rising, usually as your gorge does. The temptation is always there. Hell, we all bend the rules now and then, play God now and then. We call it "discretion" or "judgment." But it's one thing to decide to look the other way, or take it upon yourself to teach someone a lesson, or con yourself into believing that breaking and entering or some similar transgression is justified by your ends—and quite another thing to start meting out your own private brand of justice. Especially of the capital variety.

I had danced with that devil myself, most recently—and most zealously—just a few months ago. The man responsible for sending the unsavories who had hospitalized Robert Olson and later Pat Costello was out to get me, to hurt me, probably in a permanent sort of way. The fastest, cleanest, and surest way to resolve my problem was to take him out of the game. Over a period of some weeks, while I sought a less radical solution and at the same time tried to keep my friends and myself safe from harm, that fast, clean, sure alternative cropped up time and again, each time more insistently.

In the end, I found another way. I'm probably too chicken to have gone in for cold-blooded murder. But sometimes, when I've slaved over a hot typewriter into the wee hours and collapsed into bed exhausted but not sleepy, I stare at the shadows on the ceiling and wonder what I would have done if more weeks had passed without my finding that other way. I wonder what I would have done if the unsavories had killed Pat. I wonder what I would have become if I had simply rung my enemy's doorbell and blown his head off when he answered.

And I thank God that I don't know for a fact.

Elmo had been my friend for many years. Having come right up to the edge of doing something irretrievably stupid, I wanted to help him avoid making the mistake I almost had. If I possibly could.

I had started the car and was just backing out of my parking space when the Sub Standard's delivery girl, Crystal, came running out of the building, yelling and waving her arms.

CHAPTER

13

Down the street, near the project's eastern wall, a young man lounged in the noontime sun. He had on a long overcoat with a big fake-fur collar, black leather gloves, and black leather pants crammed into expensive black high-tops. A single earring dangled from one lobe. It might have been a silver cross, it might have been a silver dagger. The corkscrewed top of a brown-paper bag was sticking out of the left-hand pocket of his overcoat. It wasn't a street-king's scepter, a bottle in a bag; rather it was a bag full of small medicine vials. I know because as I wedged the Impala into a space too small for it along the curb across the street, another car idled past me and over to the curb near the young man. There was a hasty conference through the passenger-side window, then a flash of green and a flash of orange as money and vial, respectively, changed hands. The car continued down the street.

The young man shoved the folding money into his right-hand coat pocket, then screwed the bag shut and stuffed it back into his left-hand pocket. Once again he shrewdly left the very tip of the bag protruding, in case he needed to whip it out in a hurry and slam-dunk it over the wall against which he now resumed his position. I wondered what was in the vials. The list of possibilities was long.

I got out of the car and walked up the block.

This was the tree-lined residential block that Elmo and I had sized up yesterday. The houses were fifty- or sixty-year-old cottages. Originally, most of them had had open porches across the front. Now several of them that I could see were enclosed, and in a few cases made into living space. Of the ones that were still open, several were repositories for garbage and junk that looked well on its way to being garbage. Some of the houses had simply been let go to hell. But some of them were in decent shape, maintained as well as circumstances and resources allowed.

The house I wanted, number 2315, belonged to the latter group. It was a tidy little place with narrow clapboard siding that needed painting, small beds for flowers on either side of the porch steps, and two men on the porch steps, one of them Elmo.

I let out a cab-hailing whistle and they turned. Elmo raised a hand in salute. I caught up with them.

"How'd you know where I was?" he said.

"I was just going to ask you the same thing. Great minds, and so on, I guess."

He smiled politely. "W.R. O'Neal, V.Z. Nebraska." I shook hands with Elmo's oversized companion. "Reverend O'Neal is pastor of a church a block or two over," Elmo was saying. "He thinks he might be able to help us find out what Darius was doing here the other night. What's your excuse?"

"I visited Sub Standard, the place where Darius worked, and found out there was a girl who used to come in fairly frequently when Darius was working. Manager thought it looked like more than just good customer-relations. A delivery girl there knew the girl. They were at high school together. Yolanda Harris. I did a little creative work with the phone book—I am a trained detective, after all—and here I am."

"I showed Reverend O'Neal here that picture of Darius," Elmo said. "He thinks it looks like a young man he saw once or twice with Ms. Harris."

"I'm almost positive," O'Neal said. He had a big voice.

"We're about to find out," Elmo said. He nodded, and

O'Neal prodded the doorbell button.

An old-fashioned speakeasy-style peephole door opened and a pair of eyes behind bifocal lenses peered out. O'Neal raised his voice even louder than its normal level in order to be heard through the glass. "Good afternoon, Lucy!" he thundered. "These gentlemen here would like to have a word or two with you."

Behind the bifocals, the dark eyes moved to Elmo and me in turn, then back to the minister. Then the miniature door closed, a series of locks and bolts were unlocked and unbolted, and the bigger door opened. "Reverend O'Neal," the woman said, a little flustered. She slid the glasses from her nose and let them dangle from a gold chain around her neck. She was a tiny black woman in her mid-fifties. Her hair, which was graying, was straightened and swept away from her face, which displayed her high cheekbones to good advantage. She wore a pink pant suit reminiscent of some kind of uniform, with a cranberry-colored sweater over her shoulders. "I was getting ready for work. Yoli will be home in a minute…"

"Lucy is a hospital aide," O'Neal said for our benefit. To her he said, "This won't take but a minute."

"Actually, it's probably Yolanda we need to talk to anyhow," I said helpfully. "Your daughter, I think?"

She looked us over again, and there was a mixture of suspicion, fear, and curiosity in her eyes. She nervously fingered the glasses resting on her chest and turned again to O'Neal. "What's this all about, Reverend?"

"This young man," O'Neal said gently. He showed her the picture of Darius LeClerc.

She took it, raised her glasses without putting them on, and glanced at the photo. "That's that boy who was killed the other night," she said, not really making it a question. She handed the picture back to O'Neal. "I saw him on the news. But I don't see what this has to do with me. I never knew the boy." She was fidgeting with her glasses.

I looked at Elmo and he at me, and while we communicated

this way O'Neal took a more direct approach: "Lucy Wheeler Harris," he said, and his voice was big and deep enough to dive into. "I have known you for nigh well twenty years now, and I believe this is the first time I have ever heard you lie through your teeth like that."

Mrs. Harris recoiled as if struck. Her mouth opened, but she didn't protest.

O'Neal could see the surprise in her face. "You expected me to stand here silently and help you lie? You know me better, Lucy! Now this here is Mister Elmo Lammers of Chicago, Illinois, and this is his friend, Mister, um, Nebraska. Mister Lammers is the uncle of *this boy*." He held up the picture the way Raymond Burr holds up Exhibit A on *Perry Mason*. O'Neal softened his voice. "He's trying to find out why the boy was here when he got killed, Lucy. He's trying to find out for the boy's widowed mother. I didn't bring him here because I thought he would like to meet you. I brought him here because I knew you could help him."

The Harris woman had stood silently through this, immobile except for fiddling with her glasses. Her dark eyes glistened with tears, and now she blinked a few times to clear them.

"You'd better come in," she said thickly.

The living room was small and cluttered, but comfortable. As if to testify to that, a tortoise-shell cat reclined on the back of a sofa, where a thin rectangle of sunlight came through a gap in the drapes over the front window.

I realized that all the windows were covered with draperies or blinds, even on this relatively sunny afternoon. I suppose it was safer that way.

There was a makeshift enclosure in the middle of the room, formed of pillows and furniture cushions. In the center of this, on a blanket on the floor, an infant slept in that totally-out-of-it, check-back-with-me-later way that only infants manage, and only at a time of day when everyone else in the house is not trying to sleep.

"That's my granddaughter," Mrs. Harris said, smiling softly.

"That's Yoli's baby. Emily June. Eight months old." She didn't whisper or even lower her voice. She knew that when they're out like that, kids can sleep through a naval barrage.

We went with her through open French doors and into a dine-in kitchen. Like the other room, it was cluttered and comfortable. We sat at a round oak dining table and she distributed coffee from a Norelco coffeemaker on the counter. She didn't sit.

"I—I'm sorry about the way I acted before," she said, going at her eyeglasses again. "I don't..." She dabbed at her eyes with a wadded tissue she pulled from a pants pocket. "Yes, I knew Darius. I met him a few times. He kept company with my Yoli some."

"Why did you lie, Lucy?" O'Neal said.

She sighed. "Yoli said it would be a good idea to keep quiet. You know what it's like, living in this neighborhood these days," she implored. "There's so much trouble all the time. So many people getting hurt, killed..." Her eyes had fastened on the baby sleeping in the other room. "It's so *trying* sometimes. What these people have done to our home..." She looked at O'Neal. "When that nice boy was killed, when I saw his picture next day on the TV, I told Yoli we had to call the police. But she said we should stay out of it. There was nothing we could do to help Darius, she said. All we could do was get ourselves in trouble."

"In trouble with whom, Mrs. Harris?" I said.

She looked at me as if she didn't understand the question. "Why, the gangs," she said after a few moments.

"Was the boy down here to see Yoli that night, Lucy?" O'Neal asked. "Is that what he was doing down at the corner?"

"No, Yoli was in all night Sunday. I always try to keep her in at night. It's not hardly safe out there even in broad daylight. But you know how young girls are.... Sunday she stayed in, though. All day she stayed in. She had an exam next day she was worried about. She's learning to be a court reporter," Mrs. Harris added with pride.

There was a small stenography school not far from Sub Standard. They had, or used to have, a couple of public stenographers on staff there, which I employed a few times back in the olden days. I said, "Did your daughter first meet Darius at the restaurant where he worked?"

"Yes, that's right," she said, thus explaining the nylon case Harry Hanley said Darius's friend habitually carried.

"You say your daughter didn't see Darius on Sunday," Elmo put in impatiently.

"That's right. Yoli stayed in. It was cold Sunday anyway. She practiced for her exam, and played with the baby, and in the evening we all watched a movie on the TV. We went to bed after the ten o'clock news, like we usually do."

"You must have heard the shots; you're no more than half a block up the street from where Darius was killed."

"Yes," Mrs. Harris said quietly. "We heard them."

"And what did you do?" Elmo pressed. His jaw was tight.

She looked at him calmly for a long moment. Then she said, "I didn't *do* anything, Mister Lammers. I don't know how things are for you in Chicago, but if you lived in this neighborhood you'd soon learn that curiosity is something that can get you killed. You be especially careful if you're the widowed mother of a twenty-year-old daughter with a eight-month-old baby."

Her voice was not quiet by the time she finished. The Reverend O'Neal was saying, "Now, Lucy, it's all right," and I flashed a hot glance at Elmo, who ignored it, and said, "Mrs. Harris, you said that you met Darius only a few times."

"Yes," she said, her eyes still locked on Elmo. "He called on Yoli here a couple of times, but usually they met somewhere."

"Could they have planned to meet on that corner?"

Slowly, as if reluctant to take her eyes off of Elmo, she turned to face me. "What would be the sense of that?" she demanded.

"What was the sense of meeting *anyplace* besides here?" Elmo said. It was a legitimate question. Darius had kept Yoli a secret from his family, but obviously Mrs. Harris knew about him; why should they meet someplace else? Elmo had a point, all right, but by acting as if Mrs. Harris had pulled the trigger herself, he wasn't making her feel too kindly disposed toward providing helpful answers.

"I *guess* that's how they *wanted* it," the woman said crossly. Then she seemed to remember that her pastor was in the room, too, and limply added, "You know, young people like a little privacy sometimes, time to themselves…"

I was thinking about Darius slipping out of the Reedys' house in the wee hours Sunday night-Monday morning. There was no telling how many other times he might have done the same, to meet with Yoli Harris or for some other purpose. I started to ask Mrs. Harris if it wasn't possible that her daughter had similarly sneaked away after lights out Sunday night, but was preempted by the opening of the front door.

"Mama, I'm home!" a feminine voice called out.

"In the kitchen, baby."

Yoli came into the living room, tossing her things into a cushionless chair, and crouched to caress the baby when she caught sight of us around the kitchen table. She shot up as if fired from a cannon.

"*Who are these men?*" she demanded hotly. She was small, like her mother, and pretty, much as Harry Hanley had described her. Except for her eyes, which currently were wild and shot flaming bolts at anyone she aimed them at.

Mrs. Harris was taken aback by her daughter's belligerence. "Why— Yoli, you know the Reverend, and this man here is Darius's unc—"

"Darius! What have they been asking? What do they want to know?" She flew into the kitchen and grabbed her mother by the arms. "*What have you been telling them?*"

"Why, I—"

The girl turned on us. "Uncle," she spat at Elmo. "What sort of proof did he show you?" Back to her mother. "As if living in this neighborhood with everything isn't dangerous enough!

You let these strange men into the house with the baby asleep in the next room!"

"But the Reverend brought them, baby, and—"

"And he can take them with him as he leaves," she said, turning yet again and fixing a significant gaze on the big man.

"Yoli," he said reasonably, "they only want to know why the man was in this neighborhood that night. Was he coming to see you? Was he leaving from seeing you?"

The girl's eyes narrowed. "You pious son of a bitch. You're like all the other so-called Christians in this neighborhood, think because my baby's got no daddy her mama must be a tramp."

"Yoli!"

"Let me tell you something, *Reverend* O'Neal. You and your friends. I didn't see Darius at all Sunday. I wasn't planning to see him, in the middle of the night or any other time. I'm sorry he's dead, but there's nothing I can do about that. You take what you get, you go messing around with those people."

"What people?" Elmo said.

"You just walk into the room?" she said scathingly. "What people you think we been *talking* about! The gangs, mister whatever-your-name is, the *street gangs!*"

"You say Darius was 'messing around' with the gangs..." I ventured. I felt it was pretty brave, under the circumstances.

Yoli wheeled on me. Then she paused, inhaled deeply, and let it out, as if trying to calm herself preparatory to explaining something to an imbecile. "I don't know," she finally said. Her voice was far from calm, but it no longer was raging. Her left hand went for a large soft curl that wound below her ear. She tugged at the curl without seeming to know she was doing so. "Okay?" she said. "I do not know. All I know, you don't go hanging around street corners in this neighborhood at two in the morning *except* that you're messing around, okay?"

"When was the last time you talked to Darius?" Elmo said. "Did he say or otherwise indicate anything that might explain why he would be—"

"Okay, that's enough!" the girl exploded. She looked at her mother, who stood, wide-eyed and quiet, in a corner of the counter. "You *see* why I said we should keep quiet! Look, I knew Darius, I dated him a few times, I liked him, he was a nice guy, I'm sorry he's dead—but that's it, okay? He's not like the first person I ever knew who got killed. It happens. It's too bad. But all I'm concerned about is keeping my baby, my mother, and me alive and in one piece. *We're* the ones gotta live with these people. They even *think* we're crossing them up some way—" She shook her head angrily, and her hands turned into small fists. "So you just do us a favor—get the hell out of this house and stay away from us!"

The baby woke and started to cry.

CHAPTER

14

As we moved away from the house, we could hear the sound of voices inside—*a* voice, really: Yoli's. It was impossible to make out the words, but it seemed safe to guess that she was unhappy with her mother.

Elmo fired up a cigarette the minute we hit the pavement. His antique lighter had a pop-off lid. When he shoved the cap back on, he used so much force that I thought he wanted to compress the machine down to a small gold marble. "She's lying," he pronounced after a preliminary puff. "She knows more than she's telling."

"Come on, man, what could she know?"

"Do I know? She acted like she barely knew Darius, but that isn't the impression I got from the mother. Why the act, if she doesn't know something?"

"Peter denied Jesus, whom he loved, three times," the Reverend O'Neal contributed. "The reason was fear."

"Oh, great," Elmo said peevishly.

"Makes sense to me," I said. "The girl said it herself—they have to live with these bastards every day, and there's hell to pay if you get on the wrong side of them. Someone you know gets killed and it looks like maybe the gangs are involved, the smart move is to keep quiet and not get curious."

"I still say something stinks," Elmo snapped, moving down the sidewalk.

O'Neal and I followed. The dealer was still in position across the street. He leaned against the graffiti-blemished wall, motionless except for his eyes, which were locked on us.

"I may know what you smell," I said. "The girl from the sub shop, Crystal, was in high school with Yoli. Back then, Yoli was kind of wild—"

"She kind of wild *today!*"

"—and she was involved with a gang kid."

Elmo stopped. "What do you mean, involved?"

"Oh, complex, intricate, elaborate—what the hell do you *think* I mean, involved? Involved!"

"What gang?" His eyes were narrow behind the thin streamer of smoke rising from his brown cigarette.

I shrugged.

"The Bloods," the Reverend O'Neal supplied. "It's fairly common knowledge, I suppose. When Yoli was a little younger, she hung around with the Bloods. She became involved, as you say, with one or two of the boys. She was doing drugs. She dropped out of school." He shook his head. "It's the Lord's doing and nobody else's that that baby of hers was born whole and healthy. Yoli quit doing just as soon as she found out she was expecting, quit the hard way, but I still say it's only by the grace of God that little Emily June wasn't born with a habit."

"Who's the baby's father?" Elmo said.

"I don't think even Lucy knows," O'Neal said. "That's one secret Yoli has never shared with anyone, as far as I know."

"How long since Yoli dissociated herself from the Bloods?" I wondered.

"Oh, let's see... A good year, eighteen months, I'd say. Lucy was coming to me pretty regularly back then, naturally upset about what was going on with her girl. Her first two, they turned out just fine—Maurice sells computers in Saint Louis, Felicity married an Air Force man and they got transferred down to Colorado. But that was before the gangs and everything, and Lucy's husband, Aldo, was still alive... Yes, if Yoli's twenty now, then it's a good two, three years since she was heavily involved with the gang, 'long about a year and a half since she eased herself away from them and started trying to get her life back together." He paused. "From what Lucy tells me, Yoli's trying to be a good mother to that little baby girl."

"If she had a habit," I said, "and dropped it cold when she found out she was pregnant, I'd say that says she's trying hard."

We had continued moving slowly down the sidewalk and now were standing near my Impala, which was parked at the curb. I was doing some mental arithmetic. The baby would have been conceived roughly seventeen months ago. That was right about the time Yoli severed ties with the gang, according to O'Neal. Which may or may not have meant anything.

As I mulled this, I unconsciously turned and looked across and down the street, toward the corner where Darius had died. Then I looked at Elmo. "Are you well-known in the African-American community?" I said.

He frowned crossly, then let it ease back into one of mild puzzlement. "I'm legendary in my own household," he said, "but I don't think my fame has spread much further. Is there a reason you ask?"

"I notice that whenever we're together a small crowd gathers, and they don't look like members of *my* fan club."

Elmo followed my gaze across the street, where half a dozen or so boys hung out on the corner at the entrance to the project. They might have been the same kids from yesterday afternoon. Either way, there was something different about them today. A posture, an attitude, strong enough to fill the short distance between us. Yesterday all I sensed in them was curiosity. Today I was picking up a kind of aggressive possessiveness.

"No, they're with me," Elmo was saying calmly. "I had a run-in with them earlier, as I was telling the Reverend here." He squinted at them. "Yeah, looks like the same bunch. Except for the one in the kufi."

"Is *that* what you call those hats." It was a sort of tall crown, very colorful, mainly red and green with irregular strips of yellow. "What's with the bandannas on the forearms," I said. "Colors?"

"Not exactly," O'Neal said heavily. "Gang colors, as they're called, are distinct from an actual *color*. A gang may decide they'll all wear sleeveless denim jackets—that's their *colors*, regardless of what color the jackets are. Now, gangs like the Bloods and the Crips, they make a big deal of particular colors—red and blue, respectively. They usually figure into their *colors* in a big way." He nodded toward the group across the street. "You see those two in the jackets? They're members." The jackets in question were expensive-looking silk, something like baseball jackets. Red. "Those boys with the bandannas," O'Neal was saying, "they're not members, but they aspire to be. The bandannas—'rags,' they call them—are the way they show their loyalty. It's like my brother-in-law wearing his cherished Royals cap."

No wonder parents groups were urging schools to adopt uniforms. It wasn't just a matter of avoiding this or that color of shirt. There was a code, a whole language at work, and you could find yourself in a world of hurt if you unluckily missed the latest fashion bulletin.

One of the red jackets was the fellow in the kufi. "He looks older than the others," Elmo was saying.

"Oh, yes, he's an old man by gang standards," O'Neal said. Twenty-two."

This kid slowly peeled off from the rest of the group and, followed by the other red jacket, disappeared into the project.

"Just curious, you think?" I said.

"I do not. When I rousted the junior team, they went off to report to the big kids. These two came to see what all the fuss was about. Now they've gone to report back to the others."

"That's probably about on the money," O'Neal said. "The one in the hat, his name's Richard Dayton, but his street name's FlashMan D. He's one of the top men in the Bloods. Seems to see himself as the recruitment director or something. He's the one who deals with the younger kids, decides who will and who will not be considered for membership, and oversees the initiation rites."

"Christ, it's a damn fraternity!" Elmo snapped in disgust.

"The fellow with him is a newer member. Donald Lee. They call him Little Flash, on account of he's FlashMan's charge. That's how they work it: an older member takes a new recruit under his wing, and the recruit usually derives his street name from the older member's."

"This FlashMan," I said to O'Neal. "Bad news?"

"None of 'em's good. He's part of the L.A. bunch, the devils who brought this blight upon us in the first place. FlashMan and another three or four L.A. Bloods run the show here. Call themselves the Council. The leader—what they call the Top Prez or even the Supreme Prez—he's getting up there in years too. He has to be twenty-four if he's a day."

"What do these kids do when they get too old to gangbang?" Elmo mused.

"So far none of them has lived long enough for us to find out," O'Neal said.

"Just like rock-and-rollers," I said. "Who's the Top Prez?"

"His right name is Gerard Jones. But he likes to be called Wizard."

"Gizzard," Elmo said derisively.

"Wizard," O'Neal repeated gamely. "Like a magician."

"Gizzard's more appropriate," Elmo said.

"Low self-esteem is at the heart of the gang problem," O'Neal said like a man who had given it much thought. "The fact that so many gang members adopt ostentatious nicknames for themselves shows they feel the need to pump themselves up. It's a way of compensating for their poor self-esteem."

"Well, goodie for them," Elmo said curtly. "What about everyone else? What about the people who keep their blinds drawn in broad daylight because they don't want to be a target in their own homes? What about *their* self-esteem, Reverend?"

With that he turned and stormed off down the sidewalk, leaving O'Neal—and me—more or less speechless. I felt obliged to say something about Elmo's outburst, and put together a little fat-headed folderol about how this investigation was hitting a little close to home for Elmo.

O'Neal was neither offended nor angered by Elmo's vitriol. All I read in his face or heard in his voice was concern. "I'm not sure it's such a good idea for you two to be poking around this neighborhood," he said. "No offense, but I don't think either of you knows the sort of animals who have claimed this territory." He looked down the sidewalk at Elmo's retreating back. "And since he'll never take my advice, and you won't let him go it alone, then at the very least make sure he has his head on straight. 'Anger lodges in the bosom of fools.' " He looked at me. "Keep your wits about you. You probably won't stay alive, but at least you'll have a prayer."

CHAPTER

15

"You know what the hell of it is?" Elmo was saying. "I *agree* with O'Neal."

"Which you cleverly disguised by jumping down his throat. Good thinking. He'll never suspect a thing."

He grinned sheepishly. We were in a back booth of a hole-in-the-wall bar I like, in the shade of the Mutual of Omaha tower. What I like about the place is it doesn't have a "theme." It's just a bar, dark, dank, and quiet. It was still early enough in the afternoon that we had the place to ourselves, except for a couple of sales types who were drinking up their commissions.

Elmo sat with his hands loosely encircling his J&B and water. I was sitting sideways in the booth, sipping Michelob Dark from the bottle. It was the sort of bar where you feel prissy asking for a glass for your beer. Elmo frowned into his glass like he was reading a crystal ball and said, "I know you don't have much in the way of family, but let's say you have a brother or a kid, somebody close, and he gets sent to jail. After one of those big, splashy trials the news people like so much, so everybody knows about it. How do you feel?"

He was in earnest, so I gave it some consideration. It was a little tough to imagine, since in my family, what there is of it, *I've* always been the bad apple. Finally I said, "Embarrassed?"

Elmo nodded. "And angry. And confused, and sad, and hurt, and God knows what all else."

"Okay."

"Okay, when you're black, you feel like that about half the time. You flip on the boob tube, every dumb cop show has a whole army of pushers, pimps, hookers, and users—all black. If they show any 'good' blacks, well, then, naturally they're fatherless, dirt-poor families trying to eke by on welfare—even though in sheer numbers, there are lots more whites than blacks on the dole." He lowered the level in his glass by perhaps an eighth of an inch. "Then, about the time you get good and worked up over Hollywood jackasses and their short-sighted, racist, stereotyped images of minorities, you turn to the evening news and it's all about street-gang members—black, usually— blowing each other away for drug money! *That's* what I meant when I was talking about everybody else's self-esteem."

I couldn't honestly say I knew how he felt. The best I could do was to say I had an idea of how he must feel. "I suppose the real problem isn't that you feel embarrassed because such-and-such ne'er-do-well is black and so are you. The real problem is that you know the world is full of malletheads who are going to think that because such-and-such ne'er-do-well is black and so are you, *you* must be a ne'er-do-well too."

Elmo nodded. "This is where the phrase 'you people' usually comes in."

"'You people' are all alike. Insert 'black,' 'Indian,' 'Italian,' 'teenagers,' 'women drivers,' 'Jews,' 'Catholics,' 'abortionists,' 'anti-abortionists,' or whatever other readily identifiable group you happen to be down on at the moment. That's why they call it prejudice, my friend. Pre-judging. Not that that makes you feel any better."

He shrugged. "More and more, I find myself reminding myself that not everyone is like that."

"That's true. Some of us didn't start disliking you until *after* we got to know you."

"Hey, I'll take that over the other any day," he said, laughing. Then, after a bit, he said thoughtfully, "I should probably call O'Neal when we get back to your place, apologize for blowing up. Not only was I rude, but he was right. The problem—gangs, drugs, the whole ball of wax, since they're all tied in together—is more an economic and social problem than a law-and-order problem. Yeah, you need to bounce a whole lot of these bastards into the slammer, but you can't bounce them *all*. Even if you could, more would just spring up to take their place, since you haven't gotten at the real problem. Do something positive about providing decent jobs, decent living conditions, decent family life, and I guarantee you have taken care of half, maybe three-quarters of the drug problem right there. *And* you've cut the ground right out from under the gangs."

"That's a long, hard, uphill climb, Elmo. It will take tremendous resources, and it will take generations to accomplish. That doesn't mesh well with the public temperament, which is, We want it now! What's worse, it doesn't make for good pictures on *World News Tonight*. Military planes and 'advisers' landing in Colombia—*that's* good pictures. It satisfies our short attention spans' demand for 'action,' which is to say activity. And best of all, it pins the problem on someone else. If 'you people' didn't make the stuff, we wouldn't have a crisis on our hands."

"Like drugs don't come from anywhere else, including the good old U.S. of A."

We sat a little longer, doing our strictly legal, well-taxed liquid drugs, until I said, "What next, Kemo Sabe?"

"Beats hell out of me," he said fatalistically.

I said, "I don't suppose you're thinking of telling your sister that it looks like Darius had a late rendezvous with a girl in that neighborhood, a rival gang was cruising through looking for trouble, and Darius was unlucky."

"The girl denies it."

"The girl is scared."

"The girl is *too* scared." Elmo sipped a little more liquor. He is the last of the great drink-nursers.

"Living where she lives, I would be too. Having been involved with the gang doesn't help. And she doesn't know either of us from the man in the moon."

"All she'd have to do is say, Yes, I'd been with him and he'd just dropped me off. That's it, she's out of there, no problem." He had his smoking supplies and bar change near his elbow; now he was arranging various elements of them on the table. "Here's the other thing bothers me. The Harris house is here." He placed his lighter midway between us. "Darius's car is parked here." He placed a quarter a few inches from the lighter, closer to me. "Darius is killed here." He placed a dime closer to himself. He looked at them, then at me. "What's Darius doing way down here when his girlfriend lives up here and his car's parked way up *here*?"

"He forgot where he parked?"

"Uh-huh."

"Okay, Yoli and Darius made plans to meet. There must have been a certain amount of cloak-and-dagger in all of their arrangements, since Darius certainly couldn't take any calls from Yoli at the Reedys' and would have to be pretty cautious about making any to her, too. He knew he was under a microscope. So they made their plans and agreed to meet on that corner. It's a convenient place."

"Not as convenient as Yoli's front stoop. They weren't keeping their friendship secret from Lucy Harris. Why couldn't the boy just come up to the house?"

"They weren't keeping it a secret on Yoli's end, but they weren't exactly advertising it either. Because of Yoli's past history with the gang, I would guess."

"Kind of stupid to meet on a corner in the middle of gang turf then, ain't it?"

"Oh, only if you want to look at things rationally." He was right, of course. I thought about it a moment, then said, "I can turn the pieces around until my fingers drop off but they're not going to fit together right, are they?"

"It's not looking too promising," Elmo said.

"And there is the nagging question of why the Crips haven't been bragging about the drive-by, if they're responsible for it."

"There is that."

"So I move the previous question: What next, Kemo Sabe?"

He scratched ruminatively at his beard. "I would like to have a long talk with Yolanda Harris."

"What's your second choice?" He gave it half a laugh, which was all it was entitled to. I said, "Your friend W.R. O'Neal thinks we've got rocks in our heads. Not that that makes him the first. But I think he's right when he says we have to keep those heads, rock-filled or not, screwed on tight if we're going to stick our mitts any farther into this little hornets' nest."

"I'm sure he's right. But look. This is kinda my thing, my problem. I don't feel right about you helping me for nothing..."

"You can lose that idea right now."

"But I know I'm keeping you away from your other work, your writing projects and so on. It isn't right, imposing on you like this. I can't afford your day rate, but I think I should be paying you something."

I smiled at him. "You'd be surprised how cheaply I can be had. The truth, Elmo, is that for once I'm actually fairly flush. My first book has been reprinted in paperback, and I got a little loot for that. My second book has been accepted for publication, and I'll get a little loot for that. I've cranked out a couple of short magazine articles in the past few weeks—amazing how much work you can get done when you're good and pissed off at bureaucrats yanking you around—and there'll be loot coming for them too." I didn't mention that as a result of a recent escapade, one that had brought me to the brink of homicide, I had a briefcase full of ill-gotten money carefully stashed away, nice unrecorded, unreported greenbacks that totted up to a sum greater than I earn in an average year. Average, hell: a *good* year! By my standards, at least, I was rolling in it. "But if it will make you feel better," I said, "go ahead and give me money. I'll take a quarter."

He looked puzzled, but went ahead and slid the quarter that represented the Harris house toward me with his index finger.

"Thanks. I have to make a phone call."

CHAPTER

16

I let Elmo buy dinner. Steak, naturally; this is cow country, after all. Chicago is cow country too, as Elmo pointed out, but somehow no one else in the Midwest makes quite as big a deal of it as we do. I've always maintained that the only reason this is the Cornhusker State is that the Steak State is too hard to say. We convoyed down to Ross' Steak House, one of the old standbys in a town that's lousy with restaurants, many of which don't seem to last more than a season. Koosje met us there. I wanted her to meet Elmo, I wanted her to give her account of our meeting with Dr. Nielsen and the conclusions she had drawn from it, and above all I just wanted to be around her. We put away a few drinks, God knows how many milligrams of cholesterol, and a gallon of coffee before wad-dling back out to our cars for the trip back to Decatur Street.

About half an hour after we got back to my place, Kim Banner stopped by. She's one of the few cops who remembered my name after the bureaucracy came down on me. If I ended up losing my license, most of the cops I knew could be counted on to refuse to give me the time of day. Even if I won my appeal, or eventually wound up getting my license fully reinstated, plenty of cops would forever consider me a pariah. Them's the breaks, and it's no good whining about it. I knew I could count on Banner no matter what happened to my PI permit— though I also knew that she had her career, her duty, and the opinions of her fellow officers to think about, and that was bound to have its effect on our relationship. It was no good whining about that either.

Banner knew Koosje—as it happened, I had met both women at the same time, in the course of a case I had handled a little more than a year earlier—and she had spoken with Elmo on the phone, so introductions took only a couple of seconds.

It was Banner I had called from the bar, using Elmo's quarter. She promised to check on a few things for me.

Banner was currently in Homicide. Though assigned to the LeClerc killing, she was no expert on street gangs—no more so than any other cop who isn't assigned to that detail. But the circumstances of the LeClerc case required her to work closely with those officers who were, or who were working to become, experts on the gangs. What Banner had to say had as much authority as anything anyone else had to say.

"Wizard, né Gerard Jones, has a file as thick as a dictionary," she said, parking her purse and slipping out of her long coat. I hung it over the back of a kitchen chair. "Most of that comes from LAPD and the feds, but we've been adding to it ever since he showed up here about three years ago."

"Let me guess," I said. "You've had a lot of suspicions, maybe even enough to haul him in a time or two, but nothing to book him on."

"Give the man a cee-gar. Give the woman a beer, too, while you're standing there."

I popped open the fridge and handed her a bottle of Harp. She peeled the magnetic bottle-opener off the refrigerator door, used it, then poured the contents into the tall glass mug I set on the counter in front of her.

"Thanks. We know that Wizard is the main man in the local Bloods outfit. They run these things with a pretty solid hierarchy, you know—the Council, the Top Prez, all that malarkey—which makes it easy for us. We always know who's who among the main guys at least. We know Wizard's involved in interstate transport of illegal drugs—sending as well as receiving—and we know he is directly and indirectly responsible for hundreds of thousands of dollars' worth of drug sales in and around this town every year. We are certain he has been involved in or responsible for dozens of crimes here and in other cities, including at least three capital offenses. Unfortunately, 'we know' and 'we are certain' don't go very far in courts of law. You need a little something that we in law enforcement like to call evidence. Your friend Wizard appreciates that, and is very good at keeping himself far removed from evidence that can tie him into any serious offenses."

"Maybe that's why they call him Wizard," I said.

"Gizzard, you mean," Elmo said.

Banner smiled grimly. "He's seen the insides of plenty of police stations, but the only time he's ever been hammered for anything is when he was fifteen. He did time in juvey for participating in an armed hold-up. Thirteen months, whoop-te-do."

"I thought juvenile records weren't supposed to follow you into adulthood," Koosje said.

Banner, Elmo, and I exchanged glances. "Cops talk shop," Banner finally said. "You know how it is."

Koosje shook her head. "Yes, I believe I do."

"What about Richard Dayton, alter ego of the incredible FlashMan D.?" I asked, following Banner into the living room.

"That file's only a little easier to lift," Banner said. She flopped on the couch and crossed her ankles on the coffee table. I perched on the arm of Koosje's chair. Elmo was propped against the living-room side of the kitchen counter. "FlashMan is the number-two man in the local gang," Banner said. "He's done time for transporting drugs, a thirty-six-month sentence, of which he served fifteen. He's been arrested twice more, same charge, but both cases were dismissed. Also's been arrested twice for assault, both times dismissed when the victims changed their minds about pressing charges." She took a sip of beer. "He was picked up last year, accessory to murder.

A drive-by. Kicked for lack of evidence."

"He sounds worse than his boss," Elmo said.

Banner pursed her lips. "It could be he's just not as good at shielding himself. Wizard didn't get to be Top Prez by being the most popular, you know. He got there by being smart, mean, and a completely cold-blooded son of a bitch. We have a Blue snitch—Blue is Crips; Red's Bloods—who says the reason Wizard came out here in the first place is that the Bloods in L.A. are afraid of him. They think he's crazy. Goes back to his supposedly icing an L.A. streetwalker who owed the gang money. That probably happens every Tuesday, but it's the way they say he did it. He goes to talk with her, they negotiate, and they end up slipping into an alley where she goes down on him. She no sooner gets him zipped back up than he shoves a .45 against the side of her head and pulls the trigger."

"Christ," I said.

Elmo looked bored. "Come on. You said this comes from someone in the rival gang; you expect he's gonna give the man a glowing recommendation?"

Banner looked at him. "Among these bastards that *is* a glowing recommendation. The word I get is that even among the Crips this story is told with a kind of grudging admiration. It's part of Wizard's legend."

"Then he's psycho," Elmo said flatly.

Koosje opened her mouth as if to comment, but said nothing.

"No argument here," Banner said. "But if he's crazy, he's crazy-smart. That's why L.A. exiled him instead of taking him out of the game. He delivers. He's sure as hell delivered this town," she added grimly. "You wouldn't hardly believe there was *no* gang activity here seven, eight years ago."

"That's progress for you," I said. "How about Yolanda Harris?"

"All we have on her is that she associated with Jones, Dayton, and some of the other Bloods."

"A member of the ladies' auxiliary," I said, "serving coffee and doughnuts after the rumbles."

"Rumbles," Banner said. "I love the way you talk."

"What about Darius?" Elmo said.

"Based on our investigation so far, and having talked with our sort of resident authority on the local gang situation, I'd say it's shaping up that your nephew probably wasn't involved with either the Bloods or the Crips."

"Probably," Elmo grunted.

"Hey, that's about as good as it gets. They don't give them membership packets, you know, with ID cards and everything. Anyhow, everyone who knows him swears up and down that Darius was clean—"

"Do tell," I said.

"—and there's no evidence at all that he was dealing. Not even a hint. What's more, he had neither contraband nor big cash on his person when the first unit arrived. That pretty well rules out the idea that he was there to make a buy."

"Unless he was robbed before the police showed up," Koosje said. We looked at her. She shrugged and looked up at me. "I suppose it's what I get for hanging around you," she said.

"When a drive-by goes down, people scatter," Banner said. "Besides, the sidewalk and everything around him was"—she glanced at Elmo—"a mess. No way anyone could get near the body without leaving tracks." She looked at me. "From what you told me of your afternoon's work, I'd say Darius was there to see his girlfriend, Yolanda Harris, and got stuck."

I looked at Elmo. He was expressionless, which was not a good sign. "I'm not buying," he said tightly.

"We keep turning it around and around," I told Banner, "but we can't get it to make sense that way. It's all well and good to say that Darius was down there to see Yoli Harris. She denies it, but she's scared, probably of getting in dutch with her former friends, so you can maybe discount her denial. But even if Darius was down there for that reason, it doesn't explain what he was doing on that corner. Given the location of Darius's car and the Harris house, the corner would be out of his way. It also doesn't explain the shooting itself."

"Who can explain a drive-by shoot?" Banner said. "It's an act of terrorism, or retribution, or both. Innocents get caught in the crossfire all the time."

"That's the other thing that isn't going down too easily for us," I said. "How come the Crips haven't taken credit for the shoot? How come the Bloods haven't retaliated?"

"You said you have someone inside the Crips," Elmo said. "What does he have to say about the drive-by?"

"We don't have someone inside," Banner said. "I wish we did. What we have is a snitch, a little fish who wishes he was a big fish and who occasionally calls us—we don't even have a name for him—when he thinks it suits his ends. And he hasn't called us. There's not much being said about it on the street, either, from what I'm told. Oh, a couple of the loudmouth wannabees have taken credit for it, but no one believes it. Of course, there's another possibility."

"Namely."

"Namely, a contract hit financed by Darius's pals back in Detroit. That would explain why no gang's taking credit for the shoot even though the MO says gang. Also why it went down in the middle of the night, on a deserted corner, instead of broad daylight in a busy place, which is more common with a drive-by. Anyhow, it's a theory. We're liasing with the Detroit PD."

"Liasing," I said in disgust.

"You have a problem with that?" Banner said.

"With turning nouns into verbs? You bet."

"I'm not buying," Elmo said again. "I can't believe that Darius was important enough, or burned anybody important enough bad enough, that they'd go to the trouble and expense of putting a price on him."

Banner said, "Sometimes the badguys think they have to go to the trouble and expense, just to make an example of someone."

"Darius has been here for almost eight months. Why'd they

wait so long to kill him?"

"Maybe it took them this long to track him down."

"Bullshit. If someone really wanted the boy that bad, they'd've leaned on his family back in Detroit—my sister and her kids. That'd be the fastest and easiest way. But no one's so much as *asked*, much less gotten ugly about it. Anyhow, that's beside the point. The point is, someone killed Darius right here in Omaha. It's your problem. You can't be pushing it off onto the Detroit police."

"Nobody's pushing anything off onto anybody, mister," Banner snapped. "The investigation is still open, and in this town that means that it's being actively pursued. Unfortunately, nobody knows much of anything right now, so about all anyone can do is come up with plausible-sounding theories and then check them out. That and keep the heat on the gangs as much as possible. If *you've* got any better ideas, I'm sure we'd love to hear them."

"Yeah, I've got a better idea." Elmo's eyes flashed. "Start hauling the little bastards in one by one and cook 'em till you sweat something out."

"Oh, that's just perfect," Banner said scathingly. "Can I bring my whips? Anyhow, which little bastards do you want us to haul in?"

"Shit," Elmo said. "Does it make any difference? They're all the same. Start with the top guys on both ends and work your way down."

"Uh-huh. No problem. Except we got no cause."

"Christ, lady, you got a *corpse*."

"And what else?" Banner's face was red. "It isn't a matter of us not doing our job—or not doing it right. It's a matter of the goddamn answers just not being there. All the rubber hoses and high-intensity lamps in the lower forty-eight isn't gonna change that."

Elmo opened his mouth, but I interrupted him. "I think this would be a good time for us to head to neutral corners," I said. "Did you happen to bring us any visual aids, Sergeant?"

128

"What?" It would have decapitated someone less sturdy than me. "Oh. Yeah." She reached into a side pocket of the red blazer she was wearing over black slacks and a black turtleneck, and came out with two sheets of paper, folded together, which she handed over with some force.

I flattened them out on my thigh. The top one was a photocopy of a standard booking-photo, one Richard Dayton, front and profile. The photo was not quite a year old. Dayton had a round face and broad features, which were slack and emotionless and downright bored as he stared into the camera. He had been through it before, and he would go through it again, if he lived that long, and he wanted us to know it didn't impress him.

The second sheet was also a photocopy of a photo, but not a mug shot. It looked like a surveillance shot of several young black men standing around somewhere. The background was out of focus, suggesting the shot had been taken with a long lens, and the images were grainy—even allowing for the graininess of the copier—suggesting that the picture had been enlarged. A lopsided oval had been drawn around the head of one of the men. He appeared to be very thin, with a face so long and narrow that it looked like his head had been caught in some kind of compacting machine. He had a full, round mouth surrounded by mustache and chin-whiskers, and narrow, almost squinty eyes. He was wearing a wide-brimmed hat. At the bottom of the picture there was a rectangular label bearing the typewritten legend JONES, GERARD A.K.A. "WIZARD."

"Personally, though," Banner said as I handed the sheets over to Elmo, "my money's on Crips or wannabee Crips."

Elmo said nothing, studied the literature.

"If it was Crips," I said, "or someone who wanted to impress the Crips, they'd have claimed credit for it before now. That, plus the way the Bloods' groupies tried to lean on Elmo this afternoon, suggests it's something going on within the Bloods."

"They're territorial animals," Koosje said. "I don't mean

that in a derogatory sense, only to say that gang members are very conscious of their territory, their turf. Your being there may have been the issue, not what you wanted there."

"Maybe. Still, my money's on it being a set-up, a hit, for whatever reason." I nodded at the pages in Elmo's hand. "Whether they did it themselves or not, it wouldn't come off on Blood turf without the Top Prez's okey-dokey. That's why I wanted the stuff on Wizard and FlashMan."

Banner shrugged, stood up, and went for her coat. From the look of her jaw, which was set like concrete, I knew she was still hacked off at Elmo. Banner is a team player, a "company man," if you will. It's okay for *her* to gripe and moan about Omaha Police Division and the lazy, incompetent chowderheads therein, but if you screw up and start agreeing with her she'll hand you your hat, with your head still in it. Elmo's accusing OPD of trying to palm off the job blew his chances of ever making Banner's Christmas card list.

"Rushing off so soon?" I said brightly, and was treated to a look that could have cut diamonds. "I'll see you down to your car," I added, grabbing my jacket.

"Your friend there's a real diplomat," Banner said as soon as I closed the door behind me. She has a hoarse, almost rasping voice that thins out when she gets annoyed. It was thin now.

"Well, we can't all be like you," I said soothingly. "I'm not apologizing for the man—he doesn't need me to do that—but keep in mind this is his sister's kid we're talking about here. Elmo wants answers, and as you said, there aren't any so far. It'd make anyone a little testy."

"Is that the word for it. Would it do any good for me to tell you that you are poking around some very dangerous people?"

"Probably not, but I don't suppose it would hurt any."

We were down to the ground by now.

"I would just as soon not have to attend your funeral, Nebraska."

"I would prefer that, too."

"Yeah, I always forget what a tough guy you are. A regular

130

Sam Spade. Well, be careful anyway, huh? Don't do anything foolhardy just because your friend is overeager. I'll help you any way I can, you know that. Just like *I* know you like to do things on your own hook."

"Us hardboiled private-eye types—*pro tem.*, at least—are like that."

She was driving a white Miata these days, and had found a place for it in the tiny lot on the north side of the building, just under the sign that said this was tenants' parking only.

If she had had to park on Decatur, we probably would have been killed.

Banner heard it before I did—the growl of a big engine. She turned toward it, and I turned in response to her movement. The engine sat under the hood of a Lincoln Town Car, a big burgundy box on wheels. The Lincoln must have been idling along the curb up the Decatur Street hill a little; now it flew down the narrow, pot-holed street like it had someplace to be. Its luxury-car suspension was getting a workout.

Guns fired. Automatic weapons, rifles, two or three of them—scores of individual explosions merging into one paralyzing ataxia of noise. Bullets shattered against the side of the building and slammed into the tails of cars parked there, the cars Banner and I dived behind as soon as we realized what was happening.

The mind, frightened and confused, does insane things at times like this. Mine ran through a short what-if list. What if these cars hadn't been parked here? During the day, mine's frequently the only one in the lot. What if Banner had parked on the street instead? Any night but Friday, the lot probably would have been full of tenants' cars.

The list was short because the answer to those what-ifs was soberingly obvious: We'd be first and second runners-up in a Swiss cheese lookalike contest, that's what.

Although it seemed longer because the noise was so excruciating, the gunfire lasted no more than a few seconds. Banner was on her feet before I even realized that the firestorm was over. She had her pistol out and was running toward the street, toward the intersection of Decatur and the Radial.

The Lincoln had hit the intersection. Then it was in turn hit by a Dodge van that had the right of way. The van driver hadn't even had time to stamp on his brakes. The guy behind him did, but it was too late for him too.

I followed Banner. My knees were simultaneously stiff and rubbery. Neat trick. I fumbled in my jacket pocket—the .38 was there, in its holster—and praised myself for not being one of those compulsively neat people who would have put the gun away in its proper place as soon as he got home.

Banner had reached the intersection; it's barely a hundred feet from the front of the building. Horns were blaring, courtesy of drivers who couldn't see what was causing the bottleneck at the light and thought noise would help clear it. Someone was trying to start a stalled engine: the driver of the Town Car. Suddenly a plume of blue exhaust burst out of the tailpipe and the engine came to life.

I reached the intersection. Banner was at the rear of the Lincoln. "Police," she yelled. "Everybody out of that car, hands up."

I saw a movement on the far side of the car, the passenger side. A wiry black kid in a red jacket was snaking up through the front-seat window, trying to get his rifle in position to shoot down at Banner over the roof of the car.

"Watch it," I hollered, but Banner had seen it too and was already dropping to a crouch behind the car. It was big enough and she was small enough that she had plenty of cover.

Standing near the curb, I fired one round at the kid hanging out the window. It plowed into the roof of the car, startling the kid, who fumbled his gun.

Then the car's back-up lights came on and I was about to holler another warning to Banner, but in the same heartbeat the back window of the car exploded outward, a clatter of gunfire following it. It flew wide of me, probably because the driver had chosen that instant to put the car into gear. I dropped and rolled toward a big maple I had purposely positioned myself near. The tree trunk was a good three feet in diameter, both wide enough and thick enough to shield me— as I discovered a second after I got behind it, when several rounds slammed into the wood. It felt like someone had hit the tree with a sledgehammer.

Banner had been crouched behind the car when it started to move. The rear bumper bumped her, knocking her down. She rolled away from the car. There was a hideous screech of metal as the Town Car extracted itself from the van. The driver took it back two or three feet—Banner was well clear of it—then crunched it into drive and peeled out up the Radial, northbound. The left fender had buckled in the impact and was rubbing against the front tire, but I had already guessed that the joy riders had borrowed the car for the occasion and didn't care what sort of shape they returned it in.

I walked out into the street, where Banner was dusting herself off.

CHAPTER

17

"I gotta get this on the air," Banner said.

"It's done."

We both turned. Elmo was perhaps four feet away, coming toward us. He strolled nonchalantly enough, but I saw the Browning in his right fist, alongside his leg. "I called from upstairs as soon as I saw what was going down. Officer needs assistance—ought to bring 'em running."

Koosje was right behind him—and then she was ahead of him. Her eyes were wide. "Are you all right?" she said, a little breathlessly. Before I could answer she wrapped her arms around me. When she ended the embrace and stepped away from me, her face was wet with tears that still flowed.

"I'm all right," I said. "Are *you* all right?" She laughed wetly.

We heard a siren just then, and turned to see a patrol car racing down the curved slope of Happy Hollow Boulevard, just across the road. Happy Hollow angles in to the southwest quadrant of the Decatur-Radial intersection. The intersection was still half-blocked by the Dodge van and the station wagon that had plowed into its rear, as well as six or seven other cars that had screamed to a halt during all the excitement of thirty seconds ago and whose drivers couldn't think what to do now. Once it reached the intersection the patrol car had to carefully crawl between the stopped vehicles, which made for a pretty ridiculous picture since the cop at the wheel hadn't shut off the lights and noisemaker.

Elmo said, "You didn't really have to go to all this trouble just to convince me you've been leaning on the gangs."

Banner looked at him and half-smiled a half-acknowledgment of his half-apology. Then she looked back at the patrol car threading its way through the carnage. "I'll get him on the trail of that Lincoln," she said, mostly to herself, and strode off. "Probably find it abandoned in the next block."

She was wrong. They eventually found it off of the Radial on Fiftieth Avenue, a whole mile away.

"You okay, man?" Elmo was saying.

I had my arm around Koosje's waist and gave her a squeeze and a wink. "I'll have to have a change of underwear," I told Elmo, "but I think I'll pull through all right." I glanced at the cars that Banner and I had hid behind. "I wonder how long before the other tenants get together and run me out of the building."

"Them or their insurance companies. You get a look at anybody?"

"In this light? I couldn't see into the car, even if I'd had time to look. Only one I saw was a kid who popped up through a window to try to draw a bead on Banner. Skinny black kid, eighteen or nineteen, wearing a softball cap backward. Also a red silk jacket."

"Should make a lot of headway with a description like that."

I grunted. "Know what's bothering me about this?"

"You mean besides a carload of kids with enough firepower to finance a good-sized revolution trying to saw you in half? Can't imagine."

"How did they come to be here? And the answer is not *By automobile*."

"Easy," Elmo said. "They followed one of us from the project."

"Only we didn't come straight home from there. First we stopped at the bar, then we stopped at the restaurant."

He frowned. "A coupla sharpies like us would've spotted a tail in that amount of time."

"You betcha. And I was looking, not so much for a tail but to make sure my friend Elmo was keeping up with me through the barely controlled mayhem that passes for traffic in this town. I had you in my rearview mirror the whole time. I couldn't have missed a tail."

"And they'd've needed time to steal that car," Elmo said.

Koosje, in between dabbing at her eyes with a Kleenex, had been following the exchange. She was frowning. "You're forgetting you're in the phone book," she said to me.

"The thing with the book is, you kinda have to know a guy's name before you can look him up in it."

Elmo had put away his gun and fished out his smoking supplies. Now he lighted a cigarette and slowly capped the lighter. His eyes were narrow, and not on account of the smoke. "Only people we introduced ourselves to were O'Neal and the Harris woman—"

"And Yoli."

"And Yoli. I've got a feeling about that girl."

"You're old enough to be her father."

He grunted a laugh and practiced his frowning a little more. People were coming out now in little groups, as people will, rubbernecking. More cops had shown up, as well as a trio of paramedics who didn't seem to be needed. I felt an itchy, prickly agitation, a hopped-up state about twelve notches above your worst case of coffee-nerves. I credited it to adrenaline and that strange reverse-shock that comes when you narrowly avoid injury or worse. I tried some deep breaths.

Elmo said, "Whether somebody shadowed us from the project or whether someone over that direction ID'd us— either way—it had to be Bloods just now."

"Yep," I said.

"Not Crips."

"Nope."

"Red jacket says Bloods."

"Yep."

"Crips aren't taking credit for the drive-by Sunday night."

Elmo's words were unhurried, reflective, and punctuated with occasional pulls on his brown cigarette. "Bloods, or wannabees, tried to scare me away from the project this afternoon. Now Bloods come by and try to put holes into you."

"Don't feel bad; I'm sure they would have tried to put holes into you too if you'd been out here."

He smiled humorlessly. Then he looked at Koosje and softened his expression. "Hate to say it, Koosje, but you were wrong before. Those kids didn't try to dust me off just 'cause they don't cotton much to strangers on their turf."

"Yes," she said slowly. "This"—she looked toward the intersection and the mild pandemonium there—"this is a little extreme for a simple response to your invasion of their territory."

"And the Crips don't know us from nobody," Elmo said. "We haven't been anywhere near their turf yet. Only people on Bloods turf know us. Only three people."

"The Reverend O'Neal, Mrs. Harris, and Yoli Harris," I said. "Just to refresh your memory. I can't see O'Neal finking on us."

"No. I don't like the man much, I don't like that loudmouth hot-air type, but he went on and on about the gangs—a plague of godless, soulless people, he called them—and I believe he was sincere. What do you think of Mrs. Harris?"

"Yeah, she seemed just a little too *much* like a nice middle-aged lady. I bet she's the brains behind the operation."

"Don't you ever have to land for refueling?" Elmo said, laughing. "She did lie to us, you know, about recognizing Darius in the snapshot—until O'Neal called her on it."

"Sure, but after that she was talkative enough. Until Yoli came in, that is."

"And lying was Yoli's idea."

I chewed on that for a minute. "You know, her excuse for having told her mother to lie is okay as far as it goes. Keep quiet, mind your own business, pretend you barely knew the guy who got killed. Even kick out a couple of nosy Parkers who come snooping around. But it doesn't cover siccing the dogs on us."

"Not a very good way to avoid attention, either, come to think of it," Elmo said. It hung there awhile, and then he said, "Gotta be the girl."

"Maybe she wasn't given a lot of options," I said.

"Maybe you should ask her," Koosje said.

"Maybe we should ask her," Elmo said.

"Maybe we should," I said.

CHAPTER

18

The cops chewed up nearly two hours before they decided they were finished with me. Hassling me? No, let's just say they were being a tad more thorough and a tad less expeditious than they might have been. Certainly more so than they would have been had the event transpired before I angered the great god Bureaucracy. Still, having Banner around helped. She told her story and I told my story, for two or three different audiences, and since the stories matched up and the only way anyone could give me a hard time was to give Sergeant Banner one too—and no one was prepared to do so—there wasn't a whole lot more to it than that. They would need to get my statement typed up all nice and neat and official, of course, but they decided I could stop downtown later on and sign it. One of those at-your-convenience-first-thing-in-the-morning deals.

The light on the answering machine was blinking when we got back upstairs. The built-in robot voice told me I had one message, then played it: "Uh, hi. I found something out maybe you guys want to know. Um, I'll see you later, I guess..."

"Sounds like your panhandler friend," Elmo said.

"Jeff." I'd've recognized that whiny tone anywhere.

Koosje had been lying on the sofa. She had gotten bored with the police business and come back upstairs almost an hour ago. Now she propped herself up on one elbow. "What time is it?"

"Friday, nine forty-seven P.M.," the robot voice said smugly.

139

"That's when the call came through," I said, and automatically checked my watch. "Ten to midnight now." To Elmo I said, "You remember the name of that laundry?"

"Yeah, but your friend ain't gonna answer that phone."

"Why not, the office'll be closed." I was flipping through the Yellow Pages.

"He just won't, that's all. Too risky."

Elmo gave me the name of the laundry whose telephone line Jeff had tapped into and I dialed the number and let it ring twenty-five times. "I hate when he's right," I told Koosje, cradling the phone.

"He probably leaves the thing unplugged except when he makes a call. That'd be safest." He went part way down the hall to the coat closet and retrieved his topcoat. He's one of these people who actually hangs his clothes on hangers, and he had already done so.

From the sofa, Koosje said my name. I went over and sat next to her. She put her hand against my cheek, her fingertips against my left ear, the one that a bullet had creased a couple of years ago. The wound was long since healed, but the tip of the ear looked like a piece of pink plastic that someone had held too close to a heater. The doc who had patched me up back then said reconstructing the tip of the ear would be a simple matter, but I had had neither the money nor the interest to follow up on it. Besides, it's good to have some reminders of the close calls.

Koosje's hand was smooth against my face. She smiled tiredly, almost sadly. "I lost you," she said. "A few months ago, I mean, when you had to leave suddenly. I didn't know where you were or what you were doing. I had no way to contact you. I had Pat Costello's daily assurances that you were all right— but neither of us could know whether you were *still* all right until the next day when you exchanged your signals again."

She was talking about my forced exodus last autumn, when for my friends' safety and my own I went to ground, left town, and stayed virtually incommunicado until I could find out who wanted my skull bashed in and how I could convince him otherwise. I kept in touch with Pat in a roundabout way via my answering machine. Every day he would call it and leave a nonsense message that was my signal that all was quiet on the home front. I would call at a later hour and erase his message via remote control, which was his signal that I was still alive and ambulatory. So much for the next best thing to being there.

"I was surprised at my reaction to that," Koosje was saying. "To being cut off from you. In a way, it was as if you had died. In a way, I grieved for you. And for us. Which was surprising, because I had thought that we were through. I had thought that what we had—our relationship—had died. I had thought that I already went through the grieving process, months earlier. But here I was now, grieving, and keenly. Which could only mean that I had not truly grieved, because it—us—had not truly died." She smiled up at me, sadly. "It had been injured, and I may have given up on it, but it wasn't dead. Only I didn't or couldn't see that until you were gone, without warning, and I realized that there was a very real chance I might not ever see you again." She smiled. "It's a cliché, isn't it? Like something that happens in the movies."

"Things don't get to be clichés unless there's some truth in them," I said. "Quite a bit of truth, usually."

It was when I emerged from hiding that we had gone to work on the relationship, spending as much time together as schedules permitted, having long talks about ourselves and our beliefs, hopes, and fears, getting reacquainted. It was work, and having done it for these last few months I understood why so many people give up on relationships. When they go off-track, it's hell trying to get them up and running right again.

"I don't want to lose you again," Koosje said.

"You won't."

Her smile was faint. "Don't make promises you can't keep," she said.

I kissed her. "I never do," I said, and stood up.

Elmo was waiting decorously in the hallway. We went back outside.

• • •

The Impala had suffered some bullet-damage. There were three holes neatly punched through the back end, between the tail-lights. We found two slugs in the trunk; the third was probably there somewhere, perhaps still in the wreck of the spare tire, which had been rent by a flying bullet.

"And to think, I only just bailed her out of the body shop," I said sadly, and Elmo made sympathetic sounds.

The car was parked on the eastern end of the lot, the direction from which the Lincoln had come down on Banner and me. The two or three cars on that end got off easy—Robert Olson's, parked next to mine one slot father east, escaped unscathed. The cars on the western end, where Banner and I had stood when all hell broke loose, got the worst of it.

Their owners would be the ones burning me in effigy later on, I assumed.

Although damaged, the Impala was still perfectly drivable and got us down to the project in good shape.

Because of the gangs and the related drug activity, all Omaha public housing projects were under a strictly enforced curfew. Between six and eleven P.M., youths under the age of nineteen were not to "congregate, loiter, wander, stroll, or play in" common areas on Omaha Housing Authority property. After eleven they weren't to be out at all unless with a parent or guardian or in case of emergency. Residents of the projects praised the curfew roundly, but on that Friday night it was hard to tell exactly what good it was doing. There was a lot of activity; it just wasn't on OHA turf. Rather it was on the streets and sidewalks, a lot of people, a lot of cars. An OPD patrol car cruised through while we hunted for a place to park the Impala, but at most its presence caused only a slight pause in the festivities.

"Festivities" is an appropriate word: the night air was charged with a festival feeling. Mardi Gras. A grim carnival.

I was not the only white person out on the street, but I was one of only a few. And definitely a stranger. I felt the eyes on me as we went from the car to the first building, from the first building to the second. I felt the eyes on me, and wondered if this was what it's like to be a member of a minority group. I felt the eyes on me, and I felt the revolver in my pocket.

The landlord had patched the shattered door since the previous afternoon. He was getting smart. This time he used a sheet of corrugated steel. Someone had already painted KILL CRIPS on it in drippy red letters.

We went down the block and into the building next door, the one whose upstairs rooms were rented out. We went upstairs. There was a narrow steel ladder bolted to the wall in the upper hallway. It was hard to climb, the ladder being too close to the wall to get your foot on the rungs properly, but we climbed it anyway, up to the roof through a trapdoor. There was a lock on the trapdoor but it was broken. That seemed to be the norm around these parts.

No one else was on the roof, but the amount of junk up there indicated it was a popular spot.

The building butted up against the one east of it, so it was only a matter of stepping over an eighteen-inch-high wall to get from one roof to the other. Then down the ladder bolted to the east wall of that building and in through the window where we had met Jeff the previous afternoon. There was no light in the hallway—no heat either—but enough illumination spilled in through the window that we could see the door. The padlock wasn't on it. That meant the padlock was now on the inside. Jeff was home.

I raised my arm to tap on the door. Elmo stopped me. "I just thought of something. You gave your card to this character. That makes him a fourth person who could have sicced the Bloods on us."

"My card's just got my name and number," I said. "No address."

"You're in the book," he reminded me again.

I thought about it, then shook my head. "Can't see it," I said. "He lives in the neighborhood. No telling who he knows, who he's tight with."

"Still can't see it," I said, but we both got well to the side of the door before I rapped on it. Nothing. "Jeff," I whispered loudly. "It's us. We got your call." More nothing. I got out one of my cards and slid it under the door. Within thirty seconds we heard the scrape of a key in the padlock and the door opened.

"I never talked to an answering machine before," he said. "It's weird."

Elmo and I looked at each other. I hoped we hadn't come all the way up here just because Jeff had felt like playing telephone operator.

"You said you found something out," I said.

"Yeah. I found something out maybe you guys want to know. Um, come on in."

We did, and he shut the door. It was gloomy in there. He had the sleeping bag rolled out and the battery-operated lamp going and a copy of *People* open on the floor. The magazine looked like it had been rescued from somebody's garbage. I saw what the clothesline running the length of the room was for: blackout curtains. Jeff had an old wool blanket pinned to the line. It was far enough back from the windows that no observant soul on the street was likely to notice it; far enough up that from the outside the windows were dark even when Jeff had his little lamp on.

The tenant buttoned the place up, then turned and looked at us. There was expectancy on his bearded face.

"*You* had something to tell *us*," Elmo finally reminded him.

"Oh yeah. You know, I kinda work the downtown, like around the bus depot and stuff... Well, I was kinda resting in the men's room at the depot, only I wasn't asleep, and these two dudes come in and I can hear them talking even though they're trying to be quiet. There's like this echo in there."

"Oh yeah?" I said a few seconds later, since he seemed to be waiting for some comment.

"Yeah. So I could hear them pretty good. They didn't know

I was there, on account of when you go rest in the bathroom, you sit on the seat and prop your feet up on the wall 'cause when the cop comes in to check, all he does is kinda see if the doors are half-open and look under the stalls and if he doesn't see any feet he figures no one's there."

"For crimeny's sake," Elmo hissed near my left ear.

"So these guys were talking…"

"And I could hear them pretty good. They were talking 'bout something that went down on Blood turf a few nights ago. Right away I think about that boy who got killed, you know, the one you were asking me about?"

"We *know*," Elmo said with some force.

"Okay," Jeff whined, pulling back in his characteristic don't-hit-me stance. "Okay… So like this one dude says he heard talk that it was a Blood shoot even though it happened on Blood turf."

Elmo looked at me, then back at Jeff. "You don't crap in your own nest," he said, playing devil's advocate.

Jeff nodded. "Yeah, the other dude says that's bullshit, why'd they wanna do anything like that? And the first dude says it was to throw off the cops. He says everyone knows the cops don't care 'bout gangbangers blowin' each other away."

"He say why they wanted to throw off the cops?"

He shook his head. "The other dude says, 'That's just jive, man, it's gotta be the Crips' and the first dude says, 'Ain't what I heard' and the other dude says, 'That's 'cause your ears fulla shit.' And the first dude says he heard from some guy whose brother's like tight with the Bloods that a lot of guys are frosted 'cause it wasn't a righteous shoot, and then the second dude says, 'Your friend's brother's fulla shit too.' "

This had all come out at one go; then he stopped. "Then what?" I prompted.

"Then they left the bathroom."

I looked at Elmo, who was frowning in the gloom. "Fits what we were saying before," he said.

"Sort of," I said. "But what's un-righteous about a contract killing? If someone in Detroit hired the local Bloods to kill

Darius, why would the rank-and-vile complain about it?"

Elmo shook his head. "Yeah, it just doesn't work, thinking of it as a contract. It could explain some things—why the Bloods are so worked up about us, for one. But it still leaves us with what Darius was doing on that corner. Or why anyone'd go to the trouble to make it look like a gang thing."

"Anything else, Jeff?"

"No, that's all I heard. Like I said, the guys left then."

"What about around here?" Elmo said. "What do you hear on the streets?"

"Like I told you before, I don't hang around these streets much," Jeff said. "I don't want people knowing I'm around. People get kinda curious… I've had to move a lot. Sometimes I haven't had anyplace to stay. I like it here. So I kinda keep out of sight, you know? I wouldn't'a been here yesterday except I had to come back for my medication from the free clinic—"

Elmo had got his wallet out, a sleek burgundy cowhide tri-fold; now he interrupted Jeff's rambling explanation as he separated some bills from the wallet. "Tell you what, Jeff," he said kindly—far more kindly than he had addressed the man to date. "We need to know more about what you just told us—about the Bloods doing the drive-by on their own turf. So here's the deal: Here's ten dollars for what you already told us." He handed over the note. The look on Jeff's face was identical to the look that would be on your face if Ed McMahon showed up on your doorstep to tell you that mailing in those sweep-stakes forms had finally paid off. The comparison is probably accurate. Jeff was used to getting a quarter here and there, maybe even as much as a dollar on a rare occasion. I wondered if he cleared as much as ten dollars in a week's time.

Now Elmo peeled off another ten and handed it over. "This is for keeping your ears open around the neighborhood and letting us know what you hear. And this"—another ten made the transfer—"is for showing us where they crash."

"Uh, who?" Jeff was a little dazed.

"The top guys in the Bloods," Elmo said. "Giz— uh,

146

Wizard. FlashMan D. The Council. Whoever else is important that you know about."

Jeff looked from the money in his hands to Elmo to me. "Oh, man, I don't know..."

"You don't have to do anything but show us where they live," I said. "Or even just where they hang out."

"Oh, man." He was whining again. "Man, these are bad people. You don't know how bad. I knew this guy—" He broke off suddenly and clutched his arms to his chest as if he was afraid he might come flying apart. The money was crumpled in his fist. He was trembling.

"What's the matter, Jeff?" I said, gripping his shoulder.

"There was this g-guy I knew..." His teeth were chattering. It was cold in the room but not that cold, and he was dressed warmly. It wasn't the temperature that chilled him. "I like didn't h-have anyplace to stay, s-so I was hangin' out with these guys down by the river. One of them, his n-name was Fred... These boys came and they dragged him off a-and—" He broke off and drew a trembly breath and looked at me with eyes that looked through me. "*They set him on fire,*" he whispered hoarsely.

"Jesus," Elmo breathed.

"Who were these boys?" I said. "What'd they do a thing like that for?"

"Bloods," Jeff said. "We heard next day. Someone said they heard the p-police talking and they said it was, um, a nitiation. They just needed some o-old bum to set on fire." He looked at each of us in turn. His eyes were a little wild. "It could've been m-me," he said.

I looked at Elmo. He was looking at Jeff. Now he reached out and took the man by his shoulders. "Jeff, nothing like that's going to happen here. We're going to be in a car, you're going to show us where these guys live. That's all. We'll put you in a disguise if you want." He smiled and, after a bit, Jeff smiled too, shakily. "No one's going to get hurt," Elmo said.

Slowly, Jeff pulled his arms away from his chest. He wasn't

trembling so violently now. His hands were still balled up into bloodless fists, though, and the three crushed ten-dollar bills were still trapped in his right fist. He looked at them now, looked at them very hard. I felt a little ashamed. I said, "Look, Jeff, that's all right. We don't want you to do anything you don't want to do. Right, Elmo? I don't blame you for being scared. Why don't we all just forget about it, huh? You can keep the money. Right, Elmo?"

His eyes were still on the other man. "Right," he said emotionlessly.

Jeff continued to look at the money in his hand for some time. Then he looked up. "No, I wanna help you guys," he said quietly.

CHAPTER

19

The route Elmo and I had taken to get up to Jeff's sad little flop wasn't the route Jeff used. He had a "back door" that didn't require him to be seen on the street out front. Elmo and I left the way we had come—there had been at least a little curiosity about us when we came down the block, and we didn't want it suddenly occurring to anyone that we had gone into the building and never come out.

So we went out, got into the Impala, and drove away.

"One good thing about driving a car like this," Elmo said as we pulled away from the curb. "No one's ever gonna steal it."

"Especially not with the cops hanging around this neighborhood." Another patrol car, a different unit than the previous one, glided smoothly down the cross-street.

I drove far enough to make sure we were clean, out into the tired residential blocks beyond the project, then doubled back and met Jeff where we had agreed, about a block east of the Reverend O'Neal's little church. It was a quiet, poorly lighted street, virtually deserted at twelve-fifty-five A.M. Jeff got into the back seat, locked the door, and hunkered down into his coat, a worn and faded army parka. I handed him my Irish walking hat and he pulled it down over his long hair. The hat was too big for him, which was good: it hid more of his features. Elmo had a white silk scarf around his neck, which he now passed back to Jeff along with instructions that he wrap it around the lower part of his face, to conceal his straggly beard.

"Give him your shades, too," I suggested. "Then everyone'll just think we're chauffeuring Claude Rains."

Jeff gave directions. I took the scenic route. We were clean.

The directions landed us in a neighborhood a little west and north of the project, not too far from Prospect Hill Cemetery. Not too far from my place, come right down to it. The block Jeff steered us to, south of Lake Street, was similar to my neighborhood—in other words, it had seen better days although it wasn't the worst place to live either. Of course, you'd have a tough time selling that to some of the west Omaha crowd who think that everything east of Seventy-second and north of Dodge is a bad part of town. We cruised past older homes, circa World War One, in varying states of repair. Jeff directed us to an apartment building constructed in the days before someone decided they all had to look like big brick shoeboxes. This one, a gray peaked-roof affair, had a vague colonial look to it, right up to four fat columns across the front.

Scrunched down in the back seat, although there was hardly anybody out to take notice of him, Jeff raised himself up far enough to look out the side window, then dropped back down. "That's the place," he whispered.

"Not too shabby," Elmo said. "This is where Gizzard lives?"

"They all do," Jeff said. "All the top guys. The Council. They own it—the Bloods, I mean."

"Beats paying rent," I said. "How do you know about this place, Jeff?" I didn't think he would deliberately deceive us, but there was no denying he had been badly frightened when we first asked him to help us.

He shrugged—not an easy feat, considering that he had shoved himself over into a corner of the back seat and slid down about as far as he could go without kneeling on the floor. "You hear things," he said. "You know, around."

"Thought you didn't hang around the neighborhood much," Elmo said.

Jeff looked from Elmo to me. Elmo was impassively studying the hood ornament; I was half-turned toward our passenger.

"You don't believe me," Jeff whined. "You guys don't believe me."

"Christ," Elmo breathed.

I said, "Come on, Jeff. First you tell us one thing, then you tell us another. You say you don't spend a lot of time out in the neighborhood—and this is a few blocks from where you live, anyway. How do you know this is where they crash?"

He was silent for a long time, and when he spoke the panhandler's whine had bled out of his voice; it was calm and almost flat. "Because I checked, okay?" He sighed softly. "Guys like you, you don't understand. There are things you gotta know and things you gotta do and not do to stay alive on the street, okay? And it gets harder all the time. You gotta know where it's safe and where it isn't. You gotta know where's Blood turf and where's Crips turf. You gotta know where they hang out. Where they live. What they care about. You gotta know when there's gonna be a fight, when there's gonna be a nitiation—so you can be somewhere else. Me, I don't go around the project 'cause that's where a lotta Bloods live. They care about it. I don't go to the Mini-Mall 'cause that's where they hang out, a lot of them. I don't come over here 'cause this is where the real bad ones live. I checked, man. I gotta know where they are so I can be somewhere else."

He was sitting up now—still huddled in the corner, but sitting taller. I made eye contact with him, then nodded and turned back to the wheel.

"What's this Mini-Mall?" Elmo said.

It was a glorified grocery store a few blocks east of the apartment building—roughly midway between the apartment and the project. The building was carved into two unequal halves, a convenience store and a liquor store. The former was open round the clock. According to our tour guide, the place was a hang-out for the local kids, gang and non-gang alike, partly because there was a small fountain with a few booths, mostly because the owner was too scared of the Bloods—or too smart, which might be the same thing—to throw anybody out.

The front of the building was bathed in the cold bluish glare of fluorescent lights. Perhaps a dozen people lounged in that unearthly light, although the night was far from a warm one. Young men, mostly, and a few young women. From what I could tell on our drive past—slow, but not too slow—they all were at least partly of African-American heritage. They leaned against the white brick façade, under the red letters that spelled Robb's Mini-Mall; they leaned against or sat on the cars parked facing the front of the building; they sat or slept or, in one case, made out on the wide walk between the building and the parking lot. Most of them wore red jackets; the few who did not, and some of the women, wore "rags" on their arms.

A thin, narrow young man leaning casually against the building, his right arm draped around a woman's shoulders, captured my attention. "Wizard," I said.

Elmo had Banner's photocopies on the seat between us. He grabbed Wizard's sheet and flashed the beam of his penlight across it.

"It's him," I said as we glided on down the block, out of the cold glare of the lights and back into the comforting cloak of darkness. "Got a head looks like it got caught in a vise once. That could have been FlashMan he was talking to, the guy on the hood of the car with his back to us. Looked like the same kind of hat FlashMan was wearing this afternoon—what'd you say it's called?"

"Kufi," Elmo said distractedly. He was reaching inside his coat. "Turn the car around," he said.

I waited for yet another patrol car to pass before I made my U-turn at the next intersection. As we came back toward the Mini-Mall from the other direction, I kept an eye on Elmo's right hand. I didn't think he planned to take a shot at Wizard. Not really. That wouldn't have been in character. But, then, Elmo had been slipping in and out of character the whole time he'd been in town—and he would be on the Mini-Mall side of the car now. It would be longish range for his Browning, but not impossibly long.

He came out of his inside pocket with a small, square, flat pack. It might have been an old-fashioned cigarette case, but Elmo didn't use a cigarette case. As we came up on the Mini-Mall again, Elmo thumbed a hidden release and the pack popped open into a kind of wedge-shaped parcel. He put the narrow end to his eyes. Binoculars.

We were not quite even with the store again.

"Shit," Elmo hissed, dragging it out.

"Now what?"

"Take a look, man," he said in disgust, and handed the binoculars to me.

There wasn't any traffic to speak of, and we were traveling slowly; I held the wheel steady and put the glasses to my eyes, craning to see past Elmo's head. Wizard's uncommonly narrow face jumped into close-up. I could see his features clearly, and they did not resemble those of a happy fella. He was having words with the man facing him.

I handed the glasses back to Elmo. "Looks like a difference of opinion between FlashMan, if that's who it is, and Wizard."

Even as I said the name, he looked up toward the street, toward the Impala. The store was not far back from the street—no more than twenty feet from the curb; this part of the block was brightly illuminated; and the Impala's windows were not tinted. Wizard looked right into the car. He may not have been able to see me, but Elmo was closer. They must have made eye contact. From the look that came over the gangbanger's face, I would say he recognized us. He looked even less pleased than he had a moment earlier.

"Looky," Elmo drawled. "We famous."

Wizard said something—spat something—and the man on the car hood turned. It was FlashMan, all right. I didn't have to be much of a lip-reader to decode the single one-syllable word he uttered. He turned back to Wizard and there was another volley between them.

"You get the feeling FlashMan's job for this evening was to see to the whacking of a couple of private eyes?" Elmo said.

"They must figure we're rubbing their noses in it, cruising through the neighborhood like this."

"I know," Elmo said. "Ain't it great?"

We laughed. That is, Elmo and I laughed. Our back-seat driver didn't see the humor of the situation.

"You're gonna get us all killed," Jeff whined.

"Nah," Elmo said. "Not after they loused up the hit earlier. They're off-balance now. They'll move more slowly next time."

He had no sooner said it than most of the young men suddenly went for the cars parked at the front of the Mini-Mall. While we were laughing it up, a quick council had been held and a decision reached.

"Elmo Lammers, ladies and gentlemen, the man who assured us that talkies were just a passing fad." Even as I said it I was leaning on the gas pedal.

Behind us half a block, six or seven car engines grumbled.

"No heavy artillery," Elmo was saying. "They'd've used it. Probably had to stash it—all the cops crawling around."

"That cheers me up a bunch. Speaking of artillery, you'll find some in the glovebox."

He popped the latch and got out the canvas bag that contained the equipment. He put it on the seat near me. The Browning, I saw from the corner of my eye, had appeared in his hand.

I didn't know the neighborhood, but it was an old one. That meant the streets were laid out more or less in a grid and the north-south streets were identified by numbers, as God intended, and not by too-cute names. Getting over to Thirtieth Street was my immediate goal—it was the closest major street. The badguys would probably figure that was my intent, but I wasn't comfortable enough with my knowledge of that part of town to try any clever diversionary tactics.

Maybe I should have. I ran out of straightaway at a dark T-intersection, made the left that I hoped would enable me to zigzag over to Thirtieth, and was promptly cut off. These old streets are narrow, and the length of an old blue Pontiac Catalina was more than enough to block it off.

"Uh oh," Elmo said.

I put the car into reverse, but somehow they knew to come up behind us. A pair of cars formed a V between us and the intersection. I slammed on the brakes.

A picture flashed across my mind, the bumper sticker from the other morning: IF YOU DON'T LIKE THE WAY I DRIVE, STAY OFF THE SIDEWALK! I looked left: cars parked along the curb ruled that out. I looked right: no parking here, but the houses along the block sat up above street level eight or ten feet; most of them had concrete retaining walls to keep the front yard from playing in the street. There might barely have been enough room to squeak through, but the first time we encountered a utility pole or mailbox, we were dead in the water.

I shut off the car, pocketed the keys, and looked at Elmo. He nodded.

"Stay in the car, Jeff," I said. "Stay down." As if he needed the encouragement.

Then Elmo and I got out.

CHAPTER

20

The three cars trapping us produced thirteen Bloods. More than had been hanging out at the Mini-Mall. They were carrying handguns but, as Elmo had predicted, no heavy metal. About half of them, front and back, were moving toward the Impala, cautious, alert, waiting to see what our move would be.

The reason you always hear so much about the element of surprise is that, as they say on TV, it's proven effective. I don't know what the first thing our friends expected might have been, but the last thing was for us to bolt from the car. Which we did—me left, west; Elmo right, east.

I had it easier: two feet to the shelter of the parked cars along the curb, then a short sprint into the blackness between the houses. Elmo had to run uphill, in effect, and had no shield. I paused between two cars long enough to glance back. He had made it as far as a set of concrete steps that bisected the retaining wall in front of the nearest house. The concrete wall gave him a little cover, but only for an instant. Then he had to dash up the steps, into the open, and around the side of the house into the blackness.

The shots I held my breath against didn't happen. Either our friends were too surprised or, more likely, didn't want to alert the police who had been making themselves a presence in the area.

When I couldn't see Elmo anymore I figured the badguys couldn't either. Then I continued my getaway.

There was a shuffle of feet behind me, the dull *whump* of rubber-soled shoes on pavement. Some coming my way, some going the other direction.

I kept moving, but not for long.

Three cars had blocked us off on the street. At least twice that many had left the Mini-Mall. I'm a big believer in coincidences, mainly because they keep happening all the time, but even I could not swallow the idea that cars one, two, and three all just happened to show up in the right place at the right time to head us off at the pass. The cars had been in contact: in this great age of two-way radios and cellular phones, all things are possible. And if cars one, two, and three were in contact, it was inconceivable that cars four-through-whatever were not. I couldn't see the advantage of running away from one set of pursuers and into the arms of another set in the next block.

I stuck close to the side of the house, where it was dark. But not too close: the darkness that concealed me could hide all sort of unknown obstacles. Clumsiness could be fatal.

Behind me I heard the crisp rustle of hard dry grass; beyond that the whistle of heavy breathing. Someone didn't get enough exercise.

The soft sounds were no more than fifteen or twenty feet back.

They were moving slowly, as was I, trying to be quiet. I did a better job of it than they did. There was only one of me.

The night was overcast and very black; the moon was no more than a silvery smudge against the indigo sky. Even that, though, would be enough to silhouette me. I took a quick inventory: the moon was behind me, and behind my hunters, so I took a chance and moved away from the deepest shadows at the side of the house, diagonally across the eight or ten feet between it and the house to the south of it, and went around the back of that house.

They would not expect that. They would expect me to keep going straight, to the alley that bisected this block. Or they would expect me to go north, around the back of the house I had originally been glued to.

I liked that. It was an encouraging thought.

The house I was now behind had old-fashioned cellar doors, double-doors in a wedge-shaped box against the back wall—the kind of doors Dorothy didn't quite make it to at the beginning of *The Wizard of Oz*. I nearly tripped over them. Then I skirted it and crouched behind the wide end, in the angle between the box and the back wall of the house.

The rustling of dry grass stopped. There was a hiss of sibilants as whispered words were traded.

I was well-armed. I had two .38s, the one I usually carry and the one I always keep loaded in the glove compartment. I also had the speed loader and box of cartridges I keep there, too, in the canvas bag with the gun. Sixty-eight rounds, all together—plenty to take out the four or five guys I figured were behind me. If there was enough light to see by, which there wasn't. My first shot or two, even if I had a target, would give me away. Even if I prevailed, the noise would summon the other Bloods I knew had to be beating bushes nearby. Bring the cops, too, maybe, but the Bloods were closer.

Nevertheless, I had one gun ready and the other ready to go, in my right-hand pocket.

Then the hunters moved again—half of them straight toward the alley, by the sound of it; the other half north around the back of the other house.

There was no time for self-congratulations. After a decent interval, perhaps a minute, I moved away from the house, out into the yard. There was a detached garage eighteen or twenty feet back from the house and I affixed myself to it. Another ten feet ahead of me I heard the scuff and scrape of shoes in the alley.

At the far end of the alley, to the south, a weak light burned. Other than that there was virtually no light at all. Shot-out street lights were an ongoing problem in that part of town. Very few of the houses had lights on, and those that did had heavy curtains over their windows, showing at best only yellow slits. There was no traffic. It was as black as it gets in the city. Still, my eyes were adjusting to it: I could make out the twisted scrap of an ancient bicycle out in the yard; it had been invisible seconds earlier, when I passed within three feet of it. Although I was dressed in dark colors—blue jacket, black gloves, gray slacks, black demi-boots with soft black soles—my face was as white as a cueball. Once the Bloods got used to the darkness, all they'd have to do is follow the bouncing ball: it would be my head.

I moved around the front of the garage, into the long, narrow driveway. Back toward the street.

This house had a row of scraggly fitzers along the front. They should have been trimmed last autumn, and probably a few before that, but now I was just as glad they hadn't been. I wriggled in behind them, parallel to the front of the house, and found a good peephole.

Not much had changed in the old neighborhood while I had been away. The cars were all still in place. There was no sign of Jeff: if he stayed quiet and out of sight, he might be okay. There was no good reason for the two Bloods who stayed behind to guard the intersection to get interested in my car. There were good reasons not to, in fact: Elmo and me, and the possibility that we might double back on them.

The two guards looked very alert.

I had a much clearer shot here than I'd had in the backyard: the Bloods' cars' headlights were on, throwing a bright spotlight on my Impala. The guards stood inside this spotlight. They carried handguns, not rifles. There was some comfort in that, I suppose.

From my hidey-hole I could probably have picked off at least one of them.

And achieve exactly what? I would still have the other one to contend with, and the cars would offer him plenty of cover.

I would have given my position away. I would by no means be in the clear. Neither would Elmo, wherever he was.

As I mulled this over, another set of headlights appeared, from up the street, behind the Catalina. They belonged to a red Porsche with a black top and vanity plates showing a single character: W. The Porsche stopped near the tail of the Catalina. Wizard got out of the driver's side. FlashMan D. came out the other door. Another man climbed out of the back seat.

They all wore the red silk jacket. FlashMan wore his kufi and showed a lot of medallions and other jewelry. Wizard had a military-style black beret on his impossibly narrow head and carried a pair of black gloves. The third man, a tall, rangy youth I hadn't seen or noticed before, wore a camouflage softball cap, backward.

The two guards moved away from the cars and toward their leaders.

I was too far back from the street to hear much of anything—an occasional sound, not even a full-fledged word. The guards gestured off the way Elmo had fled, then the way I had fled. They made expansive circling gestures that I took to mean that men were combing the neighborhood.

Not very encouraging.

After a few minutes of this there was a soft, high-pitched warble, the electronic bird-song that today stands in for a telephone bell. FlashMan peeled away from the quartet and went back to the Porsche. He sat sideways with the door open, so I had a clear view of him talking on a slim black handset on the end of a coiled cable. He listened for a moment, then said something into the mouthpiece, then put down the phone. He came back over to Wizard and said something in his ear. Wizard just nodded.

I hoped he wasn't acknowledging the news that they had found the black guy. They did not strike me as the sort of people who take hostages.

At times like this, you list your options. It didn't take long. I could attack, maybe take out a couple members of the quartet before they nailed me. I could slink away and come back with the law. Or I could sit tight and see whether they eventually found me.

I didn't like any of them much. First, suicide wasn't my bag. Second, there was no guarantee that I could successfully evade capture a second time. Finally, could I really stay where I was until sun-up—if they hadn't found me by then—and would daylight really improve my situation all that much?

Meanwhile, what about Elmo?

And what the hell was that—a flash or a glint or something, across the street somewhere. It had attracted my subconscious attention a minute ago; now there it was again, on the periphery, like a stray thought that vanishes the instant you try to capture it.

Down there somewhere, across the street...

Probably a cat. Cat's eyes flash like that, when the light hits them just right.

There it was again. A tiny dot of white. On. Off. On. Gone.

I waited. A long wait. Then there it was again. On. Off. On. Gone.

Elmo had had a penlight in the car. If he wrapped his hand around it so that only a pinpoint of light escaped past his little finger... I smiled to myself. Of course he would double back around, as I had, and for the same reason. Great minds, and so on. He had found a good hidey-hole, too. Only, unlike me, he'd had the foresight to guess that I would do as he had done, and to signal me that he was okay. He didn't know where I was—I knew I was too well hidden for him to see me from clear across the street—but he figured I must be over here somewhere.

I squinted through the fitzer branches and caught the signal again. There was no way I could answer it. Where was he hiding anyway? I studied the tiny, almost invisible light, its strange pattern. The uncle who raised me lived in a big old house, not too different from any of these up and down the block. Like most of these, his had a porch across the front. The foundation of the house didn't extend under the porch—they seldom do—so the space under the porch floor was hollow. It was all enclosed, but there were wooden grilles, two in the front wall and one on each side wall, for ventilation. My uncle had hinged one of the side vents, turning it into a trapdoor, and stored tools, scrap lumber, a ladder, and all kinds of other neat junk under the porch.

That's where Elmo was now, under the front porch of one of the houses across the street, moving his penlight slowly back-and-forth behind a vent cover, which explained the on-off pattern.

Shrewd. Gutsy, too: no telling what sort of nasties live under a porch.

I wished there was some way to return the signal, but I didn't have so much as a match on me. The surgeon general never points out the dangers inherent in *quitting* smoking. There was no way to let Elmo know I was safe. More to the point, there was no way for us to hatch a plan for getting the hell out of there. Any move I might make to show myself to Elmo would undoubtedly attract the badguys' attention, too.

Which, come to think of it, was not necessarily a bad thing.

I made some preparations.

The spare .38 was still in my right-hand jacket pocket. I got it out, unzipped my jacket a few inches, and put the gun inside my left sleeve, along my triceps. The jacket's sleeves were oversized: the gun fit easily, and the Thinsulate lining helped conceal its bulk. If I kept my left arm bent a bit, I wouldn't have to worry about it sliding down past my elbow.

I had the canvas bag with the ammunition rolled up and tucked in the waistband of my pants, inside my jacket. I got it out, removed the speed loader, and put the bag with the shells back where it had been. The speed loader I put in my left front pants pocket.

Then I wormed out of my hiding place, got to my feet, and walked across the front yard, toward the street.

I had the other .38 in my left hand, letting it dangle by the trigger guard, well away from my body. My other arm, too, was slightly raised and stretched away from my body.

The two guards, conferring with Wizard, FlashMan D., and the third man, had their backs to me. FlashMan was facing me almost dead-on, and it was predictable that he would notice me first.

He said something to Wizard, who turned and looked.

The others turned too.

The looks on the guards' faces were looks of astonishment. I couldn't have surprised them more if I had been the ghost of Jacob Marley, rattling chains and all. FlashMan was frowning; he said something to the third man, who edged away from the little group.

Wizard, though, seemed unperturbed, as if kamikaze stunts of this sort were to be expected.

FlashMan produced a weapon, a handgun, and turned his attention from me to the surroundings. He was thinking in terms of ambush. I was hoping we wouldn't disappoint him.

Elmo would have seen me—he would have seen me first, in fact, because he would have been looking for a signal from me. He probably expected a more furtive signal than the one I was sending, but why do things halfway? By now he would be out from under the porch and working himself into a position from which he could get the drop on the badguys. I would re-arm myself during the diversion. And we would ride off into the sunset, to live and fight another day.

In the meantime, all I had to do was stay alive. Luckily, I had had a lot of practice.

The Bloods didn't open fire: I had been counting on that. Shots would bring cops. At a word from Wizard, the guards approached me. FlashMan, I noticed, was still scanning the environs, like the nervous wagonmaster in an old Western. *It's just too durn quiet, Clint.* The third man had produced a handgun and was imitating FlashMan.

I stepped into the lopsided circle of light. The guards and I met about ten feet from where Wizard and FlashMan stood, about five feet off the front end of the Impala. I wondered how Jeff was doing. I wondered how Elmo was doing. I wondered how *I* was doing.

One of the guards, a tall, wide-shouldered young man with a Maynard Krebs beard on his chin, handed his gun to his partner, a sawed-off guy who had decided to make up for it by being ugly. The bearded one took the .38 from my left hand and pocketed it. As expected, he patted me down. As expected, he did it wrong, the way he'd seen it done a million times on TV. First he slid his hands along my sides, and found no holster under my arms. Then he patted across my chest and belly, finding the bag with the shells, which I purposely left there as a present for him. You throw them a little chickenfeed, they don't keep looking so hard.

He ran his hands down the outside of my legs and up the insides. That produced the empty holster on my right hip. Next, I thought, he would pat down the outsides of my arms—which is why I had tucked the gun behind my triceps—but he didn't even do that much.

"He clean," he told Wizard over his shoulder.

"He crazy," the short guy said, and they both laughed.

I made myself smile. It would have been easier to make myself have red hair.

Wizard came over, very slow and cool. FlashMan was off his right shoulder, pistol up and ready. His eyes never stopped moving.

Wizard smiled blandly. "That it, Jack? You crazy? Or you got some kinda angle?"

"Angle?" Where the hell was Elmo? I hadn't expected to make conversation, just a diversion. "Yeah, I guess I've got some kind of angle. I'm angling to do you a favor, Gerard."

His faint smile vanished. Was it the name he didn't like, or my insolence? Either way, I didn't blame him.

"I don't need no favors from Whitey," he said. "And you, you shoulda did yourself a favor and kept goin' when you had the chance."

The night was cold, but there was a film of sweat down my back.

"I thought of that," I said truthfully. "But what would that have accomplished?"

"Would've accomplished your stayin' alive," Wizard said. The guards, who had moved around behind me, laughed. FlashMan did not join in. I did, though, and that pretty much spoiled everybody's fun.

"What, I'm supposed to be scared of you?" I said, still smiling. "After the way you guys fucked up in front of my place tonight?" I shuddered theatrically. "Ooh, nothing frightens me more than a display of brute incompetence."

"Shut up, motherfucker," FlashMan said.

I ignored him. "Must be really great for inspiring the troops too, huh? How 'bout it, guys, you inspired?" I said to the two over my shoulder.

"Man, I tole you shut up," FlashMan said, more loudly than last time.

I looked at him. The big-yard stare. I said, "Somehow I had the idea he was in charge." I nodded toward Wizard.

FlashMan's jaw tightened.

I looked at Wizard. "For the time being," I added.

"What you sayin', fucker?" FlashMan demanded.

Wizard's flat little smile was back now. "Man, one word from me, you're dead meat," he said. His voice was almost gentle.

"Only 'cause I gave you a second chance," I said. I was vamping like mad, ad-libbing all the way. If Elmo was going to charge in tooting a bugle, I thought now would be a good time for it. If he'd missed his cue, then my task changed from creating a diversion to creating enough curiosity, or uncertainty, to induce Wizard not to say that one word that would transform me into, as he so artfully put it, dead meat.

"Shit, you just crazy," Wizard decided after a longish interval. He looked past my head, at one of the guards behind me. "Do it, Hamfat."

"Here, man? Cops everywhere?"

"Fuck, *I'll* do it," FlashMan said. He handed his gun to the third man, who was standing to the side and slightly behind him. When FlashMan's right hand reappeared there was a knife in it, blade up. He came forward a step.

"Sure," I said rapidly. "Anything to keep him from finding out."

Wizard raised his right hand sharply and a second later I did not feel a searing spike of pain as the switchblade slid up between my ribs. I kept my sigh of relief inaudible, and willed my knees to remain in their semisolid state.

Wizard put his narrow face very close to mine. His dark eyes were as they had been all along: flat, disinterested, even lazy. There was none of that in his voice, though. "What you talkin' about, Jack? Findin' out what?"

I looked at FlashMan. His eyes were glued to me. I don't know if I'd had a clear idea of what to say next, but something in his eyes now made an idea crystallize in my head. "Here's that favor I told you about, Gerard: Last time I saw your playmate here, he was downtown, sitting in a car with another guy. I know that guy." I looked at Wizard. "He's a cop."

"Bull*shit*, fucker," FlashMan exploded. "You fuckin' *lie*. Don't be payin' no attention this asshole, Wizard."

Almost enough commotion for me to make a grab for the gun in my sleeve.

"Almost enough" wasn't nearly enough.

Wizard looked long and hard at his lieutenant. Then he looked at me.

"Like he's gonna break down and confess," I said. "Seems kinda jumpy, though, doesn't he?" I added conspiratorially.

"Goddammit," FlashMan yelled. "Goddamn mother-fucker—" He moved forward a step. The knife was still in his fist. Wizard raised his right hand again, but this time that gesture alone was not enough. He was forced to actually touch the back of his hand to FlashMan's chest in order to restrain him.

FlashMan stopped then, and contented himself with trying to stare me down. He was breathing hard. I might have felt bad about fingering him, but it's tough to work up sympathy for someone who wants to put a shiv in you.

After a long time he threw up his hands as if this wasn't worth his bother. "Fuck, man, he just sayin' that to confuse you. Save his own skin." He turned and strode toward the Porsche.

Wizard's eyes were still on me. "He must've seen me too," I said. "Explains why he's in such a big hurry to whack me."

FlashMan D. turned as if to lodge another protest, but in the end he said nothing. Wizard, meanwhile, continued to stare at me, as if words might appear on my forehead. Maybe they did, because Wizard finally took a deep breath and said, "I don't think I believe you."

"You should've stopped that sentence at the halfway mark," I said. "You don't think, period. Why would I lie?"

"To stay alive."

"Then I would've stayed hidden. Or disappeared into the night. I sure as hell wouldn't have come over here and struck up a conversation."

He considered that, stroking his close-cropped whiskers with a single finger. While he did, I went on ad-libbing: "I said I wanted to do you a favor. I already have. It's no secret that what went down last Sunday night was no righteous shoot. Everyone knows that the kid who got burned—Darius LeClerc was his name; it must be hard for you to keep track—wasn't a gangbanger, wasn't a user, wasn't a pusher. He was a citizen. But you whacked him and tried to make it look like a drive-by."

"Hey, fuckin' Crips, man, shootin' up our turf." He smiled.

"Uh-huh. That's why you hit them back so fast, right?"

Did the smile erode slightly, or was that wishful thinking on my part? He said nothing, which I chalked up as a point for the goodguys. This would have been a good moment for the other half of the goodguys to show up. In fact, any moment would have been a good one. I had the sinking feeling that something had gone off the rails while Elmo worked his way around to a good ambush spot, and I expected to hear the warble of Wizard's car phone any second now, bringing the bad news.

I wondered what I would do then.

I pushed the thought aside. "Look, Gerard," I said, improvising further, "save the fairy tales for the kiddies. Us grownups know you tried to set it up so the heat would be on the Crips. Well, from the number of cop cars I've seen around here tonight, I'd say that plan isn't working too well."

I wouldn't have minded if one of those cop cars turned the corner right now. One didn't. No wonder everyone says they're never around when you need them.

Wizard was still quiet. Weighing what I had said, I hoped. As long as that continued, I continued living.

I said, "A lot of the Bloods don't like the heat you've brought down on them. They don't mind heat in the line of duty, maybe, but they don't see why they should suffer 'cause you won't kill your own snakes."

He looked at me sharply.

I didn't know what I was onto, but it looked promising. I kept at it.

"There's already talk going around that you're on the way out, Gerard. No one's laying odds you'll stay in the saddle. The only thing worth betting on is how you're gonna go. Is someone gonna pop you and take over your job"—I looked significantly at FlashMan, who looked significantly back— "or is someone who was in on the LeClerc killing, or any of a dozen other dirty deals, gonna roll over on you?"

Wizard glanced back at FlashMan. Then he turned toward me again. "You crazy, Jack." The gentleness was no longer in his voice. I wondered if that was a good sign or a bad one.

"You're crazy if you haven't packed a parachute," I said.

"Meanin' what?"

"Meaning you're an old man by gangbanger standards, Gerard. It's time to retire while you still have the choice. It's time to roll over before you get rolled over on."

He peeled his top lip away from his teeth. I wouldn't call it a smile. "No one rolls over on the Wizard. Not without they go down too."

"A big man like you, we're talking federal," I said, warming up to my subject. "Anyone who gives you up to the feds gets immunity for anything he's ever done, all the way back to the first candy-wrapper he ever threw on a sidewalk."

"No such thing as immunity from a Uzi." He glanced back at FlashMan again. I tried not to read anything into that.

I shrugged. "There are programs."

"Haw," Wizard said.

"They work, when the guys in them make them work," I said. "The jokers you see on the tabloid-news shows talking about how crappy the programs are, they're small-change who coughed up other small-change. Now they think they're big-shots and they can't stand it that no one else thinks so. That's why they go on TV. They're stupid.

"But you, Gerard—you're not stupid. You did a stupid thing, icing Darius LeClerc that way, but that doesn't make you a stupid man. I think you're smart enough to know when it's time to pull the ripcord. You roll over first, take the immunity, get the witness program—hell, unlike most of the stiffs who go to the feds, you really *are* a big fish. The feds'd jump through hoops to hear what you could tell them. You can write your own ticket, Gerard, retire someplace and live like a king."

"I already live like a king."

"The operative word here is *live*, Gerard. You go my way, that's gonna stay the operative word a lot longer than if you go your way."

"What, you my guardian angel, like that?"

A snigger from behind me reminded me, if I needed any reminding, of the two guards and their guns.

"Hell, no: I've got my stake in it too. Maybe you know about me. I'm a private cop. I've got a small problem—"

"You got a *big* problem, Jack," Wizard said. The sniggering behind me grew up and turned into outright laughter.

"My problem is, the bureaucrats are trying to yank my license. You can check on that." He could, too, which is why I was telling him. "But if I go to the feds and say 'Look who I can introduce you to *if* you put in a good word for me in Lincoln,' well, my problems are solved." I was beginning to convince myself.

Wizard, though, was a harder sell. "You fulla shit, Jack. Why'd I wanna rat out the brothers just to help you?"

"Not just to help me," I said. "To help yourself. I just emcee the program. For a noncash reimbursement."

"Don't need you for none a this." There was a new quality in his smile now, a genuineness. He was enjoying this. That was not a good sign.

"You need me to keep my friend off of you," I said quickly. "He wants you any way he can get you. Darius LeClerc was his nephew."

Wizard took in this new information.

"You're surrounded, Gerard. The cops, your own gang, and my friend. There's only one direction you can jump: this one." I popped my thumbs toward myself.

He looked at me for some time. Then he turned and walked toward the Porsche.

"Take care of it," he said to FlashMan.

"Man, you ain't believin' none a his hook jive 'bout me, are you?"

Wizard glanced back at me. Then he headed for his car again. "Later," he told FlashMan.

I tried not to look around for some sign of Elmo. No sense condemning him to death too. If he was still alive and free.

FlashMan appeared to be considering something to say to his leader, thought better of it, and turned to the task he had been assigned.

There is great danger in leaving your enemies with nothing to lose. That's what Wizard had done with me.

170

CHAPTER

21

I moved.

I hoped that the apparent reluctance to summon the cops would overcome the guards' natural inclination to open fire. Just to be on the safe side, though, when I moved I moved toward their leader.

I dodged FlashMan and plowed into Wizard from behind. We went down. He cushioned me from the worst of the impact but the only cushion he had was cold, hard pavement. He hit and didn't move.

FlashMan did, though. He had the switchblade. Using it on me would make very little noise.

I rolled off of Wizard and onto my back. FlashMan had already covered the short distance between us. He still held his knife, blade-up. That's how you cut someone who's standing, not someone who's lying down. But he was smart; he'd figure a way around that one soon.

My gun was pinned between my arm and the pavement—useless.

FlashMan reversed his hold on the knife: blade-down.

I bicycled my legs and that kept him at bay for an instant. Meanwhile the third man overcame his temporary paralysis; the two guards were hustling forward too.

I knew how a turtle on his back must feel.

I pulled my knees into my chest, rocking back onto my

shoulders; then I rocked forward again, fast, and rolled up onto my feet.

FlashMan was right there. I slammed into him, butting him in the breadbasket. He exhaled a sharp *whoof!*, then toppled over from the force of my forward momentum.

I did a fast push-up to get off of him and came up on my heels. The .38 was where it was supposed to be, in my left sleeve, along the triceps, barrel down. I reached inside my jacket and whipped the gun out. You'd have thought I had practiced the draw.

The advancing men froze. FlashMan came up onto his elbows, saw the gun, and likewise froze.

"Fuck," he breathed.

Behind me, Wizard moaned and stirred.

"Lose the hardware," I said. I fanned the gun from the guards over to the third man, an arc that included FlashMan.

The guards carefully set their weapons down on the pavement. The third man did not. He had two guns, his and FlashMan's. He had both of them aimed at me.

"That means put down your guns," I explained to him.

"Fuck you, honkie," he said.

"This is going on your report card," I said.

I figured I had perhaps twenty seconds until the guards realized we were at a standoff and retrieved their weapons. At which point we wouldn't be at a standoff anymore.

I extended my right arm, very slowly. The barrel of the .38 was no more than twenty-four inches from FlashMan's forehead.

"Bullshit," the third man said. "You ain't be killin' no one."

"Self-defense," I said. "Man pulled a knife on me."

FlashMan set his jaw and stared at me hard.

Time passed.

"Fuck," the third man said. He crouched and set down the guns, then stood and laced his fingers across the crown of his head.

"Shit, here I was worried about you," Elmo said lazily.

172

I glanced to my left: he was coming around the back end of one of the cars that had blocked our retreat. The languor in his voice was more than made up for by his eyes, which were sharp and alert. His Browning was in his fist. There were streaks of mud drying on his leather coat.

"Worried? You mean I forgot to mention I've had myself bulletproofed since last we met?" I straightened up. Wizard groaned again and tried to wake up. That struck me as a lousy idea, but it was his head.

"I could see where a little thing like that might slip your mind," Elmo was saying.

"Everything okay?"

"It is now." He grinned lopsidedly. He came around the front of the car, into the little arena in which our drama had been played. "You boys back up," he said to the guards, and when they had backed up far enough he crouched and collected their guns and my property from the pavement. "Now you, over here with your friends." The third man moved. "Lie down, face-down, and take a nap. No, you leave your hands right where they are."

"Maybe you should imitate them," I said to FlashMan, who was still propped on his elbows.

"Maybe you should go fuck yourself," he said.

"Imaginative little bastard," Elmo said.

"You go fuck too, Tom," FlashMan said.

"Tom," Elmo said, slowly wagging his head. He came over near him, though not too near, and crouched down on his heels. "You've got a real attitude problem, boy."

FlashMan spit at him. It hit Elmo in the shoulder and oozed disgustingly down into the creases of his right sleeve. Elmo looked at it. "Coat needs to be cleaned anyway," he said.

"Fuck off," FlashMan said. He had a one-track mind. "Or go fuck Whitey over there. Yeah, that prob'ly be you thing, let Casper climb on top a you, slide it in real deep."

Elmo looked at me. There was a languid smile on his face.

"Casper?" I said.

"The Friendly Ghost," Elmo said. "You are a little on the pale side, you know."

"Well, I work mostly indoors."

His shoulders jumped in a soundless laugh, then he looked back down at FlashMan D., almost fondly. He spoiled the effect, though, by popping FlashMan hard in the forehead with the side of his left fist. FlashMan's right elbow went out from under him and the back of his head smacked on the pavement. Almost before that happened Elmo had hold of his shoulder, and now flipped him over onto his belly. There was no resistance.

"Fuck, man, what's wrong witchoo?" FlashMan bellowed.

"I'm unpredictable," Elmo said. "Hands behind your head, fingers laced, and remember, you're a statue." He stood up and came over to me. "Sorry for the delay, man. I went around back of those two houses down there, figured to come up behind the cars like I just did. Only there was a board fence I had to get over, and when I got over it there were two of these guys I had to get by. You surprised the shit out of me when you came strolling out like that, like it was your coming-out party or something."

"I figured it was the best way to get both of us out of here intact."

"I figured that's what you figured. Thought it was the damn stupidest thing, too—then I ran into those two bruisers and realized we couldn't hang around here all night." He looked down. "This our hero?"

"The man of the hour," I said.

Elmo prodded Wizard with the toe of his shoe. Wizard groaned. Elmo prodded harder, this time with his heel, and rolled the man over. Wizard's head lolled and his eyes came halfway open and another long groan escaped him. His beret had gone flying in our collision. His hair was little more than fuzz on the sides, long tight braids on top. There was a vicious-looking scrape on his forehead, glistening with blood and grit from the street, and his nose had taken a detour from its original route. Blood and snot oozed out and across his left cheek.

"He's gonna look like the Masked Marauder come morning," I said.

"Shit," Wizard groaned.

"Could save him the embarrassment," Elmo said. He stepped closer to Wizard and took aim. "Maybe you should go tie your shoelace or something," he said to me.

"Maybe I shouldn't," I said.

He stood like that for some time, his gun aimed unwaveringly at Wizard's head. I could have said something moralistic. Hell, I already had. Elmo knew my thoughts on the subject. He knew I thought this was no way to deal with his anger and his grief. He knew I had wrestled with some close relatives of the same demons and, in my opinion, had emerged triumphant. Now he had to make up his own mind.

All well and good. But what was I going to do in the meantime—stand there and let him murder the man?

Or I could go tie my shoelace or something.

Wizard's eyes opened. He moaned. He saw Elmo, saw the gun. His eyes opened even wider. "Oh, *man...*"

"Shut up," Elmo said quietly.

"FlashMan, where you at?" Wizard bellowed.

"Shut up," Elmo said.

"Flash*Man!*"

Elmo leaned from the waist until the barrel of his gun was no more than four inches from an imaginary point on Wizard's forehead, equidistant from each eye.

"Shut. Up."

He shut up.

"I'm trying hard to think of a good reason not to blow your goddamn head off, Gizzard."

The decumbent man said nothing.

"The boy who died, he was family. I don't expect that means much to someone like you. But it means something to someone like me. It means a lot."

Wizard's eyes were wide. His nostrils were wide, and his lips were pulled back away from his teeth. A death's-head grin.

Elmo moved fast, grabbed the front of Wizard's jacket in his left fist, and lifted the man's upper body a good two feet off the pavement.

He shoved the gun up under Wizard's chin.

Elmo's eyes were wide now too, and his nostrils, but there was no grin of any kind on his face. I could see the muscles corded in his neck, and the fat thread of his carotid. His shoulders vibrated with the strain of keeping the other man suspended.

Wizard, for his part, hung there, stiff, paralyzed.

"Elmo," I said.

After a bit he looked at me. There had been no expression on his face, none at all, the whole time he stared down at Wizard. There was none there now as he looked at me.

"Give me a good reason I shouldn't."

"I can't," I said. "But you shouldn't anyway."

He looked at Wizard. Then he contracted his left biceps, raising the paralyzed man another couple of inches before he straightened his arm and threw him back down against the pavement.

He straightened up and exhaled.

"I suppose I'd never get away with it," he said.

"I'd visit you every Sunday," I said.

"Another good reason to shine it by." He drew another deep breath and let it go. "I don't feel like screwing around with the law again, do you?"

"No, I've had enough for one night. Let's just get the hell out of here. If you keep an eye on the little pumpkins, I'll get that Pontiac out of the way."

Elmo nodded.

I did it, then went over to my car. Jeff was in the back seat, on the floor, face-down, his arms over his ears and his hands on the back of his head. "Show's over, Jeff," I said. He didn't move. I reached over the seat and shook him by the shoulder.

He mumbled and snorted and went on sleeping. Grace under pressure.

I started the car and looped around various prostrate bodies, positioning the car between Elmo and the badguys, except for Wizard, in case someone decided to get cute. Wizard was fully alert now, and his eyes, locked on Elmo, displayed almost palpable hatred. I angled the car in more or less behind Elmo, reached across the seat and popped open the passenger door for him.

"Come along, Watson," I said.

"Man, you are dead," Wizard said.

"Don't worry, he's always telling people that," I said. "But he does have friends slithering around here, so we should tool along..."

Elmo stepped away from Wizard.

"Shoulda killed me when you had the chance, asshole." He seemed awfully brave now that we were leaving.

"I still have the chance," Elmo said. He backed up as far as the open car door. Then he paused. He looked in at me. "You go on ahead," he said, around a wide grin.

He closed the car door, walked over to Wizard's Porsche, and slid in behind the wheel.

CHAPTER

22

On his instructions, I let Jeff out a few blocks from his flop. He got away from the car like it was on fire.

Wizard's Porsche was a trifle on the noticeable side, so I led Elmo over to the Creighton campus, where we stashed it in a permit-only lot and continued on in my car. Neither one of us was sleepy, so I cut over to Dodge Street and found a Perkins that was open round the clock. There were four other people in the place, not counting the help. We took a booth away from the front windows and ordered coffee.

Elmo said glumly, "He was right: I should've killed him when I had the chance."

"I doubt you could have. I doubt I could have let you."

"Be like stepping on an ant. 'Cept an ant's life is worth more."

"No argument," I said. "But I keep thinking there has to be something that separates *us* from *them*. No matter who us and them are at any given moment. There has to be a line that we won't cross. Even if they do. Especially if they do."

"Wearing the white hat isn't enough?" He managed a faint grin.

"Just one of the perks."

A tired-looking waiter brought two set-ups, two mugs, and a thermal carafe of coffee. I like it when they leave the pot, even when I suspect the only reason they do it is so they won't have to bother with you again. I poured.

Elmo lighted a cigarette and exhaled with relish. "You know what the worst part of being a smoker is? Those situations when you just *can't* smoke—'cause that's always when you want one the worst."

"Like when you're hiding under someone's porch while armed thugs hunt for you."

"Good example."

We drank some of the coffee.

Elmo said, "You remember when I handed you those binoculars, told you to have a look at Wizard?"

"Seems like days ago." I looked at my watch: it had probably been no more than ninety minutes ago.

"I didn't mean you should look at Wizard," Elmo said. "I wanted you to see who he was with."

"FlashMan."

"No. The girl."

"Oh, hell."

He nodded. "Yoli Harris."

I drank some coffee. "I can't figure it. You sure?"

"Positive. And it isn't hard to figure: she was blowin' smoke at us yesterday, all that hokum about wanting to steer clear of the gangs and all. She's tight with them again—if she ever really got away from them."

I considered it, thinking back on Yoli's outburst the previous afternoon, on what O'Neal had told us about her. "You really think so?"

Elmo sucked an eighth of an inch off of his cigarette, rested it in a scarred metal ashtray next to the salt-pepper-sugar rack, and exhaled. "I saw her there tonight, plain as I see you sitting here now," he said. "Gizzard had his arm around her."

"Things aren't always what they seem," I said. When in doubt, try a cliché.

"Which also means sometimes things *are*. Look, Nebraska: Darius's murder was no act of random gang violence. It wasn't a contract hit, either, not the way it was put together. It was cold-blooded, premeditated—all that courtroom jive. Gizzard and his guys planned it out, tried to make it look like something it wasn't. You know it, I know it."

"Right."

"But how'd they know Darius'd be on that corner at that time? The only reason he had for being anywhere near that spot was to see Yoli Harris. The only one who could've told Gizzard when Darius'd be there was Yoli Harris. The only one who could've told them where to hit at us tonight—the only *likely* one who could've given them your name—was Yoli Harris." He made a sound of frustration and anger. "Not that it matters. We don't have anything to pin on her. And if I couldn't kill a filthy little shit like Gerard Jones, I sure as hell can't see myself popping a twenty-year-old girl."

"You're a failure as a cold-blooded killer," I said. I reached to my hip and put my revolver on the table between us. "I'll trust you to do the right thing."

"Oh, ho-ho-ho," Elmo said snidely, but then he laughed a little.

I put the gun away before someone saw it.

"What we still don't know," I said, "is why Yoli would do these things."

"Shit, man—'cause Gizzard *told* her to, that's why!" He smashed the cigarette to death though it was only half gone.

"If it wasn't a contract—and I agree, it wasn't—then what'd Wizard have against Darius?"

He looked at me. At first his eyes nailed me to the cheap green vinyl bench, but then slowly, as my words soaked through the anger that clouded his brain, his eyes softened and grew speculative.

I said, "If Darius was clean—"

"Everyone says he was."

"—and he wasn't using or dealing—"

"Everyone says he wasn't."

"—then I can think of only one common interest between him and Wizard, based on what you saw tonight."

He shook out another cigarette but didn't do anything with it. "The girl."

"The girl."

He stared at his coffee mug, apparently fascinated by the phenomenon of steam rising from a hot liquid. When he looked at me again his face was equal parts amusement and bemusement. "That's it, isn't it? All this pain, killing, scheming, lying—Christ knows what all else—it all comes down to just plain ol' jealousy."

"I don't know why you put that 'just' in front of it," I said. "Jealousy's a powerful emotion. We trivialize it, dilute it: 'petty' jealousy. It's not a good honest emotion like love or hate. But even when it's petty it's powerful, and in the right kind of head, or the wrong kind, it can mutate into something as monstrous and as fatal as any of the other six deadly sins."

"Jesus," he said softly. He took his lighter in one hand and his cigarette in the other. He studied it as if trying to decide whether he should light it. "Be better'n they deserve," he said as if to himself.

I knew what he was thinking about. "Probably," I said. "Some of them."

"When we drove by tonight and I saw them, right away I started thinking about how I could get closer—close enough to take 'em out." He looked at me. "You know what that feels like, Nebraska? That kind of hate?"

"Yes, I do," I said, and I did. "Scary, isn't it?"

"Damn scary—like you got someone else living in here with you." He touched his temple. "Same thing when I caught up with you again, and that son of a bitch was lying there, just lying there like a worm on the sidewalk... Man, you think you got it all figured out, you know? Who you are, what you are, where you're coming from, where you're going. What you're made of. Then— It's like your mind betrays you. It thinks things, it feels things you don't want to think and feel. Like, *Why not pull the trigger?* Like, *They killed one of yours, you kill them.* Like, *There's no way they'll ever get the justice they deserve—unless you give it to them.* And then, while all that's going on, there's this other little voice, you know, very rational, very reasonable, saying, *Well, hell, why not?* And you can't think of any answer."

I said, "Try this one: *Because that's what makes me different from them.*"

He grinned sadly and fired up the lighter. "Us and them again, huh? The line we won't cross." He got the cigarette going. "It ain't easy, friend."

"That's sort of the point."

"Yeah, maybe you're right." He rubbed his eyes. "Christ, I'm sorry, Nebraska."

"What's that mean, you're sticking me with the check?"

He looked at me through his fingers. "For getting you in neck-deep with the Bloods. Tomorrow I fly back to safe, cozy Chicagoland. You got to stay here, way up on the Bloods' shit list."

"I've been on a lot of shit lists," I said with a breeziness I didn't really feel. "What's this about the friendly skies?"

"Aren't we watching the same show? Man, we're dead-ended, frozen out, and shut down. We've got no evidence, just good guesses. We've got nothing to use to *get* evidence. And if we *did* get evidence, the bastards'd just use their drug money to buy sixteen, eighteen, twenty shysters to get 'em off."

"Let's drive off that bridge when we come to it," I said. "I forgot that cruel fate deprived you of the opportunity to witness my lightninglike thinking and fancy footwork tonight. What Maugham called 'footlight sense' I have in spades—"

"Hey, I've *talked* to you about that."

"—and I used it like you wouldn't believe back there. With some interesting results—beyond increasing my lifespan, I mean."

I clued him in.

"Like this dentist I went to for too many years, I was hitting nerves all over the place," I said when I'd finished the recap. "Whenever I hit one, I kept at it as long as I could, mainly playing for time, you know, but also trying to see what I was getting. I don't know what I was getting—I've been a little too busy to stop and sort it all out—but my impression is that it's a lot of nifty stuff."

"Yeah, like Gizzard doesn't like to be called Gerard," Elmo said dryly.

"That's a good one, write that down. You might also want to note how Wizard got very interested when I said I'd seen his right-hand man socializing with the cops."

"Hmm," Elmo said. "Probably just heard the same rumor Jeff told us about."

"Might be more than a rumor, the way he reacted."

"Don't see how it helps us either way."

"Then there's FlashMan. He acted like I'd put a hundred volts through him when I fingered him."

"Wouldn't you? These dudes are bad news, man, and Gizzard's the baddest of them all. If I worked for him, I sure as hell wouldn't want him to think I was selling him out."

"Yeah, but he doth protested all over the place, to fracture Shakespeare. A simple Bronx cheer would have sufficed. I think that was one of the nerves I hit."

"Huh," Elmo said noncommittally. "You know, even if he wasn't planning on rolling over, he might have to now for his own self-preservation. I mean, if you got Gizzard to thinking that FlashMan's just *maybe* a threat…"

"Might be worth a shot," I said. "I wonder how one goes about making an appointment with Mister Richard Dayton."

"Just show up at the project, he'll come running."

"Him and fifty or sixty of his closest friends," I said. "We might want to think of another approach. Meanwhile, think of this: Yoli Harris."

"Yeah, I *been* thinking about her," Elmo said frostily. "You figure FlashMan'd know anything we can nail her on too?"

"Possibly, but I'm thinking more in terms of getting the girl to give Wizard up."

He guffawed. "That's good, man. It's the girl who set Darius up, remember? And it's the girl who tried to set us up. That puts her neck in the noose, too, right along with Gizzard. What makes you think she'd turn?"

I shrugged. "She must have felt *something* for Darius."

"You're some kinda romantic, man."

"Look, if she was in tight with Wizard, then why'd she even start seeing Darius in the first place? Has to have been something there. I'm guessing that Wizard tricked or forced her into setting Darius up. I'm guessing that she doesn't feel too great about what happened to him. I'm guessing we can play on that."

Elmo drummed the tips of two fingers on the side of his mug. It sounded like a small, muffled bell. Finally he said, "Might as well give it a shot. Sure as hell don't have anything else goin' for us."

CHAPTER

23

After some back-and-forth, we decided to go back to Decatur Street. We figured the badguys would figure that we would figure the place was too hot and would therefore crash someplace else, meaning they would leave Decatur Street alone. You could work that sort of reasoning down as many steps as you like, of course, and every other one of them would say that it was *not* safe to go back to my place, but we were just too damn tired to really have a serious go at it.

We got in shortly after four and grabbed a couple hours' sleep. Nothing happened, except perhaps a little REM. Too little, in my case. Then I dragged myself out and went downtown.

Police headquarters is a noisy, crowded, chaotic place; only slightly less so at eight-thirty on a Saturday morning. I repeated my story from last night, read the typed-up version of my story from last night, signed the typed-up version of my story from last night, attesting that it was in fact my story from last night, and had planted my posterior on the seat of an Air-Dyne bike at the Y by nine forty-five.

During my forced exile a few months earlier, I'd had to spend a lot of time hanging around a health club. I picked up some bad habits. One of them was trying to get to the gym three or four times a week for an aerobic workout followed by some time on the weight machines. To my everlasting disappointment, I had discovered that there really was something to all this diet-and-exercise crap after all. I had always sort of hoped that the paunch I'd been developing ever since my thirtieth birthday was inevitable—heredity, metabolism, bad karma, *anything* that I had no control over. Alas, such was not the case. Between the workouts and a few new eating habits, I had lost a bit of weight, put on a bit of muscle, and found I was feeling better, sleeping better, concentrating better—in general, better all the way around. Damn it all anyway.

I did my warm-up on the bike, finding the rhythm, loosening the muscles. I gradually worked up to where you'd've thought I was pedaling with some destination in mind. When I got into my "target zone," eighty percent of my maximum heart rate as indicated by the big chart on the wall, I kept my pedaling and my heart rate constant for twenty minutes. Aerobics is a very efficient exercise. Twenty minutes in your target zone three times a week is enough to maintain fitness. Four times a week will improve it. The trick is, those twenty minutes have to be continuous—no stop-and-start activities.

After twenty minutes passed, I gradually decreased speed, breathing deeply, bringing my heart rate down. Stop suddenly and all that nice oxygen-rich blood pools up in your extremities. When I was breathing normally I got off the bike and did some stretches on the muscles that I had worked hardest. Then I hit the weights, did some more stretches, and took a long shower.

By eleven-fifteen I was walking out of Mister Donut with an orange carton under my arm. What's the point of living longer if you don't enjoy your life?

Elmo was up, the exact opposite of the condition he had been in when I left. And he had company: the Reverend W.R. O'Neal, who had somehow shoehorned his bulk into one of my kitchen chairs. Elmo had unraveled the intricacies of my standing-infusion coffee pot and was just pouring. He took another mug from the cupboard when I came in.

"The Reverend was worried about us," Elmo said.

"I heard about the trouble last night," O'Neal said. "Word travels like a cyclone in that neighborhood. I tried calling several times this morning, but the line was always busy."

"I called Julie and the girls," Elmo said, "and then Francine."

"I knew the busy signal must have meant that you were all right, but..." He shrugged. "Like your friend says, I was worried."

"Your concern shall not go unrewarded," I said, and handed him the Mister Donut carton.

"Hey, I was worried too," Elmo said. I handed him my gym bag. "Get your own coffee, then," he said, and I did.

"So what's the story circulating in the neighborhood?" I asked. "Are we the stuff of legend?"

O'Neal smiled wryly. "After a fashion. You have to understand the importance these people place on image. Face. Especially someone like Wizard. He knows that to a great extent his power is illusory. It derives from what other people think about him. If people think he's important, a big man, someone to be reckoned with, well, then, he is."

"The AK-47s must help," Elmo said. He had torn into the carton and found the chocolate-with-chocolate-icing doughnuts I bought especially for him. Just looking at one made my teeth ache, but Elmo was a chocolate freak from way back.

"Certainly," O'Neal agreed. "But think about it—think of how complex the dynamics are. Wizard not only has to manage a group of people who are all every bit as violent, ruthless, and lawless as he himself is, but also make that group *produce*—hard cash—in order to keep his position with the gang in L.A. And producing, in turn, means he has to manage the general public, too, at least to an extent. The public has to perceive him as powerful, fearsome, and important. The local Bloods see that the public sees him that way, and that legitimizes him in their eyes: they follow him. That reinforces the public's perception. And the Los Angeles Bloods see the results and let him remain in power."

"Quite a balancing act." I found a bran muffin in the carton and claimed it, then I gestured to O'Neal to help himself. He hesitated, but eventually selected a jelly-filled doughnut. You don't get to be his size by turning down too many jelly-filled doughnuts.

"It is," he said after sampling his selection and blotting his lips on a Mister Donut paper napkin. "And so you can see why appearances are so important to someone like Wizard—well, all of them, really, in that life. Like I said before, it all comes down to self-image, self-esteem." He glanced at Elmo.

Elmo cleared his throat and said, "I know I owe you an apology for letting you have it like that the other day. It so happens I agree with most of what you said. But I haven't been feeling too charitable toward these people the last week or so."

"No one could blame you for that," O'Neal said. "Anyhow, my point is that gang members value image above almost anything else. They *need* it, really need it, and not just to hang onto power. For their own psyches, too. And you tarnished their image last night—twice, from what I hear on the street and read in the morning paper."

Elmo handed me the *World-Herald*. "Page three," he said. "Three! You were right about people getting blasé about these drive-bys."

"Some people," I said, skimming the paragraphs. There had been a reporter nosing around the previous evening, after our close encounter with the gangbangers, and two of the three main TV stations were represented. I had ducked the reporter and made myself scarce before the TV crews arrived. I learned the hard way that publicity is not necessarily a good thing for a guy in my racket.

"First they tried to kill you and failed," O'Neal was saying. "Then you came to *them*, on their own turf, and they had you but let you go."

" 'Let' isn't the word I'd use," Elmo said. He plucked a second doughnut from the box.

"The story was already spreading through the neighborhood early this morning," O'Neal said. "Word has it Wizard has a broken nose and two black eyes."

"He faw down," I said. "Go boom."

"I'm sure Wizard is trying his best, but you can't keep something like that secret," O'Neal said. "Most a person can do is make people whisper. And that's what they're doing. People are still afraid of the Bloods and especially Wizard, but that doesn't mean they mind laughing up their sleeves at his expense."

"Send for the spin doctors," I said.

O'Neal nodded. "But I'm afraid their idea of damage control is apt to be quite radical. I don't suppose I need to repeat my warning to you two. But I will anyway. They've lost face because of you, the whole gang and Wizard in particular. The fastest and most obvious way to redeem themselves would be to kill you."

Elmo looked at me. "*Told* you I should've killed him when I had the chance."

"Too late now," I said. "Reverend, we heard a rumor about some discontent in the gang, apparently because of Wizard using the gang to settle what we think must have been a personal grudge against Darius."

"And the resulting heat," Elmo added.

O'Neal nodded. "I've heard the same thing."

"Do you think there's much chance that this could lead to Wizard's ouster?"

"Especially with a little help from his friends?" Elmo said, meaning us.

The big man sighed. "The only possible answer is: Who knows? Listen, if I had a dime for every time I've heard a rumor that Wizard's on his way out—whatever the means or source of his removal—why, I'd have more money than these hateful devils could even *dream* of. Rumors spring up in that neighborhood by spontaneous generation, and once they've sprung up, look out! I have no doubt that there are members of the Bloods who are unhappy with Wizard's rule. When'd you ever hear of an organization that *didn't* have its share of grumblers and gripers? Even our Lord had to listen to complaints among the twelve."

"Funny you should make that comparison," I said. "We're sort of hoping to cultivate a Judas among Wizard's disciples."

He frowned. "That's asking a lot. Like I told you the other day, these gangs are families, in a perverse sort of way."

"Even the closest families have falling-outs," Elmo said.

We filled him in on last night's events, with emphasis on my conversation, if that's the word, with FlashMan D. and Wizard.

When we had finished I said, "Our original problem was that we didn't know why or by whom Darius was killed. Now we know the latter and even have a pretty good guess as to the former."

"But there's not a whole lot we can do about it," Elmo said. "Our 'pretty good guess' isn't gonna count for much with cops, prosecutors, judges, and all those other sticklers for details."

"You see, our curiosity was never idle. We not only wanted to find out what had happened to Elmo's nephew, we also sort of had it in mind that we'd see to it that whoever was responsible for his murder paid for it."

"One way or the other," Elmo said.

"But now it's obvious that our only hope lies in convincing someone close to Wizard, someone who has the goods on him, to give him up."

"Your Judas," O'Neal said. "How can you possibly hope to persuade FlashMan to turn on Wizard? Even if he has ambitions of replacing Wizard—especially so. To betray Wizard would make him a pariah in the gang."

"He may not have much choice. I laid it on pretty thick last night, and he rose to the bait. Even if he never had a thought of doing in his pal, he might have to now in order to survive."

"The other thing," Elmo said, "is that we're into this too far to pull back now." He looked at me. "Last night when I was talking about cashing in and going home, it hadn't hit me that that's impossible. Gizzard would never settle for that. He's got to even the score. Only way to end it now is to take him out."

"One way or the other?" I said, and he grinned ruefully.

O'Neal said, "You two do like to play with matches." He drained his mug and set it down on the table. "How can I help?"

Elmo looked at me and I looked at him. He shrugged. "Well, we need to get in touch with FlashMan D.," he said. "For obvious reasons, we can't just go knock on his door. Lousy idea even if he didn't live in the same building as Gizzard and the other top kicks."

"Wait a minute," I said. I had pulled out the phone book and was pawing through it.

"What, you think he's listed?" Elmo said. He located the third and last chocolate doughnut.

"I'm a firm believer in trying not to overlook the obvious. I read once where Ray Bradbury went nuts trying to find out the temperature at which ordinary paper ignites. He tried scientists, universities, everything. Then the light finally went on, and he called the fire department. They told him right away: Fahrenheit 451. Shit."

"Try the fire department," Elmo said helpfully.

"Maybe the Yellow Pages, under 'Gangs, Youth,' " I said, and put away the phone book.

O'Neal was slowly, pensively rubbing his fingertips along the pinkish patch of skin on the left side of his face. "There might be a good way," he said slowly.

"We don't want you putting yourself at risk."

He grinned. "Just living in that neighborhood is risky. Believe me, I have no death wish. I wouldn't be much more welcome on FlashMan's doorstep than either of you. My idea involves a young man I know. Basically a good kid, but a little confused—like too many of these kids are. He *knows* what's right, but the Bloods have an undeniable attraction for him. It doesn't help that his brother's a member. He—my young

191

friend—has sort of been on the periphery of it for months. It might be possible for me to get word to FlashMan, through my friend, without undue risk to anybody. Of course, my friend may decline. And even if he agrees to help, there's no guarantee FlashMan would agree to talk to you."

"We wanted guarantees," Elmo said, "we'd've gone into a different line of work."

CHAPTER

24

The court reporting-steno school was where it had been seven years ago—the last time I could recall having needed to make use of its public-stenographer service—and for at least ten years prior to that: in one of those anonymous, interchangeable sand-colored buildings, circa World War II, that dot the older parts of Omaha. It had a creaky old elevator I had forgotten but soon enough remembered, a steel box no bigger than a phone booth, with an accordion door you pulled shut after you closed the sliding steel outer door, and a pale ceiling light that faltered alarmingly with every vibration of the cab. Of which there were plenty on the way up to the fourth floor. What I get for being too lazy to take the stairs.

Through peerless detective work, I had determined that this was indeed Yoli Harris's school: there were only two such schools in town, and the second was clear the heck out on the south end of the city. Through unparalleled charm, I had discovered when Yoli's class took its mid-morning break: I called and lied to the receptionist, saying I had a balloon bouquet to deliver to one of the students. I was five minutes early, but by the time the elevator made its slow and rattling way upstairs, I might be late.

I had come alone. Elmo and I had spent a goodly part of Sunday afternoon kicking it around and eventually cooked up a plausible strategy. I would come at Yoli first, lean on her if necessary; if that didn't get us anywhere, Elmo would come on later with the soft soap. He was good with it, and since he was Darius's uncle he had a strong sentimental card to play.

We had heard nothing from the Reverend O'Neal. There was no way for us to know whether that was a good sign, a bad sign, or no sign at all.

We had, on the other hand, heard from Darius's counselor, Eileen Nielsen. I had almost forgotten about her—it seemed like weeks, not just a few days, since I had spoken with her. She had checked with everyone in Darius's group. None of them had been close to Darius, none of them knew anyone at the counseling center or anyplace else who might have known Darius well. It was by now useless information, of course, but I thanked Dr. Nielsen profusely all the same—partly because I did appreciate her efforts, partly for the more cynical reason that, in this line, you never know when you're going to need to go back to someone for another favor.

The elevator *ka-chunk*ed to a stop, groaned at the exertion, and wobbled slightly as if unsure how long it could keep itself suspended like that. I got the doors open and got out onto terra firma, or at least linoleum firma. The corridor was old-fashioned: wide and high-ceilinged and illuminated by school-house globes dangling from chains. AK-SAR-BEN SCHOOL OF STENOGRAPHY was painted in black on pebbled glass in the door; below it, in smaller lettering, were STENOGRAPHY, TYPING, and COURT REPORTING; and finally, in the lower right corner, WALK IN.

I walked in. There was a smallish reception area with a threadbare carpet and ugly yellow file cabinets, a thin middle-aged woman whose white hair probably was supposed to be platinum and whose eyebrows looked as if she had drawn them on with pencil, and the persistent clatter of keyboarding, lots of it, emanating from a narrow hallway to the left.

The thin woman smiled at me. She looked like the sort who had been stunning when she was younger, and had been told that once too often. Through a lot of impossibly white teeth she said, "May I help you?" in a way that almost made you think she wanted to.

"I'm meeting someone," I said.

She looked at a clock on the wall, one that must have seemed futuristic-looking when they hung it there back in 1956. "They should be out in just a minute," she said.

She wasn't far wrong. Suddenly all of the chatter from the other rooms quit, doors down the hall opened, and a different kind of chatter spilled out.

The student body was almost entirely women. I could have guessed at that, only I wouldn't have wanted anyone calling me sexist. They all came down the hall and through the reception room, laughing and talking, and went through the pebble-glassed door and, I guessed, on downstairs to the coffee shop on the street level. None of them gave me more than the barest of glances as they passed. Not even Yoli Harris. A chunky young woman of dubious hairstyle was prattling into Yoli's left ear. Yoli seemed to be doing a good job of not listening. She looked tired and washed-out; her face had no expression.

I took care of that. I drifted into the moving stream and touched her right arm. She looked up indifferently, then her eyes widened as she registered my identity.

"Yoli!" I said like we were long-losts. "They told me back at the old sweatshop you were going to school here now. That's great! How you been?" And so on in that inane fashion until we were out into the wide main corridor and the rest of the merry band had slid on by.

I had not had much opportunity to really see Yoli at her mother's house the other day; she had been kind of a blur. Now I noted that she was a small woman, slender, with smooth, rich-looking skin. Her hair, of medium length and done up in gentle curls, had almost reddish highlights. She had dark almond-shaped eyes which now were wide. "What are you *doing* here?" she whispered shrilly when the rest of the group had gone by. "What are you trying to do to me?"

195

"It may actually be that I'm trying to help you."

"*Help* me?" Her eyes were wild. "Mister, the way you help me is leave me alone, you understand?"

"Sorry, Yoli, it can't be. Every time we run a new version of what might be the real story behind Darius's murder, the Batcomputer spits out your name. Friday night, you probably know, some of your friends from the Bloods tried to kill me and Darius's uncle. Twice. Came pretty close, too. About the only way they could have known where I live is if they knew my name, and about the only way they could have known my name is if you told them."

Her eyes were on the linoleum. It was putty-gray, with red specks. Yoli seemed to sag in on herself. "No friends of mine," she said heavily.

"That's what I was guessing." I tried to make my voice as gentle and reassuring as possible. "I was guessing that they hotboxed you and the only way they'd let you out was if you did what they said."

She didn't speak, didn't move.

"And I'm guessing you just feel like a million bucks."

She looked up. Her eyes were wet. "I hate myself," she whispered fervently. "I would kill myself, I swear I would. But I got my mama and my little baby girl to worry about. That's the only thing keeps me going. I know I'm gonna go to hell, but I gotta keep on for their sakes."

I shook my head. "You gotta get out of this for their sakes. I saw you in front of the Mini-Mall Friday night." That surprised her—and shamed her. She looked away. "There's no in-betweening, Yoli," I said. "Either you're in that world of theirs or you're not. There's no having one foot on that side of the line and one on the other. It's all or nothing. Is that the life you want for Emily June—a mother who's a Blood?"

"No." Her voice was a hoarse whisper. As she had done the other day, she unconsciously tugged at the tendril of hair along the left side of her neck.

"Then you have to help us. Darius's uncle and me. You help us, we help you. That's the deal, and it's solid."

Yoli was shaking her head even before I got the words out, shaking it slowly, almost sadly. "Only thing solid is that he'll kill me if he finds out I even been talking to you."

"Wizard."

She nodded. "He'll kill my baby girl. He said he would. I know he would."

I knew it too; if Wizard's reputation was only half accurate, we could count on him.

"I got to go," she said suddenly. "I don't want the others to know... I don't want anybody to know about me." She looked at me pleadingly. "Nobody here knows about me, you know? About me and the Bloods. I don't want them ever finding out. They think...they think I'm a good person. And I can still make something of myself. I can still make a good life for my baby. I know I can."

Now it was me doing the head-shaking. "You know better, Yoli. Wizard will never let you."

She was silent.

I took a deep breath and said, "Yoli, you're about our only chance. We *know* that Wizard was responsible for killing Darius. But we can't prove it. Not without your help."

"I can't," she whispered. "My baby..."

"What about Darius? Don't you care about that?"

It was a cheap shot; it was meant to be. Her head whipped up. Her face glistened with tears and melted mascara. Her eyes were hot. "Of *course* I care," she said hoarsely. "I loved Darius, and he loved me, and he was good to Emily June. But I— I didn't have no choice."

That's never true; we always have a choice, even if it's a choice between undesirable things. But Yoli wasn't interested in a philosophy lesson. She was interested in getting away from me. I didn't blame her. I wanted to get away from me, too, when I opened my mouth and said, "I'm sorry, Yoli. I really am. But I can't give you any choice either. You have to help us."

"Or what?"

I sighed. "Or word gets around that you are helping us anyway."

Yoli looked at me for a long time, and I forced myself to maintain the eye-contact. When she spoke at last, her voice was calm. "You fucking bastard," she said distinctly, "you're as bad as any of them are."

She was right. I flashed to my conversation with Elmo after our near-misses Friday night. The line we won't cross, the line that separates *us* from *them*. Nice words. I could console myself, a little, with the knowledge that my threat, unlike Wizard's, was a big bluff. Yoli could not.

Yoli was looking off down the corridor, tugging at the curl of hair, thinking, weighing her options. Such as they were.

"We can protect you," I said feebly.

"Yeah, right."

Finally she came to a decision, sighed, and looked at the plastic watch on her wrist. "Outta time," she said to herself. She looked at me as if I were an oozing, fly-ridden pile of garbage. In fact I felt worse than that. "Not here," she said coldly. "You gonna get me killed, so I don't know why I should care what anyone here thinks of me, but not here. Not now."

"Name it," I said, "I'll be there."

CHAPTER

25

The next morning, Yoli Harris boarded the MAT near the project and, a couple of transfers later, ended up at the Doctors Building at Farnam and Forty-second, where she entered the South Tower lobby. She had the baby with her. The baby's regular doctor didn't practice there, but there was a pediatrician in the Doctors Building who specialized in ear, nose, and throat complaints.

Yoli wasn't there to take the baby to that doctor, but if anybody cared, if anybody was even idly curious, it certainly would look like it. In case anybody was more than just idly curious, I had arranged—through my friend Pat Costello, who is a pharmacist and who knows perhaps three-quarters of all the medical people in Greater Omaha—that the pediatrician's appointment book would show an 11:30 appointment for Emily June Harris, and would even show that the appointment had been kept.

I was in the lobby, watching to make sure nobody was interested in Yoli and her baby. Nobody was. We went out to the Impala and headed up Saddle Creek Road. The noon "hour," and the traffic that comes with it, starts earlier every year, it seems, and even at this hour, about 11:15, it was heavy. I took Saddle Creek north to where it hooks up with the Radial, and followed the Radial almost as far as my place, to the

Rose Bowl. It was far enough removed from both the project and the steno school to effectively eliminate any chance of our bumping into any of Yoli's acquaintances from either half of her double-life. Besides, the Rose Bowl restaurant has the best triple-decker ruben sandwich west and possibly east of the Mississippi.

Elmo was waiting for us there. In case we had to play good cop-bad cop.

There was a morning league occupying the bowling lanes, but the restaurant was only three-quarters full. Elmo had claimed a booth in the far corner. A woman with hair the color of cheap brass took our orders: rubens and Buds for Elmo and me, salad and Diet Coke for Yoli.

The baby was dozing in the car seat-carrier contraption Yoli had had her strapped into all along. Yoli loosened the pink blanket covering her, and carefully slid a pink-and-yellow knit cap from the baby's head. A crown of thin, curly brown hair popped out, and Yoli smoothed it back in a useless but maternal gesture. The sleeping baby snorted and shifted at being touched, and her delicate little fingers opened and then closed again on her blanket, but she went on sleeping.

Yoli glanced at the retreating waitress, then, her voice low, said, "What do you want from me?" She said it to the tabletop, having made eye-contact with no one since the Doctors Building.

I threw a glance at Elmo, but his eyes were on Yoli. I turned to the girl and said, as gently as possible, "We think we know what happened to Darius, and why. We need to hear it from you, though. And we need you to help us get whatever is required to take care of Wizard."

She looked at Emily June. "He already said he'd hurt Mama and my baby if I didn't do what he said." Her eyes moved to Elmo's face. "What's he gonna do he finds out I helped you guys get him?"

Elmo looked at me expressionlessly, then back at her. "I guess we'll have to make sure we get him before he finds out."

"Not just him. He's got friends."

"From what we hear, some of his 'friends' are a little frosted because he's brought the man down on everyone." The waitress brought our drinks. Elmo popped the tab on his beer and poured it carefully into a Pilsener glass the shape of an hourglass. "May be that Gizzard's 'friends' aren't so friendly when it all hits the fan."

Yoli was shaking her head. "These are the Bloods, mister. You don't know nothin' about the Bloods."

"Educate us," Elmo said over the top of his glass.

At Central High, Yoli had started spending time with a girl whose brother was a Blood. Yoli had been an indifferent student, neither good nor bad. Like a lot of kids her age in her neighborhood, she didn't so much dislike school as fail to see the point of it. It had little to do with the world as she knew it. She could only conclude that everyone, students and teachers, were just marking time until they could get out of there.

With the Bloods it was different—fast, exciting, and dangerous. The boys, the young men she met, knew what the score was. They knew that no one hands people like them anything, that they had to find what they wanted and take it. That appealed to Yoli. So did the prospect of something besides the dead-end minimum-wage job a high-school diploma would qualify her for.

Ignoring her mother's pleas, Yoli quit school. She began spending virtually all of her time with the Bloods, immersing herself in gang life—the colors, the "smack" or slang, and the violence. Somehow, though, she managed to steer clear of the drugs.

In part that was thanks to a Blood she had met and become infatuated with early on, even before she quit school. He had the attitude that drugs were for losers. Winners dealt drugs, losers took them. Beyond an occasional drink and an even more occasional toke, he never touched drugs except in the distribution chain. His name was Richard Dayton; everyone called him FlashMan D. As far as Yoli Harris was concerned, he was as smart and stylish as his street name. It wasn't long before Yoli was FlashMan's girl.

But there was another member of the Bloods whom Yoli, somewhat to her own surprise, found interesting too: a slender young man named Gerard Jones, known on the street as Wizard.

"I never loved Gerard," Yoli told us in a dull, mumbled monotone as she picked at her salad without ever seeming to eat any of it. "I loved Richie right from the first time I saw him. Sometimes I think I never did stop loving him. With Gerard though... There's nothing lovable about Gerard. His own mama couldn't love him, that's what I always thought. But, I don't know, he was exciting. You know, Richie's smooth; he's cool. That's exciting, too, for a girl—but Gerard, he's like wild. Real crazy and unpredictable. Being with Richie was nice. Being with Gerard was like insane."

It got more insane. Eventually Yoli and FlashMan drifted apart; Yoli became, more and more, Wizard's girl. "I never thought of me that way," she told us now. "But as far as everyone else was concerned, I guess, that's what I was."

"Gizzard was part of 'everyone?' " Elmo asked. She didn't answer.

Yoli had seldom done even grass or speed when she was with Richie; now, with Wizard, there wasn't much in the way of pharmaceuticals that she didn't try. Wizard encouraged this; above all he encouraged her to use crack. He sold her on the idea that it wasn't as bad or as expensive as other drugs, such as the powdered cocaine he favored. Yoli had no idea how addictive the stuff can be.

It didn't really seem to matter, though: Wizard was her source, and his supply was limitless. Nothing was said about her paying for the ever-increasing amounts of crack her body demanded. Nothing was ever said. But, inevitably, the time came when Wizard brought up the possibility of her "helping" him with a "favor" or two. There wasn't much likelihood that she would refuse. Wizard didn't even have to threaten her; she was smoking the threat several times a day now. Almost before she knew what was happening, Wizard had outfitted her with a lot of expensive clothes—"good stuff, real smart, nothing trashy"—and a round-trip ticket from Omaha to Los Angeles. She was met at LAX by a pair of Wizard's "associates," who drove her to an expensive house in the hills that belonged, they said, to a "big record executive." There a stunning, well-dressed young black woman named Marcella showed Yoli how to hide packets of cocaine and other contraband on her person, how to avoid attracting attention at airports while simultaneously keeping an eye out for anyone who might be a cop, and how to look and act so cool and chic, so uptown, so completely unlike anyone who would even dream of hiding a shipment of coke in her bloomers that it didn't even *look* like an act anymore.

"Marcella said airport cops have this profile tells them what to look out for," Yoli said. "You know, if someone acts this way he might have a bomb, someone acts that way he might be moving drugs, that kinda thing. She said all you have to do is know what the cops are looking for, and not be that way."

They practiced it for three days, including an afternoon at Los Angeles International, where Marcella showed Yoli how to spot narcs and other unsympathetic sorts, and how to "work" a baggage-claim area, sniffing out trouble before you so much as laid a hand on a suitcase that the cops might have their eye on.

On the fourth day an overnight-delivery pouch arrived from Omaha. Yoli caught a glimpse of the contents when Wizard's "associates" opened it: money. That evening she was on a flight back to Omaha, with more carry-on baggage than met the eye.

There were other flights to the left coast over the following months. Some of them were direct, or as direct as ever-changing airline schedules allowed; some of them involved a pair of round-trip tickets and planned stopovers of a day or two in another town—St. Louis, Minneapolis, Denver—en route to and from Los Angeles, just to blur the fact that she was making frequent though irregularly scheduled trips there.

Meanwhile, Yoli was hitting the pipe hard; but there weren't enough drugs on the planet to wipe away the fear she felt every time Wizard made her play courier. "I was never not scared," she told us. "Even at the start, when it was kinda fun—you know, exciting—I was scared to death. Even later, when I got good at it and you'd think it should've been routine, scared to death. From the minute Gerard handed me the airplane ticket—'cause that's how he did it, he never asked or anything first, he just handed me the tickets and said 'You're goin', girl'—from the minute he handed me the ticket to the minute I got home and turned the stuff over to him, the whole time I was just like tight inside. Scared stiff." She gulped down a lot of soda pop now, as if just talking about it still scared her. I signaled the brass-blond for another round.

Contrary to what the Reverend O'Neal had thought, Yoli's break from Wizard and the Bloods came not when she learned she was pregnant, but when terror finally overpowered her. "I was on the way back from L.A.," she said with artificial nonchalance. "I hadn't gone out there for a couple months, so Gerard thought it'd be okay I went straight out. Only I had to change planes in Salt Lake City, and there was this big commotion at the airport. They arrested this woman there; she was moving drugs, same as me. She was even on the same plane as me.

"I went straight to the ladies' room and threw up. I hadn't eaten anything all day—I could never eat the days I was traveling, I was too scared—but I kept, you know, throwing up anyway, throwing up nothing." She made a face and pushed away the remains of her salad. "I thought about flushing all the junk I was carrying," she said, "and not getting my luggage when I got back here. There was nothing to connect it to me; Gerard always used fake names and credit-cards and stuff. But I didn't do any of that." She sighed. "I stayed in the ladies' room the whole time between my planes, scared to come out. But I finally did, naturally, and I got on the plane and brought the stuff back to Gerard, all of it."

"Why?" Elmo said.

She looked at him. "Because scared as I was of getting caught, I was more scared of Gerard. I knew how much money was going out there and how much junk was coming back—I wasn't the only one muling it, you know. Just the stuff I had on me was worth thousands on the street. I fuck him over, Gerard'd take care of me but good. Me or Mama."

"He was threatening you even then," I said.

"Shoot, yeah," Yoli said. "Not so much, you know, explicitly—is that the right word?—but sort of hinting. You'd hear about someone getting iced, Gerard'd kinda smile this nasty smile he's got, say something like, 'That's what she gets for holdin' out on her old man'—you know, to keep me scared, keep me in line." She looked down at her lap. "It worked, too. I knew how Gerard was. I'd heard the stories..."

"The hooker in Los Angeles?"

"That one, others too. And I saw some things myself." She paused as if reluctant to continue; but she would continue. There is a phenomenon well-known to cops, reporters, insurance investigators, anyone who spends a lot of time interviewing people for whatever reason: a diffident subject starts to open up, sometimes even becoming expansive. It doesn't require any special skill on the part of the interviewer, except perhaps the patience to wait for it to happen. People like to talk. To Yoli Harris, Elmo and I were the badguys at the moment. Yet, slowly, she had opened up. Her reluctant monotone had taken on life. And though she might have denied it if asked, she *wanted* to tell us her story.

She said, "There was this guy owed Gerard some money, for drugs, I s'pose. He had a couple women, too, so he says, you know, take this woman for a while, she can work off my debt. Gerard says that's cool, send her over. The guy does, and Gerard just beats the living hell out of her. I mean, I'm certain that girl ended up in the hospital. Only Gerard, what he does is have her put in a car and taken over to the guy's crib. They dump her out on the lawn. Gerard says that'll teach him not to disrespect a Blood."

Elmo said, "You saw Gizzard beat up this woman."

"Part of it. I couldn't watch."

"But Gizzard did it himself. Alone." She nodded and Elmo looked at me, then back at her. "Then why all the folderol about killing Darius?"

She turned toward me, puzzled. "Why'd Wizard set it up to look like a drive-by?" I said. "Why so complicated?"

Yoli drank some of her new Coke and blotted her lips. "Thing you got to understand about Gerard, he's kind of a chicken. He's like real big on teaching you a lesson if he thinks you dis him—disrespect him—or you rip him off, something like that. But not straight-on: he'll come at you sideways, kinda sneaky-like. Like beating up that girl instead of facing down the guy who owed him money. Or having a bunch of the brothers go at someone while Gerard, he just stands back and watches. Smiling that nasty smile of his." She seemed to almost shiver at the thought of it. "He's always doing stuff like that."

I said, "Killing that hooker in L.A. was pretty direct. If it ever really happened."

"Oh, it happened all right," Yoli said. "It happened. But, see, that's just like Gerard too. He made that girl think they had an arrangement, he took his part, then he killed her when she wasn't expecting anything. Sideways, like I said. And it was safe for him: he had about ten of his friends waiting for him at the other end of the alley, and who's gonna care about a streetwalker getting blown away?"

Elmo looked at me. "Crafty little bastard."

"Charming," I said.

"You guys joke if you like, but there's nothing funny about it. He's a scary man, scary and dangerous. There's something not right up here"—she indicated her head—"and I think it's getting worse. That makes him scarier. And more dangerous."

"But you walked away from him," Elmo said. He managed to make it sound neither like an accusation nor a challenge.

"Sort of." She smiled grimly.

When she returned to Omaha after her bad fright at the Salt Lake airport, Yoli informed Wizard that she had had it—she was ending her career as his mule, she was kicking drugs, and she was dumping the Bloods as a whole and him especially. Wizard didn't think much of any of those ideas, but for once Yoli was determined. He made the usual thinly veiled threats, which she ignored, and backed them up with explicit threats, which she also ignored. They came to nothing.

In part, Yoli's ability to stand up to Wizard may have been because she was already going through hell, and Wizard's threats seemed anemic by comparison. She was kicking crack and the other crap she'd been doing so much of so long, and doing it the hard way: cold turkey, relying on a combination of willpower, fear, and help from an unexpected source— unexpected as far as Elmo and I were concerned, that is: FlashMan D.

"Richie never hardly did drugs," Yoli reminded us. "He'd seen what was going on with me, naturally, and he didn't like it. He tried talking to me, but it never did any good. I treated him real bad, but he was a true friend. He helped me kick my habit. And then…" She looked down at the sleeping baby on the seat next to her, reached out a hand and gently touched the baby's cheek with her fingertips. Emily June went on sleeping. "And then I found out I was gonna have my baby, and he helped me deal with that too."

"Were you and FlashMan back together then?"

She shrugged. "A little. It wasn't the same anymore. That was my fault, I guess. And besides, I knew I had to get away from the gang, and Richie was part of that scene. Shoot, he's a member of the Council. I stay with Richie, I stay with the gang." She shrugged again, a no-big-deal shrug; but her voice belied it: it still held a shading of pain, even after nearly two years.

There was no need for me to look at Elmo to know that he realized what I did: FlashMan, not Wizard, was the father of the sleeping baby.

"What did Gizzard think of all this?" Elmo said.

"Me and Richie? He never knew. That was part of the reason me and Richie broke up, too—Richie was real good at putting stuff past Gerard, but even he couldn't keep at it forever. Sooner or later something was bound to slip, Gerard'd find out somehow—he's got spies everywhere, all over the turf—and then there'd've been holy hell to pay, believe you me."

"Something like what happened to Darius."

Yoli sighed. "Poor Darius. Gerard didn't have anything against him, really. They never even met. It was all my fault..." Only indirectly: Yoli was not as good as FlashMan at "slipping stuff by" Wizard. She had begun seeing Darius, whom she met at Sub Standard, against her better judgment. But Darius was as secrecy-minded as she was, albeit for different reasons, and Yoli allowed herself to think that maybe after all these months Wizard didn't care what she did anymore.

She deluded herself. Wizard didn't approach Yoli anymore, he never spoke to her, but he seemed to always be around. Yoli would step off the bus, come out the front door in the morning, turn around in a store—there he'd be. Invariably, once she had seen him, he would simply turn and leave, gesturing for his entourage to follow. Besides the head games, Wizard still kept tabs on Yoli through his network in the neighborhood, and inevitably found out that Yoli was seeing Darius.

"Word gets around," she said fatalistically. "One day I get this call from Richie. He's got friends all around too, naturally, and from one of them he's found out that Gerard's found out I'm keeping company with someone, someone not from the neighborhood. Richie tells me that Gerard's trying to find out who the man is. So I say I'll break off with Darius right now, but Richie says that's no good—Gerard's talking about how I dis him, seeing another man. I can end it with Darius, but that's not gonna stop Gerard, Richie says. And he's right, I know that. When I ask him what I should do, he says the only thing to do is run away, get outta town. He said he'd give me some money. But I can't do that. There's the baby, and there's Mama—I tried to get her to move away from the neighborhood, she won't even do that, says no one's gonna force her out of her home. No way I'm gonna get her to leave town. No way I'm gonna go without her, either, leave her to face that—that animal."

She looked at Elmo. Her eyes were full and her face was wet with tears, but her voice, though thick, was steady. "I tried to warn Darius, I swear I did. Weeks before he was killed. I told him he had to stay away from me, leave town before Gerard found out who he was. He wouldn't do it. He said he loved me and he wouldn't leave me and the baby, and if I wouldn't go without Mama, then he wouldn't go either."

Elmo's face had no expression.

"I don't know if it means anything to you, mister, but Darius was a good man. He wasn't doing no drugs, he wasn't messed up with no gangs or nothing, and he was planning to go to school next fall and study restaurant management. Only thing he did wrong was love me."

The day before Darius was killed, Yoli stepped off the bus and found Wizard waiting for her near the project's eastern wall. That in itself was not strange; what was unusual was that he approached her and spoke. "He said he knew I'd been 'catting around,' he called it; that I was cheating on him with another man. I tried to, you know, slide by it: I said I couldn't be cheating on him 'cause I'd broke up with him months ago. But he said no 'bitch' throws him over, that *he* says when things are done. He said I'd insulted him and humiliated him—me and Darius. He knew Darius's name. Then he grabbed me by the arm and told me to break up with Darius. If I had, maybe things would've gone different. Or maybe not—you never know what Gerard's gonna do, no matter what he says. Anyhow, I told him to piss off. I guess he'd threatened me so often and nothing had ever happened, I thought nothing ever would. Or maybe I was just mad 'cause he grabbed me like that. I don't know. But I told him go to hell.

"And then he just went cold. I never saw anything like it. Not with Gerard or nobody. He got kind of stiff and his eyes were like steel or something. He let go of me, and he smiled—only it wasn't a smile; it made him look like some kind of animal. He kinda half-turned and waved his hand back toward the project. I thought it was a signal for his guys—he always had his guys with him—and I remember I thought, *Well, girl, you done it now.*" She smiled unsteadily. "I thought I was dead. But it wasn't a signal—he wanted me to look at the project, through the entrance there. You've been there, you know how it is. There's this little playground right inside. That was a nice afternoon, sunny, and there were a bunch of kids playing in there, and I saw my mama sitting on one of the benches there. She was sitting with her friend Mrs. Waters, who lives in the project; Mrs. Waters's little boys were playing. Emily June was in Mama's lap, all bundled up, asleep." She looked down at the baby now. It was some little time before she resumed:

"When he saw I'd seen Mama and the baby, Gerard turned back toward me and he smiled again and he waved toward off behind me. I turned around, and there was this big old van across the street there, just down from our house. Gerard, he must've made some kind of sign 'cause the windows on that side of the van slid down and a couple guns stuck out, just enough so I could see them and know what they were.

"I turned around again and Gerard kinda glanced over to the project again. I knew what he was telling me. A sign from him and that van'd come rolling down the street and swing over by the entrance, and all those people on the playground there would be dead before you could bat an eye. Including Mama and my baby."

Yoli did what any sane person would do: she caved. She agreed to stop seeing Darius LeClerc as of that instant. But, as she had said, there was no telling what Wizard would do in any given situation: at some point during the previous ninety seconds, Wizard had decided that that wasn't what he wanted after all. Shrewd and sadistic, he must have realized immediately that he finally had Yoli on the ropes; now he decided to tie her up with them. He told her that she was to call Darius tomorrow, Sunday, and tell him she needed to see him late that night, right there on the corner where Wizard and Yoli now stood. It had to be Sunday because of important gang business Saturday night.

Yoli protested, or tried to: why would she have Darius meet her out there, in the middle of the night? Wizard brushed it aside: "He'll do it," he said confidently. "He in love with you, ain't he? You just tell him you got something important to discuss, he be here."

"What do you want me to say to him when he gets here?" Yoli asked, defeated.

"Nothing," Wizard said. "You won't be around. I be talkin' to him, explain how things are. See, you say you gonna break up with him, but I can't trust you, bitch. You cat around, try'n keep things from the Wizard. I always find out, but I don't like you sneakin' like that. I tell the boy he ain't to see you no more, then I know it's done."

Yoli didn't believe him; she didn't believe that was all he had in mind. But she tried to convince herself that she had believed him: she worked on it all weekend. Without success. She knew she was turning Darius over to his executioners, but she did it anyway. There was no doubt in her mind that her mother and her child would be dead in an instant if she didn't surrender to Wizard's demands; no doubt that they would suffer if she didn't obey his instructions.

Not that that made it any easier to live with herself.

"Why didn't you call the police," Elmo said. "They could've set a trap."

Yoli laughed. "Mister, half the time you can't even get the police to come to that neighborhood." It was a common enough complaint, even though the obvious police presence

Elmo and I had seen there Friday night gave it the lie. "And anyhow, say I did call and they did come and they found Gerard and the others in their car, waiting for Darius, all of them armed. What then? Drug money buys lots of lawyering, mister. They cop some kind of jive charge on the guns, probably bargain it down to nothing, probably be back on the street again inside a week. And there's only one person could have ratted them: Yolanda Harris." She paused, and her voice, which had become almost strident, went down a level. "If it was just me I had to worry about, I think I could've stood up to him. I think so. But it was my mama and my baby, and I couldn't let anything happen to them."

So she made her call as instructed, and Darius LeClerc died.

Elmo said, "One thing I got to know. Who. Exactly."

She looked at him for a long time. Her fingers went for the hair that curled below her left ear. Then, in a low voice, she said, "Richie. Two other guys from L.A., guys on the council. Hamfat and Soldier—Michael Perry and Walker Freed. And a local guy named Donald Lee. They call him Little Flash on account of Richie was his ace kool when he joined the Bloods. And Gerard—I guess he figured it'd be safe for him. He drove."

In a way, Yoli Harris died too when Darius died. In the hours before the ambush, she felt herself growing numb: she said it was as if there was nothing inside her anymore. Since then she had been going through the motions as best she could, but she felt like she was looking at everything from very far away. It was as if she wasn't present; it was as if she wasn't alive.

Nor did she any longer have the will to even attempt to resist Wizard. What would be the point? What he said was true, he always found out about her. He was always there, watching her; he always would be; he would never let her be free of him. So why fight?

And what would be the difference anyway? Darius was dead; she was dead: a zombie. When Wizard told her that she was his now, that she was expected to be with him when he wanted her, she obeyed. None of it made any difference anymore. As long as Wizard left her baby alone, none of it made any difference.

"Richie tried to give me money again, said I should take the baby and start over somewhere else, whether Mama wanted to leave or not." Her voice was again the listless monotone it had been at the start; we were coming full circle. "But Gerard, he'd just find me, make me come back..."

It was growing late; the lunch-hour was ending. The worker-bees had all pretty much departed the restaurant, and the morning-league bowlers, their games wrapping up, were filing in to replace them. Emily June had been squirming and stretching in her sleep, off and on, for the last few minutes. Now she woke and, with wide eyes, looked around as if trying to figure out where she was. Yoli freed her from the carrier and hoisted her up into her arms. The baby smiled and squeaked and batted her mother's face once or twice until Yoli could catch her little hand. She turned Emily June and sat her on her lap, facing the table. The baby, of course, went immediately for the remnants of Yoli's lunch, and Yoli calmly moved everything out of the way. Then Emily June noticed me, across the table, and stared hard.

Yoli laughed a little. "Sometimes she does that, if we're out somewhere or something. I guess she doesn't usually see too many white people." She nuzzled the back of the baby's head.

Elmo said, "Yoli, the only way you're ever gonna be rid of that snake is to help us put him away. Between what you know and what the police in two states know—the feds too—we can get him locked up until your baby girl there is a grandmother."

"No way, mister." Some of the fire and steel that was in her voice when she threw us out of her mother's house crept back in now, but under it was still a note of tired fatalism. "Only reason I agreed to talk to you at all was so's your friend here wouldn't make a scene down to the school. I also was hoping that once you knew how things stand, you'd leave me and my family alone. Things are bad enough without you poking around, stirring things up, making everything worse."

"We can pack it in, Yoli," I said, "but the cops are going to keep the heat turned up all the same. They think Darius's death stinks too."

"Cops don't worry nobody; nobody down there talks to cops, leastways not anybody who ever knows anything. Look, I'd really like to help you—really—but I just can't. Me and my family, we're as good as dead if Gerard finds out I even talked with you. That's why I acted the way I did the other day, up at the house, but you already figured that."

I said, "We'll get you protection. OPD will put you and your family someplace safe. Wizard's wanted by the feds too: if you testified, they'd relocate you, give you new identities, get you set up—"

"Yeah, I hear all about them kinda programs," Yoli said derisively. "Problem is, *first* you gotta go through all the—what'd you call it?—folderol making a case, bringing it to trial, appeals, all like that. That could take years, couldn't it? Meanwhile, Gerard's got friends…"

"You'd be under constant protection," Elmo said.

"Uh-huh. Let me ask you straight, mister, and you tell me straight: can you absolutely, positively *guarantee* nothing would happen to Mama, Emily June, or me—ever?"

He said nothing.

I didn't seriously contemplate threatening her again. I doubt it would have worked, and after what she had told us I simply didn't have the stomach for it anymore. I had reached the line I wouldn't cross.

"Like I said, I'm really sorry," Yoli said. Again silent tears flowed down her face. "For Darius."

There were no tears for Yoli. None that were shed, at least.

CHAPTER

26

By the time I had redeposited Yoli at the Doctors Building and doubled back to Decatur Street, it was half past one and beginning to snow. The sky was an ashen canvas across which dust mice chased one another. The snow was as thin and sparse as an old woman's hair. There was no wind.

Elmo was in the living room when I came in, dividing his attention between the telephone, his Leatherette notebook, and a bottle of Harp. I threw my jacket in a chair and appropriated a beer for myself, then took it and the mail back to the desk in the bedroom.

I drank most of the beer and threw away most of the mail. If every letter I got that hit on me for money contained money instead, just a dollar or two, I would be wealthier than Donald Trump used to be. Alas, they did not. I saved the bills that absolutely had to be paid, the new issue of *The New Yorker*, and a letter for Jennifer, my wife, whom I hadn't seen in more than a year and whose whereabouts were currently unknown to me. From the return address, I gathered her high-school graduating class in Arlington was planning a reunion. Twentieth, that would be. It was hard to believe that it had been nearly twenty years since I first met her, in college; nearly fifteen since we were married. I wondered, idly, how many of those years we had actually spent together; it seemed that by now we must have spent the majority of them apart. But math was never my best subject, and there were cartoons to be looked at in *The New Yorker*, and I knew from experience that there was no point dwelling on my marital status. Ultimately it always came down to the same realization: that one of us would have to grow up sooner or later, face reality, and take the big step that neither of us wanted to take.

Elmo appeared in the doorway. "I was talking to a friend of mine, a U.S. Marshal in Chicago."

"Am I the only one who always thinks of James Arness whenever someone says 'marshal?' "

"No, that's what most marshals think of too," Elmo said, seating himself on the fold-out sofa against the wall. "My friend's guess is that neither FlashMan nor the Harris girl would have any trouble cutting some kind of immunity deal in return for testimony against Gizzard, and they'd be accepted right into WitSec without a hitch. I didn't name names, of course, just circs."

"This part of the country is crawling with relocated wiseguys who rolled over on hoods back east," I said. "Makes sense: you want to find Sal Manella, who ratted out Tony 'Big Chicken' Tetrazzini back in Brooklyn, you're not going to start looking in Spearfish, South Dakota. Question is, where do they relocate badguys *from* the Midwest?"

Elmo shrugged. "Julie had a good idea for taking care of these gangbangers: sic the Mafia on 'em."

"Even those guys have too much sense to want to screw around with the bastards."

"Yeah?" Elmo said. "What's that say about us?"

I drank some beer.

"My friend's gonna check with someone he knows in the U.S. Attorney's office," Elmo said, "but he said that everyone's in a sweat 'cause the 'war on drugs' has been nothing but a lot of talk. Sooner or later the big talkers are going to be up for election, so he figures they'd bend over backward for a chance to nail a big-time gangbanger like Gerard."

"The possibility that they might not only get Gerard but also get him to roll over on some of the L.A. crowd ought to make them salivate, too."

"Oh my, yes," he agreed, and tipped back his bottle.

I leaned back and put my feet up on the corner of the desk. It had come to expect that kind of treatment. " 'Course, it's all pretty academic at the moment, isn't it. Yoli won't sing, and FlashMan hasn't exactly been ringing the phone off the hook."

"This isn't Western Union we're dealing with," Elmo said. "We don't know how long it might take for O'Neal to get word to his friend, how long before his friend can get word to FlashMan—"

"If he does it."

"—or how long before FlashMan can get word to us."

"If he does it."

"Pessimist."

"Realist."

"I figure if we haven't heard from O'Neal by tonight, we should call him and see where's he's at with it," Elmo said.

"And meanwhile?" I said.

"Wait."

I spent most of the afternoon on the living-room carpet, my back against the sofa, going over the editing job on The Next Book. This was only the first step in the protracted process known as publishing—well, second step: the first was for me to write the damn thing. Each step was more tedious than the last. At this stage, my job was to go over my editor's comments and suggestions on the manuscript, see what I thought about what he thought. I didn't mind that so much: though a chore, it was a chore that allowed for and even required some creativity. Besides, my editor—who was also my publisher, his being a small, independent house that continued to exist only because of a distribution arrangement with one of the big publishing companies—was one of the rare sort who thinks his job is to help a writer make his manuscript as good as it can possibly be, not make it the book that *he* would have written if only he had the time. Most of his recommendations were worthy; and when I decided one wasn't, it didn't seem to cause him undo ego trauma.

The fun, and the creativity, would start to evaporate fast, though. In a few weeks, I'd get the copyedited manuscript to review, which would involve all the nutsy-boltsy *who-or-whom?/that-or-which?/comma-or-semicolon?* minutiae that most people think of when they hear the word "edit." That can be sort of fun, since the "authorities" all disagree with one another and, as with doctors, you can always find one who agrees with you if only you have the patience to keep looking. But after that I would receive the galleys, uncorrected photocopies of the actual type for the book, and then it would simply be a matter of trying to catch typographical and other out-and-out errors. No room for creativity here—just two solid days' worth of tedium.

Yes, it is a glamorous life.

Elmo, for his part, spent part of the time sprawled in an armchair with a book he'd filched from my shelf, *The Ambition and the Power* by John M. Barry, about the fall of Speaker of the House Jim Wright. It was a pretty fat book, which made me wonder if Elmo thought he was going to be there awhile.

But he couldn't stay with it for more than a few paragraphs at a time. He'd get up and go after a cup of coffee. Then he'd read. Then he'd look through my tapes and CDs. Then he'd read some more. Then he'd go for his coat and step out the door for a smoke. Then he'd come back inside and begin the cycle, or a slight variation thereof, all over again.

Although he hadn't taken me up on the offer, I had told Elmo it was all right if he lit up indoors: it wasn't an afternoon you'd want to be out in if you didn't have to. The snow had picked up; so had the wind. By three-thirty it was dark enough in the living room that we needed the lamps on. When the snow had started, the temperature was close enough to the freezing mark that the snow melted on the pavement as soon as it hit; as the afternoon progressed, the temperature dropped and the wet pavement iced over and now was collecting snow on top of it. That sort of road condition makes grown insurance-company executives break down and cry.

At six I knocked off for the day, did some stretches to soothe my aching back and neck, and made some inquiries of a supperly nature. Neither of us could work up a lot of enthusiasm for venturing into the great outdoors. I prowled through the cupboards and the fridge and came up with three chicken breasts, a package of linguini noodles, and some other odds and ends. I put Elmo to work skinning and boning the chicken and cutting it into small pieces while I cooked the pasta and cobbled together a kind of Alfredo sauce. Since I didn't have any cream, I had to use milk and let it reduce. I laced it with Chef Paul's Louisiana Cajun Magic, which I also rubbed on the chicken before I shoved it under the broiler. Elmo sliced a green pepper and grated carrots and a little parmesan while I called the boys to see if they'd care to join us. A couple of minutes after they arrived with a six-pack of Grolsch, I split half a dozen wheat buns and put them in the oven. French or Italian bread would have been better, but you make do. I divvied up the noodles, put the vegetables, chicken, and cheese over them, and ladled the quasi Alfredo sauce over the works, with the wheat buns on the side. It must have been okay; there were no leftovers.

We talked about my literary escapades, Elmo's girls, Robert's on again-off again memory, and the outrageous price hike at Jim's health club. We talked about movies and TV shows; Robert, as usual, chided me for being one of the few people in North America who doesn't own a VCR. I pointed out that I'd had color TV only a couple of years, and then only because I couldn't get replacement tubes for the old DuMont. We listened to a new Mannheim Steamroller "Fresh Aire" disc Jim brought with him. We talked about whether the Metrodome could, would, or should lure the College World Series from

Rosenblatt Stadium to Minneapolis-St. Paul. We drank all of the Grolsch and some of my Harp, and two pots of coffee.

None of it made the phone ring.

The following day was Tuesday. At eleven A.M. the phone rang. I answered it. There is a rhythm to the universe.

"You the white guy or the black guy?"

"The white guy," I said.

"Lemme talk to the black guy."

I hit the hold button and held the receiver out to Elmo. "I think it's your pal. Give me a minute to get on the extension."

He nodded, took the handset, and waited with his finger poised over the hold button.

I trotted back to the bedroom and sat down at my desk. I had a plain old no-frills beige desk phone back there.

As with most things, there is a right way and a wrong way to eavesdrop on a phone conversation. The wrong way is the way they always do it on TV: pick up the receiver *real slow-like* and clamp a palm over the mouthpiece. No matter how light a touch you have, there's going to be a pop or click when the line opens, and clamping your hand over the mouthpiece creates a heavy, swirling sound in the other guy's receiver. It makes him think he's got hold of a seashell instead of a telephone.

The right way to do it is the way we had set it up already in anticipation of FlashMan's calling. I had previously un-screwed the mouthpiece from the phone on my desk and put it in a drawer. Now, when I got sat down I called out, "Three, two, one," and lifted the receiver. At almost the same instant Elmo hit the hold button in the other room and said hello.

Since there was no microphone on my extension, I could sit there and sing sea chanteys and FlashMan would hear nothing. I, on the other hand, could plainly hear both sides of the conversation.

Such as it was.

Elmo said, "Hello."

"You the black guy?"

"Yeah. This FlashMan?"

"Don't be stretchin' this out. No way you can trace this."

"Why would we want to," Elmo said, "since we know who you are and where you live?"

There was a brief pause.

"Heard you wanna talk to me."

"Yes."

"Maybe I don't wanna talk to you."

"Then why'd you call," Elmo said.

There was another brief pause.

"What you wanna talk 'bout," FlashMan said.

"Keeping you alive."

"I already 'live," FlashMan said.

"I said 'keeping,' " Elmo said. "After that business Friday night, keeping you alive might take some doing."

"Yeah? Whyzat?" He sounded like he wanted to know almost as badly as he wanted to know what made the Big Bang go bang.

"Because my friend threw some mud at you, and I think we both know what will happen if Gerard Jones thinks even a little of it stuck."

Another pause.

"Wait," FlashMan said. "Call you back."

"He's interested, at least," Elmo said when I came out of the back room.

"That's what you call being interested?" I said.

"He wouldn't have called if he wasn't a little bit curious about what we had to say to him."

"Or unless he's planning something fun for us."

"Shit, man, *you're* the one said this was worth a shot," Elmo said.

"It probably is," I said. "I just wonder who's going to be doing the shooting."

CHAPTER

27

I parked as close to the front door as possible and took the car out of gear.

"Early," Elmo said, checking his watch. It was just shy of 1:30 P.M.

"The streets weren't as bad as I expected," I said. "Anyhow, you won't have to wait." I jerked a thumb over my shoulder. Elmo turned and saw what I had already seen in the rearview mirror, a shiny red BMW with the license plate fLASH.

"Shit," Elmo said in disgust. "Man, used to be if the cops saw a black kid nineteen, twenty years old driving around in a car like that, they'd pull him over, figuring he stole it. Probably had, too, kid that age. Now, they don't even bother. They know he not only didn't steal it, he probably owns it free and clear. Meanwhile, I'm making payments on a '92 minivan. Used. No personalized plates."

"Vanity plates are just bumper stickers that don't come off at the car wash," I said.

"That supposed to make me feel better?"

"I know I'd feel better if I came in with you," I said. "To cover your back." We had already had this conversation—about fourteen times in the last forty-five minutes, since FlashMan called back.

"Seeing you might spook him," Elmo said. "You're pretty

ugly, you know. Anyhow, he said he would only talk to me."

"That supposed to make me feel better?"

He grinned. "Look, if this was a set-up, they'd be setting us both up."

"I still don't like this. I don't know this place, and he conveniently didn't give us enough time to case it." We were parked in front of a restaurant called Helen's Kitchen, which may or may not have been a pun.

"Relax," Elmo said. "How could FlashMan know you didn't know this place? He's probably just worried about being seen talking to me, and picked this place 'cause it's so far away from the project." It was that, being located clear the hell past 132nd Street off of Center. There isn't too much of Omaha west of that.

"You carrying?" I said.

"The pope Polish?" Elmo said. "Everything's cool. You sit tight, listen to the radio or something." He got out of the car and went up a kind of gangplank to the building's entrance. You entered sideways to the front of the building, through a glass-and-wood vestibule that did not suit the rest of the structure. Except for the vestibule, it was a dark rustic-looking building with a vaguely nautical look—the gangplank, complete with a "handrail" of fat roping, porthole-like windows and a few other such touches—that said it had begun life as the home of one or another of the seafood chains.

I hadn't been inside it in any of its incarnations, so I didn't know if it featured a good position from which I might have seen but not been seen. With FlashMan already on the premises, there was no safe way of finding out. We couldn't afford to spook him: he was our only chance to get Wizard. Not having me watching his back didn't concern Elmo, or at least he didn't let on that it did. He pointed out that the short notice was probably just a matter of scheduling: FlashMan saw where he could be away from the turf for a while with no one thinking anything of it.

That made sense. Why didn't it make me feel better?

I let the car run so I could keep the heater going: the day was cold and blustery, occasionally flinging a hard, gritty snow that sounded like handfuls of fine sand being thrown against the side of the car. We had received about four inches of snow overnight. That meant six or eight real inches on the ground in most spots: I don't know what sort of ruler the Weather Service uses. Either way, it wasn't much, but it was enough to throw the city into near-paralysis. You'd think it never snowed in Nebraska. But the first snow, or the first one after a long dry spell, invariably produces among even lifelong residents roughly the same effect that four inches of snow might elicit if it fell on, say, Honolulu.

The radio was playing the latest great pop tune from the sixties to be "improved" by some adenoidal teenager whose biggest gig till now had been as opening act at a shopping-mall ribbon-cutting. I realize that the people who originally cut those songs were themselves adenoidal teenagers at the time, but they were adenoidal teenagers who possessed something that today's adenoidal teenagers lack. Talent, let's call it.

I turned off the radio, sat back, and waited for my friend.

It was just as Elmo had expected. The lunch hour passed, the restaurant was only thinly populated. FlashMan D. was seated in a corner booth at the back of the dining room, away from the tinted round windows, his back to the wall. He was dressed conservatively, by his standards: black leather pants, baggy dark-gray shirt with a small irregular neon-green pattern running through it, bolo tie, blue-lensed sunglasses, and a black hat something like the one Zorro wore. No red silk jacket. But the clip on his tie was the color of blood.

He didn't wave when Elmo entered the room, nor did he make any sign of recognition as the man came over to the booth. For all Elmo knew, he could have been asleep behind the shades' round lenses.

Elmo slid into the booth, his back against the other wall of the corner. He wondered if FlashMan had planned it that way, that neither of them would have his back exposed, neither of them would be in a vulnerable position, and immediately decided that of course he had. The man was a seasoned gangbanger, had lived long beyond the life-expectancy for a member of his profession. That doesn't happen by leaving many things to chance.

Which made Elmo wonder which of the few other patrons was FlashMan's "shotgun," his backup. Elmo had been certain all along that this meeting was not a trap for him. But he was just as certain that someone in FlashMan's position would have someone watching his back. If there was someone he felt he could trust.

Elmo glanced casually around the quiet, dimly lighted room. That slender man across the room, was he the one who had been so reluctant to surrender his weapons Friday night? Possibly—it was hard to recognize these guys when you saw them in mufti. But it didn't matter.

FlashMan had continued to stare straight ahead, as if unaware that Elmo had joined him. The blue shades made him look like a blind man. A waitress materialized and Elmo took it upon himself to order coffee for them both. When she had gone, returned, and gone again, FlashMan finally spoke, without turning his head or altering his expressionless expression in any way. "You wanna talk," he said. "Talk."

"The boy you killed was my nephew," Elmo said. "My sister's oldest. Family, you understand me?"

FlashMan inclined his head the barest fraction of a degree.

"I want the animals who killed him—all of you. But I'll settle for Gizzard."

FlashMan showed his teeth. "Uh-huh."

"Here's how it plays, Richie." The younger man turned his head slightly toward Elmo, but said nothing. "I know about Gizzard and Yoli Harris. I know how he used her, I know how she broke away from him. I know about her and Darius, too, and I know that burned Gizzard, hurt his pride. I know he forced Yoli to get Darius to the project that night so he—you, the Bloods—could kill Darius. Gizzard thought it'd look like another drive-by, that the cops wouldn't push it too hard. He was wrong. He was stupid. The whole business reeked from the beginning: the cops *had* to push. They have to keep pushing."

"Man don't bother Bloods none."

"Bullshit. You got so much heat on you, brother, you've lost ten pounds since I saw you Friday night. You wouldn't be sitting here if that wasn't so."

FlashMan remained silent for some time. His broad features—what Elmo could see of them—were placid. In time he said, "Still ain't heard you say nothin', man."

"All right, then hear this: You're on thin ice. I got a rope to pull you in with."

"Uh-huh."

Elmo shrugged, tried to make it look casual, unimportant. "Man, you were there Friday night. You heard what my friend said about you. You saw how Gizzard reacted."

FlashMan's upper lip moved. Not a smile, not exactly. "Shit, that so lame. That asshole, he just stallin' for time— stallin' for you to show up." He shook his head slowly.

"You saw how Gizzard reacted," Elmo repeated.

"He no fool," FlashMan said, but only after a moment. "He see what goes down."

"Really? Feel like betting your life on it?"

FlashMan said nothing.

Elmo said, "Here's the thing, Richie. Even if you're a stand-up guy, Gizzard can't afford to take the chance. Not with the heat on the way it is now."

"Bullshit. That honkie jive dint fool him none."

"What makes you say that? 'Cause you're still alive enough to be talking about it? Man, Gizzard's just thinking it over, thinking about every time you and him had a disagreement about something. Like Friday night in front of the Mini-Mall."

Another long moment passed before FlashMan spoke. "Been me an' Wizard a long time now."

226

"How much does that count for? With the pressure on. With Gizzard crazy as a junebug and getting crazier every day."

FlashMan angled his head ever so slightly toward Elmo. Elmo had the distinct impression that the man was actually looking at him.

"You know he's crazy, Richie, don't you," Elmo said. "He's probably always been crazy, but now it's starting to drag him down. Killing my nephew, trying to kill me and my friend—twice—all of that. Crazy. It's gonna undo him, and it's gonna undo you too. Unless you move first."

He exposed his upper teeth again. "Uh-huh."

Elmo said, "I talked to a man I know. He said the feds want Wizard real bad. You probably know that already. But he also said that the guy who gives them Wizard can name his own tune. Immunity, new ID, money—the whole nine yards, man."

FlashMan's smile stayed in place. "Yeah, I hear you honkie friend tellin' Wizard all 'bout them *programs*. Shit. Don't know nothin' 'bout the Bloods, man. Don't know nothin' 'bout the *code*."

"Right, tell me about that," Elmo said, sneering. "Start with how Bloods do a drive-by on their own turf, try and make like it's someone else, not them." He grunted a caustic laugh. "Kinda pussy, ain't it, Rich? I mean, why didn't you guys maybe dress up like old women, beat the boy to death with your canes or something? Code."

The other man sat motionless. "Don't know nothin'," he repeated firmly but calmly.

"I know Gizzard's a coward; you know it too, man. He's good at beating up women—killing them, if he's got enough backup and there's no chance of him getting caught."

"You fulla shit, nigger. He the main man. He the Top Prez. He kill you, he hear you talk like that."

"Right. If he's got three, four, a dozen homeboys with him, all armed with AK-47s, assault pistols, howitzers, bazookas, boomerangs, and a sackful of sharp rocks. They pile into a stolen car, drive past me on the street, turn me into hamburger. Yeah, that's what I call real bravery, man." He leaned in closer. "That's all jive. You know it, I know it, so let's cut the crap, huh? Ol' Gizzard has a long history of hiding behind someone else when he settles his scores—except with women. He's aces when it comes to pushing women around. Like Yoli Harris. He made her set Darius up. Threatened to kill Yoli's mother and her baby. Your baby, Rich."

FlashMan again moved his head a few degrees, as if looking at Elmo. The Reverend O'Neal had said Yoli told no one who the baby's father was; did that include the baby's father? And if so, how could that be used now?

"He won't deal man-to-man," Elmo went on. "That's 'cause it takes balls to be a man, and Gizzard ain't got any—that about the size of it, Rich?"

The younger man remained silent. He seemed to notice the coffee in front of him for the first time, took the gray pedestal mug between his two big, fleshy hands, and raised it slowly to his lips.

"Here's what I'm saying, Richie," Elmo went on. "This much pressure, someone pops. Always do. Maybe even Gizzard himself. If you don't move first, someone else will."

The other man sat still.

"That's assuming he doesn't first decide he can't risk it with you and has you dusted," Elmo said.

A good long time passed. Then FlashMan spoke. "Blow smoke somewhere else, nigger," he said with finality.

Elmo suppressed a sigh and poured himself more coffee from the bronze-colored plastic pot on the table. He had come to this conference armed with two proposals, and had led with what he considered the weaker. It was time to try the one that FlashMan would be more likely to go for, but which would produce less satisfying results.

"All right, try this: You don't give up the Bloods; you just give up Gizzard."

Again FlashMan's big head swiveled a few degrees toward

Elmo and his lips parted. "Same thing, man."

"No way. You won't give up the Bloods because you're loyal, right?"

"Right. That be the code."

"Gizzard broke the code when he started using the gang to fight his personal battles—when he put all the Bloods at risk because a girl dumped him. He betrayed the Bloods when he did that. He doesn't deserve any loyalty."

After a long while FlashMan gave one of his almost imperceptible nods. "May be. But I can't be doin' him in without I'm doin' in the whole gang, man. I know how it work."

"No, you don't understand. I'm not saying go to the man, testify, all like that. I think you should, but I know where you're coming from on that one. So I'm saying, okay, next best thing is you give *me* the goods on Gizzard. Everything you got—names, dates, places, all that shit. I give it to the cops, see what they can make of it with what they already have. Nobody mentions your name, ever. Meanwhile, you keep your eyes open for a time when they can move in on Gizzard and close him down for good—you know what I mean, catch him holding the bag. They take Gizzard out, you step in." He shrugged. "You're safe, Yoli's safe, the baby's safe. Everybody's happy."

That wasn't quite true—Elmo Lammers, for one, wouldn't be truly happy unless Wizard paid for the only crime that mattered to Elmo: his nephew's murder. But life imposes its compromises; Elmo was old enough, and wise enough, to understand that, even if he didn't especially like it. In this instance, the best outcome would be that everyone responsible for Darius's death would be tried for that crime. The worst outcome was that none of them would be. In between those two extremes was a whole series of compromise alternatives, including the one Elmo now proposed—nailing Wizard for *anything*. Less satisfying than nailing him for what mattered, naturally; but far more so than seeing him go scot-free.

Elmo also realized that if FlashMan had ever entertained a

thought of usurping Wizard but lacked the opportunity, this suggestion might be tailor-made. It would be far, far less risky than a direct coup attempt. FlashMan's exposure would be minimal; it would be the cops who actually effected Wizard's ouster, and only natural that the number-two man, FlashMan, would step in.

It seemed that FlashMan considered it worth thinking about: at least, he took his time before replying. When he did his voice was low and measured.

"Got a better idea," he said. "Faster and surer. Whack Wizard."

Elmo waited.

"Lotsa fat lawyers sittin' around waitin' to get the brothers sprung when the man comes down on us. You never keep Wizard behind no bars. You want him, you got to kill him."

"So why haven't you?"

FlashMan smiled lazily. He seemed to look nowhere. "Like bein' alive, man. Can't line up soldiers, 'cause no way tellin' whose side they really be on. Man got friends."

"All the more reason to play it my way, Richie," Elmo said.

"Told you, won't work. Way to play it is I tell you where and when, you score the hit."

"You want me to kill Wizard."

"What you want too, man. I see it. Seen it the other night. You like to kill me too, only you need me. That's cool. We help each other, like you been sayin'. You get what you want, I get what I want." His lips parted in his humorless smile. "Everybody happy, like you say."

The restaurant seemed to pitch and yaw before Elmo; he took his coffee mug in both hands as if to steady himself with it. It wasn't FlashMan's suggestion that rocked him—Christ, he had been fighting the same temptation from the very beginning. What threw him now was the way in which part of him—that shadowy, base part he wished he could pretend wasn't there—leaped enthusiastically at FlashMan's proposal. After Friday night, Elmo thought he had successfully quashed that part of him. Not so, obviously. It required a conscious, determined effort now to quell the impulse to go along with FlashMan's scheme. It required a few minutes, too, and FlashMan misunderstood the man's long silence.

"Make it worthwhile for you, too," he said casually.

Elmo smiled grimly. He took in FlashMan's expensive wardrobe, recalled the shiny BMW out in the lot, Wizard's Porsche, the sums of money that Yoli indicated comprised the gang's drug business. FlashMan could indeed make it worth Elmo's while, and the money would solve a lot of problems for him and Julie and the girls. But when he thought about the girls he thought about all the times and all the ways he and Julie worried about them, worried about the people they met and the pressures and temptations they faced. Like most parents, drugs were at the top of their list of things they feared most. Drugs meant operators like FlashMan—too smart to take them but perfectly willing to inflict them on others. For the money. If Elmo took some of that money, what would that make him?

He shook his head, and smiled. The smile was there because he knew that FlashMan had unintentionally made the temptation easier for Elmo to resist by offering him money. If not for that...

"Suit yourself, man," FlashMan said, and made as if to leave.

"Whacking Gizzard would only solve part of your problem, Rich," Elmo said. "You're still stuck with Darius's murder: the cops won't stop their investigation just because Gizzard's out of the picture."

FlashMan shrugged. "No problem, man."

"You get rid of Gizzard your way, you can't give him up. You've lost your ticket. But the others, the other guys in on Darius's murder, they still have a bargaining chip: you. Things get hot, they can always roll over on you. You'll probably have to kill them too. Then you're up to your ass in charges—accessory to murder, conspiracy to commit murder, three or four counts of murder one."

The other man got up and moved away from the table.

"Long as Gizzard's alive, your neck's in the noose," Elmo said. "If the cops grab him, they get you too."

FlashMan hesitated in his slow, unruffled movement away from the table, but only for a moment. Then he continued on toward the door. Elmo resisted the urge to throw his coffee cup at the back of the man's head.

CHAPTER

28

I was sprawled across the front seat of the car, feet up, back against the driver's-side door. It sometimes seems I've spent a lifetime sitting in a car waiting for something to happen. I had been keeping an eye on the restaurant entrance in case Elmo gave me the high-sign. That's why I immediately noticed the flash of reflected light as the inside door opened. I straightened up.

It wasn't Elmo but FlashMan D., moving slowly and confidently, cool, unflappable, as if he had all the time in the world. He stepped out of the vestibule and paused at the top of the rough-wood gangplank as if waiting for someone.

The inside door had barely closed when it opened again. Elmo came into view, moving through the vestibule and out the outer door. He said something to FlashMan. The other man might have been listening; he gave no sign of it and his eyes were invisible behind the round lenses of his shades. I was too far away to have heard over the wind even if I had had the engine off and the windows down.

I did hear a car engine fire up, however; I didn't give it a thought. This was a parking lot, after all.

My eyes were on the two men in front of the restaurant. Elmo was talking; FlashMan was shaking his big head, but only barely, as if he had a stiff neck. The slight motion was constant, though. Elmo wasn't making quite the progress we had hoped.

Then there was another glint of reflected light, this time in my rearview mirror. It came from the dark-tinted windshield of a white older-era Olds Cutlass that had pulled in behind me and the few other cars parked in front of the place.

The Oldsmobile's doors flew open.

I kicked open my door.

The sudden activity had already caught Elmo's attention. By the time I got my head out the door and yelled at him, he had already grabbed FlashMan's sleeve and gone into a half-crouch, half-dive for the vestibule door.

My yell was lost in the racket thrown up by perhaps half a dozen rifles and pistols.

The second-to-last thing I saw before I ducked back into the Impala and flattened myself across the seat was the glass top-half of the vestibule wall dissolve in a flash of flying shards. By then Elmo was no longer visible, so I presumed and prayed that he was lying safely on the floor, protected by the thick rough wood that made up the lower half of the vestibule wall.

The last thing I saw in that heartbeat's-span before I took cover was Richard Dayton. He had foolishly torn away from Elmo and run out toward the parking lot, perhaps in the insane hope he could reach his car and make a getaway. When I last saw him he was six feet down the gangplank, gyrating like someone with St. Vitus' dance, all but invisible inside a cloud of pink mist that had sprung up around him.

And then I was flat on my belly on the seat of the car. Somehow the .38 that had been on my right hip was in my right hand. With my left I popped open the glove compartment and dragged out the old canvas bag. I shook out the gun and the speed-loader and threw the bag and its box of cartridges back into the glovebox. If you're in a situation where you need more than eighteen bullets, you won't have time to reload.

The noise was truly terrifying, in the exact sense of the word.

It was as if the world had exploded, and the explosion went on and on without end.

A stray round took out the rear window of my car: cold air and a few beads of safety glass washed over me.

From far away I heard human sounds—screams, crying. From inside the restaurant, probably. Anyone sitting near the large porthole windows at the front must have been severely injured, even dead, mowed down by bullets or sliced to ribbons by flying plate-glass.

I wondered about Elmo. There was no point wondering about FlashMan.

As quickly as it started, the cataclysm of bullets stopped. I stayed put, though, until I heard the squeal of tires behind me: the sound must have been very clear through the gaping hole that used to be my car's back window, but my ears seemed to be stuffed with cotton batting. I poked my head up cautiously over the seat back and saw the big Oldsmobile tearing out of the lot, over a curb. I jumped out of the car to look for Elmo.

He emerged from the building, still crouched low. "I'm okay," he yelled. "I'll call it in. Get after 'em, man!"

Adrenaline is in charge of situations like this, and adrenaline doesn't think far enough ahead to wonder what the hell I would do if I caught up with them.

Miraculously, the engine was still running. I threw the car into reverse. Even more miraculously, the car was sitting on four wholly inflated tires. I backed around and aimed at the street.

The Olds had turned left out of the lot, not toward the heavily traveled West Center Road but into the neighborhood north of it. I followed.

Away from the main drag, shops and offices soon gave way to sleepier streets lined with the low-slung ranch-style houses that Realtors like to call "executive housing" in the newspaper ads. I was in trouble here: I didn't know the neighborhood, I didn't know which of the loopy meandering streets went anywhere and which doubled back on themselves. I hadn't managed to spot my quarry, and of course I didn't know where they were headed. They had surprised me by going left, north, and not straight out onto Center—surprised me and yet didn't surprise me. Center would give them a straight shot down to the I-680 interchange near 108th Street; but if they had scoped out this neighborhood, as I figured they had, they probably had a more devious, circuitous escape route in mind.

I projected a city map onto my mental movie-screen, but it wasn't much help: it had no details of this part of town. I knew that Highland Country Club was around here somewhere, north and east; I knew that Boys Town was just northwest of that. I knew that 132nd was effectively the last major north-south route on that side of town. So I wouldn't expect them to head west...except that if they had reconnoitered the territory, they might know how to pull a Christopher Columbus and get east by heading west.

Or they might head east to 120th, or north to Pacific, or double back south to Center...or they might switch to another car they had hidden along these streets that were laid out by a mapmaker with a severe palsy, and that would make things even more fun for me. There were just too many possibilities, and while I tried to sort through them—driving too fast for these residential streets that hadn't been snow-plowed or worn clear by traffic—I also managed to complete a rather lumpy circle: Helen's Kitchen was in sight now, at the bottom of a shallow hill.

No sense burning more gas; I headed for the restaurant.

A scream of car horns interrupted me. It had come from the east a few blocks.

I goosed the gas pedal and shot past the restaurant, out onto Center, just as my light turned against me. That didn't earn me any angry sounds from the cross-traffic: in Omaha, everybody jumps the pink light. When you cross the thin line between pink and red, though, your fellow motorists get peeved. As FlashMan's killers had just learned.

I spotted them a few blocks east of me. They must have

known how to wind through the neighborhood and come out on 120th, then doubled back southward to Center, undoubtedly intending to throw off any pursuers—as had just about worked.

Giving the Impala a little more gas, I made a lane-change there wasn't room for. That brought an angry toot.

The killers had caused a little fender-bender at the light. These guys did a lot of driving, but they weren't very good at it. It looked like they had decided they didn't need to wait their turn before turning left onto Center, and four lanes' worth of drivers disagreed with them. The Olds was caught in that no-man's land where the median broke for the cross-street. A westbound Toyota had clipped the Olds's rear fender; behind that a Ford pickup whose driver swerved to avoid rear-ending the Toyota had plowed into an LTD. That effectively stopped westbound traffic, and the westbound traffickers made their displeasure known.

Eastbound traffic, meanwhile, slowed to a comparative crawl. Cautious drivers wanted to see if it was safe to proceed; most of the rest of them just wanted to see.

And then there was me, slowed to two miles an hour, now about four blocks away. So close, as they say, yet so far. Not that I had yet hatched any idea what I would do if I caught them: my trusty six-shooters were no match for who-knew-how-many semiautomatic weapons.

Then I heard sirens: first ambulance, then police sirens. Maybe I wouldn't have to worry about it after all.

However, the killers had good ears too: the onset of the sirens spurred them to sudden action. With a crunch of abused metal and a new strain of horns to join the steady wail already being performed, the Olds bumped up over the median and into the eastbound lanes.

With much squealing of tires, my side of West Center Road came to a halt, too.

But I had seen that coming, and had already worked my way into the right-hand lane. Now I went up over the curb and down a snowy incline into the parking lot of one of the uncountable number of shopping centers that line the street. I skidded, fishtailing, parallel to Center, through the lot to an entrance that seemed to be beyond most of the congestion on the street, and reemerged onto Center just as the Olds screamed past.

By now even the most insane of Omaha's mostly insane driving population had realized that what was happening was beyond the pale; some of them had actually stopped their cars until they could figure out what was going on or it stopped going on, whichever came first.

That was good for me: there wasn't much in the way of obstacles between me and the Olds. I floored the gas pedal as fast as I dared; the Impala hesitated for a slice of a second, then jumped forward.

The needle on my clock surged up to the fifty-miles-an-hour mark. The Olds was going even faster.

If they had been smart, they would have headed south on 680, a nice easy right turn onto the ramp. But they had it in their heads to go north on the Interstate, which meant turning against the westbound traffic on Center. While the eastbound side of the median was relatively deserted thanks to the confusion we had left behind us, the other side of the street was even more congested than usual—thanks to that same confusion, which had slowed the oncoming traffic.

But such petty concerns are for mere mortals such as you and me: these guys didn't care a flying fig about the oncoming traffic: they just turned into it.

There was a lot of noise.

One of the oncoming cars clipped the Olds's rear fender—now it had a matched set—and the Olds skidded on the wet, slushy surface. I thought it might wind off the edge of the road and down the bank of the on-ramp. There wasn't much chance an ordinary car could drive up that steep slope, especially with the snow.

But the Oldsmobile's driver had a little more skill than I had credited him with, and managed to steer out of the spin. The car fishtailed up the long ramp to the freeway, but it was in no danger of sliding off and down the embankment on either side.

"Shit," I told the steering wheel.

Between the drivers who had sensibly stopped and the drivers who had been forcibly stopped, there wasn't much traffic flowing through this intersection now either. I had to steer a winding, hairpin course to get around the cars jutting partway into the intersection, but otherwise there was no obstacle between me and the on-ramp.

CHAPTER
29

It's a long ramp, and between my being slightly delayed down on the road and again while waiting for an opening in the freeway traffic—I couldn't imitate my friends' total disregard for courteous driving habits—there was no sign of them when I got up to the highway.

I put a little more strain on the gas pedal: sixty, seventy, eighty... The car had been built during a time when you customarily drove seventy or eighty miles an hour on the open road. But that time was now some time ago, and the Impala wasn't used to such demands. I wondered if it could take it. It was an old car—but so old that many major components were new. Even so, there were always belts and hoses and clamps that break only at the least opportune moments...

Eighty-five...ninety...

There was a fair amount of traffic, but a fair amount of that was pulled off to the side. I had my friends in the Olds to thank for removing most of the obstacles. Still, I had to do an awful lot of weaving. The driving lanes were worn clear, but between them was a three-foot-wide strip of filthy, slushy snow; every time I had to cross it the car lurched—and with it my heart, which currently resided somewhere in the vicinity of my Adam's apple. At the speed I was traveling, it wouldn't take much for the car to spin out and off the road. And I still hadn't spotted my friends.

Then there they were, at the Pacific Street interchange, their tires barely on the pavement.

The freeway here is almost straight, angling slightly to the northeast, until you get to Pacific. Then it curves fairly sharply to the east, crosses the Big Papillion Creek, and straightens again just south of the cloverleaf at West Dodge Road. Only someone resolutely committed to suicide would take that curve at ninety, ninety-five miles an hour—and the way my friends in the Olds were trying so frantically to escape proved they weren't interested in suicide. At the last possible instant, the Olds's brake lights came on. I was doing about ninety-five—at that speed, there was no time to look down at the meter—and now gave the gas pedal another goose.

It didn't do any good. After having owned the Impala for better than a decade, I finally knew what every car owner always idly wonders about, his car's upward limit. I risked a glance down: the needle hovered just shy of 100. The gauge went all the way up to 120.

Then I had to pump the brakes as I entered the curve.

The Olds's driver was braver or more reckless than me: he took the curve much faster than I dared and was already across the creek and into the straightaway. I realized there was no way I could overtake them: I had lost ground on the curve and couldn't match their speed. The best I could do was try to keep them in sight and hope that, for once, there would be a cop around when you needed one.

The freeway sort of bottoms out at the creek, then begins a long climb up to Dodge. They wouldn't be foolish enough to take the Dodge exit—the traffic there is even heavier than on Center. I was betting on them sticking with 680, which runs more or less straight north for another five or six miles, then curves eastward around the north side of the city. What their plan might be beyond that was an even bigger guess, but since I couldn't catch up with them anyway it didn't seem worth worrying about.

Only I *was* catching up.

They were just past the off-ramp to Dodge, so it wasn't that they were slowing for the turn. Nor were the Olds's brake lights illuminated. That familiar little alarm-bell of suspicion sounded gently in the back of my head, and I eased back on the gas pedal. Eighty, seventy, sixty-five—and I was still gaining on them.

I rolled down the window. Above the sound of my car's laboring and the rush of wind, I could make out a faint, faraway, rapid *putt-putt-putt* from the Olds. It wasn't the sound of a flat tire: my post-graduate work in old-auto mechanics prompted me to finger something under the hood—sticky valve, maybe, or a bad lifter. Whatever the cause, the point was that I had slowed down to a reasonable speed and I was still gaining on the Oldsmobile.

Now what?

I had one of the .38s tucked barrel-down between my thighs—very Freudian, that—and the other next to me, the barrel jammed into the groove between the seat and seat-back. I took the former gun into my right hand and steered with my left, letting gravity and the freeway's slight incline slow the car still further.

The Olds limped slowly along. I had to put the brakes on now. The rush of wind died to a whisper. The fluttery *putt-putt-putt* was louder. There were no sirens to be heard, no reassuring flashing red lights in my rearview mirror.

But there was a flash of red ahead of me as the Olds's brake lights came on. The car rocked to a stop. Then the back doors flew open simultaneously and two men jumped out. They held what appeared to be assault rifles—"appeared" because I didn't waste time making positive identification. I slammed on the brakes and dropped onto my side on the seat, wondering whether the car's firewall was designed to withstand the kind of fire it was in for.

The noise was slightly less deafening than the last firestorm, but only slightly. Bullets slammed into my car: it was as if six burly Irishmen had taken hold of the front end and were

242

rocking it, each to his own internal metronome. Glass and chrome metal flew. Though the gunmen were aiming lower, the windshield inevitably took a fatal hit and beads of glass rained heavily on me. I was on the seat with my arms protecting my head and my silly little revolver in my right hand. Among the panicky, insane thoughts that flew through my mind, one bobbed to the top: Never buy a car with a rear-mount engine.

Engine—

It was still running, but not for long.

The radiator went; a thick plume of steam billowed up. I could feel the sticky heat through the nonexistent windshield.

I reached over, winding my hand through the steering wheel, taking pains to keep my head well below dashboard level, and shifted the car into reverse. A shard of chrome sliced a narrow gutter across the back of my left hand.

My left foot was still on the brake pedal. I removed it and the car started moving, as much from the kinetic energy transmitted by the bullets plowing into it as from power of the idling engine.

A front tire went and the car lurched even more alarmingly than it had been.

I came up on my right elbow so as to be able to get a half decent grip on the wheel with my left hand. I couldn't see where I was going, of course, and I wasn't about to sit up and look. The important thing was that I was moving away from the source of destruction, and I didn't care about much beyond that.

The rearview mirror came loose with a *pang!* and flew into the back seat.

The speedometer showed five miles an hour. I gave the gas pedal a little encouragement and got it up to ten. The idiot light on the dash showed that the engine was overheating, thanks to the busted radiator, but that wasn't worth worrying about. There wouldn't be much left of the engine to salvage. My immediate concern was to salvage me.

The other front tire went, and the car spun to the right.

All of the idiot lights came on now: the engine was dead.

WILLIAM J. REYNOLDS

Immediately the wheel went stiff in my hand as the power-assist bled off. I popped into neutral and left it to momentum and gravity to keep the car moving away. It seemed that the slamming of bullets into the front end had slacked off a bit—maybe that was just wishful thinking. I waited a few seconds: the shooting stopped.

I poked my head up tentatively, over on the passenger's side, where I hoped they wouldn't be looking for it.

They weren't. They weren't looking at all. The cloud from the radiator was dense—it didn't help that it was a cold day—but not so dense that I couldn't see that the Olds's back doors were now closed: the gunmen had gotten back inside.

Then the Olds's white backup lights came on, and a new bolt of panic shot through me: They're coming to finish me off.

That terror vanished as fast as it arrived, though. Their interest wasn't me, it was getting rid of their crippled car and getting away. I was just in their way.

I sat up now, no longer worried about my safety. The Olds backed up as far as the exit for West Dodge Road. Then it *putt-putt-putt*ed up the ramp. Westroads was right there, along with a kazillion other shopping centers, office buildings, restaurants. I figured they'd ditch the Oldsmobile in a parking lot, boost another set of wheels, and be on the road again inside of five minutes.

In the course of all this, I somehow managed to overlook the fact that my car was still moving—slowly, but moving nevertheless. I was reminded of that when the horizon suddenly tilted away from me and I found myself looking at the gray sky through what used to be the windshield.

The Impala had rolled off the side of the freeway. It rolled down the embankment until the front wheels, devoid of rubber, left the pavement and dug into the snowy earth; then the back end slid a couple of feet and the whole works rocked to a stop.

I turned the ignition to off and pocketed the keys. Old habits. Slowly, on legs made of sponge, I climbed out of the car. It

244

was a total loss, of course. I had expected that, but even so the reality of it was worse than I had anticipated. There was nothing left of the front of the car—the grille, the headlights, the bumper, the front part of the hood where it curved down to meet the grille, all of it was just plain gone. The hood and fenders looked like they had been the main course for some giant metal-eating insects from hell. The side mirror was gone, mount and all. No sign of it anywhere. Probably vaporized. I knew where the windshield was: I was currently brushing it out of my hair and clothing. The shots that took out the windshield had taken their toll on the top of the front and back seat benches, too, leaving their innards exposed to the elements.

If there was someone out there who needed a rear end for an ancient Chevy Impala, I might be able to salvage a couple of bucks out of the poor old thing.

On the sides of the car there were small chrome emblems, a stylized impala leaping through a circle, next to the word *Impala* in graceful chrome letters. Real chrome-plated metal, not colored plastic, which shows how old the car was. The emblem on the driver's side had come loose somehow and was hanging by a thread. I snapped it off, looked at it awhile, then slipped it into my pocket.

I was exhilarated, of course; nearly drunk on the thought that I was still alive and whole. It was foolish to let that joy be diminished even slightly by the demise of a hunk of metal and glass, a machine—and a machine that stubbornly refused to start when the weather was too cold or too wet. But there was no denying that my eyes felt hot as I looked at the old beast, and after a while I couldn't look at it anymore. Silly. But you forget that a car is a machine, an inanimate, unthinking, unfeeling object. You begin to think of it as a friend, someone sharing your adventures. And when that friend dies, you grieve, if only a little, and you forget the times you cursed it and its expensive habits. You miss it, and you know it will be a long time before you make another friend like that—and even then it won't be like that, it'll be different. But, then, the Impala was getting up there in years, had 169,000 miles on the clock, and had reached the point where parts were going out faster than replacement parts could be located. It was time. And as ridiculous as it sounds, I like to think this was the way the old thing would have wanted to go.

A few of the more stout-hearted drivers now were creeping up upon the scene; drivers in the southbound lane, across the median, who had pulled over when the racket started, now went quickly on their way. A black Volvo stopped near where I had gone off the road, and the occupants, two women, got out to see if I was okay.

I looked at my watch, for some reason. By my estimate, less than twenty minutes had passed from the time the first shots were fired at Helen's Kitchen until the last shots a couple of minutes ago. Yet it had been a long day.

And then I heard the sirens.

I sighed, balanced both of my revolvers in plain sight on what was left of the hood of the car, and dug out my wallet.

The Guys in Ties were already trying to yank my PI license; now they'd probably want to go after my driver's license, too.

CHAPTER
30

Elmo had lied when he said he was okay. He had in fact suffered a score of nasty slashes, two of which required stitches, when Helen's Kitchen's vestibule windows shattered all over him; and even before that happened he had caught a slug in his left calf as he dived into the vestibule. But the bullet had been traveling with such momentum that Elmo's leg barely slowed it on its way into the restaurant's façade, and the emergency-room doc at Bergan Mercy was able to clean the wound and sew it up without too much fuss and bother.

By the time I caught up with him again, Elmo was lounging in a wheelchair in an ER cubicle, his eyes a little glassy from the combined effects of shock and painkillers. His left pants-leg hung in shreds from the knee, showing the fresh white bandage around his shin. A dozen or more small cuts on his face, head, neck, and hands glistened with greasy antiseptic; a few neat stitches on his right cheek and the back of his right hand shined with the same goop.

I said, "Look, Lammers, you're simply going to have to break down and put a new blade in your razor."

He looked up and smiled stupidly. "Nee*brass*kah," he said.

The ER resident, a heavy young black man in serious-looking eyeglasses, said over my shoulder, "That leg will hurt like hell for a few days, after which it'll be stiff for a couple of weeks, but he shouldn't suffer any long-term effects."

"Hell," Elmo said. "I's hopin' t' be able t' fo'cas' th'weather."

I looked at the doctor. "That will start to wear off in four or five hours. You'll want to have these filled before then." He handed me a pair of prescription slips. "Painkiller, antibiotic. There's a pharmacy in the building."

"Thanks," I said, knowing I'd fill the scrips at Pat Costello's store. It wasn't as convenient as the hospital pharmacy, nor was it convenient to my place, but Pat and I go back a long way, and I always run as much business through his store as I can. Even when he doesn't have hospital bills to pay because of the unsavories who tried to scramble my eggs last fall.

After I had signed my name to sixty or seventy forms and satisfied the woman at the desk that the hospital was going to be reimbursed for its act of mercy, I wheeled Elmo out the automatic doors to Kim Banner's white Miata.

I had met up with Banner at what we in the trade call police headquarters, to which I had been hauled in order that I might recline in comfort while I gave my statement to everybody in turn except the assistant apprentice custodian. There had been some loose talk of a reckless-endangerment charge against me, plus a concealed-weapon gripe or two for the hell of it. But the cops who had been first on the scene had to admit that my weapons were right out in the open when they showed up, and since the guys who had caused the real reckless endangerment had gotten away—leaving the police department with egg on its collective face—no one was really all that keen about prolonging the agony by bringing charges against that heroic citizen who had gone after the killers. In slightly less time than is required to ratify a constitutional amendment, they decided there was no way around kicking me loose, and I went and scared up Banner.

"I have to go spring Elmo," I said. "Can I borrow your wheels?"

"In your dreams," she said helpfully.

"Why not?"

"Because you drive like a maniac."

248

"Nonsense. I drive a reasonable and prudent five miles per hour over the posted speed limit at all times."

"How could I have been so unfair." She didn't sound the least bit remorseful. "Let me ask you a question: How come you need to borrow a car?"

"Uh, 'cause mine sort of got totaled?"

"Uh-huh. Tell you what: I'll give you a lift. It's almost check-out time anyway."

And so she was waiting for us outside the ER entrance. It was a tight squeeze, but we all three got into the little car somehow. It helped that Elmo could feel no pain.

"Not gonna be much use for a day or two," Elmo said languidly after we manhandled him up the stairs and situated him on the sofa.

"You talk as if we had some idea what we're going to do next," I said.

"Maybe we could call Jack Reedy," Elmo said, "use his pull over at SAC t' arrange a' air strike on that buildin' where the fuckers live."

"They're probably not allowed to do that sort of thing within the city limits," I said.

Banner helped herself to a couple of Harps—the second one was for me, since Elmo was on the wagon for the time being—and said, "We're leaning hard on anyone who might have anything to say about this afternoon's festivities: informants, small-change pushers, a couple of ex-gangbangers, Mad Dads, other citizen groups—the whole ball of wax. So far, exactly zip. The guess around the shop is that people are just too damn scared of Wizard. After all, FlashMan was his right-hand man, and a power in his own right. If Wizard would kill FlashMan—and who else could be behind it?—then he won't think twice about killing anyone."

"How'd he know?" Elmo said.

"About your meeting?" She shrugged and settled into a chair. She had on a blue corduroy skirt and jacket over a pale-yellow sweater and blue checked shirt. Her butterscotch hair, which she used to wear in what twenty-five years ago would have been called a "Beatle haircut," was shorter these days, almost boyish—although "boyish" is not a word that leaps to mind when I think of Kim Banner. The number of women who can carry off such a hair style is far smaller than the number of women who try. Banner could carry it off. "At least one other person besides you two and FlashMan knew about the meeting—assuming your guess was right about FlashMan having had a backup in the restaurant, and I'd bet money he did."

I knew that Elmo had filled in Banner and the other cops at the scene before he'd let himself be taken to the hospital, including his belief that FlashMan had someone in Helen's Kitchen watching his back. I also knew that any such someone had faded like a summer afternoon before anyone could even think of getting his opinion of current events.

"Maybe FlashMan's trust in his backup man was misplaced," Banner was saying. "Maybe someone else overheard FlashMan setting up the appointment. Maybe Wizard had someone keeping an eye on him." She shrugged again and drank some beer.

"By the way," I said, "has anyone polled our lad?"

Banner nodded. "You'll like this: From one o'clock until nearly two-thirty Gerard Jones, a.k.a. Wizard, and two 'financial advisers' were with a real-estate agent. Viewing 'investment properties'—Mister Jones's phrase—downtown near the Central Park Mall. You know, all those old warehouses and shit they're renovating? The Realtor and the money guys back him up. Everyone's story meshes with everyone else's. Well, heck, they might even be telling the truth—Wizard wouldn't have to be on hand to be behind the shooting."

"He would want to *not* be on hand," I said, "and you wouldn't expect him to be alibi-less in any case."

"Could be why FlashMan gave you such short notice," Banner said. "He found out Wizard would be occupied, thought it'd be safe for him to be AWOL for an hour or so."

Her voice took on a note of longing. "Sure would've been nice if you'd talked him into rolling over on Wizard and the rest of that lot."

"We wouldn't be any better off," I said. "FlashMan would be just as dead; we'd merely have the satisfaction of knowing he *would've* helped us."

Banner looked glum. "Did I tell you we found the car? You called it: one of the Westroads lots. I feel sorry for the owner. We're going over it with a fine comb, and knocking on every door within six blocks of where it was stolen. That might lead to something," she said optimistically.

The phone rang. Elmo had dozed off on the sofa; he flinched when the bell sounded, but he didn't really wake up. I grabbed it before the second ring.

"I just heard about Richie," Yoli Harris said without preamble. Her voice was not hysterical but it was extremely animated: her words climbed over one another in their effort to get out. "Sweet Jesus, I can't believe it! I can't believe he'd really go and kill Richie. They were so close… It was Gerard done it, wasn't it?"

"A lot of people would go along with that," I said vaguely.

"Oh, Lord—" She broke off in a kind of choked sob. "It's my fault, too. If I'd helped you like you asked, you wouldn't've had to try Richie and he'd still be alive."

"No, that deal was already in the works." I was well aware that, while I was talking with a woman who was implicated in a murder, another woman who happened to be a sworn officer of the law was sitting roughly four feet away. "One didn't have anything to do with the other."

"First Darius, now Richie," Yoli said stubbornly. "They'd both be alive now, except for me."

"Now that's no good," I said firmly. "Listen, I've got some people here; I'll have to call you back later."

"I know what you must think of me," Yoli said. "But I swear to you I didn't know one thing about what happened to poor Richie. Gerard, he never said or did anything while I was around—else I'd've warned Richie."

"Everybody knows that."

"That man is an animal," she said. "He's gotta be locked up, just like a mad dog. I don't care what it takes or what it costs: I will do anything you want me to do to help put that bastard behind bars where he belongs."

"You should maybe think about that some more," I said. "Conditions haven't improved any, you know. Maybe they're worse, in fact."

"I don't care." There was a hard, defiant recklessness in her voice. When you considered her almost tangible fear when we talked to her the previous afternoon, this new determination to stand up to Wizard was especially admirable. It crossed my mind that if more people were willing to stand up to the gangs—a majority of people instead of a relative handful, and not just in afflicted neighborhoods but everywhere around town, all across the country—the situation would be a lot different than it currently was. Of course, that can be said of any case of terrorism, despotism, or oppression. And, as always, it's easier said than done.

"Well, there's more to it than just that," I said.

"I don't care," she repeated. "You help me make sure Mama and my baby'll be safe and I'll do whatever you want."

"I'll get back to you real soon. Meanwhile, you just hang loose, okay?"

"I won't do nothing till I hear from you," Yoli promised, and hung up.

"Yeah, and say hello to Susan and the kids for me," I said to the dead air.

I smiled at Banner. "My insurance man," I said. "Can't wait to see what my new premium's gonna look like."

"Uh-huh," she said. "Too bad, too, after you just got it out of the shop again."

I got up and went after another beer, which gave me a moment to think. Roughly thirty hours ago I would have jumped at Yoli Harris's offer to help nail Wizard. Between what she knew about the transfer of drugs and money between the Bloods on the coast and the Bloods in the Heartland and what she knew about Darius LeClerc's demise, Yoli's testimony could put Mr. Gerard Jones away for a goodly time. No matter how many high-test lawyers the gang had on retainer.

But in a single afternoon I had witnessed, and too closely, just how ruthless these bastards really were. And how thorough. And how well informed. Richard Dayton presumably knew even better than Yoli just how dangerous Wizard was. Presumably he had taken pains to keep his dissatisfaction and burgeoning treachery secret; presumably he had taken precautions before going to meet Elmo. Yet look what had happened.

And that, of course, was the message that Wizard wanted to send; that's why FlashMan died where and when and the way he died.

Well, I received that message loud and clear. And having received it made me a lot less enthusiastic about employing Yoli Harris, no matter her feelings now. I kept coming back to the question she had asked Elmo: *Can you absolutely, positively* guarantee *nothing would happen to Mama, Emily June, or me—ever?*

Yesterday we knew the answer was no. Today we *damn sure* knew the answer was no.

But with FlashMan gone, what other weapon did we have?

Banner came into the kitchen. "What's the hold-up, you bottling that stuff yourself?"

I pried the lids off a couple of bottles and handed her one. "How good's witness protection?" I said. "Really."

She looked at me. "Your insurance man planning to blow the whistle on someone?"

I shrugged.

"Uh-huh. Well, the answer, I'm sure you know, is: It depends."

I jerked my head and she followed me down the hall to the back room. I closed the door.

"Pretty sneaky way of getting me into your bedroom," Banner said.

"I didn't want to disturb Elmo."

"Yeah, that's what they all say." She sat on the sofa and pursed her lips. "The programs work as well as the people in them make them work," she said. "Hoods, some of them, don't do very well. They get tired of being ordinary slobs and do something stupid. Citizens do better. But, you know, you're asking them to give up home, family, even their own identity. That's a tall order for most people."

Yoli had told us that her mother wouldn't even leave the neighborhood, much less town. Would she be willing to leave that and more, if her daughter's life, her granddaughter's life, and her own life were at stake? Not just in the sense that everybody's life is at risk in a dangerous neighborhood, but in a literal, concrete way.

"The other thing," Banner was saying, "is that it depends on how badly someone wants to find someone. I don't need to tell you that there's always a trail. But always. You make it as hard as possible for anyone to follow, but if they have time, patience, and lots of money, and they think the lesson is worth teaching…" She shrugged and drank some beer. "It might help if I knew what the heck we were talking about," she said after a while.

"We're talking about how good the feds are at hiding people," I said. "Now let's talk about how good they are at protecting people before they go into hiding."

"You've got someone who's willing to roll over on Wizard," she said.

I said nothing.

"Yolanda Harris," Banner said after giving it a little thought. "That was her on the phone, wasn't it. What does she know?"

I said, "Anyone who'd try to go up against Wizard and the Bloods is putting his neck in a noose. You have to keep them alive during all the courtroom shenanigans, then you have to keep them alive forever after. The Bloods have lots and lots of money, as you say. And I suspect they'd consider the lesson worth teaching."

"Look, Nebraska, I will personally guarantee—"

254

"There are no guarantees," I said. "That's the problem."

She was silent a long while. Then: "You're right. There are no guarantees. All we can do, all the feds can do, all anyone can do is promise to do their best."

"I'm not sure that's good enough."

"Hey, life doesn't come with *any* guarantees," Banner said. "You do what you do and you take the consequences."

"I hate it when you quote me to me," I said.

"Well?" she said.

"Off the record?"

"Hell." She thought about it. "I can't promise. You know that."

Yes I did. I also knew that we were in a no-win situation. Yoli was the only thing we had that gave us a decent shot at nailing Wizard. But to expose her that way was to expose her to a risk that I no longer could make myself think was tolerable. But if we didn't nail Wizard, then sooner or later he would nail us.

"Looks like Elmo maybe had the right idea all along," I said aloud.

"From the beginning," Banner said.

I gave her an abridged version of things, concluding with the gist of Yoli's call this evening. "I've been talking Elmo out of plugging everyone in sight ever since he got here," I said. "Now I'm thinking I may have been a little hasty."

She smiled faintly and ran a hand through her short hair. "Yoli can testify that Wizard forced her to set Darius up for the kill," she said. "But no one can corroborate that. She didn't tell anyone. She didn't tell the police."

"She was scared."

"She also was a drug addict."

"That ended a long time ago."

"Says her."

"And Wizard was her source."

"Says her. The way the defense goes is this: Yolanda Harris, an admitted drug addict, was involved in a romantic relationship with the defendant, Mister Jones. Mister Jones, disgusted by her drug habit and suspecting she was involved in the narcotics trade—the plane tickets, the hotel receipts, all of that stuff will mysteriously appear, phony names or not—broke off with her. When Mister Jones repeatedly rebuffed her attempts to renew their relationship, Yolanda Harris decided to punish him. She used as her device the slaying of Mister Darius LeClerc, the innocent victim of a street-gang drive-by killing. She attempted to implicate Mister Jones—some time after the fact—even though it's been documented that Mister Jones and Mister LeClerc never even met. In addition, she has tried repeatedly to tarnish Mister Jones's reputation by portraying him as a trafficker in narcotics and a cold-blooded killer, among other things, but no such charge has ever been proved."

"In other words," I said, "there's no reason for Yoli to risk it."

"As much as I'd like to see that s.o.b. take the fall—and as sure as I am that I should be on that phone right now arranging for someone to go pick up the Harris girl and squeeze her till she squeaks—I can't see where her testimony alone is gonna make the case. He's set it up nicely: the only one she'd hurt is herself."

"But you've got other stuff on Wizard."

She sighed. "Almost all circumstantial—the same box Yoli's testimony would end up in. Of course, you can hang a guy with enough of the right kind of circumstantial evidence—"

"*There's* a cheery thought."

"—but I don't think we have enough of the right kind, not us, not the feds, not nobody. Would've been different with FlashMan. He'd've had lots of good stuff—names, dates, places... Hey, why so glum? I thought you didn't want her to sing."

"I don't want her to sing," I said. "I also don't want Wizard to walk."

"Yeah, you're probably not one of his favorites right now."

"There is that," I admitted. "There's also the fact that Elmo and I think somebody—namely, Wizard—should pay *somehow* for Darius LeClerc."

Banner put the lip of the bottle against her lower lip and

blew softly, creating a faint low hum. "There's the other three guys who were in on killing Darius—whatever you said their names were."

"Hamfat, Soldier, and Little Flash. I love these gangbanger handles."

"They all mean something," Banner said, "but I guess you had to be there. Anyhow, we could try squeezing them—play it the way you guys played it with FlashMan. Roll over before you get rolled over on. Their testimony *plus* Yoli's would be solid enough to build a case on."

"Wizard broadcast a message this afternoon," I said, "and the message was *This is what happens to traitors.* Anyone with half a brain will think twice—at least—about turning. Give the guy credit: he snatched that card right out of our deck."

Banner tooted another little tuneless tune on her makeshift pipe. "Then you'd better think of another game," she said after a while.

CHAPTER

31

Koosje and I were in her living room, with brandy and coffee and a fire. Koosje was frowning at the fire.

Her CPA had finally convinced her that she might as well run her money through a paper-shredder as pay rent, especially in her tax bracket, and the result was this house, an old two-story number on Blondo near Fiftieth, about three miles from my place. It had lots of woodwork, hardwood floors that had miraculously escaped the wall-to-wall craze, a full attic, a backyard big enough to turn around in and a smaller front yard, and walls made of real honest-to-God plaster, cracks and all. To my considerable amazement her furniture—light, vaguely contemporary stuff that I always think of as Scandinavian although Koosje assures me, with some verve, that it isn't—worked just fine in its new home.

We were making a point of getting together at least weekly, usually on Wednesday, usually for dinner. We had finished the meal and I had asked her a question and she was considering it. Which is why she was looking at the fire as if she was about to give it what-for.

Now she gave me the same look. "I don't suppose it's occurred to you that you could just leave it alone," she said.

"You don't get into the Goodguy Hall of Fame that way," I sniffed. "Besides, it won't work. We've given Wizard a black eye—two, from what I'm told, and a broken nose. He's not apt to forget about that and let bygones be bygones."

"Mm," she said sadly. "You're probably right. From what you've told me, he has a long history of settling every score, seeking redress for every slight no matter *how* slight."

I nodded. "He killed Darius LeClerc just for seeing a girl who had broken it off with him."

"And he forced the girl to participate," Koosje said. "A naked and sadistic display of his power over her." She looked at me. "A kind of rape."

"Yes."

"People like that can be very dangerous."

"Yes."

"And Wizard has already demonstrated, time and again, that he possesses more than the *potential* for danger." She nibbled her lower lip. "But you have some sort of plan."

"Some sort, yes." I sketched out for her some ideas that Elmo and I had been knocking around. She listened silently. "It was the Reverend O'Neal who provided the inspiration," I said when I'd given her the gist of it. "Last weekend, when he was talking about the gang's obsession with image and how Wizard's power is largely derived from people's perception of him as someone with power."

"Mm," Koosje said over her coffee cup.

" 'Power is perception,' " I said. " 'If people think you're powerful, you are powerful.' Tip O'Neill." Elmo had quoted that to me out of *The Power and the Ambition.*

"Mm," she said again.

"Point out that the emperor is naked, everyone else sees it too."

"Everyone else *may* see it," she said, correcting me. "They may choose not to notice. You're asking people to effect a change of attitude, belief—as you say, perception. Any kind of change is difficult; a change of attitude is perhaps the most difficult. People naturally resist change, we all do, in favor of the status quo. Even when the status quo is unpleasant and even threatening to us. Believe me, I know. Also, I doubt that

Tip O'Neill was thinking about armed terrorists when he said that power is perception. Power is perception *among other things.* 'Other things' includes guns and knives and the willingness to use them."

"I'm getting the feeling you don't think much of my master plan," I said.

Koosje sighed and stood up and went to stab the fire with a brass poker. She was wearing a long wool skirt, forest green, and a matching vest over a paisley top of rust and gold. She had on no jewelry and very little makeup. She had given her contact lenses the night off and was wearing the round horn-rimmed spectacles that make her look like Hollywood's idea of a woman lawyer, but her dark hair was loose around her pale face, softening that look.

She finished punishing the logs and parked the poker in its brass stand. She looked at me and smiled. She knew I had been looking at her while she worked.

"You have an irritating habit of asking me to give you a psychological profile, prediction, or diagnosis based on your sketching out a few select details for me," she said without rancor.

"What's the irritating part?" I said, and she laughed. "I've told you before, I'm not looking for statistical probability; I simply value your opinion. No pressure—you don't have to be any more accurate than a TV weatherman."

Koosje was shaking her head and smiling faintly.

"So what would you say our chances are," I said. "Even? Better than even? Less?"

Finally she sighed and said, "Less."

"Bummer."

"While it's possibly—probably—true that these are insecure personalities in that they depend on image or reputation to a greater degree than we would like to see in a healthy personality—"

"*God,* I love it when you talk that way."

"—it is *not* necessarily true that you may easily exploit those insecurities. You can damage their reputations, injure their pride, and that will upset them terribly, but I think they will be less likely to fall on their swords than to try to run you through with them. We've seen evidence of that already."

"So we have," I said. "We're not expecting them to wet their pants and run away if we say boo. In fact, we're not expecting *them* to do anything. We're only interested in one of them."

Koosje nodded. "Chances are, Wizard is the least insecure of the lot. He's lived this kind of life a long time, he's been in a position of leadership a long time. He holds a great deal of power, real power, and the perception of his power is wide-spread."

"The bigger they are," I said.

"Mm," Koosje said.

She came back to the sofa and I put my arm around her. Her back was hot from the fire.

"Besides," I said, "how self-assured can he be? He never goes around except with an entourage, armed; he never exposes himself to a potentially dangerous situation; he uses others to fight his battles unless he's positive he's dealing with someone powerless and absolutely nonthreatening. I think Yoli Harris is right; I think Wizard is basically a coward. An armor-plated coward, maybe, but a coward. We want to see what happens if we punch some holes in the armor."

"If you take him on and lose, you will only increase his power."

"That's what Elmo says. If we fight him, we've got to kill him."

"Figuratively speaking," Koosje said.

"I hope so," I said. "That's the whole point of all our schemes. It'd be comparatively simple to put a bullet through Wizard's head, but that's not much of a solution. Moral aspects aside, it would only inspire his survivors to pursue a vendetta. They're good at that. We can't just walk away, for reasons already enumerated. Besides, Elmo and I have this peculiar idea that the guy ought to pay for what he did—to

Darius and God knows how many others. Ideally, Justice-with-a-capital-J would take care of him—but Elmo and I are both grown up enough to see that that just ain't gonna happen here. The odds were slim to begin with and they've only narrowed. It stinks, but there it is. Our next best bet, maybe our only next bet, is to try to hit Mister Gerard Jones where it really hurts. And given what we know about him and his friends, that's probably the worst punishment anyone could devise for him."

Koosje was silent for some time.

Then she said, "You are proposing to play a dangerous game with a deadly adversary. I don't have a good feeling about it." She looked up from the fire and into my eyes. "I told you the other night, I don't want to lose you again. I haven't changed my mind."

"I told you the other night, you wouldn't," I said. "I haven't changed my mind either."

I held her. In time, her lips found mine. Her mouth and tongue were cool. I eased her back onto the cushions and put my weight on her.

A while later she said, "Do you have to be getting back to your patient?"

Koosje and I had spent several evenings together since we'd gone off-track last year, but by tacit agreement we never spent the night together.

"Jim and Robert are keeping an eye on him tonight," I said.

"I like those two," Koosje said.

CHAPTER

32

On Thursday, the Reverend O'Neal was busy. In addition to his regular daily routine, he had taken on an assignment from Elmo and me.

That morning he dropped by Robb's Mini-Mall for a pound of coffee he didn't need, and made a point of striking up a conversation with the proprietor, a wizened old man who wore the same moth-eaten shawl-collar sweater day in and day out, summer, winter, spring, and fall. Starting a conversation with old Mr. Robb required absolutely no effort whatsoever; the tricky part was trying to get a word in edgewise. O'Neal managed it, though—managed several well-chosen words, in fact—and was on his way well before any of the local gangbangers rolled out of the sack. He did not want them to know he had been talking to Robb.

That afternoon he called on several members of his congregation. This was not unusual; O'Neal believed that a minister who stayed cloistered inside his church building and did not venture out into the community and into people's lives wasn't much of a minister. He frequently "made the rounds," as he put it, visiting not only members of his church who were ailing but also other residents of the neighborhood, churchgoers or not, "just to be sociable." O'Neal's list of calls was never entirely random, but he had composed today's with special thought: it included three individuals whom he carefully selected because they, along with Robb of the Mini-Mall, all possessed a particular gift.

"Forgive me, Lord," O'Neal said to us, eyes rolling heavenward, "but these people are the worst gossips this side of the Platte River."

We needed the busybodies to help us spread a rumor that Elmo and I had studiously crafted. The rumor was that FlashMan D. had sung like Caruso, that he had actually gone along with our wildest-dreams scenario the other day and agreed to rat out the Bloods. That wasn't much of a threat to anyone now, of course, so we sexed it up by adding to it the "fact" that FlashMan had provided names, dates, and commentary on any number of Blood activities, especially Darius LeClerc's murder.

"I told it not in Gath," O'Neal said, "I published it not in the streets of Askelon. But I sure put the word out in that neighborhood. And as I told you before, a rumor needs only the slightest push to get going around there. Then it picks up speed and circulates, and as it circulates it takes on a life of its own. It grows. It becomes credible." He smiled. "And like a homing pigeon, sooner or later it returns to the source."

"Two days," I said. "Not too shabby."

This was Saturday afternoon. We were in Koosje's office in the Old Market. The Old Market—the old city market, ancient brick structures along wide old cobblestone streets, disused for years but more recently converted into trendy boutiques, restaurants, antique shops, and other establishments—may have been designed originally for tourists, but in recent years it had found favor with the town's yuppified contingent, too, which worked in our favor today. There was too much risk involved in O'Neal's coming to my place or us to his; too much risk in meeting in a public place. Koosje's office provided security both ways: even on a cold and uncongenial Saturday, the Old Market is a busy place, so it wouldn't seem strange to someone who might have been paying attention that we had gone down there; but Koosje's office was private, so that same someone would never know that we had connected up.

Elmo was with me. Three days of convalescence had made him a little stir-crazy. He was supposed to be using at least one crutch, but he wouldn't hear of it. He wouldn't even look at the steel cane that Pat Costello loaned him from inventory. He said he didn't need any of it. But I noticed that he didn't waste a lot of time getting into a chair whenever one presented itself.

"By the time the rumor came back to me this morning," O'Neal was saying, "I learned that FlashMan D. was an undercover federal cop who infiltrated the gang years ago, back in L.A." He shook his head, chuckling silently. "What next, I wonder."

"Could try resurrecting the guy," Elmo said.

I said, "We let the rumor have the weekend off. Let it rest up, run its course, build some more, whatever it wants to do."

"All systems go for Monday, then?" Elmo said.

"I talked with Banner again yesterday afternoon," I said, nodding. We had spent most of the past days on the phone, Elmo and I, conferring with various people. In between phone calls we conferred with each other. To keep his wits about him, Elmo had been giving his pain pills the cold shoulder. After three days, it showed in his face.

O'Neal said, "What more can I do?"

"Your next assignment is to do absolutely nothing. Sit tight and keep your head down. With any luck, all hell or a goodly amount of it will break loose Monday morning. We'll need you again after that, and in the meantime we can't afford to have anybody get the bright idea that you're in cahoots with us."

I had made a pot of coffee in the little galley in the alcove between this room and the other one, where Koosje sees people. O'Neal had a cup of it in front of him, but he hadn't touched it. It must have been quite cool by now, for he half-emptied it now at one go. He set the cup down, looked at us in turn, and said, "I applaud what you two gentlemen are trying to do. I think I understand your reasons for doing it. But as far as your chances for success..." He shrugged his meaty shoulders.

" 'The race is not to the swift, nor the battle to the strong,' " I said. "Ecclesiastes."

" 'But that's the way to bet,' " O'Neal said. "Damon Runyan. You know I'm with you all the way. I said that when you first told me your plan the other day, and I haven't wavered or changed my mind. But don't underestimate Wizard. He may be the coward that you and Yoli say he is. He probably is. But you have to understand, though Wizard and all his unholy disciples are loathed by every decent person in that neighborhood, they are also feared and, in a grudging way, respected."

"We'll have to see what we can do about that," Elmo said.

CHAPTER

33

Monday morning the cops moved in.

It took a little cajoling, most of it handled by Kim Banner, since I didn't have a lot of goodwill with OPD anymore. Meanwhile, Elmo had worked on his friend with the U.S. Marshall in Chicago, I had worked on a man I know named Jurgenson, and on Monday we had four white OPD cruisers on the scene, plus two imposing-looking Ford Broncos from the U.S. Marshal with the lights and the decals and everything all over them, plus a more discreet dark-blue Buick sedan with U.S. GOVERNMENT on the front doors and Elmo and me in the back seat.

The cars, federal and local, convened with all the tire-screeching, light-flashing, and general merriment they could muster. All told there were fifteen cops of one uniform or another. Some of them were off-duty volunteers. All of them were armed. The morning was sunny and crisp.

Bill Jurgenson, rumpled and weary as always, sat behind the wheel of the Buick and watched as the cops stormed the colonial-looking apartment building where Wizard and the other top dogs lived. It was early. We figured that was the best time to catch them at home.

"Is anyone keeping track of how many laws, ordinances, policy guidelines and—oh, yeah—civil rights are being violated here?" Jurgenson said lethargically.

"Except for your being parked a little close to that fireplug," I said from the backseat, "virtually none."

"Everything's been cleared through channels," Elmo said. "All the paperwork's been processed. Everything's kosher. The locals and your bosses both thought it'd be a nice idea to show a presence in the neighborhood, in light of recent events."

"Our guys have search warrants, which will produce exactly what previous search warrants served on these premises have produced: zip. And they have been authorized to invite the occupants downtown to talk about the late Richard Dayton, a.k.a. FlashMan D., for they have it from a usually reliable source—he said modestly—that the late FlashMan was a victim of his own former friends."

"For this you need the Fifth Army?" Jurgenson said.

"We be showin' a *presence*," Elmo drawled.

"Yeah. Well, I get paid the same whether I'm wasting my time or not."

A little of that time passed, and half a dozen cops emerged from the building with the occupants: Wizard, two other black men—one of whom I recognized from our hide-and-seek game a week ago Friday night—and a young black woman in a yellow bathrobe. Everyone looked rumpled. The woman was swearing inventively at the cops. The men were stoic. They probably knew their lawyers were already flying into action.

A tall, silver-haired OPD sergeant with a small mustache ambled over to the Buick. His name was Donnelly, he was the division's resident expert on the gangs, and he was coordinating the local side of the event. He leaned down and rested a forearm on the edge of the open window and said to Jurgenson, "Full house. They were all sacked out. Gerard Jones, Michael Perry, Walker Freed—the whole L.A. cadre."

"What's left of it," Elmo said.

"The girl's name"—he glanced at his notes—"is La'tisha Duchar. Lives over in the project. She's a friend of Mister Freed's."

"Need her for anything?" Jurgenson said over his shoulder.

"Never even heard of her before," I said.

"I'll kick her," Donnelly said. "Zorinsky, right?" The Justice Department offices were in the Zorinsky Federal Building. The badges were taking the little pumpkins there in the hopes that the lawyers would descend on the police station, and that the confusion would give the cops a little time to question the gangbangers before the shysters showed up screaming bloody murder. No one expected to gain anything from that exercise, but as long as the authorities were going to all this work they figured they might as well play it out and see what happened. Besides, it helped justify this outlay of tax dollars.

Donnelly lingered a moment, looking back toward the cars they were about to load the Bloods into. He sighed heavily. "I sure wish I could figure out a way to arrange a nice fatal car accident on the way downtown," he said. "Selectively fatal, I mean." From Kim Banner I had learned a little bit of Sgt. Donnelly's story. His youngest daughter had died of a drug overdose her senior year in college, almost ten years ago. To say that Donnelly had no use for drugs or the people who pedaled them was to put it mildly. Based on what Banner had told me, I figured that if there had been any way to engineer a "selectively fatal" accident on the way downtown, Donnelly would have figured it out.

Now he walked back over to the group, and apparently informed Miss Duchar that she was free to go; she seemed to think she should stay for the last reel. Finally one of the men—Walker Freed, I assumed—spoke to her and she reluctantly stepped aside while her friends were escorted to the cars.

Just before he got into one of the cruisers, Wizard glanced toward our Buick. He had dark bruises beneath each eye; they made him look like he was wearing a domino mask. Elmo had his window rolled down and his chin resting on the backs of his hands. Their eyes met. Wizard tried the stare-down, but the cop escorting him was impatient. He gave Wizard a shove. Wizard gave him a mountain-incinerating look, then turned slowly to look at Elmo again. Elmo hadn't budged.

"I *want* you, nigger," Wizard said loud enough to be heard across the distance.

"Here I am, boy," Elmo said softly.

I called O'Neal from Jurgenson's office. "The eagle has landed," I said.

He chuckled. "Onward and upward," he said.

"You and Yoli be damn careful," I said. "This is where it starts getting hairy."

"True," O'Neal conceded. "But their attention will mostly be on what happened this morning. It not only gives them a bloody nose, it also gives credence to the rumor about FlashMan. They'll need to digest this new development. That will give us a little more protection."

"All the more reason to be extra careful," I said.

"Aw, *geez*, ma," Elmo said when I put down the phone.

"Someone's got to mother-hen," I said. "Enough people are dead already. And now we're putting Yoli at risk too."

"She's a big girl," Elmo said. "She knows the score." I hadn't quite figured out where Elmo stood on the subject of Yoli Harris. He was a damn sight more sympathetic toward her than he had once been, but he hadn't lost track of the fact that she had set up his nephew for the kill. Chances were, Elmo hadn't himself figured out where he stood on the subject of Yoli Harris.

Jurgenson said, "Talking about people getting killed: You ever stop to think that your little maneuvers here might push Wizard over the edge?" Jurgenson knew the plan, or most of it; I had had to fill him in before he would even halfheartedly agree to help. "Guy's not too stable to begin with, from what I hear. What happens if he goes ape-shit and starts whacking everybody in sight?"

"That would be a damn shame," Elmo said.

"*If* innocent bystanders got in the way," I added. "Anyhow, conceivably *everyone* in the gang is a potential threat to Wizard.

Everyone must know something he could sell to the cops. Not even Wizard could be psycho enough to wipe out the whole gang. And if he is, well, the Bloods will take steps."

"Fine by me," Elmo said. "Long as the bastard takes the fall."

Jurgenson looked hard at Elmo, then at me. I looked at my watch. "We're a long ways away from that point yet," I said. "They'll probably be able to hang onto our friends another forty-five minutes, sixty at the outside. Ten o'clock at the earliest before they can get back to the neighborhood. By then the next step should be underway, and we'll have a clearer idea how this thing is shaping up.

Jurgenson, slouched in the high-back swivel chair behind his cluttered desk, folded his hands over his belly and said, "I keep trying to decide whether this is a brilliant plan or the most hare-brained scheme that's ever come along."

"It's that way with most of my great ideas," I said.

CHAPTER

35

Yoli was afraid. Not with the terror that had paralyzed and nauseated her back in the days when Gerard Jones used her to transport drugs. Nor with the fear that had overpowered her and left her empty in the hours before Darius LeClerc was killed. The anxiety she now felt was different, simultaneously sharper and yet somehow less threatening. The difference was that on those earlier occasions she did not know what would happen. She did not know—did not *really* know—what Gerard would do. Her fear then was born of ignorance. Now, however, she knew precisely what he would do. His killing Richie Dayton removed the last vestige of uncertainty from her mind. Gerard had threatened to kill and Yoli had submitted to his threats; Gerard had killed anyway. There was no one who was sacred, no one who was safe—no one whom Gerard would not kill, if killing was what he had decided to do. There was no appeasing him. There was no trying to reason with him.

He was an animal, a rabid animal.

He had to be destroyed.

It was late morning, gray and blustery. Yoli snuggled into her short jacket as best she could and hurried along toward the project. There were people milling around, more people than you would ordinarily expect out in miserable weather like this. Yoli knew why. The neighborhood had been abuzz all morning. *They busted the Bloods. Wizard, all of them, man. Hey, my cousin was there, he saw the whole thing. Fifty cops. No shit. I heard the other day FlashMan a fuckin' cop, man, like undercover. Kill a cop, brother, that it for you. Fuckers never let up on you...*

That was the intended effect, that was the point—get people talking, wondering, questioning. But Yoli didn't like it. It made her nervous. Talk like this, it disrupted the stability of the neighborhood. It upset things. It upset people. There was no telling what would happen if the wrong people got upset the wrong way.

La'tisha Duchar lived in the project, third building in, second floor, back. She lived with her mother and her mother's husband and two brothers and one half-sister in a two-bedroom apartment. One of the bedrooms was so small you couldn't get anything in there but a twin bed, no other furniture. La'tisha didn't spend a lot of time there. She spent most of her time with Walker Freed—Soldier.

Yoli knew La'tisha well enough to not like her. She was a stupid, venal little thing. But Yoli's voice held nothing but concern—worry, even—when La'tisha's half-sister opened the apartment door. "La'vonna, honey, is your sister all *right? There* you are, girl!" She swept into the room, uninvited, and hugged La'tisha. She put on the disguise she always wore around the Bloods and their sympathizers—the smack, the attitude. "I done *heard* what went down and came straight home," she said. "Done heard they busted everyone. You too. How'd you get sprung so fast?"

"Fuckin' pigs dint take me in," La'tisha said with disgust. "Took Soldier, Hamfat, and Wizard."

"Fifty cops, I done heard."

La'tisha made a noise. "More like a hunnert. Need a hunnert cops, you want to be bustin' Bloods on some hook jive like that—'questionin' in connection with the murder a Richard James Dayton.'" She spat. "Bullshit, man."

"They sayin' somebody rolled over."

"Bull*shit*," La'tisha said with conviction. "Well, maybe FlashMan. They been sayin' he a cop or somethin'. I don't believe none a that. Hey, Yoli, you and him, you be pretty tight once. You think FlashMan a cop?"

It had taken longer than Yoli had expected for someone to get around to asking that dangerous question—not even Gerard had remembered that connection, or let on that he did, at any rate—but Yoli had been expecting it and was prepared. "Shit," she drawled, "I don't know, girl. If he was, he was damn good. Not even Wizard caught hip. Anyhow, I'm hearin' someone's ratted out to the man. Sold out the Bloods."

"Who?" La'tisha demanded.

"Don't know *who*," Yoli said patiently. "Nobody know who. But they sayin' *someone*, sayin' that's why the man come down this morning."

"No way. My brother, he talked to Little Flash just like twenty minutes ago. Little Flash say everything bogus, fuckin' pigs got squat, man, they gotta kick the brothers like right now."

Yoli frowned. "Little Flash? How come they didn't bust him?"

"Shoot, girl, *I* don't know! He be downtown with some of the brothers, findin' out what's goin' on."

"Funny, they be bustin' everyone, alla main players, 'cept Little Flash," Yoli said musingly. "FlashMan that dude's ace kool."

"So what?" La'tisha said. "Whatchoo sayin', Yoli?"

"Ain't sayin' nothin'," Yoli said. " 'Cept things goin' on— all kinds of things we don't know nothin' about. You be damn careful, Tish. You, me, everybody—we gotta be damn, damn careful."

La'tisha Duchar had never been on any list of people who were in danger of letting their brains overheat. But by the time Yoli left the tiny apartment, La'tisha was frowning deeply. Yoli took that as a hopeful sign.

Yoli didn't head for home, though that's what she wanted to do. Instead of going back the way she had come, she continued

on west, through the project, out through the western entrance, on to the little apartment building where Gerard lived.
Where Richie used to live.

She looked at the pink plastic watch on her wrist. La'tisha's
brother had talked to Little Flash about twenty minutes ago…
Yes, they should be back by now.

The front door was locked, as always. It was a beat-up steel-
core door with a small pane of bullet-proof glass at eye level. All
the windows in the place were either bullet-proof or boarded
over and barred from inside. Yoli rang the bell and the little
door behind the heavy pane opened. An incurious eye looked
at her, looked left and right to make sure she was alone. Then
the little door closed and Yoli heard the familiar sound of locks
and bolts being unlocked and unbolted.

Yoli didn't know the doorman, except by sight. Doormen
rotated frequently: it was a boring job. But one that had to be
done. The man on the door was armed, as always. So was his
"shotgun," the Blood who stayed out of sight in the darkened
alcove off of the lobby in case the man on the door was
overpowered. The odds of anyone getting past those two and
upstairs to where the Council members lived were slim.

"He back?" Yoli said, and the doorman nodded.

The house smelled. It always smelled; they never aired it out,
hardly ever cleaned it. There was junk everywhere, junk and
cobwebs and trash, and dust all over everything. Too bad, too, Yoli
thought: the place could be real nice if someone gave a damn.

No one lived on the ground floor. Too dangerous, Gerard
always said, even with all the windows covered. They used the
downstairs rooms sometimes for meetings; mostly, though, it
was just storage. Nothing hot—Gerard was insistent on that,
too. No big guns, no heavy drugs, no stolen property. That
stuff was stashed in an old house about a block away. That was
the rule. Anyone forgot that rule, Gerard flew through the ceiling.
The brothers used to laugh about it behind Gerard's back.
They wouldn't be laughing anymore, after this morning's bust.

Yoli went up the staircase off of the small lobby.

Like the rest of the place, the staircase was lighted up like it was the middle of the darkest night of the year. Gerard had to have all the lights on all the time. Partly that was because the boarded-up windows and the heavy curtains everywhere made the place so dim—but only partly. Even when he slept, Gerard kept lights on in the room. Yoli figured he just needed to see what was going on all the time.

There were four apartments on each floor, off of a wide, short corridor, but really there was only one big apartment with a lot of rooms, because the Council had punched holes between the adjacent apartments and put in connecting doors. Everyone—even Gerard—joked about that. They said Hamfat was just too lazy to go out into the hall and knock on Soldier's door when he needed to see him. Gerard said no, that wasn't it, they did it so that if someone was in one of their bathrooms, they could just go next door and use the other guy's. But Yoli knew the real reason: the connecting doors meant no one could ever be pinned down in an apartment: there was always a back door.

Bloods never did anything for no reason.

Gerard's apartment was number eight, back of the building, northeast corner. Right across the hall from Richie's apartment. Yoli paused, staring at Richie's door as if he might emerge. Behind her, noise came through the steel door to number eight—voices, loud and angry. Yoli drew a deep breath, turned, and knocked lightly.

"What the fuck is it," Wizard yelled from inside.

"It's me, baby. You okay?"

"Open the fuckin' door, Player."

Locks and chains clattered, and Yoli went in.

It was a gathering of the Council, what was left of it: Wizard, Hamfat, and Soldier. The latter two sat on the scuffed-up leather sofa next to the wing-back chair that Wizard always occupied. Always until now, that is. Now he paced the narrow space behind the chair. Yoli had never seen him pace before.

Three other Bloods hovered on the periphery: Little Flash,

Player, and C.K. With FlashMan gone, one of them probably would be promoted to the Council. Everyone always figured that Little Flash would be next in line. FlashMan was his ace kool, the brother who took him under his wing and taught him how to be a Blood. But the way FlashMan had died, and the rumors that spread about him after his death, made Little Flash the longer shot now. Yoli was a little surprised he was even allowed in on this meeting.

"I heard what happened, babe," Yoli was saying as she entered. "I came right home from school soon's I heard. You okay?"

He looked at her hard, and her heart moved into her throat.

"Yeah, everything's cool," he finally said. He exhaled loudly, and some of the tension in the room seemed to bleed out. "Everything's cool."

"Motherfuckin' pigs, man," Soldier grumbled.

Wizard looked at him. "No way. Cops got nothin'. Squat. They had anything, they'd'a kept us. They just hasslin' us, 'cause them two cocksuckers told 'em to. Black guy used to be some kinda cop, sheriff, somethin'. Pigs stick together."

"Like fat on ham," someone said, and everyone laughed, Hamfat loudest of all.

"We gotta take care a those fuckers," Soldier said.

Wizard nodded.

"Do a drive-by," Soldier said. "Do it right this time."

Wizard's face was immobile. "Could," he said after a while. "No." He smiled. "They be lookin' for that. No, we choose two of the brothers, send them out. Not a drive-by. A hit, like in the movies." He looked at Soldier. "Find two of the brothers who can do it right. Tell 'em they can earn a stripe."

"Problem is," Hamfat said, "them two fuckers be too smart to hang out at their crib. Gotta be like hidin' out, you know, layin' low. How we find 'em?"

Wizard's face went still again. It was always like that when he was thinking hard, like all of his energy went into his thoughts and left nothing for his nerves and muscles. "Sonofa*bitch*," he finally yelled. He took a full ashtray from the top of the TV set and flung it across the room. "Do I gotta do all the thinkin' for you fuckers?"

No one said anything, no one looked at anyone, no one moved a muscle. Ashes settled over the room. The tension that had abated earlier returned in force.

Wizard came around and flopped into his chair. "Shit," he said in disgust. "We'll think of somethin'." He looked at Soldier. "Line up the talent. Now you guys get lost. Try'n think up somethin' on your own for a change."

The gangbangers filed out.

Wizard looked at Yoli. It was impossible to tell what he was thinking; it was always impossible to tell. You never knew where you stood with the man. The way he looked, the way he acted, even sometimes the things he did had nothing to do with what was going on inside his head. Now he smiled. It was the smile she hated and feared. "You worried about me, huh, girl?"

"Sure, babe. I heard somethin' like a hundred cops—"

"Haw. 'Bout ten. Bogus bust, they ain't gonna waste much money on it."

"Well, I was worried anyway. You okay?"

His eyes held her. "Yeah, I'm okay. Come over here, girl."

Yoli stepped closer to his chair. He took her hand and smiled up at her. "Show me how much you were worried 'bout the Wizard."

She held his eyes for a moment, then slipped her hand from his and backed up a step. She slid out of her jacket, letting it fall to the floor. Then she unbuttoned and unzipped her jeans, skinning them and her panties off at the same time. She stood before him in her turquoise turtleneck and bright-blue heels. That was how he liked her.

Then Wizard gestured with his left hand and she moved forward, sinking to her knees. That was how he liked her more.

• • •

Later on, after she had fixed her face and Wizard had smoked a little bo and was feeling pretty good, Yoli said, "Babe, it true what they sayin' 'bout Richie?"

"What they sayin'?"

She looked at him and smiled. "Oh, *you* know—him bein' a cop and all."

He watched thin smoke drift toward the ceiling. "Who sayin' that?"

"Everybody."

"Everybody's stupid," he said eventually. "I knowed the man like six years, somethin' like that. From back in L.A. May be he was tryin' to stick it to me, but he wasn't no cop. If he was, he was a shitty one, 'cause they didn't have nothin' to pin on us today."

Yoli sat on the couch. The leather was cold against her bare backside. At least it always warmed up quickly. "Then is Richie the one they sayin' rolled over?"

Wizard looked at her languidly. His eyes were a little unfocused, but she knew better than to be fooled by that. Whether he was stoned or drunk, only his physical processes were affected; his brain kept on working just as smoothly as ever. "Shit, girl, I just *told* you the pigs got nothin'. What's the difference what FlashMan maybe told anyone. Can't hurt no one."

"No, babe, I heard this just this morning. They sayin' someone—not Richie, just *someone*—been talkin' to the pigs. One of the Bloods. They sayin' that's how come the bust this morning."

He was out of his chair faster than Yoli would have thought possible. He covered the short distance between them before she could react and grabbed hold of her arm, bending it back the wrong way.

"*Who?*" he yelled.

"E-everybody—"

He slapped her. "Bitch. Who ratted us out?"

"I don't know, ba—"

He slapped her again. She willed herself not to cry out. Tears spilled down the fresh makeup on her face.

"Nobody knows," Yoli stammered quickly. "Nobody *knows*. They all just sayin' *someone*—you know. It's just people talkin', babe, it's just a rumor. Prob'ly don't mean anything."

Wizard was silent. There was nothing unfocused about his eyes now. They were as sharp and as hard as a bird's.

Yoli had expected a reaction—a reaction is what she had hoped for, the whole reason for everything—but nothing like this. She had never seen Gerard this way before. Angry, yes, abusive too; scores of times. But never so churned up like this. Never worried. It frightened her. It also gave her a certain cold satisfaction.

"Babe, you hurtin' me," she whispered after a long while.

He seemed to have forgotten she was even in the room, much less that he had her arm. Now he looked at her and smiled. *The* smile. "Hurtin' you," he said softly.

"Baby—"

Wizard flexed his arm, and a hot bolt of pain flashed up into Yoli's shoulder. Despite her resolve, a gasp of pain escaped her lips.

"Please, baby—"

"Say it."

"Please, Gerard."

"*Say* it, bitch."

"Please. Please. It hurts. *Oh*—"

He pushed her onto the floor. She heard him stand up, heard the snaps, the zipper. She got up on her hands and knees.

Taking her that way, he couldn't see the look in her eyes.

CHAPTER
36

What the Reverend O'Neal said about rumors, about their taking on lives of their own, can be said of plans, too. Elmo and I, with the help of some other people, had developed a plan. The plan was designed to move toward a specific event. As near as we could tell, the plan was humming along nicely. But there were so many pieces, so many actors, so many unknown variables. And we could feel the plan accelerating, building a head of steam. Almost as if it had acquired a will of its own and was preparing to exercise it. We were nearing the point, we felt, where we had to step up the timetable, move toward the event, finish it, before the forces we had put in motion nudged our Juggernaut in an unanticipated direction—and yet we had also reached the point where speed literally could kill.

Monday night, the week after FlashMan was killed, two weeks since Darius had been killed, someone shot Gerard Jones.

It happened in front of the Mini-Mall. As usual, a group of locals, Bloods and hangers-on, were loitering around the place. Wizard had just arrived, had just climbed out of his Porsche, when half a dozen shots sounded. There was the usual pandemonium. Wizard fell to the pavement. He had been taken to St. Joe's. Kim Banner called with the news, and Elmo and I came running. The hospital, on the west end of the ever-sprawling Creighton campus, is only about five minutes from my place.

Banner was in the ER waiting room. Donnelly and another uniform I didn't know were hanging around the hallway outside the examination rooms. There were three other uniformed officers in attendance, too, but they weren't hanging around. They were keeping a close eye on the six or eight young men, most of them in Bloods colors, and three young women who crowded the waiting room.

Yoli was one of the young women. We made eye contact, but then she made a point of staring through me, as did all of her friends. I turned my attention to Banner.

"He'll live," Banner said.

Life is full of these little disappointments.

We drifted up the corridor, away from Wizard's friends, though neither too far nor too fast, out of respect for Elmo's left leg.

Banner gave us the few additional details she had acquired. "Five or six shots, according to the witnesses," she said when she'd finished her recap. "Four accounted for. One hit our boy, but it looks like it didn't do much besides bust up a couple of ribs and throw him on the ground. The other three hammered the car. One took out the windshield."

"Serves him right," Elmo said.

"Him, maybe, but it's just sheer luck that Yoli wasn't standing next to him," I said. "The slugs that went into the car could have gone into her just as easily."

"Yeah, but they didn't."

"Yeah, but they *could* have." When I play mother-hen, I bury myself in the part.

"The Bloods are blaming it on the Crips, but that's hooey," Banner said. "It makes sense that the Crips might take advantage of the recent, uh, disarray among the Bloods to wreak a little havoc—and they still might do it—but they wouldn't do it this way. Five or six shots, most of them wild, almost certainly from a handgun—we'll know when they get the slugs dug out of Wizard and his car—that doesn't say gang."

"Individual," I said.

"Amateur," Elmo said.

Banner nodded. "Donnelly's guess is that it probably was one, maybe two kids who *want* to be Crips, and figured they'd earn big stripes by whacking the Blood's Top Prez. Should've put in a little range-time first."

"You guys think it's at all likely that one of Wizard's own tried to do him in?" I asked Banner.

"You can't rule it out," Banner said, "but it isn't real likely. The Bloods who are most apt to want Wizard gone are the ones toward the top, the Council and them. After all, they're the ones taking most of the heat from the fire you two have been building. But those guys all know guns like you know your own ZIP Code. None of them'd botch the job like this."

"But you're collecting alibis anyway."

"Everybody should have a hobby," she said. "The Council's in the clear, at least: both Hamfat and Soldier were with the group in front of the Mini-Mall when the scene went down. We're working on that tier of up-and-comers, the guys next up for a seat at the table. Player, Little Flash, and C.K."

"Could be one of them decided to free up yet another chair and take care of the Wizard problem at the same time," I said.

"One or more," Elmo said. "Or all."

"Still too damn amateurish," Banner said.

"We're losing control of this thing," I said to Elmo.

"Control?" Banner said. "What the hell did you ever expect to control? All you can do with a situation like this is keep tightening the screws until something cracks. It looks to me like that's what's happening."

Elmo and I exchanged glances.

There was some movement behind us then and we turned. A few of the people from the waiting room had come up the corridor. The three young women, and two of the men. One of the uniform cops was hovering behind and off to the side of the little contingent, waiting. They stopped about six feet from us, all except for Yoli, who slowly continued toward us, right up to me. She looked at me expressionlessly for a long moment. Then she spat on me.

"You fucker," she said in a low, grating murmur. "This is all your fault."

I said nothing.

"Gerard's got a contract out on you," she continued in exactly the same tone of voice. No one more than two feet away could have heard, unless he had ears like a spaniel's. Yoli's eyes moved to the left, including Elmo in her warning. "Two guys. One's that one in the red cap. They think you're hiding out somewhere."

She looked at Elmo with the same chill detachment, and then slapped his face.

Then she calmly rejoined her party, which, with many significant glances our way, returned to the waiting room.

"I thought you said steno school," Elmo said. "You must've meant acting school."

"Hasn't this girl ever heard of using a telephone?" I said, wiping my lapel with my handkerchief.

"What the hell was all that?" Banner said.

"That fire of ours you spoke of? Yoli's carrying buckets of hot coals from it directly to the Bloods."

"Gizzard especially," Elmo said. "Only she can't let on she's working with the goodguys."

"Jesus Christ. You two are crazier than I thought. And I thought you were pretty crazy. I also thought this master plan of yours was just to put the pressure on Wizard and the others and see if anything snaps loose."

"That's the general idea," Elmo said. "But we've got to keep the pressure turned up, and we need help to do that."

"Although we have powers and abilities far beyond those of mortal men," I said, "there's still a limit."

"What?" Banner said. "You mean you *can't* make that girl and whoever else you've recruited for your harebrained crusade bulletproof?"

"Nobody wants anybody getting killed," Elmo said testily.

"We're taking precautions."

"Oh, good," Banner said. "Precautions."

I said, "What Elmo said is true—we've got to keep the pressure on Wizard. That's what our whispering campaign is designed to do. Your and the feds' contribution lent a nice air of credibility to the rumors we're circulating, but the key to the plan is the rumors themselves. The only way we have of spreading them is through the people up there who want Wizard and his pals out of their hair. Yoli, O'Neal, and some of O'Neal's friends."

"Wouldn't be too cool for us to go up there and stand around on the corner kibitzing with the locals," Elmo said dryly.

"We know that even just spreading these rumors is dangerous. So do the people who are helping us. We've tried to plan things out so that the misinformation can't be traced back to the source. We're hoping to keep Wizard jumping to such an extent that he doesn't even think to try it."

"And we're doing it," Elmo said. He turned to me. "Must be making them pretty uncomfortable, they want us dead."

"Excuse me," I said, "I thought they've wanted us dead for about two weeks now."

"Oh, they were just funnin' around before. Now we've got their attention."

"And exactly what do you intend to do with their attention now that you've got it?" Banner asked.

"Yes," I said to Elmo. "What *do* we intend to do with their attention?"

He shrugged. "Keep it."

CHAPTER

37

"I don't got to be talkin' to you, bitch."

Banner smiled benevolently at Sgt. Donnelly, who in turn smiled at Wizard. "Now, Gerard, is that any way to address an officer of the law?"

"Fuck off, old man," Wizard said.

He was a little groggy from the effects of medication and the aftereffects of shock. But that didn't improve his disposition any. The docs had removed the slug from his side without any trouble and taped up his broken ribs—there's not much else you can do for broken ribs—and parked him in an over-lighted cubicle off of the ER. They wanted him to hang around for an hour or two to make sure everything held together. In the meantime, Banner wanted to take advantage of his captive-audience status.

She said, "Gerard, certainly you want us to try and find out who shot you."

Wizard made a rude sound. "Maybe ought be askin' them." He cast a hot glance at Elmo and me. "Be askin' them where they were when the Wizard went down. What the fuck they doin' here, anyway? They ain't no cops. Got no business here."

"We didn't get to spend enough quality time with you the other night, Gerard," I said. "So we asked the nice policelady if we could visit our sick friend and she said okay."

"See, Gerard?" Elmo said. "Lose the attitude, maybe you

can start to get along with people, too."

"Fuck you, Tom."

Elmo looked at me. " 'Tom' again," he said. "You ever read *Uncle Tom's Cabin*?"

"Missed it somehow," I said.

"In the book, Uncle Tom is no Uncle Tom. He's whipped almost to death for standing up to Simon Legree. But when they turned the book into a play, that's when they took away Tom's backbone. Figured northern audiences, white audiences, would never go for a black man who's noble and decent."

"Once a producer gets hold of your book," I said, "it's out of your control."

"Fuck, I don't got to listen to this bullshit," Wizard said. "I know my rights. Don't got to talk to no one, don't got to listen to no one."

"Wrong, sport," Donnelly said. His voice was as soft and comforting as a steel girder. "Maybe you don't have to talk, but you sure as hell have to listen. Listen good. Someone put a bullet in you tonight. They didn't do a very good job of it, so maybe they'll go off somewhere and practice for a while, then come back and try again. Maybe get it right next time."

Banner said, "It's all the same to us, Gerard. But if you'd like to sort of stay alive, your best bet is to talk to us. Before your invisible friend puts in too much target practice."

"Bullshit," Wizard said.

"Hey, like I said, it's all the same to us."

"You wanna know who tried to pop the Wizard, you ask those two queens. Set it all up to get me in here, try and get me to rat out the Bloods. Shit, you prob'ly in on it too, bitch."

"*Sergeant* Bitch to you, asshole," Banner said.

Elmo said, "You work at being that stupid, Gerard, or you just come by it naturally? If we were gonna shoot you, we'd kill you. If we were gonna kill you, we'd've killed you Friday night. You got a bigger problem than us, Gerard."

"Got no problem isn't gonna be handled real soon," Wizard said without separating his teeth.

"He must mean the two guys he's got looking for us," I said. Wizard's eyes jerked from Elmo's face to mine. You could almost hear them click. I smiled. "Oh, was that supposed to be a surprise? Sorry. The man's right, Gerard, you got bigger problems than li'l ol' us. You're the captain of a leaky ship. You plan to go down with it?"

He went very still then. Only the quick rise and fall of his chest indicated that he was alive and not carved of wood. Yoli had told us how he seized up that way when he concentrated. I hoped he was concentrating on the rumor that someone in his organization had been doing a Benedict Arnold impersonation.

Eventually his eyes refocused. They zeroed in on Elmo with undisguised hate.

"Tired a you, asshole," Wizard said. His voice was tight, little more than a harsh whisper. "Tired a your ugly face. I see your ugly face again you dead, you got that, fucker."

"You say that every time you see me, ace. I'm still here."

"Fuck you," Wizard said. "Get outta my face. All a you. Get the fuck outta my face. Wizard don't gotta listen to none a you, don't gotta look at none a you."

"Gotta come naturally," Elmo said. "No one could *make* himself that stupid, no matter how hard he worked at it."

"Get this fucker away from me," Wizard said, his voice the same as before. "He got no right bein' here. Get him away."

A nurse materialized. "*What* is going on back here?" she demanded.

"Nice going, Gerard," I said. "Now you got us *all* in trouble."

The nurse threw us out.

Out in the main corridor Banner said, "Wait a minute, you two." She came over to us. "I smell something cooking, and it does not smell like the recipe we discussed last week. Exactly what are you two brewing up?"

"It's like we said all along," I said. "We're trying to apply enough pressure to get Wizard, one of his friends, or all of the above to crack."

"Yeah, yeah," Banner said. "That include taking pot-shots at him, sort of help things along?"

"No," I said, "that was just lucky happenstance."

"Not too lucky," Elmo said. "Guy's still alive."

"It's that kind of talk that worries me," Banner said. "I know you"—she jabbed a finger at me—"have a problem with authority and like to go riding off on your own like the Ajax Knight or something. And you"—she turned her attention to Elmo—"have a nephew who was killed by that pile of dog droppings in there, and I don't think you've done a good job of adjusting to the fact that there's not a hell of a lot anyone can do about it. Shut up," she said to me.

"I wasn't going to say anything," I said.

"Really? Well, then save it for some time when you are. Now look. I know you want this guy. So do I; he's a real wrong number. But there are ways and there are ways, and there are rules that I'm supposed to play by. I don't mind cutting corners, but there's a limit. And whatever you two jokers cook up flies back on me too when it hits the blades, 'cause *I'm* the one who went along with your little scheme and sold it to the big guys. What the hell, I thought, maybe if we shake the tree something'll fall out. Only now I'm getting the feeling that maybe you're not just shaking the tree, but looking to cut it down. There's more stuff going on here than I thought there'd be."

"Meaning what?" Elmo said. "You thought we'd spread the rumor that FlashMan sang before he croaked, then you and your friends'd come in with lights and sirens and Wizard'd curl up into a little ball? You thought that'd take care of everything?"

"I didn't think you'd keep running innocent people as players," Banner said. Her voice was tight. "I didn't think anyone'd start taking shots at anyone."

"We've already discussed the former," I said, "and no one could have predicted the latter."

"Not that either of you is real broken up about it."

"Would crocodile tears make you feel better?"

"What would make me feel better is if I had some reason to think that *whatever* you two characters have started in motion was under *somebody's* control. That you guys were playing it straight with me. And that there wasn't going to be more blood spilled before this is all over."

Neither of us said anything.

"That's what I thought," Banner said.

CHAPTER

38

Wizard's entourage had thinned out. The guy Yoli identified as one of the pair assigned to taking care of us was missing. So was Yoli.

There was a pay phone near the ER doors. I cadged some change off of Elmo and dialed Decatur Street, then keyed in the numeric code that made my answering machine cough up its messages. There was only one. It was from Yoli.

"I didn't have time to call you before," she said. "That's why I couldn't tell you about Gerard sending those two men after you. They won't try another drive-by. They figure you must be hiding someplace—they think you're too smart to stay at your place."

Guess we showed them.

"They probably followed you home from the hospital, so you got to be extra careful," she went on. "Maybe you ought to be hiding out someplace. Anyhow, I'm going to try and talk to Donald tonight, right now, before Gerard gets back to the neighborhood. I'll call you later."

"Hell," I said, hanging up the phone. "She's gone ahead with the next part."

"She was supposed to wait."

"No shit." I looked at my watch. It was about a quarter of ten. "The time-stamp on the answering machine said she left the message at nine twenty-three—probably as soon as she left here. She's up there by now."

"Well, maybe it's just as well she do it before Gizzard gets back on the scene."

"That's what she's thinking. But I don't like the idea of her hanging out there by herself."

"She would be in any case," Elmo said. "You just don't like it that she went ahead with the next part of your big plan without clearing it with you first."

"I don't like it that things are moving on their own. Banner was right—this is turning into a misguided missile. Anyhow, this part was your idea, remember?"

"I'm big enough to share the credit. What do you want to do now?"

"Damned if I know. Let's get out of here. Not that way—Yoli thinks those two bad apples will be hanging around to follow us from here, see where we're hiding out."

"Getting subtle in their old age?" Elmo said. "More likely they plan to pop us in the parking lot."

"Either way," I said, and Elmo nodded. We turned and went back through the maze of the hospital, exiting at the front doors. The corridors at that hour were hushed, the lighting muted, and yet there were people about—hospital personnel, bathrobe-clad patients walking slowly with family members, and, once we came out into the chill night, smokers who were forbidden to indulge their habit inside the building.

Elmo and I circled the building. The area around the hospital was very well illuminated. Here again there were a few people out, but none of them appeared to wish us any ill. We came around to our parking lot, came up to Robert Olson's Honda, and got in.

Elmo reached into a pocket of his overcoat and pulled out his folding binoculars. He popped them open and scanned the area, panning from the ER entrance to the left, then to the right.

"There," he said. He pointed and handed me the glasses.

It was an old telephone-company van, two-tone, olive and white, with the shadowy remnant of the German-helmet bell decal on the one side visible to us. There was a bumper sticker on the back end: I ♥ MY GRANDKIDS. The van was parked four rows of cars ahead of us and off to the south, facing the hospital. In the big mirror mounted on the driver's-side door I saw the reflection of an intent looking young black man, the one Yoli pointed out to us inside. His eyes were glued to the ER entrance.

"What do you think, is his pal in the van with him or waiting in another car?" From our angle, there was no way of telling whether anyone was seated on the passenger side. There were no rear windows.

Elmo took back his binoculars. "My guess is the van. I think we're supposed to come out those doors, they jump out and take care of us, then they pile back into the van and disappear."

"Seems cruel to leave them waiting out here all night."

"Uh-huh. Also means we got to keep watching our back."

"Plenty of cops inside," I said. "They could haul 'em in on weapons charges."

"Yeah…" Elmo said, giving it three syllables. "But the Bloods would just appoint some more buttons. We've already started Wizard to thinking that we know everything going on inside his organization. Feel like reinforcing that idea?"

"Oh, why not," I said. "Beats having to walk clear around the hospital again."

We got out of the Honda and split up. There were plenty of parked cars to offer cover, and though we each stayed hunched down behind them, that kind of stealth wasn't really called for. The side-mounted mirrors were the van's occupants' only way of seeing what was going on behind them. All we had to do was fan out wide, outside of the mirrors' fields of vision, and come in more or less perpendicular to the van. The gunmen were so intent on the ER doors that they didn't even notice Elmo until he was six feet off the port side.

By then I was one car over on the starboard side. That gave me a clear profile-view of the two men in the front seat. When the guy on the passenger side spotted Elmo, he alerted his pal.

They both turned. I saw a sawed-off barrel.

I came around the front end of a T-bird and closed the gap between me and the van. If the driver's door wasn't unlocked I'd just shoot through the glass.

The door was unlocked. They wanted to be able to hop right out and mow us down without any pesky hindrances.

I yanked it open and shoved my gun behind the driver's ear. He jerked stiff and offered no resistance when I took the shotgun from his hands.

During the distraction Elmo came up on the other side of the van and similarly lightened the other guy's load.

"*Damn* but I'm getting tired of you people," Elmo said. "Like a buncha gnats. You don't do any harm but you're a nuisance."

"I don't know whether you guys ever had anything going for you," I said, "but it looks to me like you could fuck up a one-car parade these days. Why don't you tell Wizard to save everybody a lot of embarrassment and just pack it in."

They kept quiet, which was to their credit.

I reached around the steering column and plucked the keys out of the ignition switch.

"Thought you'd like to get in a little hot-wiring practice," Elmo told them.

The Reverend O'Neal met us in front of his church. We had called him en route.

"Get in quickly, before anyone sees you," he whispered. His whisper was about the same volume as your or my conversational voice.

We went in and O'Neal locked up after us. He led the way to his little office at the back.

"I tried to talk Yoli out of going ahead before she talked with you," O'Neal said, echoing what he had already told me on the phone, "but she was determined. There was nothing I could do. I don't even know where she was calling from."

"All we can do is hang on and enjoy the ride," Elmo said in

response to the sour look I probably was wearing.

"At least I made her promise to come back here when she was done," O'Neal said. "I told her I'd wait up all night if need be." He smiled at us. "Like I said before, I think it's too dangerous for you to even be anywhere near this neighborhood. But as long as you're here, I'm glad of the company. I won't pretend that all of this plotting and intrigue isn't tough on my poor old nerves. Now then: I put on a fresh pot of coffee, which ought to be done by now, or there's tea, ginger ale, mineral water, or one or two bottles of some stronger stuff I keep on hand just for emergencies such as this."

"Revered O'Neal!" Elmo gasped.

He laughed. "As I said, this whole business has been tough on the nerves. Tonight, I expect, will be the worst of all."

"The worst so far, maybe," I said. "Not the worst of all."

CHAPTER

39

Far away, as if in someone else's dream, a bell tinkled softly and clearly. The Reverend O'Neal straightened in his chair, looked at a big steel alarm clock on the corner of the desk, looked at Elmo and me. We were in the orange barrel-chairs in front of the desk.

"That's the back door," he said.

"Man has ears like an elephant," Elmo said, following me following O'Neal out of the office and through a double-hinged door into the kitchen.

This was a small, strictly utilitarian space; unlike the rest of the house, virtually untouched in the conversion from dwelling to church. I assumed the windows were barred, as all of the windows at the back of the house were. Heavy roller-shades pulled down over the glass prevented me from seeing. The back door was windowless, and secured with three deadbolts and a bar. O'Neal went up to it and bent down to put his eye to the peephole lens. He looked back at us.

"It's Yoli. Get that light."

The only illumination in the room was from a bulb above the electric range. Elmo extinguished it, and except for a sliver of yellow beneath the door to the office, the room was dark.

O'Neal worked the locks by touch. Cold air and a thin gray light came into the room, along with two dark shapes. I transferred my revolver from the clip-on holster on my hip to my hand.

296

Then the gray light was shut out again, metallic *clunks* and *clacks* signified that the bolts were being shot, and a second later the ceiling light came on. Yoli Harris blinked against the sudden glare. She had a companion, whom I recognized as the third man with FlashMan D. and Wizard in the Porsche that Friday night. Tall and thin, he was nineteen or twenty tops. He was wearing his colors, a camouflage cap reversed on his head, baggy black pants of some shiny material, and black high-tops. Almost every gangbanger I had seen in the past two weeks had been wearing high-tops. Just about every brand available, too. Except British Knights. Crips wear British Knights. They pretend the "BK" emblem stands for "Blood Killers."

"This is Donald Lee," Yoli was saying. "His street name's Little Flash."

He was eyeing Elmo and me with undisguised suspicion.

"What're *they* doin' here?" he said sullenly.

"Helping," Yoli said. She turned to us. "Donald and me had a long talk. He's in trouble. He needs to get out of town."

Elmo and I knew what that meant.

This stage of the operation had two parts. Part one was to sow confusion, suspicion, and even a little fear in the ranks of the Bloods and especially in the heart of their Top Prez. In an effort to accomplish that, we had arranged the morning raid on the Council's headquarters; floated the rumor, with the Reverend O'Neal's help, that FlashMan had been cooperating or worse with the police; and, mainly through Yoli's efforts, started the rumor that someone else in the Bloods was currently talking to the police. Part two was to capitalize on the effects of part one by convincing someone in the gang that Wizard had decided *he*, the someone, was the rumored informant, and persuade him to disappear before Wizard helped him disappear. When that as-yet-unelected someone vanished, it would lend credence to our rumor about the informant. And it would give Gerard Jones something to think about—namely, whether the vanishee was now singing to the police and, if so, what tune.

We had discussed that angle at length with Yoli, during our

planning stage, and she had nominated Donald Lee, Little Flash, as our most likely candidate. Because of his closeness to the late FlashMan, FlashMan having been his "ace kool" or mentor, Little Flash now truly was under a certain amount of suspicion. That made him fit the circumstances we had invented, and also put Little Flash in some danger, or potential danger, which was the other reason Yoli had tossed his hat into the ring. She liked Donald Lee. Because of her closeness to FlashMan, she had of course known Lee well for some time, and I got the impression that she looked on him as a younger brother.

Despite that, despite the common bond they shared—their close friendship to FlashMan—Yoli had warned us that convincing Donald Lee to betray the Bloods would not be easy, maybe not even possible. As the Reverend O'Neal had reminded us, gangs are a kind of surrogate family for gang members. But we hoped that our various actions would cause the Bloods to close ranks, and that when they did Little Flash would be on the outside. When that happened, Yoli would go to him as a friend, convince him that Wizard distrusted him, and make him see that his only chance to survive was to disappear.

That would happen, we hoped, at some point in the not-too-distant future. But tonight Yoli jumped the gun. Yoli knew that Little Flash had not been at the Mini-Mall when Wizard was shot, and realized that his absence would raise suspicion about his having had something to do with the shooting. The fact that Little Flash hadn't even heard about the shooting until Yoli told him, several hours after the fact, was an indication of the extent to which he had already been shut out by Wizard and the Council. Yoli sensed not only that this might be the right time to approach him, but also that if we delayed, Wizard might settle his suspicions by simply having Little Flash whacked. It would be completely in character.

Without waiting for our go-ahead, then, Yoli had gone to work on Little Flash—and apparently with some success.

Complete success would have been her convincing Little Flash to actually roll over on Wizard. Elmo had proposed it, and Yoli agreed to try, but we all knew it was the longest of all possible shots. By telling us now that Donald Lee needed to "get out of town," Yoli was indicating that she had failed to persuade Lee to squeal, but at least had convinced him to let us help him disappear. In our own inimitable style.

Right now, though, Lee looked like he needed re-convincing.

He pulled away from Yoli and looked at her hard. "You settin' me up here, Yo?"

"Yeah, stupid, I'm setting you up to stay alive."

"These the guys got FlashMan offed."

"Wrong," Elmo said. "These the guys tried to get FlashMan to save his own neck. Didn't work."

"Son, these men are working hard to stop all the killing," O'Neal said. "They'll help you if you let them. We all will. We've got it all planned out how you can get away, get way out of town before Wizard or anyone else is the wiser."

Lee looked from him to Yoli. She nodded.

"I've got a brother-in-law in Kansas City," O'Neal was saying. "He's in the furniture business. He's got some things to take up north, on up to Winnipeg, but he's been waiting to get a full load."

"You're the load," Elmo said.

O'Neal nodded. "You can stay here. We'll fix up a bunk in the basement. The windows have been bricked over for years, and no one would ever think of looking for you here. I'll call my brother-in-law, he'll load the truck and come on up. Might take a couple of days. We'll sneak you out of here, meet up with him somewhere —we'll work it all out—and he'll take you as far as a town called Morris."

"In friendly Manitoba," I said.

"Canada?" Lee said, like we'd just invented the place. "Shit."

"No gangs in Morris, Manitoba," Elmo pointed out.

"No nothin' there, I bet."

"My brother-in-law knows people there," O'Neal said. "He can get you a job loading furniture and carpeting. Stay put and you'll be fine. Later on, when things have cooled down, we'll get in touch and you can decide what you want to do from there."

He thought it over. "Got no choice, do I?"

"Sure you do," Yoli said. "Stay here and get your fool head blown off. Or tell the police what you know."

Lee shook his head. He looked lost, a little scared, and for all his toughness somehow vulnerable. He looked at Yoli for a long time, and she met his eyes. Something passed between them, in the silent language that friends sometimes share. Then he looked at O'Neal and sighed. "I'll need some money," he said. "Clothes and stuff."

We had already considered that. "We'll let you have a few dollars before you go," Elmo said. "Enough to get you going, get some clothes, get a place to stay."

"But you know," I said, "there's no such thing as a free lunch."

Lee looked at me, sizing me up. He shrugged, a world-weary gesture. He knew how things went.

"What do I got to do," he said.

CHAPTER
40

Having peppered the project and environs with our home-made rumors, it was a little surprising to us when we caught wind of one that we hadn't crafted ourselves.

This one came to us in the form of a late-night phone call on Tuesday, from our old partner-in-crime, Jeff. "I been hearing that the big guys in L.A. are gonna replace Wizard," Jeff said. "I been hearing that things are like real churned up. I heard where they told Wizard to come out to L.A. and explain everything going on back here, but he's stalling, so like this guy I know, he says two Bloods from the coast are coming out here next week and see for themselves."

"Rumors," Elmo said. "You can't believe everything you hear."

"I don't know," I said, grinning. "This isn't one of ours. That gives it credibility."

The next day both O'Neal and Yoli called to say they'd heard the same thing. But that didn't make it true. Yoli reported that Wizard, though recovering nicely from his injury, was also running in tight tiny circles. As we had hoped—and as we had helped—the word up and down the block was that Little Flash had gone over to the goodguys' side. Everyone knew that Little Flash knew enough to take Wizard down hard.

On Thursday it was Wizard's turn to receive a phone call.

301

Yoli was with him. That was no coincidence.

"Yeah, man, this's Little Flash."

Wizard went very still, the way he did. "Hey, brother. Where you been?"

"Never mind that," Donald Lee said. "We got to talk."

"Sure," Wizard said. "I'm listenin'."

"Not on the phone," Lee said. "Face to face. Man to man—alone, catch?"

"I catch." There was something in Wizard's voice, a tone that might have suggested a scowl crossing face—or was that just what we wanted to hear? "Yeah," Wizard went on, "this a good idea. Get ever'thing sorted out, man. Clear the air. All this shit goin' on, nobody know what the hell's goin' on no more. You and me, Little Flash, we got no problem can't be talked out."

"Glad to hear that," Lee said gravely. "I know what everybody's been sayin'. Know what you been thinkin'. I figure I can't get square with you, then I got to go and do what everybody's been sayin'. Got to go and talk to the man. Don't want to. I always been loyal to the Bloods."

"I know that," Wizard said earnestly. "You shoulda never been thinkin' I didn't. Now, don't you be doin' nothin' to regret later on, man. You and me, we'll get ever'thing sorted out. You just tell me where and me, I be there."

He put down the phone.

On the other end of the wire, Donald Lee hung up the phone and looked across the desk where O'Neal, Elmo, and I had been monitoring.

"Perfect," O'Neal said with enthusiasm. "Wizard's had two days to stew about Donald's disappearance. He'll jump at this."

Lee smiled skeptically and shook his head. "No way he'll come," he said. "Not alone. He ain't *that* crazy."

"Us neither," Elmo said.

• • •

Gerard Jones stared at the phone for a long minute. Then he looked at Yoli Harris. She was on the leather couch, half naked, the way he insisted she be.

"Man, I don't believe it," Wizard said. "That dumb fuck Donald Lee. He ain't been talkin' to the cops—he been *hidin'* for two days. Now he say he got to talk to me. Say it all a big mistake." His upper lip peeled back in that sneer of a smile that Yoli loathed so much. "Got that much right."

He picked up the phone again.

"You gonna talk to him, babe?" Yoli said.

"Like I told him, gonna get ever'thing sorted out." He stabbed the intercom button on the phone and punched in two numbers. "Soldier. You and Hamfat get in here. Get Player and C.K. too. We got plans to make. I just got a call from Little Flash. Never mind, you just get your lazy asses in here." He hung up.

Yoli got up and reached for her clothes.

"No one told you go anywhere," Wizard said.

She stared at him. "Gerard, I'm naked."

Starting at her shoes, he slowly moved his eyes up to her face. She felt her face burning, felt her lips go bloodless and tingly. She felt a little off-balance.

"Ain't got nothin' every other bitch don't got," Wizard said flatly. "Sit your ass back down till I tell you get up."

Uncertainly, jerkily, Yoli returned to the couch and waited for the men to arrive.

CHAPTER

41

The Omaha economy balked, stalled, and crashed in the early 1980s. Major employers abandoned the city; others threatened to. Companies slashed their workforces. The Union Pacific repair shops closed. Literally thousands of workers, from laborers to middle managers, were displaced. In 1983 unemployment reached a ten-year high of 6.8 percent. No one but the most die-hard civic boosters predicted anything but a continued tailspin for the near future. But by the end of the eighties unemployment was at a ten-year low, and Metro Omaha had gained 25,000 new jobs. Now, as the midpoint of the decade fast approached, the nineties were shaping up to be the economic mirror-image of the eighties.

What was invariably overlooked in all of the "Omaha miracle" articles was that the new jobs were just that: *new* jobs, replacements for hundreds, perhaps more, that were gone for good. Plenty of businesses had sunk like rocks and, again like rocks, would never bob back up to the surface.

The G & O Asphalt Company was one such business. Unable to endure the construction slump of those dark days, it had been closed for nearly six years now. Its remains sat moldering along the Missouri River a distance north of the I-480 bridge, in a flat and inhospitable area crisscrossed with railroad tracks and permanently inundated with the smell of oil, tar, grease, and burned fuels. It's easy enough to forget that

Omaha is one of those quirks of the American frontier, a city whose roots are both agricultural and industrial. A cowtown and a railroad town. The bleak and almost alien landscape around the late G & O Asphalt Company served as a good reminder of the second part of those roots. And of what fragile things economies are.

There was no earthly chance that Gerard Jones would come to this place alone and unarmed, no matter what he assured Donald Lee. Elmo and I would have bet all our worldly possessions on that even if we hadn't had Yoli Harris's report of Wizard's council of war.

According to Yoli, Wizard would be well-armed. That was a sign of how thoroughly we had shaken him up over the past couple of weeks. Usually Wizard went about unarmed except for what he called his "emergency kit" strapped to his right ankle. He had come to depend on his entourage to handle any unpleasantness that might occur. But he was taking no chances for his late-night meeting with Little Flash.

Also according to Yoli, Wizard would have six "shotguns" with him, the six Bloods he felt most inclined to trust in the climate of distrust we had fostered. Soldier and Hamfat, who were all that remained of the Council; Player and C.K., who were next up for membership now that Little Flash had taken a powder; and two new recruits from the ranks, names unfamiliar to us. Wizard's inner circle had contracted over the past couple of weeks.

It was a safe bet that they would have enough firepower among them to take down a government.

I was lying on my belly on cold, broken pavement under what looked like an LP tank with a pituitary problem, waiting and watching, soaking up the oily atmosphere and keeping half an eye on the luminous dial of my wristwatch. It was half past midnight. Lee and Jones had agreed to meet at twelve. Jones was late. That was forgivable: Lee wasn't going to show at all. At the moment he was somewhere on I-29, probably about midway between Fargo, North Dakota, and the Canadian border.

By the time the big hand on my watch swung around to the nine, I had begun wondering whether Wizard had gotten a better offer for the evening. That was unlikely—it was unlikely he would believe that he could afford not to deal with Little Flash. Little Flash could hurt him badly if he decided to. All of our machinations were geared toward making Wizard realize that, make Wizard think Donald Lee might in fact decide to turn on him, make Wizard decide that he had to preempt him.

And in person; that was of cardinal importance.

Most likely Wizard and his friends were out there somewhere, beyond the fenced-in grounds of G & O Asphalt, likewise waiting in the frigid darkness of this moonless night. Perhaps convincing themselves that Little Flash would be foolish enough to trust Wizard and come alone to this rendezvous. Perhaps devising tactics. Perhaps simply trying to psych Little Flash out, make him jumpy before they descended on him.

We had decided to give Wizard until two A.M. I shifted position in my small snowless patch and settled back in.

The area that had been the G & O Asphalt Company was an irregular square with the river as its eastern boundary. The center part of that square was empty space, sort of a compound where in better times trucks and other heavy equipment maneuvered. What was left of the operation—tanks and other containers, unlovely utilitarian buildings, and whatever else couldn't be sold off when G & O went down the tubes—more or less ringed this compound. The whole area was contained by eight-foot-high chain-link fencing with another ten inches of barbed wire above it. That hadn't presented much of a problem to us and we didn't expect it would deter Wizard.

We had reconnoitered the place, Elmo and I, before having Donald Lee place his call to Wizard. We assumed Wizard would do likewise after the call—in fact, we had invited him to do so by giving him a day between Lee's call and the time of the rendezvous. His reconnaissance would reveal the best places for his people to enter the grounds. Our reconnaissance had showed us the best places to wait for them.

The whole eastern end was secure. Beyond the fence the embankment down to the river was too steep for a quiet approach. The western side was secure, too. That's where the main entrance was, and Wizard was supposed to meet Little Flash just inside that chained and padlocked gate, near a small brick building that had served as G & O's front office. Wizard wouldn't risk Little Flash seeing his friends on the front side and rabbiting. That left the north and south ends. The northeast, northwest, and southeast corners were the more likely points of entrance. Tanks, buildings, and other obstructions guaranteed that someone near the gate could not see anyone coming over the fence in any of those corners.

I was positioned near the southeast corner, under one of half a dozen huge capsule-shaped tanks. Elmo was nearby, near a short, squat tower that might have been a water tank except for the thick, shiny black lumps of dried tar all over it.

The wind came up, as it had been doing occasionally the two hours we'd been in position, rattled the chain-link fence and made leaves, dirt, and litter scurry across the pavement. The past two days had been sunny and mild, taking care of much of the snow, and when litter scuffs across a stretch of bare blacktop it sounds an awful lot like a pair of shoes doing the same thing.

The wind eased and so did I.

At one-ten the chain-link rattled again, but the wind was down.

I looked across my left shoulder and saw two figures at the fence. One of them was coming up with enough grace to make a cat envious. He straddled the barbed wire like it wasn't there, then slid on down inside. His friend was less nimble, but he got over too. They didn't make much noise—scarcely more than made by the intermittent whisper of the night breeze.

Elmo may have seen them too. If not, he would soon enough. I waited.

When they were both on terra firma, they quickly got themselves organized. Weapons came into view. Hard to tell, in the gloom, but I guessed a small military-style rifle, perhaps an M-16, and a sawed-off shotgun. You could about bank on them having a pistol or two each, too. Well, why not—they had come to hunt down one whole guy, after all.

They crept slowly northward, hunched and ready, making good use of the deep shadows offered by the capsule-shaped tanks. They passed by the one I was hiding under, so close I could have bit them on the ankles. I resisted the temptation.

When they disappeared around the end of my tank, I slowly eased myself out, got to my feet, and stretched muscles that had gone stiff. This would be a bad time for a charley horse.

I moved down to the end of the tank.

The tanks formed one edge of a kind of rough path that led from this end of the yard to the bigger open area farther on. The path was about eight feet wide. The other side of it was delineated by the tower and several short round bins of corrugated steel.

Elmo emerged from among the crisscrossed support beams of the tower's base and nodded at me.

Then he disappeared back into the shadows.

I mirrored his movement, moving quickly down to the other end of the tank. Between the row of tanks and the east fence there was a narrow space, a kind of alley, maybe three feet wide. Crouching, I hustled as fast as I dared along the fence.

I came even with the two gunmen.

I passed them by two tanks, then turned left into the darkness between the last two. About eighteen inches from the end along the path, I went into a low crouch, not to hide myself—the tanks were easily seven feet high, and the shadows between them were virtually impenetrable—but to give myself a good footing.

The gunmen crept up even with my position, moving

slowly, eyes open, weapons ready. Their goal was obvious; it was what we expected; it was what we intended. Wizard was supposed to meet Donald Lee inside the main gate, near the office building. These guys would sneak in from the south, no doubt other gunmen would sneak in from the north, and all of them would come up behind Little Flash and, with all their firepower, turn him into something of roughly the consistency of a Slurpee.

I hoped Elmo was in place.

I hit the guy nearest me low, behind the knees, just as they passed. He pitched forward, landing hard on his knees. He automatically put out his hands to catch himself, and dropped his weapon. A shotgun. He scraped some skin off his palms, inhaling sharply. I had a .38 in my right fist and swung it hard in a horizontal arc that ended at the back of his head. He went slack.

That took about four seconds. I turned, gun ready, though I didn't want to use it, to face the guy's partner. Elmo had already taken care of him.

He smiled at me, rubbing his sore leg. "Thirty-three and a third," he murmured.

"Hope so," I said. He knew what I meant—that we had eliminated a third of Wizard's force. Yoli had told us there would be six men, plus Wizard, but she couldn't tell us what she didn't know. If Wizard had changed his plans and added more guns later, when she wasn't around, then we could be in for a nasty surprise. It was a calculated risk. Paranoia might tell Wizard to bring more men; paranoia might also say don't trust anyone else.

Elmo and I each had black nylon bags strapped around our waist. Not as keen as Batman's utility belt, maybe, but equally functional. We each took out a pair of Smith & Wesson handcuffs and fitted them on our playmates. Then we got out adhesive tape and made sure their lips were sealed.

• • •

Elsewhere in our little amusement park, Wizard's other friends came over the fence about where we had predicted. The northeast contingent had it easiest, because from the top of the fence they could step across to the low, slanted roof of a kind of pavilion, probably an equipment shelter, and shimmy down a support pillar to the ground, but the northwest group made it over without too much trouble.

Like their opposite numbers on the opposite end, they were heavily armed. They met up in the shadows, then crouched low for a moment, waiting, watching and listening for some sign of their quarry. They received none. Furtively, then, they moved along the rough path toward the open compound.

They didn't get far.

When Elmo and I finished our handiwork, we got our playmates to their feet, sort of, and half-marched, half-dragged them into the blackness between the tanks. Once we were concealed, Elmo unzipped his black bag and got out the walkie-talkie, as elegant and gracefully designed as a brick. It had a fat black whip antenna and settings for voice or Morse. It was set for the latter. Elmo sent three distinct dashes, and promptly got three back in return. Nothing that walks on fewer than four feet could have heard the Morse pulses from a distance of ten inches or more.

Elmo nodded in the darkness and put his back against one of the tanks. "Good thing we're so good at waiting," he said softly.

Our playmates weren't badly incapacitated. They were little more than stunned, and a four- or five-minute break there in the night air would be enough to revive them.

Midway through the break Elmo's walkie-talkie emitted a short sequence of dashes and dots.

"Your boss is over the fence," he told our guests.

"Real sweet," I said. "Let the artillery get into position, then show yourself and lure the target out into the open. Guy's cagey, you have to give him that."

"Only *one* thing I have to give him," Elmo said.

The gunmen glared at us with unmasked hatred, but it'd been a long time since either Elmo or I let that kind of thing hurt our feelings.

A couple more minutes passed. Then the walkie-talkie spoke again. And again, almost immediately.

"One hundred percent," Elmo said, sending the answering signals.

I stood up. "Your friends ran into our friends," I told the gunmen. "Small world, isn't it?"

We hauled the guys to their feet.

"Let the games begin," Elmo said.

CHAPTER

42

"Yo! Little Flash!"

It was louder than a whisper, softer than a yell, the voice you use when you're not sure how much volume is called for. The next utterance, a few seconds later, was louder and more confident.

"Hey, Donald! Where are you, man?"

Wizard had come over the gate and dropped to the ground, with no noticeable attempt at stealth. Now he wandered slowly along the wide strip of pavement that led past the office building and connected the gate to the big open space at the middle of the yard. In the poor light, the shapes of disused and forgotten tanks, sheds, bins, and Christ knew what other junk hunched darkly, as sinister and as silent as gargoyles.

He appeared to be unarmed. Appearances can be deceiving.

"Hey, come *on*, man! Thought you want to talk to the Wizard, Little Flash."

Wizard paused near the far corner of the office building. From his posture, I realized he had expected Donald Lee to be waiting there, along the east wall of the brick building, safely out of sight of the front gate. That Lee hadn't shown himself must have set Wizard to wondering. Was Little Flash waiting around the corner, waiting for Wizard to walk past, waiting to mow him down?

Wizard didn't move.

Except to cast a quick glance left and right. Looking for his pals.

"Shit, Donald, it's *cold* out here, man! Ain't got all night."

His voice was louder now, but not with confidence. Tension. It had wanted to crack on the word "cold."

He retreated from the corner of the building, slowly, back toward the gate.

"Lose this bullshit," Wizard said to the night. "Got *better* things to do."

He paused again. What if Little Flash *had* been hiding on the east side of the building? And when he saw that Wizard wasn't going to pass by that corner, went around the north side of the building and now was hiding along the *west* wall? Then when Wizard went past *this* corner...

He stopped, turned, and then slowly backed away from that end of the building.

"Hey, come on, Donald," he said, trying to make it sound light. "Let's talk, man."

He hung there, afraid to go past either end of the little building.

The wind put in another appearance. A brittle scrap of newsprint skittered up the path. Wizard turned on it as if it might attack him.

"Soldier!" he squealed. "Hamfat! Where the fuck *are* you guys?"

I didn't know the name of the gunman I had tackled, but I figured any familiar face would comfort Wizard. I gave my guy a push and sent him stumbling out into the open.

Wizard whirled on him and whipped out a foreshortened little semiauto rifle of the sort we used to call a burp gun.

"Shit!" he bawled. He took a couple steps forward, then checked himself.

Across the way, Elmo stepped out of the blackness.

Wizard didn't drop his teeth or leap out of his skin or fall down. Some people are no fun at all.

"Fuck," he said. "Shoulda knowed."

"Shoulda," Elmo agreed.

"This's personal now, nigger," Wizard said. He raised the

rifle. "Gonna blow that shit-eatin' grin off your ugly face."

"It's been personal all along, asshole. You hurt my family, I hurt you. That's the game, Gizzard. You lose."

"What, you change your mind, decide you got balls enough to kill me after all?"

"Killing an animal doesn't take balls," Elmo said pleasantly. "You're living proof of that, Gizzard."

"Tired a you, Tom," Wizard said, aiming.

I showed myself.

On a clock face, Wizard was at the nine o'clock position, Elmo at three, and I at about six thirty-four. Elmo wasn't showing any weaponry, but I lacked his sang-froid. I had my .38 in hand and ready, and its twin was nestled securely in my jacket pocket.

Wizard jumped. He arced the weapon from Elmo to me, me to Elmo, doing a little jig like a kid trying to get his cap back from two bigger kids.

"Fuck," Wizard said again. "Don't you go nowhere without your boyfriend?"

"Look who's talking," Elmo said. He reached behind him into the darkness and dragged out the other gunman we'd captured.

"That won't help you none," Wizard said.

"He's not a shield." Elmo pushed the man forward. He stumbled and fell. "I know you'd shoot through him in a second."

"He's an observer," I said, and Wizard spun on me.

"He gonna observe me blowin' both you away."

"Use your head for once," Elmo said. Wizard looked. So did I. He now had the confiscated M-16 resting in his arms, lazily, familiarly. He knew his way around such ugly machines. We had both been carrying rifles like that one the day we met, and we continued to carry them every day for a lot of days afterward. "You shoot me, he shoots you. You shoot him, I shoot you."

"Standoff," I said.

Wizard's lips pulled away from his teeth. "You wanna see

how many rounds a second this mother shoots?"

"We do not," Jack Reedy said.

Wizard pirouetted.

Reedy stepped out from behind the west end of the office building. Wizard had been right to suspect someone was using it as a hiding place, wrong to assume Donald Lee was that someone, wrong to assume a deadly intention—although Reedy's bearing made it clear he would not be afraid to fire the big Colt .45 in his hand if Wizard forced that action on him.

"Fuck!" Wizard yelled into the night. "Fuckers gangin' up on me!"

"Ganging up," Elmo said.

"Comedian too," I said.

Wizard turned from one to another of us, back and forth. It was a wonder he didn't get dizzy and fall down. The other thing I wondered about was whether we had pushed him too close to the edge, too close to that point where he would snap, or with deliberation decide he had nothing to lose, and either way start spraying indiscriminately. Surrounding him as we were, one of us would certainly drop him before he took us all down. But that would be small comfort to the one or two of us he did manage to clip first.

"Relax, Gerard," I said, knowing it was probably futile. "Nobody's going to shoot anybody unless you do something stupid first."

He whirled and glared at me hard, as if deciding whether to test my claim. From the corner of my eye I saw Elmo train his weapon on Wizard.

I met Wizard's gaze for a long while, then I looked at Reedy and nodded.

Wizard spun again, probably expecting I had signaled Reedy to plug him in the back. All he saw, though, was Reedy thumbing the Morse button on the walkie-talkie in his left hand, while he kept his eyes and the Colt in his right hand unwaveringly on Wizard.

And then the shadows began to move.

CHAPTER

43

Purplish shapes detached themselves from the shadows and drifted forward. Wizard started. I didn't blame him. It made the hair on the back of my neck go up, and I was expecting it.

Reedy was at about the eleven o'clock position. Now two other forms emerged from the shadows, one to my right at about five o'clock, the other to Elmo's right at about one o'clock. Five o'clock was a tallish, sandy-haired guy with eyebrows like Richard Gephardt's; one o'clock was a square block of a man, black, with almost no hair on his head and a look in his eye that could bore through a mountain. Their names were Gianelli and Johnson, respectively, and they were friends of Reedy from the air base.

Johnson melted into the shadows for a second, then re-emerged with the two gunmen he and Gianelli had subdued on the north side of the yard. He shoved them out into the open area.

Wizard danced a couple of steps backward, as if punch-drunk. He didn't lower the burp gun, though.

Another bound figure stumbled out of the gloom and fell to the dirt near Wizard. This time I was certain he'd start blasting, but he had more of a grip on himself than I thought. He merely stared at the man on the ground, as if in disbelief.

Sgt. Donnelly, who had propelled the gangbanger into the open area, stepped out of the shadows a couple of yards to my left. Kim Banner and her charge materialized near the southeast corner of the little building, and Wizard danced around to face them. Banner was less violent with her captive than the rest of us had been with ours; she merely prodded him with her shotgun and he stepped on out into the open to join his friends.

It was a bad idea for the two cops to be there. It violated every rule, regulation, and guideline in the division's book, as well as a handful of civil laws. They knew it, we knew it, and all the arguing we had done hadn't changed anybody's mind. We hadn't planned to tell Banner anything about our evening's plans, but she had started to develop suspicions the night Wizard was shot—suspicions that we were up to more than we were letting on; accurate suspicions, as it happened—and she only had grown more suspicious in succeeding days. About the time she threatened to put us under twenty-four-hour surveillance unless we told her what we had up our collective sleeve, Yoli learned that Wizard's team would contain two more players than we had lined up for our team, and on short notice there was nothing we could do except fess up and hope Banner wouldn't close us down.

Which was her first inclination, of course. I don't really know what changed her mind. Maybe we convinced her that, contrary to the way it looked, our aim was not to make Wizard the lead duck in a shooting gallery—we could do that with far less elaborate planning. Maybe she realized that closing us down was tantamount to giving Wizard a free pass. Or maybe she reasoned that we'd go on ahead with or without her help, and thought that her being on hand would give her a measure of control over the outcome. Whatever her thinking was, and for better or worse, there she was. Donnelly, too. He had been a lot more enthusiastic about the idea from the start than Banner ever would be.

The Reverend O'Neal appeared now, near Banner's left shoulder. If it was a bad idea for the cops to be there, it was a terrible idea for O'Neal to be on hand. We hadn't wanted to involve "civilians": the potential for disaster was too great. But O'Neal had argued convincingly that he was already involved, and then some, and since he knew the whole plan, and had from the beginning, there was no good way to lock him out.

Wizard had seemed stunned, almost numb, for the last few minutes, but now the sight of O'Neal seemed to snap him awake. He took a few steps toward the minister. Banner hefted her shotgun.

"What the fuck *you* doin' here?" he demanded of O'Neal.

"Witnessing your demise," the big man boomed.

"You fuckin' *dead*, old man," he yelled. "You fuck with the Wizard, now you *had* it!" He spun—it was more of a stagger—and took us all in. "All a you—dead. You had it."

O'Neal remained silent. So did the rest of us.

Wizard's chest was pumping. The night was cold enough that his breath emerged in little white clouds, but there were beads of sweat on his forehead along the band of his beret. His eyes were wild.

He backed away from O'Neal. His movements were jerky. I held my breath against the rifle suddenly spitting. I had been holding my breath, figuratively at least, ever since our observers started showing themselves.

Wizard looked at O'Neal. At Reedy. Me. Gianelli. It was as if he recognized none of us.

Then he got to Elmo. "What the fuck you pullin', man?" Wizard demanded. There was something new in his voice now, almost a plea.

"The plug," Elmo said.

Wizard stared at him.

"Sending you down the drain," I said.

Wizard's head snapped around to me, then back to Elmo.

"Shut up!" he yelled now. "Just everybody shut up and lemme think!"

"Too late for that now, Wizard," O'Neal said. He made the last word a sneer. "You should have done your thinking a *long* time ago. In fact, you should have thought twice. About a lot of things."

"We've had it with you," Reedy said.

"We've been putting up with you and your kind too long," O'Neal said. "We thought there was nothing we could do to stop you, thought there was no alternative except to try to teach kids to stay the hell away from you. But we were wrong."

"Take away your guns, take away your friends and *their* guns, what's left of you?" Johnson said.

"Nothin'," Donnelly spat. "Just a bully. Just a scared little boy." He laughed. "Look at him," he said to no one in particular. "Twenty-five degrees out here, he's sweatin' like a butcher. He's a coward even when he's *got* a gun."

"Shut up!" Wizard cried again.

"Truth hurts, don't it, Gerard?" Elmo said.

"Shut *up!*"

"That's what we're here for, Gerard," I said. "To get the truth out in the open. To let these people—and your own people—see the truth. And take it back to the project and the whole neighborhood."

"By noon tomorrow, *everybody* will know what we know," Jack Reedy said. "Gerard Jones is nothing but a lot of hot air."

Wizard seemed to remember he was armed. He brandished the rifle. "All a you *shut the fuck up!* Kill all a you—"

"I don't think so," Reedy said. Wizard looked at him, looked at him hard as if he was having trouble focusing. He seemed to take in the gun in Reedy's fist, aimed directly at him. He jerked around and looked at me. At Gianelli. At Elmo. He stopped at Elmo.

"*You* the coward," he said. "All these people—all these guns—"

Elmo smiled. "Learned it from you," he said. "Difference is, we don't *want* to use them."

The Reverend O'Neal's big voice boomed across the yard. "All we want is to show you for what you really are—nothing—and tell you that we are *through* with you."

Wizard whirled.

"Better shut up, old man. Wizard got friends..."

"Yeah, we know there's more where you came from," Banner said.

"Too many more," Donnelly said.

"We're up to our necks in garbage like you," O'Neal said. "I don't know whose fault that is, but it doesn't matter. What matters is, *we're* the ones who have to take control. We're the ones who have to take out the garbage. One bag at a time."

With the hardware he was carrying, Wizard could have sawed O'Neal in half in the time it takes to draw a breath; O'Neal was obviously unarmed; but it was Wizard who seemed to cower away from the big man. I didn't half blame him. When O'Neal spoke again, his voice was like thunder from a long way off: "We know there'll be others like you," he said. "Dozens, scores, even hundreds. You're cockroaches. Always been around, always will be around. But you always step on a cockroach when you see one, even though you know there'll be more."

"I think you done wore out your welcome, Gerard," Elmo said.

Wizard whirled on him, and once again I braced myself for gunfire that didn't come.

"That's our show for tonight," I said, eager to wrap things up before something nasty decided to happen. "Everyone drive carefully on the way home."

"What?" Wizard rasped.

"We've seen what we wanted to see," I said. "And we made sure your own people saw it too. Like the man said, by noon tomorrow—at the latest—everyone in the Bloods, everyone in the project—well, damn near just about *everyone*, period— will know what happened here tonight."

"People have been laughing at you behind your back, Giz," Elmo said. "People in the neighborhood, people in the Bloods. They laughed behind your back on account of they were afraid of you. Soon as they hear about this, though... Well, they'll go right ahead and laugh in your face. If you're stupid enough to show it."

"Some of'em will do more than laugh," Jack Reedy said. "If you're dumb enough to still be around tomorrow, you *won't* be around day after tomorrow. I'm willing to put money on that."

"Sucker bet," Johnson said, laughing. "I don't think you'll find anyone willing to take that one, Jack."

"Fuck, man..." Wizard mumbled. He turned from one of us to the next, from face to face. "Man, you don't know what you messin' with," he said, a little louder. His voice cracked. He was panting like a long-distance runner. "I'm the Wizard. You know that? *Wizard.*"

"Then make yourself disappear," Elmo said. He gave the high sign, and Reedy melted back into the shadows. Then O'Neal and Banner. Then the other men, slowly, as slowly as they had appeared. I breathed a little easier as each one of them vanished from view.

"Fuckers!" Wizard yelled. "You *dead.* You *all* dead! Nobody fucks with the Wizard—"

It was a surprisingly satisfying form of justice, I felt, not just the second-best alternative we had conceived it as. Gerard Jones, the mighty Wizard, had been humiliated. The humiliation had been witnessed by his own troops—been witnessed and would be reported, as he well knew. Now Jones would be perceived as the coward he really was. The façade was gone, and there was nothing to the man but the façade. Perhaps there had been once, but if so it had been a long time ago. Depriving Wizard of his fearful façade was a far greater punishment—and far more fitting justice—than depriving him of his life or liberty. Power is perception. We had, this night, changed the way people would perceive Gerard Jones, and changed it permanently.

Perhaps Jones realized that already, perhaps not. He ranted on, cursing and threatening the shadows. Finally, all that remained were his defeated soldiers and Elmo and me.

And something moved near the west end of the little building. Jack Reedy had been on the east end; why would he...

Yoli Harris stepped calmly from the shadows.

Elmo and I traded quick glances—all the time we dared spend with our eyes anywhere but glued to Wizard.

He saw the girl, stopped his jerky, pointless movements as if he had slammed into a wall, and stared at her.

I had no idea what Yoli was doing there. I had had no idea that she even knew about this part of our plan, or where or when or how it would go down. O'Neal had said it was impossible to keep a secret in that neighborhood around the project; maybe Yoli had heard something, guessed at something, put several somethings together... It didn't matter now. There she was, gazing serenely at Wizard as if idly wondering what it was she was looking at.

In time, Wizard came out of his reverie.

"Bitch," he said. It came out quietly, almost gently. His voice was hoarse, raw from shouting. He had the rifle but it wasn't aimed at anything. "You deadest of all, bitch," he said.

I eased forward. Elmo did likewise.

"It's all over, Gerard," Elmo said.

He didn't hear. "You set me up, girl," he said.

"Yes I did," she said, quietly but defiantly. "That's why I'm here. I wanted to be sure you know that. I set you up." Her eyes filled, then overflowed. "Set you up the way I did with Darius—" She choked on a sob. "The way you *made* me do with Darius. You made me do so many things... You terrorized me, you threatened my family, you abused me. You treated me like a whore—worse than a whore. And I let you. First 'cause I thought there wasn't anything I could do about it. Then, later on, 'cause I knew there was."

Elmo and I were close now, me about eighteen inches off of Jones's right, Elmo about two feet back from his left shoulder. We both had our guns aimed at him. Although he seemed oblivious, perhaps he recognized us in some fashion, for he still held the rifle aimed at the pavement.

322

He was staring at Yoli as if hypnotized, or trying to hypnotize.

"Dead," he said softly. He glanced back at Elmo and smiled. It was the smile that Yoli had described as making him look like an animal. She had been accurate. "These two queens ain't always gonna be around," he said. His hoarse voice was almost soothing.

Like most people who were alive in the sixties, I carry in my head an indelible picture of the assassination of Lee Harvey Oswald. There is Jack Ruby, the back of his head, the extended gun arm. There is Oswald, collapsing in on himself, his face distorted in pain. And there is the unlucky escort, the cop in the light-colored suit and hat, his eyes and face wide in the surprised realization of what is happening right before him, right beside him, and which, proximity notwithstanding, he is powerless to prevent.

Now I felt the way the cop in that picture looks.

Gerard Jones had been smiling at Elmo. He turned back to give Yoli some of the same. Her right hand came out of her jacket pocket, where it had been all along. There was a flat .22 in her hand. Its chrome plating caught a stray particle of light from somewhere and threw it across Elmo's left sleeve.

She emptied the gun into Gerard Jones's midsection.

He caved in on himself and fell back.

I caught him. He didn't care.

I put him down on the cold ground, groping for the pulse I knew would be dropping off. His blood was hot on my hand and face.

I looked over my shoulder. Elmo had taken the .22 from Yoli. She offered no resistance. She looked down at Gerard like he was just another body on the six o'clock news.

Banner and Donnelly appeared from somewhere. Reedy and his friends must have already left, as they were supposed to. O'Neal was crouched next to me, his big hands cradling Jones's head, softly murmuring a string of words that I couldn't hear.

I said to Banner, "You people get lost."

"Forget it," she said.

"He's right, Kim," Donnelly said.

"If you get kicked out, there's no one left in the division who'll give me the time of day," I said.

She looked at Jones, then at me. Her face was tight. "Your concern is touching," she said.

They disappeared, and Elmo knelt next to me, pocketing Yoli's handgun. "CPR, man," he blurted.

He started to rip open Jones's clothes and O'Neal said, "There's nothing left to resuscitate," and we looked at the unholy mess that six .22 calibre slugs had made.

And Elmo pulled the edges of the red silk jacket back over the man's chest.

CHAPTER
44

The following Saturday afternoon, I drove Elmo to the airport. It had been a long week. He checked his baggage at the counter, keeping his briefcase, which was very heavy. It contained four quart jars of Mrs. Galas's homemade pickles.

We went up the escalator to the bar on the boarding level. It was dark and cool, even at two in the afternoon.

"I'll buy," Elmo said. "Least I can do."

"Got that right," I said.

He smiled ruefully behind his nappy beard.

"What's your lawyer friend think about your chances of keeping your permit?"

"Kennerly?" I said. "Oh, he's not worried. He's never worried. Me, I'm not worried either. I figured my chances were slim in the beginning. Now they're fat. So what's to worry?"

Elmo grinned and shook his head. "What will you do now?"

"I think I will order a bourbon on the rocks."

A woman with legs that wouldn't quit, wearing the sort of cocktail-waitress outfit that wouldn't let them quit, came and took our orders.

"I wouldn't discount your friend until he's played all the cards up his sleeve," Elmo said when the woman and her legs had gone. "I've had more opportunity than I'd've liked to watch him up close while he works. He's good."

He was. The various lawyering publications consistently

put Mike Kennerly in the top ten. Kennerly had been able to convince the authorities, more or less, that we had not lured the late Gerard Jones to the late G & O Asphalt Company for the express purpose of murdering him. It helped that the Reverend O'Neal corroborated our story, and Yoli stated that we had not known she planned to be on hand, that we hadn't even told her where and when the confrontation was to go down. We all somehow neglected to mention the presence of other participants and observers that night, and oddly enough the surviving Bloods, whom we released before the cops showed up, likewise neglected to come forward and set the record straight.

That still left Elmo and me facing half a dozen other charges, from trespassing on up—including a weapons beef against me that probably would stick—but once you've stared down the business end of a murder rap, everything else seems pretty tame.

Yoli was not so lucky. There was no way she could avoid being charged, but Mike Kennerly was upbeat. He had witnesses willing to testify that Wizard had been extremely well armed and was in fact in the middle of threatening her when she killed him. Kennerly thought he might actually get her off on a self-defense plea. His worst-case scenario was voluntary manslaughter and a suspended sentence.

Then some bright thinker downtown had the brainstorm of comparing the slugs that killed Jones to the slugs that were pulled out of him and his car the previous week. They matched, of course. Yoli had taken the ineffective pot-shots at Wizard that night at the Mini-Mall, using a pistol Richie Dayton had given her long ago, when Wizard first began threatening her. That punched a big hole in her case, but Kennerly was confident that he could patch it up.

" 'He pulled a knife on me so I shot him' is nice and straightforward as a defense," Kennerly told us, "but it isn't the only possibility. A threat isn't necessarily an event; it can be a process, too, a long ongoing series of intimidation and abuse.

That was certainly the case here—over a period of several years, actually. It's not necessarily a less valid response than shooting someone who pulls a knife on you. It just takes more work to make a court see it."

"There's not a jury in this country that wouldn't be sympathetic to her," Elmo said now, stirring his scotch with a short plastic straw. "If it even gets to a jury trial. Which I doubt."

"I hope you're right. The sooner Yoli can get this behind her and get on with her life again, the better."

"What do you think the Bloods'll do?"

"For the moment, nothing," I said. "Too much heat, too much publicity, too much discombobulation. They'll need to regroup, recharge. That will take time. But it's for damn sure the Harrises can't go on living in that neighborhood. Or even this town."

"Says you," Elmo said. "Anyone told Mrs. Harris?"

"You mean besides you, me, Kennerly, Banner, Donnelly, et al.? She ought to be getting the picture by now. No one likes to have her home taken away from her." I paused, and drank some bourbon, and thought about that time a few months ago when someone did take my home away from me. And how hard I had fought to get it back. "But I think she'll come around." I smiled. "I think Yoli will *bring* her around."

Elmo nodded. "Might be a good time for you to take a little vacation, you know."

"Might," I said. "But if I'm going to start having to support myself entirely as a freelance writer, I'd better hit the typewriter instead of a beach."

"What made me think you might say something like that? Well, look at the bright side. Maybe you'll get that bookshelf of mine filled up after all."

We drank to it.

Then we sat silently for a while. You can do that with old friends. Finally Elmo said, "I keep wondering if we did a damn bit of good. If what we accomplished was worth what we're paying."

"And what Gerard Jones paid."

"Yeah, him too."

"Well, let's see," I said. "We all of us put ourselves in physical danger, got ourselves in hot water up to our ear-lobes, got Gerard Jones killed—and all of it counts for exactly zip in the grand scheme of things. We may have injured the Bloods, but a damn sight short of fatally. We may have helped the people of the neighborhood around the project achieve a certain renewed sense of control over their own lives, but they'll still have the gangs and the violence, the drugs, the poverty, the hopelessness—the whole interwoven mess. We did not clean up this town. We did not see Gerard Jones brought to justice for murdering your nephew, among others. We don't even have the satisfaction of being able to say we achieved our own brand of justice by rendering Darius's killer impotent. We came *that close*," I said, "but then Yoli knocked us off the board."

Elmo nodded. He looked out the tall tinted windows that overlooked one of the runways. "But did find out about Darius," he said around the plastic straw in the corner of his mouth. "We did find out what really happened to him and why." He looked at me. "We found out what sort of a kid he had become."

"We found out what sort of a man he would have been," I said.

Elmo turned back toward the windows. "And we tried," he said. "We tried to even things out, balance the scales, make things better. It got away from us at the end there and we ended up failing. But we tried, and maybe that's what counts. We tried, and other people helped us, and because of that, no one can ever say Darius died for nothing."

He looked at me again. His eyes were wide.

"God help me," he breathed. "I'm sounding just like *you*."

I laughed. "We can only hope we've caught it in time."

The P.A. made a noise slightly reminiscent of a human voice calling Elmo's flight.

We went out to the gate.

"See you in a couple of months when my court date comes up," Elmo said.

"I'll be around."

He got his boarding pass, got in line. After a bit an agent lifted the velvet rope and let people through to the jetway.

Elmo paused in the doorway and looked back at me.

"Thanks," he said.

"Hey, what are friends for?" I said.

On my way back to town, I noticed something strange: I was feeling pretty good. I tried to analyze it. I was washed up as a PI, but it wasn't my first career change. Our plans for taking care of Gerard Jones had laid a big egg, but he was out of the way and a kind of rough, lopsided justice had resulted. I was mud as far as most of OPD was concerned, but if there were more than three people in the division whose opinion counted for much with me, I was hard-pressed to name them. Koosje and I were not back to where we had been before I loused things up, but we had begun settling into a new groove, not the old, good one but a different one that might ultimately prove better. The sun was out, spring was on its way, and when I came up behind a Ford Probe with a bumper sticker that read HONK IF YOU LOVE JESUS, I thought what the hell and gave the horn button a couple of friendly taps.

The woman in the Ford looked in her rearview mirror and flipped me the bird.

About the Author

William J. Reynolds was born in Omaha, Nebraska, and was raised there and in Sioux Falls, South Dakota. He graduated from Creighton University in Omaha with a degree in Political Science. He has worked as a magazine editor and a writer. He currently lives in Sioux Falls with his wife, Peggy, and two children. *Drive-By* is his sixth Nebraska mystery.